Hero Risen

ANDY LIVINGSTONE

Book Three of The Seeds of Destiny Trilogy

HARPER
Voyager

Harper*Voyager*
An imprint of HarperCollinsPublishers Ltd
1 London Bridge Street
London SE1 9GF

www.harpervoyagerbooks.co.uk

This Paperback Original 2017

First published in Great Britain in ebook format by Harper*Voyager*
2017

Copyright © Andrew Livingstone 2017

Andrew Livingstone asserts the moral right to
be identified as the author of this work

A catalogue record for this book
is available from the British Library

ISBN: 978-0-00-818151-2

This novel is entirely a work of fiction.
The names, characters and incidents portrayed in it are
the work of the author's imagination. Any resemblance to
actual persons, living or dead, events or localities is
entirely coincidental.

Typeset in Sabon by Palimpsest Book Production Ltd, Falkirk,
Stirlingshire

Printed and bound in Great Britain

Hero Risen

Andy Livingstone was born on New Year's Day in 1968 and grew up with an enthusiastic passion for sport (particularly football) and reading. An asthmatic childhood meant that he spent more time participating in the latter than the former and an early childhood encounter with *The Hobbit* awakened a love of epic and heroic fantasy that has never let him go. He is a press officer and former journalist and lives in Lanarkshire, Scotland, with his wife, Valerie, and two teenage sons, Adam and Nathan. He also has four adult stepchildren, Martyn, Jonathon, Melissa and Nicolas, and four grand-bundles-of-energy: Joshua, Riah, Jayden and Ashton. He can be found on Twitter @markethaven and at his website, www.andylivingstone.com

For Valerie

Prologue

He paused before the door, running his fingertips slowly down the wood smoothed as much by years as by the plane, letting them fall into the curving groove of the traditional mark of luck in its centre. He was prolonging the moment.

The sounds of early evening were all around him, stark in the deserted village, but he heard none. The smells of dusk drifted over him, but he noticed none. Still he stayed his hand from pushing the door.

It was a strange mix of feelings that coursed through him on the final night of a story:

Nerves – that he might not do justice to those whose tale he told.

Pleasure – that the crowd waited on his words: the result of his efforts the previous two nights.

Sadness – that tonight this telling would come to an end.

And eagerness – a quickening of heart and breath. He would be drawn into the telling, the exhilaration confining his awareness within each moment and shortening time.

It was always so.

It was, these days, what he lived for. Keeping the past alive. Ensuring the deeds he had witnessed did not drift and fade with the shifting winds of memory. Helping the lessons of before to be learnt afresh, the mistakes understood, the heroics and sacrifices appreciated.

He pushed on the door, letting the remaining light spill within and hush the murmur of the throng. He moved inside, his adjusting eyes revealing rings of faces turned his way. Close by, one caught his eye. A boy who had decried the stories outside the hall on the first night; the challenging cynicism in his voice now replaced by eager anticipation in his eyes.

He stepped forward.

He was a storyteller. And he had a story to tell.

Chapter 1

She sat beside him each afternoon now. Two high-backed chairs were paired on the balcony, fine sand gathering around their short legs of finely carved wood.

It was curious how change eased its way into your life before awareness caught up. He could not remember when her companionship had become routine; he could only recall the day when, with her called on other business, it had seemed strange that she was not there.

The other servants made no comment. They would not dare, of course, in his presence but he knew from his sources that her companionship provided no domestic scuttlebutt in the corridors. Why would it? Nobles, in particular, royals, had a habit of demanding services far more intimate from servants. Gossip is not born in the commonplace.

Her whisper drifted in the baking air. 'You hate this.'

'The heat?' He snorted. 'It is the only weather I know.'

'Not the heat, as you know quite well.' It was uncanny how a hoarse monotone could yet convey chastisement. 'The waiting.'

3

He rested his head against the chair and raised his eyes to the deepness of the sky. The same sky that sat above all countries, above all people, and some more specific than others. 'You think you can read my mind, crone, but you are wrong. Not the waiting. Waiting lies within the course of every strategy.' *He frowned at the sky.* 'I hate the not knowing.'

She gave a soft grunt. 'And the not controlling.'

'I would that I could control you and your prattling tongue.'

It was even more irritating when she did not reply. He let the silence draw out, as if it had not irked him.

'And you miss him.'

He cursed inwardly, as much at the involuntary start her words had given him as at the suspicion that she could read his mind after all. He turned slowly and looked at her for a long moment. Her gaze never wavered from the horizon but the slightest twitch at the corner of her mouth hinted that she was aware of his stare.

'On pain of death, do not ever say that in the presence of anyone,' *he rasped.* 'Especially him.'

* * * *

Pain thumping and rebounding within his skull, Brann forced open his eyes and found himself lying in hell.

The stench of gore was so pervasive that he could taste it filling his throat; enough to make him retch, had he not become accustomed to the sensation that seemed half a lifetime before. He heaved at a body – cold, clammy, and limp and as naked as he felt himself to be – to force its weight away from his chest. It slipped from him with a wet slither, allowing him to drag in a breath of welcome depth. Pain flared across his ribs as he sucked in the air, but a pain of a battering and, thankfully, not of broken bone. It was not so much the breaking that worried him, but the piercing and tearing it so often caused inside. Bones could mend, but blood coughed up all too often prophesied the end. He twisted, feeling lifeless limbs shift beneath him, to look further around. He was in a pit as deep into the dry crumbling earth as his father's mill had been tall. The darkness of night above was tinged with the glow of fires beyond the lip and either the flames or the moon or both combined to lessen the gloom just enough to reveal the silhouettes of arms and legs and bodies and heads, a layer of nightmare shapes with the promise of more hidden beneath.

Low voices approached and Brann lay still, tense and alert. A glow grew brighter at the lip of the pit until the flickering light of a torch brought the detail of the scene around him to his eyes in all its stark gore. Faces stared back at him, some hacked almost beyond recognition as human, while others appeared ready to start a conversation until he saw the eyes, cold and dead as stone. Limbs were strewn at angles, attached still to bodies or not; skin was rent and pierced, and everywhere, coating all, was blood, a dark lubricant that saw the corpses – stripped of everything whether of value or none – shift as, with a scrape of movement at the edge of the pit and a harsh slap on impact, another body was flung onto the pile.

A long moment of silence and shifting shadows was broken by a grunt of satisfaction.

'That'll do for today. Tomorrow will see us fill it enough to put the dirt back in over them, then we've done our bit.

I'll put the stew on to heat, and you two can start sorting their gear. We'll divide it once we've eaten.'

A harsh laugh and a younger voice: 'Sounds good to me. It's hungry work, this. Bodies are heavier than I thought.'

A third voice: 'But worth it for the loot. Don't matter that the bodies are heavy when the loot pays you back. You city cut-throats are all the same when you come to this – you don't realise you can't just leave the dead in an alley for the watch guards to pick up in the morning. Now you know why I told you it's good to stick with the sergeant who's the best cheat at dice. Won us a pit to fill, didn't he?'

The first voice was further away, presumably at the stew pot: 'Say again that I cheat and you'll be in the pit yourself and as dead as the others.' The sergeant finished with a barked laugh.

The torchlight started to recede but Brann forced himself to lie still; steeling himself against rising bile at the feeling of a cold arm pressing against his face, and waiting until the pit returned to safe darkness. The voices were still relatively close.

'Of course, boss. You're just very good at it. But before you start rolling those dice again, I want my name on those black weapons.'

Brann's eyes jerked wide open.

The sergeant's voice: 'Good try, but we all do. I'll take the sword. You bastards can roll the dice for the axe and knife.'

The young voice: 'I am happy with the knife.' A snicker of a laugh. 'I like knife work.'

'And the axe is fine for me. So we're agreed. We can roll for the rest.'

The sergeant grunted. 'You can sort the rest now, or the

food will be ready before you're done. Get your arses over here. You can use the knife tomorrow. At least the black one won't take you four tries to cut a throat like that blunt apology for a blade you were using today.'

Brann growled as rage flared, overwhelming the horror and disgust prompted by the gore-smeared bodies pressing around him. He made to rise, but his left arm gave way beneath him as a shock of pain ran from his elbow into his shoulder. He could make out the dark shape of a wound on the arm, and a burning on the side of his ribs led tentative fingers to the split skin of another long gash. Either the bash on his head that was causing the headache or the loss of blood had been the reason he had passed out and appeared dead. Either way, it had saved him from being finished off by a looter's blade. He had to hope it hadn't been blood loss, or the strength to even escape the pit would have drained from him with it. He grunted softly. There was only one way to find out. The pain wasn't enough to stop him from forcing movement had it been necessary, but while he had another good arm, there was no need.

Brann rolled to his right and pushed himself against a torso, chest hair slick and matted with blood and the jagged end of a rib pressing against his hand, and levered himself into a crouch. He tested his legs beneath him. They ached, but only through the stiffness of immobility. Hands and feet slipping and slithering on corpses, he moved towards the side of the pit. The body parts shifting beneath him made progress awkward, but the slick covering of stinking fluids saw them move quietly – just a squelch or a small slap as cold flesh met cold flesh. With almost every movement, his foot, then a hand, then a foot slipped between bodies – corpses that clung on, unwilling to let him go. His head told him that they were dead, that they were empty pieces of meat and bone, that they could not hurt him. But the feeling that they were trying to drag him down among them, to lose him in their midst and accept him as one of their own, overwhelmed him. Panic rose and he started to scrabble faster, one foot sinking even deeper into the grasping cadavers. He dragged in a gasp and forced himself to stop moving, desperately trying to control his impulses. He could feel his leg encased for most of its length against still, cold, wet dead skin. But it was the stillness that he forced his thoughts to accept. While he didn't move, nothing else did. There were no spirits trying to pull him into their embrace, no fingers grabbing his ankles. He slowed his breathing and withdrew his leg gradually, pushing down within him the revulsion at the feeling of what it slid against. He was no stranger to death or broken bodies; the gods only knew how many he had caused and the brutality involved. But those were dealt with in the moment, reaction and action born of necessity, and driven by the urge at the core of nature to survive. This was the cold eternity of death, and it reminded him of everything he fought to avoid. He blew out a slow breath and moved slowly, each movement placed with deliberate care. A face, eyes dull but staring, almost allowed the panic back in, but he forced his concentration away from what the bodies had been and made his eyes see them as nothing more than a surface to cross. The entire journey was no more than the length of two long spears but to his straining nerves it seemed the distance of an arrow-shot. He glanced ahead – he was almost there. A leg that bridged unseen between two bodies snapped under his weight, the splintered end of the shin puncturing the side of his heel. He caught his balance by throwing himself at the pit wall, bracing his good arm against it and finding it steep. Stomach heaving, he twisted and wrenched free the broken shin bone. He let his vomit go; there was no point in fighting it in this hellhole. Most of the bone was intact, and he stabbed the jagged end into the wall, using it to pull himself up, injured arm dangling and one foot finding a root that protruded enough to let him push against it, dried earth rubbing against his front and mixing with the gore that coated every part of him. His arm found the lip and, legs scrambling behind him, he dragged himself over.

The nightmare apparition – naked body, heaving chest, and snarling face caked and smeared and matted in mud and blood, and broken bone in hand – that he must have presented as he rose to his feet, eyes glaring from a head lowered from effort and shoulders hanging low to one side to favour the left arm held tight to his chest, was reflected in the dread filling the stare of the man who must have been the sergeant. The man froze, a ladle dropping against a rock with a dull clang that alerted his companions.

His reaction stopped the other two also, despite their backs being towards Brann, giving him a moment to absorb what lay before him. The sergeant, crouched beside a steaming pot suspended over a fire, was a wiry veteran, with little hair and fewer teeth. The fact that he had reached this age told of skill with arms or ruthless guile, either of which was as dangerous as the other. The other two, a skinny youth and a taller man, broad of shoulder and girth, were closer to him and had been moving items from a heap of all the plunder stripped from the bodies and sorting them into smaller specific piles.

'Son of a poxy whore,' the sergeant breathed.

The other two turned.

The youth's eyes widened, and his voice was shrill. 'The dead. Gods save us. The dead are rising.' He had been handing Brann's axe to the other man when Brann's appearance had frozen them, and it hung forgotten in his hand.

Brann growled at the sight.

The broad man tried to speak, his mouth working soundlessly.

Brann started towards them, the stiffness easing from his legs with every step. His movement broke through the men's shock but, before it could turn to panic, the sergeant recovered enough of his senses to growl at the other two.

'Back-from-the-dead or never-dead, make sure the bastard stays dead this time. I want a head to fall.'

The boy hefted the axe but still hung back, waiting for his companion to move. Clearly the sort who preferred his victims with their backs to him. His voice was still high and shaking. 'Should we get help?'

The brute beside him grabbed the nearest weapons to hand: a halberd with a broken tip and an axe-blade with more nicks than edge, but no less dangerous for either. 'And let them demand a share of our loot in return? Help me gut him and we'll get our dinner in peace.'

Brann's eyes narrowed. For all his initial dumbness, this one's nerves had steadied the quickest. He was the first threat. He angled his approach towards the youth, panicking the boy even more as he fixed him with a stare that seemed intent on him alone. With a roar, the burly man shouldered the youth to the side, sending him staggering, and raised the pole of the halberd high to strike.

Brann's grin was savage. They may be useless and unskilled, or they may be anything but. Regardless, they

10

were better one at a time. 'Got you,' he said, his voice rough and dry.

The man's eyes widened in surprise, for an instant, before he started to swing the weapon. In that instant, Brann was inside his swing and the jagged end of the shin bone had buried half of its length up under his ribs. Brann had spun away and towards the youth, the bone pulling with it a sprayed crescent of blood before the body had even started to collapse. A wild swing of the axe, born of panic, was easily avoided and the bone was left a hand's width deep in the youth's throat as Brann closed his fingers around the familiar haft of his axe and pulled it from already nerveless fingers.

The sergeant spat and crouched, a sword drawn back in readiness. 'You won't catch me by surprise, bastard.'

Brann stepped forward and, in a blur, raised the axe high with both hands, gritting his teeth against the sharp agony of the stretched wound along his ribs. As the man swung his sword up to parry the downwards swing, Brann changed to slide one hand up towards the dark metal of the head of the weapon, grasping the wood and slamming the shaft end first into the man's face. The sergeant barely had time to register his smashed nose and shattered teeth before the axe swung and his head bounced in the dirt beyond the firelight.

Brann, his chest heaving, looked down at the corpse. 'That was what you said you wanted, wasn't it?'

He sat the axe against the ground and rested on it. His wounds had sapped his energy, but he had proved that the blood loss wasn't life-threatening just yet. He needed clothing – he could wash and attend to his injuries once he was safely clear of the area – and, looking around, it was clear that the looters had been diligent enough to provide him with a large selection. He had another concern first, though. You can't meet an attack so easily with a tunic or a pair of boots. He wiped clean the black axe head on a ripped tunic and moved to the pile of sorted weapons, grunting in satisfaction to see the distinctive black metal of his sword and dagger. Lifting them to one side, he turned to the next pile, one of weapon accessories: scabbards, belts, sheaths, and the like. The three men may have been callous, but they had certainly been meticulous. It didn't take long to find his belt and the strapping and sheaths he had become accustomed to using to fasten knives to each of his forearms, between his shoulder blades and on his lower legs, inside his boots – he always felt better if a blade was to hand, no matter where that hand may be. His sheaths had been near the top of the pile, so he guessed his knives would be likewise in the heap of weapons. He must have been one of the more recent bodies to have been dragged to the pit.

He chided himself. Of course he had been. If he had been brought earlier in the process, he'd have wakened under a layer, maybe several layers, of corpses. Unless suffocation had seen to it that he never wakened at all. He grunted in annoyance. His thoughts were slow and he needed to be away from this place as soon as possible. Ensuring his main weapons were always within reach, he quickly flicked through the assembled collection of edges and points and soon had assembled his collection. Now for clothes.

As he straightened, the wind shifted and drifted smoke in his direction. There was a strong smell of burning meat, but there was too much smoke for it to have come from campfires. Some of the corpse collectors apparently favoured pyres over pits.

He tensed. The smoke was not all that the shifting wind had brought his way. A sound, no more than a scuff of boot on a loose clod of dirt, mixed for a moment with the crackling of the late sergeant's cooking fire. He crouched, feeling for his sword and axe, his eyes straining to see beyond the fire's light. He cursed himself, not only for the time he had taken but more now for his position – he was perfectly lit beside the fire, whilst those approaching could be encircling him and approach from any or all angles with little warning. He whirled back and forth, fighting to see, but all he could discern was a shadow, then two more, slightly vaguish, and all from the same direction as he had heard the noise. He bent his knees, pushing through the pain in his left side to hold the sword forward to parry and the axe back to strike. This time he might not get away with using one weapon.

'Steady, chief. Not everyone thinks it's a good idea to fight you.'

Brann relaxed with a sigh, and Gerens stepped into the light. The rangy boy turned and whistled softly into the darkness. 'He's over here.'

Konall emerged from the gloom. 'The gods save me,' he gasped. 'There's an image that will haunt me to my deathbed. For the love of all that's dear, please get dressed.'

A guffaw exploded as Hakon followed close behind. 'Little friend, the weapons in your hands are sufficient. One more would not make a difference.' He reached down and threw a pair of breeches to Brann. 'Put these on and stick to the weapons you can do harm with.'

Brann grunted and started to dress. 'I was a bit distracted by these other three. If I'd known you were coming, I'd have tidied up.'

'I'd have settled for just getting dressed,' Konall said drily.

'Wait,' said Gerens from behind. 'Don't put them on just yet.'

'Oh, make up your minds!' Brann objected. 'First you can't wait to get me to cover up, now you... argh!' His yelp turned to spluttering as cold water drenched him from his head down. He whirled to find Gerens solemnly regarding him, a now-empty bucket in his hand.

'Your dead companions had left this water, and it may rinse some of the worst from you until you can wash properly. I don't know if you had noticed, C, but you are in a bit of a mess.'

Brann just looked at him.

Gerens's eyes widened with concern as some of the grime rinsed from his arm. 'You are wounded!'

The other two stepped forward in concern, but Brann waved them away and ignored the pain to pull the tunic over his head. 'It's fine, it can wait. We need to leave.'

'You are right there,' Konall said. He found a sack. 'Fasten your black weapons to your belt and put your many knives in this. You can sort them later.'

Reluctantly, Brann did so. He buckled on his belt and slid the weapons home, sliding the leather hood, dangling from the loop for his axe's shaft, over the weapon's head.

Hakon tossed over a pair of boots. 'These do? They look like they'll fit your dainty little feet.'

Brann felt a smile pull at the corners of his mouth. 'So says someone who would need to have his footwear made at the boatyards.' He looked at them. 'They're actually better than the ones I had.' He tried them on. 'And comfier.'

'Good,' Konall grunted impatiently. 'Now grab another set of clothing and let's go.' Brann wondered why, and it must have shown. The tall blond boy added, 'The state you

14

are in, all that those clothes you are wearing will be good for when you take them off will be the fire. No use being a change of clothing down when we set off.'

Brann nodded his understanding and quickly gathered what he needed, adding it all to his sack of knives.

Konall turned to go, but Brann hesitated.

'Wait just a moment.'

Konall threw his hands in the air. 'Oh for the love of the gods. What now?'

'It won't take long.' Brann crouched by the sergeant's headless corpse and reached under the man's tunic until he found what he was looking for: a pouch that had hung on a thong around the man's neck when there had been a neck fit for that purpose. He pulled out a handful of coins and a set of dice.

'Brann!' Hakon was aghast. 'We needed the clothes, that was fair enough, but this is not you. I've never seen you loot the dead before.'

'And you won't now.' He scattered the coins on the ground and dropped the dice among them. 'If you came across this scene, what would spring to mind? That they had fallen out over dicing or that one of the dead woke up, hauled itself out of the pit and slaughtered them?'

Hakon beamed. 'Good thinking. Wait, is that what you did? The crawling out the pit and killing thing?'

Gerens cocked an eyebrow at him. 'You think he stripped naked and smeared himself from top to toe in blood for the fun of it? And that these three committed suicide?'

The large boy grinned and slapped Brann on the back, prompting an un-noticed wince. 'Good man! This will make an excellent story for the others.'

Brann picked up the sack. 'You tell it then. There is much in it I'd rather not be reminded of.'

Konall snorted. 'You and me both. At least you weren't greeted with the sight that we were. Now can we go?'

Without a further word, they left the light of the fire, Konall leading them unerringly into the gloom. They skirted telltale campfires and their progress proved straightforward. Brann could remember nothing of how he had come to be in the burial pit, but it had been obvious from the start that there had been some sort of battle, although the only men remaining were those tasked with clearing the dead, and paid for their troubles with the loot. Those who had fought would seem to have moved on. He glanced around and counted no more than six or eight campfires, two of them with large pyres burning beside them. He pictured the pit he had been in, suppressing a shudder at the memory of slick bodies moving and sliding beneath him, and estimated the dead within it. Even if the men had doubled the number the following day to complete their pit, and assuming that all of the similar groups around them were allocated similar numbers to deal with, then the dead numbered in the low hundreds rather than the thousands. So not a major battle, then.

It still didn't explain his involvement, though. Or his failure in combat, which worried him more. It was only luck that had kept him alive, and chance was the most unreliable of all factors, and the one he generally tried to avoid having to consider.

His thoughts were interrupted as he stumbled.

Instantly, Gerens caught him by the elbow, taking the sack from him with his other hand. 'Steady there, chief.'

'Thank you. I'm fine now.'

But Gerens maintained his hold on Brann's arm. And Brann, feeling a weariness, hitherto banished by the energy of combat, creep over him, said nothing to shake off the support.

They left the fires behind without incident and found the horses picketed by the three boys in a copse on the far side of a hillock from the small valley where the conflict had been fought, dark shapes scattered in the gloom below and the noise of scavengers – human and animal – moving among them proving that the work to clear the bodies would continue into the next day. Brann shuddered. Had he not wakened when he did...

Gerens sat Brann in front of him, the wiry strength in his arms providing a calming security. As they moved off, Brann decided they were far enough from danger to be able to gain some idea of how fate had led him to a burial pit. The swaying of the horse, however, the weight removed from his legs, the companionship of his friends... it all felt so welcome that he decided to enjoy it for a few moments before questioning Gerens.

He was woken by a shout of alarm. Breta's familiar booming tone was not happy as her powerful arms lifted him from the horse. 'What do you bring me, you fools? You return him to us in such a state? He is barely conscious.'

'Small wonder,' said Cannick's calm growl as his fingers pulled the blood-soaked tunic away from Brann's side.

The sharp pain as the material pulled away from the wound on his ribs dispelled the torpor of his recent sleep and almost immediately threatened to send him back there as his head swam.

'That's an impressive nick you've got there, son. Looks like more on your arm, too. Breta, lay him by the fire where I can see better. And cut that tunic from him. Marlo, bring me my pack. We'll see if we can get him sorted out before the others return. No need for them to get the shock we did when we saw him.'

'Be grateful,' Konall's voice said from behind them, 'that you did not suffer the shock we endured when we first saw him. I have seen some unpleasant sights in my time, but...'

Brann almost laughed, but the pain it caused stopped him. He settled for a weak smile. 'Glad I made an impression.'

Konall grunted. 'Fear not, it was one I will struggle to forget. Though believe me, I will try.'

'At least you can smile.' There was relief in Hakon's honest voice. 'I don't feel right when you are not smiling for more than a few heartbeats.'

Breta laid Brann beside a small fire set in a small depression cut into the ground to minimise its glow. It had been allowed to burn low – the night was warm enough as it was, and, cooking time over, it served only to provide what little light was safe enough for them to allow. Gerens squatted silently beside him, his dark eyes burning with as little hint as ever of the thoughts behind them, but deep concern born in hope filling the way he leant forward. Cannick brought a water skin and a clean rag, and started washing around the two wounds and the lump on the back of Brann's head. Satisfied that the bump was no more than that, he turned to the wounds, starting to clean them with short efficient movements. Brann sucked in a sharp breath through gritted teeth as the cloth touched the open wounds, and once more as water was again poured over them. His head grew light, but he forced his breathing to be deep and slow and, the more Cannick's work was repeated, the more the feeling became bearable and more sensation than pain. Similar, he mused, to the cold plunge pools in Sagia – what seemed an overwhelming shock, at first, soon dissipated against all your expectations to a bearable level. Similar, but a bit more painful in this case. Still, the aftermath of every gladiatorial contest in the Empire's capital had involved work of some sort to a variety of wounds, so he fell into the familiar process of concentrating on his breathing. The slice along his ribcage was attended to first, and the pricks when the needle and thread pulled together the deep cut on his arm brought him relief, as he knew the ordeal was close to an end.

Cannick grunted, peering at his handiwork. 'It'll do. Now get in the river and wash the rest of you before I pass out from the smell.'

Brann smiled his thanks. There was something he had to do first, however.

The horses were restless as he approached, the scent of death that still encased him making them shift nervously against the ropes tethering them but the noise helping him to find them in the darkness. His own horse whickered as he stopped in front of it, eyes widening and nostrils flaring. He stroked its face just as it liked, and spoke softly until it calmed. Moving to the side, he felt in the darkness behind the saddle to feel the familiar heavy cloth of a cloak. His fingers traced the line of a repair, feeling the marks of his mother's careful stitches.

A throat clearing behind him made him jump. He turned, and then relaxed when he saw Marlo, receiving an apologetic smile in return.

'You've learnt to move quietly!'

Marlo shrugged. 'It was something I always could do, but Sophaya has been helping me improve, just as you help me with my weapons.'

'Really? I never noticed.' He saw Marlo's look, and raised his eyes to the sky at his own slowness of thought. 'Of course. That is the point of her speciality.' Brann nodded, considering. 'It is good. It helps to be as skilled as you can at as many things as you can. Especially the things that help you to stay alive.' He ducked to one side and came up to flick the back of a hand at the side of Marlo's head. The boy fended it off with a flick of his wrist and they both laughed. 'I hope she is a more patient teacher than I am. And there are at least three others who have trained for years longer than I have.'

'But you are the best at finding a way to win.' Marlo grinned.

'Mongoose moves more similarly to you. She would understand what works for you.'

'I would not like to upset Hakon. He still has ambitions.'

Brann's laugh burst from him. 'You mean he still doesn't know?' Marlo shook his head, his eyes twinkling in the moonlight. 'We really should tell him, but it's too much fun.' He laughed again, softly, as his mind pictured an image. 'Anyway, Gerens is fine with you having private time with Sophaya?'

'Of course. You know Gerens. Everything is taken as it is.'

'True. But Breta – she is expert with weapons I have never even seen.'

'I am quite happy with both of my tutors, thank you. Each is equally adept.'

'Ever the diplomat, trying to keep us all happy.'

'Why not? It is only fair, as you all make me happy by allowing me to travel with you.'

Brann gripped the boy's shoulder. 'Marlo, never be

mistaken. You are as much a part of this group as any of us.' The silence stretched, almost awkward. Brann turned to the horses. 'Saddled?'

'We kept them ready and the essentials already on them, in case we needed to leave in a hurry after we found you.'

Brann's hand strayed to the bundle behind his saddle, and Marlo smiled. 'Your father's cloak is most definitely one of the essentials.'

Brann smiled. 'Thank you.' He made to start unbuckling the saddle. 'Perhaps we can now make the horses more comfortable for the night.'

'Indeed, but I am afraid that you must have become accustomed to the way you... well... not to put too fine a point on it... stink. It is not good for the horses. Even your own is finding it hard to stay calm.'

Brann paused. It was true. 'I should wash.'

'You should wash. I will see to the horses.'

It was only a short walk to the river, a small effort little more than a brook. Kneeling waist deep in the water, Brann savoured the refreshing cold, a welcome contrast to the hot humid air that was oppressive even close to the middle of the night. There was a splash behind him and he whirled, wary of the day's danger not yet being finished. But it was only Breta he saw, striding through the water as if it were a puddle. He turned his back as quickly as he had first turned, clutching both hands to conceal his groin.

The girl laughed. 'Fear not, little gnat. It is your arse that my eyes have always preferred to feast upon.' A massive hand slapped the relevant part of him to emphasise the point. It also served to immerse him, face first, in the water, before the same hand caught his arm – thankfully his uninjured right one – and hauled him back upright. 'That's you rinsed. Let's get you washed. You do the front and I will tend to the side you cannot reach, which also of course contains this firm little arse.'

Brann couldn't help but laugh. 'You really are just like a female Hakon, aren't you?'

An even harder slap answered that, but this time with the other hand holding him in place. 'He is just like a male me. A pale imitation. Ask the men of the last town we visited.'

Brann grinned his amusement. 'Only you and he would use a town in the nightmare grip of a siege as an opportunity to bed as many locals as possible.'

'He did try hard to follow my example with due enthusiasm, I'll grant him that. It is always good to spread good feelings where otherwise despair would rule.'

'You have a good heart.'

'It was not the heart I was seeking,' she guffawed, slapping him a third time. Brann resolved to end the conversation while he could still walk, and concentrated on washing himself while Breta did likewise on his back.

As soon as he had dried himself, and before he could fully dress, Cannick inspected his wounds and wrapped them in clean cloth. 'This should keep them clean. I'll check them each morning and night, but as long as the cleaning has kept infection at bay, they should heal without restricting your shield arm.'

Brann grasped the older man's arm as a surge of emotion swept through him. 'Thank you, Cannick. I don't know what I'd do without you. What any of us would do.'

The broad shoulders shrugged. 'One day you will have to. Learn enough from my infinite wisdom until then.' He winked, passed Brann his clean tunic and carried his pack back to the rest of his belongings.

Tended and washed, Brann felt a weariness sweep over him. The others were pottering about with minor tasks, their attention on the minutiae of camp life. He moved to where his pack lay on the edge of the fire's light, and spread his blanket on the ground as far from the heat of the embers as possible. The night was still warm, but the glow of light was also welcome. He took off his boots, curled up and closed his eyes.

Brann woke slowly but realised quickly that he would not find sleep again easily. His mind filled with thoughts, one racing on to find another waiting, and he tossed from one side to another before deciding a change of scene might help.

He rose and moved to the river bank, dangling his feet in the welcome cool of the water. The eddies swirling before him were lit by the full moon, and his mind whirled in tandem. Images of the pit of corpses merged into the degenerate fighting pits below Sagia where Loku had sent him to die and where the horror had forced him from his own mind to let his body survive. Dead bodies beneath his feet faded into dying bodies at his feet. And all the time, blood ran down his face, smeared his body, dripped from his hands.

Gerens sat beside him, his arrival causing Brann to jerk in surprise. 'Have you all been practising creeping up on people?'

The other boy's expression was as implacable as ever. 'I don't need to practise that.'

Brann's irritation had already dissolved. He smiled softly. 'I'm certain you don't.' He sighed. 'Every time I go to do something since I got to the camp, someone seems to appear beside me.'

'You wonder why?' The tone was matter-of-fact, not challenging. 'You were not in a good state when we found you.'

'I was in a better state than when Grakk pulled me from the pits of the City Below after Loku had sent me down there to die.'

'*Better* is not necessarily *good*, chief.'

'I did learn a lot in those pits, right enough. Not so much in the pit of corpses this time.'

'I suppose you learnt this time that you weren't a corpse, which is a fairly good discovery to make.'

Brann almost smiled. 'I was lost to myself in the City Below, Gerens. I will never be able to repay you all for what you did to bring me back.'

He sensed more than saw Gerens's shrug. 'You did what you had to do to survive. We did what we had to do to help you live.'

Brann paused to push aside the reluctance to say the next words. 'There was a change in me, left by the pits. You know that, don't you? There is a killer inside me.'

Gerens snorted. 'There is a killer inside us all for when we need it. Some indulge it, some use it. The difference in you, chief, is that you are very good at it.'

'And that is actually a good thing?'

'In the world we live; on the road we travel?' Gerens jerked and there was the sound of a soft plop as a small stone was cast into the water. 'Without doubt.'

They sat in silence for a while. That Gerens was a more familiar companion than Marlo was reflected in the fact that quiet lay more easily over this pair.

Silence, until Gerens cleared his throat. 'Warm weather.' Brann looked at him. 'Heavy air, hard to breathe sometimes, don't you think?'

Brann nodded, looking back at the water. 'It is. Need a storm to clear the air. Rain would help it.'

'It would. Just enough to clear it. It has been pleasant to be free of quite as much rain as we have in our land.'

'Indeed. These lands do have that advantage.' Brann yawned. 'It's late, I suppose. Probably best to go back to sleep.'

'Indeed.'

They walked back to the group of sleeping figures beside the fire. Konall's space was empty – he would be somewhere in the darkness, keeping watch. Brann lay down once more on his blanket.

'Gerens?'

'Yes, chief?'

'Thank you.'

'Any time, chief. Every time.'

Dawn was starting to fade the darkness when he woke again. The camp was stirring as Grakk, Sophaya and Mongoose rode into their midst.

Mongoose stopped her horse close to the rising group around the fire. 'So you found him then.'

Konall grunted. 'Be glad it was us and not you who found him.'

The girl raised her eyebrows in question, but Hakon cut in. 'Please do not start Konall on this subject again. He has been badly affected by the experience. He may never be the same again.'

Konall grunted. '*Will* never.'

Mongoose slid wearily to the ground. The other two also, Brann noticed, looked bowed by fatigue as they dismounted. She led the three horses to the river, while Grakk glanced at Brann, then looked pointedly at Cannick. The grey-haired old warrior nodded back briefly, enough to satisfy the wiry tribesman for now. Grakk nodded in return, the soft light enough to make visible the intricate tattoos on his shining scalp that marked him as from the people of the deserts beyond Sagia – people who allowed, and indeed fostered, the misconception of them as simple uncivilised nomads, to maintain the secret that they harboured the accumulated knowledge of the known world.

Gerens's query was more audible, though barely in more words. 'You took a while. Trouble?'

Sophaya shrugged. 'Avoiding trouble, more like. We were on the far side of the field of dead, and had to lay low to avoid a patrol. We also took a trip into the main camp to see if Brann was among the prisoners, which by necessity was not the fastest of visits.'

'You went into their camp?' Gerens was aghast. 'Do you realise how dangerous that was?'

Breta's laugh boomed across the fire pit. 'You say that as if we have a safe and dull life as it is.'

Gerens was not to be deterred. 'But still…'

Sophaya smiled sweetly. 'Oh, darling dearest, are you worried about me?' She patted his arm softly. 'Fear not, the three who were there were the three best suited to slipping through shadows. And I am the best of the three.'

Grakk winked at Gerens. 'She is undoubtedly correct in that. She is like a shadow herself.'

Gerens nodded in acceptance. 'She is magnificent,' he conceded.

'So,' Cannick cut in. 'We know you didn't find him among the prisoners.'

Grakk's stare was bleak. 'We did not find any prisoners.'

'You wouldn't.' They all looked at Konall. He shrugged. 'What do you expect? This is the remains of an army, in retreat. Thanks to you,' he looked at Brann, 'they no longer have their leader, since you cut his head off in the battle that lifted the siege of the town, and they are no better than a rabble, looting to take what they can to, in their eyes, redeem a bad situation on their way, heading home. That does not include keeping prisoners to feed.'

Hakon frowned. 'That doesn't need to include slaughtering simple villagers. That was a whole settlement wiped out. Farmers and their families are hardly a deadly enemy to leave at your back.'

Cannick spat. 'Some people just enjoy the killing. Doesn't make it right, but it's a fact.'

Brann nodded. He had seen enough of that in his time to know the truth in it. He frowned, however, frustrated at the fog in his memory that was obscuring something with as much magnitude as the slaughter of innocents, but leaving his questions for now.

Mongoose had tended to the horses and accepted a hunk of dry bread from Hakon. 'Anyway, they'll get what's coming to them. If they had bothered to scout ahead, as we did after we needed to leave their camp on the far side, they'd know they are heading directly towards a proper army coming to teach them why they shouldn't have come here in the first place.'

'Good,' Brann said quietly. They had their own business to concern them, but he was glad to think of the fate that awaited such savage butchers. 'Let them meet their doom. They are heading east; we are heading north. We have Loku to catch, and we were delayed enough when we got ourselves trapped in that town's siege. We need to make haste if we are to stand any chance of catching Loku and learning of the conspiracy he is part of. Any animosity we bear him from his misuse of his position as the Emperor's spymaster and the ills he has done us personally is secondary to discovering the true nature and extent of the threat facing the lands of the North. We have to work our way up through his superiors, remember, if we are to learn both who is the leader controlling all and what actually is planned. We cannot afford to waste any time at all.'

Cannick had brewed coffee, and passed it around. 'Take some of the Empire's greatest export – after wine, of course – and settle down. These three need a rest. A few hours today won't make a huge difference.'

Mongoose stood up. 'If we stop early enough tonight, I can sit on a horse until then.'

Grakk glanced at Sophaya. She gave a defiant nod, as if any suggestion that she could not achieve the same were an insult. 'Agreed,' the tribesman said. 'Let us saddle the horses.'

Conscious that they should be well clear of even the remnants of the army before they could feel safe, Brann waited a good hour before moving his horse beside Hakon's to broach the subject he had been given little chance to address since being found the previous night. In truth, he could have asked any of his companions, but Hakon's affable and guile-free manner would ensure he received the most open of answers.

The large boy proved the point before Brann had even opened his mouth. 'You want to know how you ended up where you did, don't you?'

'Yes.' He desperately did. He could remember all of his savage primeval time in the fighting pits below ul-Taratac, and thanks to the administrations of the most learned of

Grakk's tribe in bringing him back from the creature he had retreated into as a means of surviving the pits, he had accepted his experience for what it was – a part of his life that had, at its most simple, happened. What it had changed in him, he could never change back, but the shaman Grakk had taken him to had rescued and returned Brann's soul, his persona, his essence; whatever word was applied to it, and whatever the man had done to him, he had brought *Brann* back from where he had been hiding from those very changes. Now he was in control, he was the real Brann in normal life. But in combat the other Brann – the animal living only to survive – would re-emerge, only to subside, satisfied, when the danger was past. Or, at least, emerge as much as he would allow. He could not resist the rise of his other self in times of danger, as it was as much a part of him as any other part of his character, but in having the original side of him, the side of emotions, of civilised thought, of memories and the nuances of character that they create – in short, *his personality* – having that returned had given him an element of control over the cold efficiency of the side buried deep. When that other element rose, it dominated, but there was still a thread connecting him back to himself, like a cave explorer's rope fed back in his wake to the outside world. But retaining that awareness when his primeval self took over, that knowledge of how he was behaving... did it remove the excuse that acting in such a coldly brutal way was outwith his true personality? Did it mean that he could not escape responsibility for what could, at times, be ferociously savage? And did that make him evil? A killer? Insane? But if those same savage actions and coldly efficient decisions were all that stood between the survival of himself and those he deemed good people, did that then justify them, make them morally the right thing to do? He had spent countless hours agonising over such questions before realising that it made no difference. He could not change it, so to wonder as to its label was immaterial. What did matter was how he acted towards those around him, and that this had indeed kept him, and at times them, alive. The rest of the time, he was much the same person as he had been before his time in the lawless pits in the caverns below Sagia, albeit hardened and less naïve and with lapses into melancholy and occasional nightmares – not all of which were when he slept. He could live with that.

And the thought of surrendering that tenuous link to himself, of allowing the darker side of him to assume total control, to swamp him, to open up the possibility of his true self never finding its way back – the thought made him shudder.

But what worried him more immediately was his lack of memory of the recent events. It reminded him too much of the immediate aftermath of his time in the vicious pits of the City Below, when his mind's response to the blood-soaked and death-laden distortion of the more skill-based gladiator fights in the mainstream arenas above ground had been to abandon any concept of his real self. Was he slipping back into that shell? Was the cold killer asserting control? Was he losing himself?

'Yes please,' he said to Hakon.

Hakon's look was appraising. 'How recently can you remember? Sagia? Or the journey along the coast and then turning north through all those really nice small villages with the nice village girls? Or taking the boat into Markethaven during a siege because there had been news of a man matching Loku's description having been seen

30

there? Or becoming trapped there for the duration of the siege only to find that he had left before it started? Or leaving the city after the siege, and reaching the valley where the village was attacked? Or...'

Brann cut in. 'The journey from Markethaven: I remember until that and everything before. I don't remember the village, or setting up camp at that place, or anything after.'

'Well, you weren't with us when we set up camp, so you wouldn't remember that.' Hakon regarded him again. 'So you don't remember coming out of the trees to see those bastards cutting down the villagers. It was only a portion of what is left of the army, maybe a thousand soldiers or so, but the poor sods had no chance. The place was bigger than the smallest villages, but not as much as a town, just a few hundred ordinary folk living off the surrounding farms and the trades that go with their produce. The men were barely armed with working tools, never mind the women and children who were totally helpless.'

Brann stared into the distance. 'Sounds like what happened to my village.'

The big Northern boy gave a grunt. 'That would explain your madness. Before we knew it, you were galloping off to take on a couple of hundred armed men single-handed. You didn't even have your mail on – it was a warm day, and we hadn't expected trouble. We went after you, of course, but we were beaten back by the numbers. It was just too many. I'm sorry.' He fell silent, but just as Brann started to reject the need for any apology, Hakon drew a breath and continued. 'The last we saw, you had worked your way through to a group of men, maybe fifty, who were outside a hall where their families had taken refuge, defending it as best they could against many times their number. By the time we had regrouped, your horse had found its way clear, but you hadn't.'

It was Brann's turn to fall silent. Doubtless his companions in the burial pit had been drawn from those brave men.

'It is I who should be sorry. I could have condemned us all.'

Hakon shrugged. 'Sometimes the good in us overpowers the sense. This was your time for that. Those people were already dead. They didn't know it yet and you just didn't want to accept it.'

Brann frowned. 'It was stupid. I should have seen that.'

'We all have a demon inside us. The good you showed is what keeps it under control. It was our fault for not being quick enough to stop you. We know we are all capable of doing what you did, so should have anticipated it in time. But we didn't, and you did what you did. *Should have* changes nothing, and pondering it only delays the solution. So we regrouped, waited until we *could* do something, and then did it. Except that we expected that the something we could do would be to find you and bury you properly – that's what your people do, isn't it? Bury your dead.' Brann nodded. 'It seemed your time had come. Only Marlo was determined you were still alive, but that's Marlo for you.' His face split into a huge toothy grin. 'Turned out the wee mad bastard was right, after all, which we were all very pleased about. Especially me – I shudder at the thought of telling my sister I had returned but you had not.'

Brann couldn't help but laugh. For the second time in a few hours, he was grateful for the counsel of his friends, no matter the form it took. And Hakon's mention of Valdis gave him an extra eagerness to hasten their journey northwards. 'Thank you, Hakon.'

'No, thank you. It was worth all of it for the look on Konall's face when we found you.'

Brann laughed again. Remembering that expression didn't make the time in the pit worthwhile. But it did help.

Konall reined up his horse where the road crested a rise, and the others bunched around him. A walled town rose from the plain before them, buildings at this distance seeming to have been crammed in by a giant hand, so tightly packed that only a jumble of rooftops could be seen within the grey walls. The morning sun was high in the sky, and glittering around the outskirts suggested a moat of some sort. Farms dotted the plain as if the same giant had strewn them in one scattering sweep of his arm, but they were the only habitation outwith the protection of the walls. This place did not welcome intruders.

'Belleville,' Cannick said, staring at it. 'The beautiful town. In reality, it is anything but. It is drab, dour, and unpleasant, and has the people to match. But the northern coast before we take ship for the Green Islands juts out into the seas at its north-west corner, so if Loku hasn't wanted to sail round it and is instead cutting overland to sail the short distance to the islands, he will pass through this town. So, to my distaste, it is advisable that we do too.'

Hakon grinned. 'So you've been here before then, Cannick?'

The old warrior leant to the side and spat on the dry ground dismissively. 'More times than I would have liked. Two major routes, north-south and east-west, meet here, so it holds an important position, and don't they know it. Still, passing through has been a necessity before, and it's a necessity now. Might as well get it over with.'

The others readied themselves to move. Most were still mounted, but Brann's pack had worked loose in its bindings and its rhythmic bumping against him for the past few miles had been irritating him, so he had slipped to the ground to take the chance to secure it more tightly. Grakk also was on his feet, picking a stone from his horse's hoof, and Brann cast an eye over the road ahead. They were on the highest point and it undulated through a series of ever-lower rises until it met the floor of the plain. On the next rise, a man struggled alone to fix a cart that had lost a wheel. Brann nodded in his direction. 'Looks like he could do with a hand.' He glanced at Cannick. 'I know you want to get in and out of this place as quickly as we can, and pick up Loku's trail as soon as possible if he has indeed passed this way, but it wouldn't take us long if it isn't too badly damaged.'

The broad shoulders shrugged. 'We are passing that way anyway. We can see when we get there.' He kicked his horse forward without hesitation, accepting Brann's opinion.

Brann swung himself into the saddle, his mail shirt clinking slightly as he did so. The pain from his ribs irked him more than that from his arm, not only because it hurt however he moved but also because it was a reminder of the folly of charging unprotected into a battle where blows will come from all unseen angles. Although ironically, he mused, had he not suffered wounds enough to render him unconscious, he would probably have fought on to his death. Still, he had donned his mail at the first stop to water the horses after Hakon had recounted his story, hot sun or no hot sun.

His hands automatically checked the helmet, shield, and bow hanging at vantage points around his saddle, and eased his sword in its scabbard, while his eyes fixed themselves on the scene at the cart. His gaze flicked to the area around it, searching for any sign of movement or disturbed wildlife, but his attention was mainly on the working man. Just because the distant figure had his back to them didn't mean he was unaware of their presence. And just because he worked alone didn't mean he was alone. Brann watched the man through the shimmering of the hot air, and continued to watch as they moved forward, waiting for a telltale glance towards hidden companions, or even the unnatural pretence of remaining oblivious to them beyond the point where he could not have failed to notice their approach.

His mind settled comfortably into the watchfulness. He felt happier to be putting more thought into a situation as opposed to reacting in line with the impetuous side that had been born in the pits of the City Below; born, admittedly, as a necessity in an environment where stopping to think was the first short stride in a one-step march to death. Thinking was a small sign that his darker side was not extending its control, but it was a small sign that he grasped and held tightly.

They moved at a trot, not wishing to move any faster lest it seem too aggressive. Brann's eyes continually scanned for movement or shining metal in the area around, returning always to the man, but all that he could see was a carter labouring over a repair in the mid-day heat, the cargo, four large barrels, standing at the side of the road. When they were two bowshots away, the man straightened and turned, his face scarlet with effort and awash from pate to waist in sweat. If it was a ruse, the effort he was putting into his act was impressive. He watched their approach warily – a sizable group of riders, all armed, was a sight to make any stranded traveller nervous – and his hand strayed into the back of the cart for a hammer that, presumably, he had been using in his vain efforts to mend the wheel. He would know it would make no difference in the face of the odds he faced, but Brann guessed that he felt more comfortable with something, anything, but preferably something heavy, in his hand. Brann himself would.

The others drew up in front of him but Brann rode past, circling the area until he was happy that no hidden cut-throats lay waiting for their chance. Not that there was much cover among the small and sparse trees that the road cut through on its way to the plain, but it did no harm to be sure, and took only a moment. He walked his horse up from behind the cart as Cannick climbed stiffly from his saddle and slapped the road dust from his clothes.

'Look like you could do with some help, feller,' the griz-zled veteran said. 'Hot enough riding in this heat, never mind trying to sort a wheel on your own.'

The man, around the same age as Cannick but around half his width, relaxed. 'That I could, friend, that I could.' He wiped his brow with the back of one hand, but Brann noted that he still held the hammer in his other. These were not totally peaceful lands. 'It is indeed a touch warm today, but the problem is not so much the heat as the weight of the cart. I have not the strength I once did...'

Breta and Hakon strolled past Cannick. 'I wouldn't worry about that, little man,' Hakon said cheerfully as he continued beyond the carter, slapping him gently on the shoulder and causing the hammer to drop from the man's hand and narrowly miss his toes. 'We'll take care of that.'

The man's eyes widened and lifted high to follow the pair, regarding them as if a couple of trees had donned clothes and sauntered by. 'That's, er, very kind of you,' he said to Cannick, his eyes still flitting to the large couple. 'The pin snapped and the wheel just fell off the axle. Nothing else actually broke, so it is just a matter of lifting the cart to let the wheel be slipped back on. I have a spare bit of metal that will serve as a replacement pin in the meantime, if the cart could just be lifted by your two, er, enormous companions.' He looked quickly at Breta. 'No offence meant, madam.'

She frowned in confusion. 'Why would a compliment offend?' She shook her head as if some people were bewildering and turned to grip the underside of the wagon. Hakon did likewise, and in a heartbeat the pair lifted the heavy wagon level, allowing Brann and Gerens to slide the wheel back into place. Mongoose took a heavy iron nail, around a hand-and-a-half in length, from the man and dropped it through the hole previously meant for the pin, and Hakon lifted the hammer from the ground, bending the pointed end with a single blow to sit neatly flush with the axle and hold the nail in place.

Mongoose looked at the nail appraisingly. 'Nice work.'

Hakon beamed. He glanced at Brann and Marlo, and winked. Brann avoided catching the Sagian boy's eye – his own straight face was under enough pressure as it was.

The carter was also beaming, his smile containing considerably fewer teeth than Hakon's, but no less engaging with simple happiness for it. 'You are angels of the road, scions of the good gods sent to save a traveller in need. Jacques extends his thanks to the gods and to you for bringing you this way. May fortune bless your every step! May the road bless you with effortless passage! May the sky bless you with fair weather! May your boots bless you with feet free of blisters!'

Mongoose sidled up beside Brann, her voice a murmur. 'Should have stopped after three blessings. Got a bit desperate by the fourth.'

Brann turned away, his shoulders shaking, as Breta and Hakon eschewed the planks that the carter had used to roll the barrels from the cart and lifted them directly back into it.

Grakk had been quietly watching, having taken the opportunity to seat himself on a rock at the side of the road. 'Your gratitude is gracious, but unnecessary, my friend. When a man with a predicament such as yours meets a group with capabilities such as ours, there should be only one outcome.'

'Perhaps in your experience, but not in mine, holy man,' Jacques said, mistakenly assuming Grakk's mode of speech and tattooed scalp to be based on religion. He sat on the back of his wagon, clearly glad of the rest before he was on his way. 'Most armed groups that are met on these roads are wont to take what you have of value and pay you by allowing you to live. If they allow you to live.'

Cannick frowned. 'And Belleville allows this?'

The man spat. 'Belleville protects Belleville, and its farms on the plain, nothing more. They patrol the plain and hide behind their walls. It is up to us to get ourselves there intact. In truth, the bandits are fairly harmless and not overly numerous. They are no more than lads made desperate by poverty, and if they get enough to keep them going, they are satisfied. The real crooks are in the town. When we do,' he spat again, 'they pay a pittance for what we have and charge a fortune for what we want.'

Brann turned, humour forgotten in the face of injustice. 'Can you not take your goods elsewhere?'

Jacques shrugged. 'Nowhere else close enough to make it viable, young man.'

Brann still found it hard to understand. 'Can you not refuse to sell unless they raise their prices? And refuse to buy at the prices they set?'

The man smiled sadly. 'They grow their necessities for life; what they buy from us is over and above that, such as this oil I carry today. These goods enhance their life and they would not like to be without them for any length of time, but they can afford to survive on basics, just to make a point, and are stubborn enough to do so. We, however, need what they sell to produce what we do, and need their coin to buy what we eat. If I had a farm that produced all I needed to live, I would never soil myself with visiting that accursed town. Too late in my life, though, to change what generations of my family have done. We are carters, pure and simple. We transport, we are paid for transporting, we buy from our neighbours what we can avoid going to town to acquire, and then we transport some more.'

'So,' Brann said slowly, a thought growing. 'If you didn't have to go to the town today, you would not be distressed.'

The gap-toothed grin returned. 'If I did not have to go to the town today, I would be bloody overjoyed, young man. Sadly, however, a consignment must be delivered for the fee to be paid, and the consignment will be paid for in the town.'

Brann looked at Grakk, then Cannick. 'Unless the consignment and the cart are both bought at the side of a road and delivered by its new owners in your stead.' His eyes had returned to the carter by the end.

The carter shrugged. 'Should that be a possibility, it would be a welcome possibility.'

'What are you thinking, Brann?' Cannick was cautious.

'I am thinking that a band of armed riders at the gates of a town renowned for its less than welcoming attitude would arouse suspicion. But a band of armed riders escorting a cart through dangerous bandit-ridden countryside would make more sense.'

'Could we not,' Konall said, 'just escort this man to the gates of the town and pose as an escort in that way without having to pay for it in the first place?'

Hope began to fade from the old man's face.

Brann shook his head. 'Jacques has been doing this all his life, which is a considerable length of time.' He looked at the man. 'No offence meant.'

The man flashed his few teeth at Breta. 'Why would a compliment offend, eh, young lady?'

She nodded solemnly. 'Indeed.' She turned to Hakon. 'He called me a lady. Did you hear that?'

Brann continued quickly before Hakon could get himself into trouble. 'The guards at the gate will know Jacques, and would wonder why he has broken the habit of a lifetime to now employ a guard. Whereas,' he glanced at Konall, 'a new man starting his business in this area, made nervous by the stories of banditry, might panic and hire a sizable escort. That might seem natural, might it not?'

The tall blond boy nodded. 'It could make sense.'

Brann looked at Grakk. 'We have the ability to pay.'

Grakk looked at Sophaya, having entrusted to her the pouches of coin passed to them by their benefactor in ul-Taratac – as the Sagians called their empire – to fund their mission, wherever Loku led them. Who better to know how to keep safe such valuables than the one natural thief in the group?

She nodded. 'Of course. If that is what you want, it is there.'

Brann took a selection of coins from Sophaya and collected them into a pouch. He turned back to the old carter. 'Can you buy a new cart in time for your next delivery?'

'No need, young man. I have two, in case an accident befalls one with more dire consequences than today's mishap. In any case, your price is far too high. Half of that would more than suffice, even after I purchase two more horses.'

Konall made to speak, but a glare from Cannick and a dig of Mongoose's sharp elbow jolted him into uncharacteristic restraint.

Brann handed the pouch to Jacques. 'It is the right amount.'

Cannick had suggested approaching the town's main gate a little after dusk had started to fall, when the heat of the day had left the guards tired and thinking more of a refreshing drink than the duty involved in the remainder of their shift.

The wait allowed the others to rest in the shadow of the cart while Sophaya rode with the old man to a nearby steading, where he could borrow a mount to see him home. The glee on his face attested to the infrequency in his life when he could wrap his arms around the waist of a young woman. Gerens's glare removed the glee for as long as it took, Brann noticed with amusement, for the pair to move beyond the grim boy's line of sight.

Brann sat on the ground and rested his back against the recently repaired wheel. He folded his arms, rested his chin on his chest and closed his eyes, but found himself unable to snooze as the others were doing. His mind whirled and calculated, thoughts fired by his relentless impatience to reel in Loku. His thinking was hampered, though, by his nagging regret at missing the man at Markethaven by only a matter of days, only to be trapped there by the siege for weeks, the frustration driving his mind in circles.

The irritation was still refusing to leave him alone after they had moved off, the sun low in the sky but the air no less stifling for it. He nudged his horse beside those of Grakk and Cannick.

'How long do you think—?'

Grakk cut in with a smile. 'It would take Taraloku-Bana, or Loku, as he calls himself in these more norther parts, to reach here? I am only surprised, young Brann, that it has taken you so long to ask when you had time this afternoon to ponder it.'

Brann frowned. 'I was thinking about it, yes, but every time I tried to think about it, my head kept returning to the way we came so close to him, and yet still he managed to stay ahead of us, while we lost even more time. It was as if the gods were toying with us like a bully dangling a toy in front of a child: almost in reach but then pulling it away at the last instant.'

Cannick spat into the dusty road. 'The gods do not toy with us. What happens, happens. All we can do in this game that is life is play the dice the way they fall and not waste time wishing they had shown different numbers, or some other player will step in and play our turn.'

Grakk looked at the old soldier with narrowed eyes. 'An interesting theological philosophy, my friend. Can I ask your religion?'

Cannick barked a cynical laugh. 'The religion of real life. I have seen many a soldier gutted who, moments before, had prayed to his gods, and others walk from battle without a scratch who had prayed just as piously. The gods may watch us, but the only people who can keep us alive are ourselves and our friends around us, if we are lucky enough to have them. Forget that, and place trust in great beings whose workings we only know of through priests and priest-esses – other people just like us, not magical beings of great knowledge, mark you – and all you will do is let your guard down. Plenty of time for pious men to speak to their gods when they meet up with them.'

Grakk nodded thoughtfully. 'I see. You term it "their gods". And so, do you believe there are no gods?'

'Oh, there must be gods.' A brawny arm swept to indicate the fields around them and beyond, then up to the sky. 'How else can all this be explained? Someone or something must have made it all, and must keep it all working. There's enough work there for an army of gods. Why would they bother whether one of us sticks a sword in another, or falls in love with another, or recovers from a hangover, or wins a wager at the gladiator pit, or whatever else people pray for? But then I'm just an old soldier, and that's just an old soldier's opinion.'

'An old soldier who is still alive, however,' Grakk pointed out, 'and whose opinion has therefore been formed and tested in many situations of living or dying.'

Brann thought that Cannick's views sounded similar to the views of his own upbringing, where practical people lived off the land and prayed in gratitude to gods representing all aspects of nature while, at the same time, learnt to work themselves with all the unpredictable vagaries of nature that each year threw at them. The real problems came from other men, not gods. The thought of home sent a wistfulness through him, prompting in turn thoughts of urgency – and Loku.

He could see that Grakk, the learned gatherer of knowledge, was now intrigued by Cannick's straightforward philosophies and had another question about to be asked. He cut in quickly. 'Loku? Distance travelled? Length of time?'

Cannick sighed theatrically. 'Oh, the impatience of youth. All right, young man, we shall work it out.' Grakk looked crestfallen, and Cannick patted him consolingly on the shoulder. 'Worry not, old friend, we can talk more later.'

He closed his eyes, as if to concentrate, and tapped one thumb against the fingers of that hand in turn, as if calculating. 'Let's see. From Markethaven, the last place we and he both were, it would be about seven days' sailing along the south coast and another eight northwards, up the side of the country.' His eyes flicked open and must have seen Brann's dismay. 'But that is in good weather, and in straight lines. He will have been hugging the coast because of the time of year – rough weather in the sea off the south coast and fullblown storms as he turned northward into the big sea. And not only will his winding route and the difficult waters have slowed him down, but he may well have had to put into port a couple of times when the weather got too bad for them.' He nodded at Konall and Hakon, riding side-by-side in silence ahead of them. 'The Southern sailors are nothing of the ilk of their lot, who would laugh at a storm and sail through it and out the other side as if the wind were no more than a baby's fart. But then, the Northerners have such skill bred into them. Those Loku has

44

taken passage with in his journey to meet up with his fellow conspirators,' he spat again, 'are not, as I say, that sort of sailor – we already know the first ship he took passage on had needed to put into Markethaven for repairs, causing him to wait until he could leave on the first ship to be headed his way. So I reckon, a good three-and-a-half weeks all in. Then a couple of days overland, east, to this town before us, if he didn't want to go by boat around the Point of the Last Lands, and I'm fairly sure he will have had quite enough of bumpy seas by then to want to take on the worst part of the sail. Say, four weeks as a good guess.'

Grakk nodded thoughtfully, his hungry mind already absorbed in this new task. 'By contrast, we were delayed three weeks, roughly, by the inconvenient siege of Markethaven, but were then able to cut diagonally across country to here, a trip so far of nineteen days.'

'Which,' Brann said slowly as his thoughts collected, 'would put us maybe a dozen days behind him.' He brightened. 'Which isn't too bad considering he doesn't know we are chasing him. And this is his journey, so he will keep moving. We, of course, do not know what business he will conduct when he reaches his destination, as discovering that is part of our mission, but in conducting that business his progress will be slowed, and all the time we will draw closer.'

'You see,' Grakk beamed, 'I was certain we could cheer up your disconsolate face.' He turned to Cannick. 'Now, about the gods and nature. Where would you say the gods' influence ends, and the innate actions of flora and fauna begin?'

Brann groaned and slowed his horse to drop back, out of earshot. He studied the fields around them, quiet as dusk approached. The creaking and squeaking of the cart and the knock of the horses' hooves were the only sounds: loud enough to mask the few voices that chatted – only Grakk and Cannick, as a matter of fact – but quiet enough to let him realise that work had finished for the day in the fields. The crops around this part of the road swayed slightly in the early evening breeze, their colour combining with the varying hues of other, more distant, fields to form a patchwork broken only by the occasional pasture hosting, in those he had seen so far, goats or cows. It was a scene that reminded him of home despite the harder ground and the irrigation channels Grakk had pointed out to him – a feature unheard of in his own rain-drenched homeland. He sighed. Home was a thought he had tried to avoid for the past year, but it had wormed its way into his head ever more often recently as they moved towards the islands. Depending on Loku's movements and where they led Brann and his party, he may never travel any further north than the South Island, but even just to head in this direction made repressing memories more difficult by the day.

He shook his head in annoyance. He had to focus on the danger this town presented now. He fixed his attention on the approaching gate, analysing the situation, to force aside his self-indulgent maudlin musings.

Two guards lounged at the entrance, one leaning against the gatepost, his jaded gaze resting on the approaching party. The other rested a shoulder against the outside of the wall, facing his companion as they passed the time, and seeing nothing in the first guard's expression to cause him to feel the need to turn his head towards the cart and its escort.

Brann's eyes had already scanned their weapons, though – they were well-tended and to hand. His own hand strayed onto his belt, close to his own sword hilt. Just because someone looked lazy and disinterested now did not mean they would stay that way. And just because they looked as if they would take an extra second to lower a spear or draw a sword did not mean that they did not know how to use them once that second had passed. Just because they obviously did not expect trouble did not mean they were unable to deal with it were it to appear before them.

The hooves of the lead horses clattered for a moment as they passed over the stone at the start of the bridge across the moat, then gave off a deeper rumble as they moved onto the wooden main section. Brann's eyes narrowed in curiosity, glancing from the bridge surface and then at the gateway, where a stout metal portcullis was ready to be dropped and where thick gates, banded with iron, could further block the way... but where no chains ran to the timbers of the bridge. He moved his horse beside Cannick's.

'No drawbridge?' he said quietly. 'Strange, given their desire to protect themselves from outsiders.'

'Look where the bridge meets the other side,' Cannick murmured.

Brann saw that the wood of the bridge led into a slot in the stone of the gatehouse. Cannick slowed his horse, pretending to check with a glance at the tailgate of the cart, to avoid closing on the guards while they were talking, and Brann followed suit.

'It slides in?'

Cannick nodded.

Brann's curiosity awakened. 'But why? It seems a great deal of extra effort to construct this. And a normal drawbridge provides an extra layer across the gateway to penetrate.'

'A normal drawbridge remains exposed when lifted.' He smiled as Brann felt his face light up in understanding.

'A lifted drawbridge prevents attackers from crossing the moat, but also prevents defenders from doing the same,' Brann said. 'If those besieging the place can damage the drawbridge while it is raised, defenders cannot issue in numbers from the main gate for a counter-attack, and if the intent is to starve them, then it will also help to trap them within.' Brann brightened with enthusiasm as his understanding unfolded. 'This way, it can be withdrawn and protected. They already have a strong portcullis and gate to protect the entrance, not to mention the moat.'

'Good lad. I thought you'd get there eventually. The moat flows in from the north and out at the south, but they stop the exit during these drier months to keep the level high, only letting water escape as they need to.'

Brann thought back to the towns of Konall's and Hakon's homeland, ingeniously designed to make an attack virtually a suicide mission. 'Looks like they could give our friends in Halveka a run for their money in designing defences.'

Cannick grunted. 'No one touches the Halvekans on that score, and certainly not here. When you get inside, you'll see.'

Marlo reined up the horses in front of one of the guards, who had managed to rouse himself to confront them. The man looked sullenly around their company.

'What's this?'

Marlo cleared his throat hesitantly. 'I am bringing produce intended for the merchant, Patrice, in the Third Quarter, sir.'

The guard grunted. 'Don't know your face. And it is not a face that was born anywhere near here.'

'My family moved here from the Empire, good sir. I work for my uncle, who heard there was good work for carters here.'

Brann had already noticed that, while the second guard still lounged against the wall, his gaze had never stopped watching the riders, flicking from weapons to callouses on hands, from where they were looking to how they looked. These two maybe didn't expect danger, but they were watching for it.

'Why so many swords with you?' the first man asked, with more curiosity in his tone than suspicion.

His eyes scanned the group once more. Hakon was trying to slouch himself into a diminished size, but was still hulking over the man from his mount. Several of the others were no less intimidating: Konall knew no other way to hold himself than with the casual arrogance of one with years of training and of being obeyed; Gerens had a stare that suggested he would cut your throat without a passing thought; Cannick had the scars and the carriage of an experienced campaigner; Grakk just looked downright fearsome; and Breta... when the man's eyes alighted on her, he froze with a slight gasp. She treated the guard to what Brann knew she would be intending as a winning smile; the reaction from the man was a nervous swallow and a tightening of his fingers on his spear as he took a slight and involuntary step back.

Brann noticed he had not been one of those to elicit a response from the guard – he was happy for that to be the case. To be regarded as not a threat was to gain an advantage before the fight even started. The sentry steadied himself and glared at Marlo, seeming to be reassured by the fact that Marlo looked as nervous under his gaze as the man himself had done when noticing Breta's intimidating appearance.

'Pardon me, sir.' The fact that the anxiety evident in Marlo's voice was entirely natural was what had made him the obvious choice for the role. 'Pardon me, but my uncle had heard there was good work for carters here, but also that there was an element of danger. He preferred to err on the side of caution, as far as security was concerned, until we better learnt the true nature of the peril, as he had heard say that there were parts of the route where transported goods attracted the attention of nefarious brigands.'

A rough laugh burst from the man at that. '*Nefarious brigands*? I have heard them called many things, but that is a new one on me. So tell me, well-guarded young carter: why does your uncle the carter not drive his cart?'

'My uncle, sir, prefers to organise the business and to let his nephews carry out the simple task of driving the carts.'

'Your uncle prefers to sit in the safety of his home and let his nephews face the dangers he sees in the shadows, more like.'

Marlo was proving so effective that Brann found himself hating the fictitious uncle and warming to the sentry.

The guard stepped to the side and flicked his head towards the gateway. 'Typical Sagian. As if we don't have enough of your lot here already. Better get yourself and your many helpers into the safety behind our walls then. On you go.'

Marlo flicked the reins. 'Thank you, sir.'

They filed in after the cart. Breta winked at the guard, winning herself a flinch of fear. The young woman looked hurt.

Cannick had noticed as well. He slapped Breta heartily on the shoulder. 'Would you help me, good lady, find a suitable inn for us? I don't know about you, but I need an ale.'

Breta brightened immediately. 'First decent suggestion I've heard all day. Hopefully there are some men in this town who are less scared of the fairer sex than that mouse at the gate.'

And hopefully, Brann thought, there were plenty of them willing to talk. They needed information, and they needed it fast.

Chapter 2

The girl was still nervous in his presence. He liked that. It was a refreshing change from the confidence of the crone, and the fact that the old woman was usually right in what she said. But since the young one had started working for him, learning from him, striving to impress him, she had grown more adept at covering the nerves from all but eyes that sought it. He liked that more.

He did not look up from the fire. He also liked to maintain the nerves. And in the fire, he also saw welcome heat in the chill of the evening.

'You have news?'

'I expect you know I do, my lord.'

The nerves may still have been there, but had lessened sufficiently to allow room for boldness to creep in. Not a bad asset if she were to be effective for him, but he could not allow her to know he approved in even a small way where the boldness was directed at him.

He barked at her, his dry voice harsh. 'You forget who you address, girl. You served the princess well, but she is here no *more and you have but one master now, regardless of what the Steward of the Household Staff may think.' His head snapped round, eyes boring into her. He could see from the slightest of flinches before she caught herself that his glare had retained its potency despite his years. Maybe the age added to it. There must be some few counter qualities to infirmity, surely.*

She dropped her eyes. 'Apologies, my lord. I do not forget your eminence, but do forget myself. Forgive me.'

If it was an act, it was the right act. He grunted and waved a hand dismissively, looking back at the fire. 'Your news, now that you have remembered your manners?'

'The boy and his companions. They were heading in the direction of a town called Belleville.'

'I know it.'

'You know a town in the north of the Vine Duchies?' The surprise was clear in her voice. 'I do remember who you are and who you were, my lord, but this town is not a part of Sagia. Not even close to the border.'

His voice grew softer – slightly – as his mind drifted decades into the past. 'Sometimes to rule an empire, you must act outwith the empire. By accident or design, that town is located with great strategic advantage. There was no need to waste resources in a campaign against the Vine Dukes to add their lands to ours. We already had beneficial trade agreements and the dukes were merchant dukes, not warrior dukes. They were no threat, and we had what we wanted from them. But it was clear to me that Belleville had potential. It did no harm at all to make a gift of enough Scribes to help them establish an effective administration.'

He could hear the smile in her voice. 'No harm at all, when there are Sagian Scribes running a town along Sagian principles.'

Innocence suffused his tone. 'We are a benevolent people. I saw a chance for our principles to enhance the prospects of the people in a town where there was potential for commercial growth. Under our guidance, many there have become wealthy by the passage of travellers and trade through their town.'

'Passage that is carefully controlled and documented, I am sure. With records available to the higher echelons of the Empire's Scribes, should it be desired. And certain individuals among those record-takers who would report instead to someone other than the higher echelons of the Empire's Scribes.'

He shrugged slightly. 'There were, of course, fortunate benefits.'

'So if the boy...'

'The boy is a man now, in life if not in years. And he had better be, or he is of no use to us.'

'Apologies, my lord. If the...' She could not bring herself to say it, he noted. The remnants of bitterness may prove useful or may require handling. 'If he does pass through there, he will find available to him records that could tell him of he whom he follows?'

'Possibly.'

'There will possibly be records?'

'There will certainly be records. But he may or may not be able to gain access to them, or even know they exist. Our associates there do not know of him, or the significance of his prey. But that prey, remember, has his own network, greater than mine in numbers.'

'That is to be expected. He is the Emperor's Source of Information, after all.'

'Greater numbers is rarely an advantage in the war of

*knowledge. To be overwhelmed with information is as para-
lysing as having too little. With spies, it is far better to have
a shrewd person picking gems than a hundred shovelling piles
of ore that take days or weeks to sift through. Fortunately,
I have pickers while Taraloku-Bana has labourers.'*

*'If I may say, my lord, I doubt it is left to fortune to
govern your recruitment policy.'*

*'That, you may say.' He grunted. 'So, the party we follow
with interest. How long before they reach the town, if they
hold to the same path?'*

*'Already or soon, given where they were and how long
it took my source to reach here.'*

'And your source is reliable?'

*'Even apprentice Scribes are meticulous. Even more so,
in fact, in that they must impress to advance.'*

*'Meticulous, but not known for being any more free with
information than a corpse.'*

'Scribes are not celibate.'

*'You took him to your bed? I understood your bed
companions were drawn from the gender banned from the
Order of Scribes.'*

*'Where information is concerned, my bed companions
are governed by necessity. But no, I did not take him to my
bed. Nor did I visit his. After several weeks on the road,
merely the suggestion of such was enough to spark his
tongue to life.' She laughed suddenly – an unusual sound
from her recently. 'I mean he talked.'*

*It took him a moment to mask his amusement – something
else that was rare in recent times. 'And did he know who
you asked about?'*

*'He did not. I had to do a little sifting and prompting
before I could pick your gem for you.'*

'*You are learning. Make sure you continue.*'

'*You require obedience and wit, my lord.*'

'*Then leave me now, and persevere to give me more of both.*'

'*Yes, my lord.*'

Three words only, but enough to let him hear that she had heard the compliment he had given her. Or, at least, as close to a compliment as he would give. The girl was growing into her role, and he could see it before him, which was good.

The one of whom she had spoken had grown into what was needed – now that one needed to rise to what he must do – and all this old man could do was sit and hope, events unfolding unseen, and unknown, until they were weeks in the past.

He hated that.

He felt the chill of the evening. He looked into the fire, and saw danger.

****

Brann thumped into a seat in the tavern, the weariness of travelling in his bones but the fire of enthusiasm in his head. Marlo was ensuring the horses were well-tended by the grooms at the livery yard across the road, and Hakon was ensuring that sufficient food and drink were going to be available from the innkeeper's wife, while managing at the same time to eye the woman in the corner with the laces of her top just loose enough to show most of her cleavage; she in turn was eyeing Hakon's purse.

'So,' Brann said, 'once we have eaten, we can start trying to gather information.'

Gerens nodded across to the stairs leading to the bedrooms, where Hakon was disappearing with the loose-laced woman. 'Looks like you may have to wait for the big man.'

Brann slapped the table in frustration. 'Does he *ever* think with his head?'

Grakk laid a calming hand on his arm. 'Fret not, young Brann. He means that it might be best to wait until Hakon has returned to plot our next move. It seems that Hakon is more keen even than you to start gathering information.'

Brann frowned. He was not convinced.

Cannick grinned. 'Take it from me, Brann. If you want to know what is happening in a town, spend a week talking in markets and taverns or spend five minutes talking to a whore.'

Brann grunted. 'Maybe you're right. But I still don't think that's all he'll be doing up there.'

Breta guffawed, startling a man behind her into almost choking on his ale. 'There is truth in that. Better give him ten minutes, then.'

It was almost exactly ten minutes when Hakon rejoined them, oblivious to the amused looks passing between his companions.

'You took your time,' Sophaya said, as Brann and the recently returned Marlo stared at the floor, shoulders shaking.

Hakon's big shoulders shrugged. 'We had a lot to talk about.'

It was too much. Brann's spluttered laughter was replicated around the table. Grakk just smiled gently and slid along on the bench to leave room for the perplexed Northern boy. 'Ignore them, they are releasing accumulated stress at your – if I can describe it as such? – method of releasing accumulated stress.' The hilarity only redoubled at that, and Grakk raised his eyes to the ceiling. 'Sit, young hearty fellow. The food will arrive soon, and once these buffoons have composed themselves, you can tell us what you have learnt.'

Hakon cast his confusion aside as an irrelevance in the face of impending food, and lowered himself beside Grakk. Brann wheezed as his laughter subsided, his face and his ribs aching alike. The learned tribesman was, as ever, correct – he had not laughed as helplessly for as long as he could remember, and he felt better for it.

The appearance of the food and another round of ale forced them to compose themselves, although the mistress of the tavern, who looked no stranger to a sharp word if she thought it warranted, showed no sign of disapproval at their raucous behaviour. Laughter in an inn spoke of happy customers, and happy customers attracted more customers who wanted to be happy. And they needed more liquid fuel than those nursing their sorrows.

'So,' Cannick said once the food was served. 'What can you tell us, Hakon my lad?'

Hakon's shaggy head leant forward conspiratorially, although the noise in the rest of the common room was enough to make even those at the other end of his own table strain to hear him, never mind anyone elsewhere.

'Loku was here.'

Brann felt himself tense.

'He stayed a few days, then left a week ago.'

Brann leant forward. 'Left for where?'

The big shoulders shrugged. 'Don't know.'

'Was he with anyone?'

'Left with two men.'

'Who?'

'Don't know.'

'How does she know?'

Sophaya snorted. 'Men lose secrets as soon as they lose clothes.' Gerens looked at her, and her smile in return was sweet and innocent. 'So I have heard, my darling. And once a secret is out, all the girls know it.'

Brann was anxious, however. 'So who did speak to him?'

'Don't know.'

He felt his palms burn as hot as his frustration as he slapped the table. 'Oh, for the love of the gods, Hakon! Do you know *anything*?'

That Hakon was puzzled was painted across his big honest face. 'Of course I do. Why else would I come to tell you something?'

'*Well why don't you tell us?*'

Hakon frowned. 'Because you keep interrupting me.'

'I'm asking questions to try to find out what you know!'

Hakon was now quite obviously confused. 'But how do you know the right questions to ask if you don't know what I have to tell you?'

Brann paused. It was a good point. 'I don't.'

Hakon nodded sagely. 'That became clear when you kept getting it wrong.'

Konall flicked a chunk of bread at Brann's head. 'Perhaps,' he suggested in his languid tone, 'you should let the boy speak?'

Brann saw Cannick looking at him as Grakk leant to speak in the veteran's ear. He realised everyone was looking at him, and felt his cheeks grow hot. 'Sorry,' he mumbled.

'Right,' Hakon said cheerfully. 'What she did know is

that her friend took money from the captain of the Duke's personal guard.'

Sophaya perked up. 'Her friend is a thief?'

Brann grinned. His brain was starting to work at last. 'Her friend was doing what whores do with captains of guards. And at the end, one purse was heavier and one lighter.'

Sophaya grunted and took a bite from a chicken leg. 'Always warriors and whores. Why do we never get to meet any nice thieves?'

'Maybe there are just no nice thieves about,' Marlo offered brightly. Sophaya glared at him. 'Oh,' he said, colouring, and taking a sudden interest in tidying the crumbs on his platter.

Hakon cleared his throat. 'Anyway, the captain of the guard is a regular customer of Joceline's friend. Joceline is the nice girl from upstairs.'

'We guessed,' Brann growled. 'Anyway...?'

'Yes, well, he told Joceline's friend that a man calling himself Loku had stayed with the Duke for several days, and had been locked away in discussions with him for much of that time. He said that the man must have been important, because the Duke wasn't rude to him.' He looked around at the questioning faces. 'Apparently, the Duke is rude to everyone, so that was a big thing.' He laughed. 'I know, it sounds a bit trivial, but it seems that he is ruder than most around here, and this is not a very polite town as it is.'

Cannick snorted. 'I can vouch for that.'

'So,' Mongoose said, 'I think we need to have a chat with this rude Duke.'

'Just what I was thinking, too,' Brann said. He looked

at Hakon. 'Do you think Joceline could arrange to let us meet with her friend, so we can work out our best approach?'

Hakon's face split into a proud grin. 'Already asked her. It cost me extra, but if we go up to her room in an hour, they'll be there. The man the friend meets with has tastes in gratification that had, of late, turned to a more, er, painful type for Joceline's friend, but while the friend would like to end the relationship, the man is controlling and powerful and, it appears, even gains gratification from his power to keep the friend visiting unwillingly. I get the impression that if we can help with this situation in any way, the friend will be amenable to helping us in return.'

Grakk filled Hakon's flagon with ale. Even in a land renowned for the quality of its wine, the Northern boy's tastes remained constant and straightforward. 'Well done, young Hakon,' the tribesman said. 'You have indeed been a credit to yourself tonight.'

Hakon drained the flagon and reached for the pitcher to refill it, burping happily. 'Thank you, Grakk. It was hard work, but it was worth it in the end. I think my father would have been proud of me.'

Marlo almost spat his own drink across the table, and the laughter of the others filled the air above it. Brann, though, felt a stillness creep through him, and he stared into the large fire in the hearth, but the flames he saw were not those warming the room. He saw a mill alight, and a man in the doorway, holding off attackers before being driven inside the building. His home and his family, burning together. He shuddered and got to his feet, muttering about needing some fresh air.

The courtyard at the back of the tavern was quiet, a place of sharp contrast against the boisterous cheer of the common room inside, and a small barrel provided a convenient seat against the back wall of the building. Night had fallen completely, and a thin crescent moon slipped occasionally into brief sight between drifting clouds. Darkness had dropped across the sky in ul-Taratac in what seemed like a single breath compared with the gradual change he had been used to as a child, and while the dusk had been longer here than in the Empire, still it seemed fleeting here than at his home.

Home. He sighed and rested back against the wall, staring at the sky. Movement from the doorway to his right saw him relax almost as quickly as he had tensed. It was strange how, on a journey, you become attuned to the tread and breathing of your companions to an extent where you know who approaches without even realising what your ears have heard.

Cannick pulled over a small crate and sat beside him, groaning as he eased himself down. He laughed. 'You know when you are getting older when you make a noise every time you sit down or get up. Every so often you forget to try to hide it from those around you.'

Brann smiled, and touched his fingers to the ribs on his left side. 'Just like an injury.'

'We all try to hide what bothers us, lest it betray a weakness.' The grey head turned in the shadows to look at him. 'Don't we?'

Brann sat for a moment, then sighed. He waved a hand upwards. 'That sky. We could be anywhere. I was just wondering if the same sky is looking down on my home.' He stopped, his breath catching sharply in his throat for a moment. 'But then I wondered if I have a home any more.'

'You have seen much. You have changed and grown and

are not the boy who left that village. You have seen and endured more than most people would ever experience in a dozen lifetimes.' A big hard hand rested itself on his shoulder. 'It is only natural you would question where you fit in.'

The hand on his shoulder felt good, comforting, protective, understanding... fatherly.

He stood up quickly, tears stinging his eyes. 'It is that, yes. I meant it that way.' He wiped a sleeve across his eyes and cleared the roughness out of his throat. 'But I also meant it in a literal way. The last sight I had of my village was to see it under attack from those pirates you fought after I... after I came aboard your ship. The last sight I had of my home was it aflame. And the last sight I had of my father was him fighting men at the doorway. They forced him inside.' He took a deep breath. 'At least he was with my mother and my sister when he died.' His voice was a whisper. 'The last words he ever said to me were to drive me away over my brother's dead body. He wished it had been I who had died. The irony is, if he hadn't rejected me, he would have got his wish – I would have been in the house with them.' He sat down again and looked at the shadow of Cannick's face. Honesty lives more easily in the privacy of dark than the glare of day. 'There are times when I wish I had been in there with them. And with them now, wherever we go after,' he waved an arm expansively, 'all this.'

Cannick sighed. 'The life we live and the things we see, boy, there are times when we all think that way. But we still cling to life, and fight to cling, and use every last bit of strength to fight. It is what we do.' His hand ruffled Brann's hair. 'You are not alone. Remember that.'

Brann leant back against the wall again with his shoulders and head, staring at the darkness of the fragments of sky and the darker clouds framing them as silence fell over the pair. The clouds filled a space they could see but could never touch. Occasionally clouds came to earth and touched people, but people could never go up there to meet them. It was a world they knew was there, but could never reach. And beyond that world... Who even knew what was there?

'Cannick?'

'Yes?'

'What you were talking to Grakk about before. About the gods, and religions, and priests, and all that. Do you think there really is something after this life?'

The silhouette changed as the veteran warrior turned towards him. 'I think we don't know if there is or there is not. If there is, and we have lived life as well as we can here, then we can face whatever lies beyond as it comes to us. But if there is not, then it would be a terrible waste being given this life if we were not to live as much of it as we could, don't you think?'

Brann nodded. It made sense. 'But what do you believe? You must have seen so much. You must have heard so many priests, and listened to men talking about their gods. Is there nothing that makes sense more than the rest?'

Cannick laughed. 'In the right words, they all make sense. But let me ask you this: you have seen a fair bit yourself, and you were brought up respecting your own gods. What do you think?'

Brann stared into the darkness. 'I think,' he said slowly as his mind worked. 'I think that it is the people who matter, because religions are guided by people and followed by people.'

'Exactly. There are temples that preach violence and hatred, but they are few and badly followed. Why? Because of what people mostly want from religion: reassurance, understanding, hope, all connected with the things we don't understand or know.'

Brann remembered a comment from the campfire several weeks before. 'But Breta said that religions have started more wars than anything else.'

Cannick barked his harsh laugh. 'Take it from an old soldier, people start wars, not religions, and for all sorts of reasons. Power and fear being two of the main ones. Religion is a tool some use to do that, but it is the most powerful tool man has ever known for that end. Like everything else, what one man can use for good, another can use for bad.'

'So it is just a sham? A tool for controlling people?'

Cannick laid a calming hand on his arm. 'You tend to overthink things, Brann. It is what it is. It feeds needs that we all have, and if it makes people get on, take care of each other and respect the world around them, if it gives people peace and calms them when they worry about answers they can never know for sure in this life, then what does it matter what names they give their gods or what position they adopt to speak to them?'

Brann sat in silence. This simple soldier's life had given him an outlook that strangely mixed common sense and cynicism to create tolerance. But there was something else. 'But what about those savages Loku had gathered in the mountains of Halveka? The ones who captured Hakon and Gerens, and who tried to overthrow Einarr's father. They seemed to worship death, and gods of death. They revelled in torture and suffering; they lusted to inflict pain and

despair, and not just there – it was the same with the story
we heard when the ship put into the South Island.'

Cannick spat between his feet. 'That was no religion, that
was Loku. That was a sham, used to control carefully
selected people, not a message of belief spread to anyone
who would listen. That bastard took the scum, the dogs
who enjoy dishing out suffering. The bullies, the cut-throats,
the murderers, the sort who revel in disorder and feed off
any opportunity to indulge themselves. You will find them
in a hysterical mob, joining for the fun of it; you will find
them in the shadows when they see a vulnerable victim; you
will find them in the crowd at an execution, baying with
bright eyes when the axe falls or the noose tightens. It is a
thrill they crave.'

A chill ran through Brann. 'Gerens?'

'No. Gerens is different. Whatever has happened to that
boy, there is not that love of inflicted pain these others have.
Were there that in him, he would not be with us. He would
not be one of us. When he does anything, he does it without
any feeling at all, like if that innkeeper in there killed a rat
in his food store.' Cannick sighed and sat staring ahead, as
if choosing the right words to fit his thoughts. 'Some people
come arrive in this world to a life that is close to nature.
For some – like him – it seems there is little difference
between animals and men in certain respects: we are all
creatures, and there is a certain amount of truth in that.'

Brann frowned. 'But he is not a monster.' His loyalty to
Gerens had forced out the words more harshly than he had
intended, and he gathered himself before continuing. 'He is
practical. The way he sees it, if something needs to be done,
he just does it.'

Cannick put a big hand on Brann's shoulder. 'No, he is

not a monster, but he is different. There is no getting away from that fact, and to deny it is to deny Gerens for the person he is.'

Brann shrugged. 'We are all different.'

Cannick smiled gently. 'Some differences make more of a difference. But you are right, and I say again, he is not a monster – he has feelings.'

Brann nodded. 'For Sophaya.'

'For Sophaya, yes. And for you.' Brann looked at him sharply, and Cannick snorted in amusement. 'Not in that way. He feels a loyalty. A protective urge without reason, without question.'

'That's Gerens, though, isn't it? He doesn't question; he just acts.'

'Well,' Cannick said quietly, 'be thankful that he acts in your favour. And I do mean: be thankful. Few men have their back guarded so fiercely.'

Brann looked at the veteran warrior pointedly. 'Einarr does.'

Cannick nodded. 'For different reasons.' He stared at the sky with the expression of a man who looked not over distance, but back through time. He grunted. 'Those are reasons for another conversation. But simply put: yes, you are right. So never forget, or underestimate, his place in your life. And never see him either just as he who would kill in aid of your safety as easily as blinking. Yes, put a knife in his hand and he is coldly efficient without compassion or remorse – but remember always that, though his emotions work in his own way, they still exist. They are as much as part of him as the other side.'

It was true. 'Like me, now.' The thought frightened him when he allowed himself to consider it. 'After the City Below.

And after the... the treatment in Khardorul. One me normally, another me when I fight.'

Cannick grunted. 'Like all of us have to be when we fight. We do not have the luxury of being able to care in those moments. It is what humans do to survive. With Gerens it does not need the heat of conflict to do that, it is there all the time, ready. But he is different from those others, Brann, the ones who Loku gathers, who he fosters. Gerens may not do it with regret, but also he does not do it with pleasure or desire.'

'But others do. We saw as much at the village in the mountains before we travelled south with Einarr: people acting worse than animals; people craving the suffering of others and finding some sort of euphoria when they inflict it. Is this common?'

'Fortunately not, son, fortunately not. There are just some people, Brann, and thankfully only a few in every hundred, who like that sort of thing but they are usually not bright enough to do anything more than inflict random violence when a chance presents itself... unless a leader finds them. Look in every army and you'll find one for every score or more of ordinary soldiers. Loku set himself up as a leader for them. The "religion" he gave them of sick and twisted viciousness was not a religion at all, of course, it just took the pleasure they already had and built up its flames with constant feeding and by surrounding them with similar people, like taking a man who is a slave to ale and putting him with others the same and giving them an endless supply of the stuff.' He spat into the dust at his feet. 'In his case, it *was* a sham and a way of controlling people to his own purpose, but they became intoxicated so much that life without it would seem lacking – and they were enjoying themselves too much to want to change it, anyway. It justified their actions and encouraged them. We were lucky you found that group in time, but there will be others in Halveka and in the South Island, as we know.'

Another memory came back to Brann. 'When I was first taken onto your ship, there were riders who came to the beach, who we narrowly escaped from. They wore masks – hideous masks – like I had never seen before.'

'I'm guessing those were leaders, recruiters, instructors, call them what you will. They were too organised for the slavering rabble we have seen in action.'

Brann's breath caught in his throat. 'But it means they were on my island. Close to my home.'

Cannick's tone was grave. 'I would expect so. They will spread, and endeavour to do so, like a pox.'

Brann felt several emotions surge through him as one. 'My family may be dead, my village may or may not still exist, but the thought of them walking on the ground where I am from... I feel sick.' He looked at the figure beside him. 'Cannick, why are they doing this?'

'That is the question that is driving this journey of ours, remember, young man? We need to find Loku, find his master and his master's master, find whoever is driving this plot that is spreading savagery and terror across entire countries and ask them that question, and then you will have your answer.'

And with that, Brann felt his resolve return. 'And first we need to find this Duke. We have plans to make.'

He stood, and Cannick laughed as he did likewise. 'And I am sure that by the time we discuss them, they will already be made in your head, young thinker.'

He was right. Brann's head was already moving, running

through scenarios, information they had and information they needed. Actions and possible consequences, consequent actions, and further consequences, and on and on. Who would do what, and who could do what best.

But then the old soldier in front of him opened the door to step back into the inn and the light spilled out over his lined and weather-beaten face, a face with eyes that had seen so much and still spoke of the caring within, and Brann's thoughts stopped.

'Cannick,' he said, and the man turned. 'Cannick, I... You...'

The creases in the soldier's face multiplied as he smiled. 'I know. An old sergeant had the same sort of conversation with me when I was not much older than you. I reckoned if he was an old sergeant then he must know a thing or two about how to get old without dying first, and he must have picked up a thing or two along the way since then. If I've helped you tonight, I have repaid him.' He winked. 'When you don't know if there is something or nothing awaiting you in death, it puts a little warmth in an old heart to know you have left something of you in those who come after.'

Brann stepped forward and wrapped him in a hug, and the brawny arms gripped him back. It felt like it said more than the words he couldn't find.

Breta's voice boomed from the passage that bent its way to the back door. 'Brann, Cannick! Are you out there?'

Brann jumped back at the thought of her seeing him that way, and his heel kicked over the small barrel Cannick had used as a seat. The lamplight from the doorway illuminated it as it rolled and spilt the remnants of what it had once contained, a trickle running through the dust on the flag-stones of the yard to mix with a small puddle in a gutter.

Watching it, a thought entered his head and he smiled, his head filled once more with plans. Again they were interrupted, this time by Breta as she filled the entrance.

'That's trollop's friend has arrived, apparently, and is waiting upstairs.'

Brann smiled. 'I note that she is "a trollop" but the handsome young men you spend time with when you pay for some pleasure are "handsome young men" when you talk of them.'

'Of course,' Breta said, a frown betraying her puzzlement. 'If the men were not handsome or young, why would I spend money on them?'

Some arguments, Brann thought, were just not worth having.

The others were still at the table and Cannick waved at them all to remain seated.

'Yes, we know: this friend of Joceline is waiting upstairs. I don't think all of us traipsing up as a group would be as low-key as we would want. Maybe just Brann and Grakk?'

Nods of agreement saw Grakk rise, but Gerens got to his feet also. 'How do we know this is not a trap? We do not know this girl. Her friend might be half a dozen armed thugs looking to cut their throats and take their coins.'

Brann looked at Cannick, who shrugged and nodded.

'Top of the stairs, turn right, third door on the left,' Hakon said.

The door creaked almost as much as the stairs and the floor had on the way to the room. There was little or no chance of sneaking up on someone here, which was probably exactly the way the inhabitants liked it. Brann had his long dagger, its black blade that seemed to absorb light rather than reflect it, drawn and he noticed that the others had done the same. The door had swung only half open, blocking their view of most of the room and, before he could move forward, Gerens shouldered him roughly to the side and pushed the door wide.

The dark-eyed boy must have seen his surprise. 'Don't want to be unmissable for a crossbow bolt, do you?'

Brann nodded that indeed he did not.

No missile had come their way, however, and Gerens pushed past him. Grakk did likewise, and it was only when the wiry tribesman had moved clear of the entrance that Brann was able to make his way into the room.

Joceline, the woman he had seen with Hakon, stood to one side, while across the room from them a couple, just a few years older than Brann and fine-featured with such similarity that they could only be brother and sister, stood nervously in front of a large bed draped in ostentatiously colourful fabrics. The man stood slightly forward and, while his fingers toyed apprehensively with the hilt of the knife on his belt, Brann sheathed his own weapon. The dagger was the only apparent weapon on the man and, although he had learnt many times that looks could be deceiving (and had used that fact to his own advantage on more than one occasion), he felt fairly sure that if this girl was placing her trust in her brother for protection from rough violence, it was trust misplaced.

He nodded past the man at the girl behind him, trembling at the sight of the three who had walked in with blades in hand, although it was not clear what scared her most: the situation, the appearance of Grakk or the stare of Gerens. 'We will not hurt you. We are grateful that you have agreed to talk to us.'

'Actually,' the young man said, coughing to try to clear his throat of nerves. 'Actually, it is I with whom you have arranged to speak.'

'Eloquent of speech,' Grakk said approvingly.

The timid girl shrank into herself even further at the sound of Grakk's own words, incongruous from a tribesman of such fierce appearance.

Brann stared at him. 'You?' He looked from brother to sister to brother in confusion. 'But...'

The man raised his eyebrows. 'You think all whores are women? That all men prefer women? You are unaware that this is not the case?'

'Actually,' said Gerens solemnly, 'you would be surprised at the number of things he is unaware of.'

The man turned to Brann and spoke patiently. 'Would it help you to know the background?'

Brann nodded vaguely. He couldn't think of anything else to do.

'I did not plan this career. My sister, Eloise, and I – I am Philippe, by the way – we came here as members of a troupe of actors. Some months before, I had met a man in another town and, to my surprise, he had offered to pay for, shall we say, what I had expected to be a fleeting experience of mutual enjoyment. I became aware that there were men who were willing to enter into the same sort of transaction with me in every town and village our show visited, and it became a more than useful method of augmenting an income that, let's face it, could have been improved by a change of career to pig herder. It became even more lucrative than I had envisaged, in fact, because these men pay for two elements, gratification and discretion, and when the transaction is between two men rather than a man and a woman, the desire for discretion transpired to be greater, and therefore more expensive. However, in this fair town, my efforts to keep my lucrative sideline hidden from the leader of the troupe ceased to be successful and, on his discovering my infidelity to him in both a professional and emotional sense, I found that I was no longer a member of the troupe. And so I stayed here, and my sister with me, this new profession replacing, rather than augmenting, our acting.'

'Believe me, my dear,' Joceline drawled as she sauntered across the room, 'all whores play a dozen parts every day. It just so happens that these two play them with more skill than most, and are lucky enough to have the stunning looks to help them along the way.'

Brann looked at the girl, a picture of nervous innocence. 'These *two*?'

Eloise straightened and gave him a brazen smile. 'Admit it, you felt sorry for me, didn't you? Would you have found it easier or harder to cut my throat with that fancy knife of yours, having felt compassion towards me?'

Brann nodded weakly at one more surprise to rock him. 'Not all would have felt so reluctant, though.'

Joceline put an arm around Eloise. 'Men as bad as that would have done what they were going to do, regardless. Better to reduce the chance though, my love, don't you think?'

Brann sat on the edge of the bed to process his thoughts. Philippe looked at him enquiringly and Grakk coughed politely.

'Should the rest of us retire from the room, young Brann?'

He looked at Grakk, then at the man standing by the bed. His eyes went wide and he jumped to his feet, taking a quick step away. 'No!' He edged closer to Grakk and

Gerens. 'No, I... er... I mean...' He looked at Philippe, waiting patiently. 'Oh! I mean no offence. You seem a very nice person and I'm sure you're very good at your job, but...'

Joceline's laugh cut through the room, and Brann saw the amusement on the faces around him. He smiled sheepishly. 'I think we had better move the conversation on.'

Brann composed himself. It did make some sense. And it opened up new possibilities for his plans. A guard captain with even more to hide...

'Please excuse my ignorance,' he said. 'We have much to discuss.'

Brann awoke the next morning in a chair in Joceline's room, having slept where he sat after plotting through the night. The others seemed to assume that Brann would devise a strategy, and he had pushed aside his initial discomfort at being left to do so by people with far more experience or education in such matters to use the time productively. In ones and twos, the others had returned to join the discussion after Brann had worked out the skeleton of the plan and, once they were all sure of the role each would play and how it connected to those of all others, most of the party had retired to the room they had taken for the night. Most of the party: Breta had decided that the large bed where they were was much more suitable than the bunks in their own room, and had thoughtfully left Joceline a small space at one side of her own mattress, where the whore was still sleeping despite the stentorian snores of the huge warrior beside her.

Brann stretched, feeling the sharp pain of the wound down his ribs as it pulled against the stitches. The gash on his arm was healing more quickly, but he had to be careful not to open the big wound whenever he twisted or reached, and it was annoying him. Still, he had suffered worse, and survived worse.

He ran back over the plan in his head. It was not intricate – the simpler, the less there was to go wrong and the easier it was to adapt as, inevitably, any plan has to do – and it didn't even involve all of their group, but he was happy it should serve the purpose. It was not even a complicated job they were attempting. After all, they just wanted to gain access to the Duke of this region in his bedchamber at the top of his tower home, with an entire contingent of his soldiers filling the grounds around the building and the floors beneath the man's quarters.

Despite Breta's sound snoring, he woke her with an ease born of a warrior's instant readiness and padded down the corridor to the other bedroom where he roused Marlo and Hakon – the three would complete the delivery of the oil before joining Cannick and Mongoose outside the town, ready to greet, and if necessary defend, the exit of the small party who would visit the Duke.

Brann thought of the barrel he had kicked over in the yard the night before, and shook Marlo's shoulder as the boy sat rubbing his eyes, slower to alertness than the experienced fighters. 'Remember, when you take the barrels...'

'Yes, yes,' the Sagian boy grumbled. 'Only take two and pick up the other two from here to take out of the town to the others. But what about the merchant? He will be expecting four.'

'Did you not hear last night?' Brann was exasperated. He only felt comfortable if everyone understood what needed to be done.

'The fire was warm and the night was late,' Marlo shrugged. 'How could I not fall asleep?'

'Next time, stay further from the fire,' Brann growled. 'All you have to say is that when the wheel fell off, two of the barrels dropped from the cart and smashed. He will only pay you for two, but we already covered the full cost to the carter, so all is fine. He'll grumble and you can look apologetic, and there will be nothing else anyone can do about it, so he'll just have to accept it.'

'Excellent!' Marlo beamed infectiously as ever, and Brann found himself unable to resist smiling back, as ever. 'I can manage that.'

Brann nodded. 'Good. We'll see you outside the walls. Cannick will organise you all out there.'

The hours of the day stretched out interminably, as waiting always did. It was with relief that night fell upon them, and they eventually left the inn, guided by Joceline and Eloise as they wound their way through the cobbled streets. It was a clearer sky than the previous night, allowing them to see their way without the revealing light of lanterns, and making for a more marked contrast between moonlit areas and the shadows cast by buildings, but Brann would have preferred by far to be moving through a deeper and more general gloom, particularly when he thought ahead to trying to remain unseen in the grounds of the Duke's tower.

He need not have bothered worrying about the weather. Moon or no moon, clouds or no clouds, it made no difference. Eloise had halted them at a corner across a narrow street from the plain stone wall around the tower's compound, around a man-and-a-half in height and with a gateway fronted by two lounging guards halfway along the wall to their left. What had caught their attention, however, was not the expected barrier but what came from behind it: even from here, the glow from lanterns or torches that must illuminate the area within was bright enough over the top of the wall to suggest that they may as well have been in daylight. Philippe's assignation with the guard captain was after the man had overseen the final shift change of the sentries, and if the young man was to be able to distract the guards from outside the door to the Duke's chambers, then the time when the captain slumbered after his exertions would be the perfect opportunity. The only opportunity.

He looked around the group. Konall, Grakk and Gerens were frowning as strongly as he was at the blazing light, but Sophaya merely squinted at it appraisingly. She looked around at the others.

'What? You thought they would create some nice shadows and maybe a hedge or two to let intruders hide on their way to the tower?'

Gerens still wasn't happy. 'You are incessantly magnificent, it is true, but you still think you can get us into that tower? With the guards watching that whole area?'

'Look at them, dear Gerens,' the girl said with an impish smile. 'Like any sentries, they look outwards, and only inwards if something should catch their attention.'

Konall's look was cold with disdain. 'We could hardly fail to catch their attention if we wander about in that light.'

But Brann looked at Sophaya and smiled. 'People only see what they are looking at. So if they are looking at something else...'

'So,' Grakk murmured, 'this would require their eyes to be diverted away to something else. Would you have a suggestion?'

'Oh, that's easy.' They all turned at the sound of Eloise's voice, which changed in the space of a breath to a tone of exaggerated despair, supported by extravagant and flailing gestures. 'Oh, how seldom people see beyond the wafer-like crust of a surface to the depths beneath! Oh, how quick people are to disregard the years that went before the last day they have seen!' She snapped back to herself, grinning. 'I am an actress. If you can somehow help my brother in his situation, then I can be for those guards whatever we need me to be.'

She tousled her hair and smeared a little dirt from the gutter across her face as if the result of a fall. That fall quickly seemed liable to be repeated as her eyelids drooped and her body sagged and swayed, working to stay upright in the face of the excess of intoxication that she had never actually imbibed. She paused, seeming not quite satisfied with the effect, then pulled at the front of her blouse, ripping it open slightly and just enough to expose an expanse of what lay within. A button fell free and she bent to pick it up, staggering as her fingers closed on it and lurching into Brann.

He felt her lean into him to steady herself and looked at the face that turned to leer up at him. 'Oh, you are a lovely one,' she drawled at him. 'I'll save you for later.' She pressed the button into his hand, and winked. 'Remember me by this, my lover.'

Joceline laughed softly at her antics as Eloise pushed herself away from Brann. He slipped the button in beside the coins in his pouch as, in a low voice, she said to them all, 'Remember, further along to our right and then, immediately around the next corner, ivy has grown unchecked on the wall. Not a great deal, but enough to let you gain the top of the wall.'

Sophaya was not impressed. 'Sloppy. I'm surprised others haven't tried to rob him.'

Eloise shrugged. 'The walls of the town protect him from those without, but it is his reputation that protects him from those within. To catch the eye of the Duke does not usually end well, and no one in this place wishes to court the possibility. Why run towards the danger they fear and hide from?'

Grakk was curious. 'What is it that is so terrible? I have seen rulers who rule by fear, but the impression you give is that it goes beyond the normal.'

Joceline spoke, her face as dark as her tone. 'He has tastes. Desires that he satisfies. He calls it study, but...' A strange look came into her eyes.

Grakk frowned. 'He does what, precisely?'

Eloise started to speak, then hesitated, looking at Joceline, who herself shrugged. Eloise seemed to gather her resolve, a troubled look on her face. 'I don't know, nobody really does exactly. Sometimes noises come from the tower, sometimes fragments of stories emerge, but not one person who is taken there has been seen to return.' She hesitated again. 'People don't like to make trouble about it, or even talk of it, because then they come to the notice of the Duke's men. And... well... who would risk losing a child?'

Brann looked sharply at Grakk and then Gerens. He could see they had the same thoughts: they had all been present on a ship off the coast of Cardallon, the southern of the Green Islands, when a shore party had returned with news of the slaughter of a village; a massacre of a sort that had sounded chillingly similar to the love of torture and killing that they had witnessed among Loku's recruits in the mountains of Konall's homeland. And prominent amongst its victims, too, had been children. 'I feel more than ever we need to have a word with this Duke.'

Eloise gathered her skirts as she continued. 'No one knows the full truth, and that is exactly why I do not like Philippe being so close to that man. If we are to do this, I would that we do it without any more delay.'

Without waiting for a reply, she pointed at them and then at an alleyway running parallel to the road between them and the wall, then slipped into its equivalent heading in the opposite direction. Moments later, the rambling shouts of a drunkard were heard arguing with a rat, before they saw her stagger into the open near the compound gate and lurch in surprise at the sight of the guards. She weaved her way towards them, her words inaudible to Brann's ears but her demeanour making it clear that the two men were targets of her desire. From the way they came alert, it appeared that the attraction was mutual.

Her less than quiet antics had, however, attracted further attention, and a shout from behind the wall saw one of the guards open the gate. A brief explanation from him and further instruction from inside saw her ushered within, much to the apparent irritation of the guards on the gate, although her swaying gait maintained their attention after she had disappeared from Brann's view.

Joceline nodded back down the street they had come up. 'At the next junction is the edge of an area where girls can be seen offering their services. I am not usually so public about my work, but I can look like I fit in there. I will wait there to guide you on your return.' She cast another look back at the gate to the compound. 'Now go, for the sake of both of them. Please ensure they come back from that place.'

Brann nodded, as did the others. The courage of Eloise had affected them all. They ran quietly along the alley and turned to meet the road at the first opportunity. They were only a bowshot from the corner, and they reached it in a few rapid heartbeats. Brann blew out his breath in relief as he saw the ivy, and before he could say anything, Sophaya was on top of the wall, lying along it on her stomach. She nodded and dropped silently from sight.

Brann tested the strength of the plant and then realised that it mattered not – he had no option but to try dragging himself up without any further delay. It held well as he grabbed large handfuls to try not to put too much pressure on individual roots, and with Konall using his height to advantage and pushing from below, he managed to haul himself to the top with his one good arm, the light dazzling from countless lamps on tall stands that were dotted across the expanse within. The wall was the length of his forearm in thickness, and he blinked his eyes shut and open rapidly as Konall started to follow. A glance down saw Sophaya moving tight to the wall, and Brann hurriedly dropped to the rough ground below to leave space for the Northern boy, looking for Eloise as he landed in a crouch. She had wandered towards a tall guard who seemed to hold some level of authority, from the way that the other two guards with him on the short flight of steps to the door of the tower moved back instantly at his wave. Two sentries between Brann and the unfolding scene were amusedly watching her, while another just inside the gate was equally engrossed.

The tall guard stepped forward and took Eloise by the arm, looking to usher her inside the building. Brann froze. He did not like the thought that she should be taken inside by those men at all, but it had been inevitable from the moment she had stepped through the gate, and should the watching men lose the object of their interest from view too soon, at least one of them would notice the four figures who would be running around the perimeter of the compound. Admiration filled him, though, as Eloise remained both in character and true to her purpose, pulling free from the man and embarking on a drunken rant. Only the occasional word reached Brann, but it was enough to understand that she was berating the onlookers for only being interested in one aspect of a woman. If that was what they wanted, she yelled, why not feast their eyes, and she started peeling off her clothes with the combination of extravagant flourishes and staggering lack of balance that only intoxication can perfect. Grinning, the tall guard folded his arms to enjoy the spectacle, and if the other onlookers had not been giving every shred of their attention to her before then, this was no longer the case.

Brann set off immediately in the footsteps of Sophaya. Konall had already landed and followed closely behind, and soft crunches in the dirt told him that the other two had dropped from the wall only a few breaths later. As he ran, his eyes scanned the area, as much in wariness of coming across guards as to discover the nature of their surroundings. The ground was flat and mostly paved, empty of any character and populated only by the tall poles supporting the lamps that bathed the area in near as much brightness as daylight and stretching from the wall the length of around a hundred paces to the tower, which had been built exactly in the centre of the compound. The building itself was square and around twenty paces on each side; Philippe had described seven storeys in all, with a roof terrace, and only the top four levels had windows, each with shutters as a means to keep the weather at bay, but each with those shutters lying open to the world to encourage what little comforting breeze the humid night offered. The Duke's chamber occupied the top two levels, accessed on the sixth level where his living quarters were, from which a stairway led to the sleeping area – a sleeping area that was sacrosanct, where no one, without exception, was permitted to set foot. If they could corner him there, it was likely they could do so without risk of being disturbed.

He cast a look back. Eloise was now completely naked and twisting with flailing arms to make it difficult for two laughing guards to take hold of her. Difficult, but not impossible, and they soon had her in their grasp, starting to lead her towards the entrance to the tower. Brann redoubled his efforts, chilled by thoughts of what may await Eloise inside the building and anxious as much to be in a position to help her as he was to escape being spotted. As he approached the next corner of the wall, the rear of the compound became visible and he could see the difference that brother and sister had described to them: a garden area that filled the space from the back of the tower to halfway to the outer wall. Trellises, low shrubs, and stone animals with decorative paths snaking among them were not the best of cover, but it was better by far than the exposure that lay on every other side.

The three following caught him as he rounded the corner. Sophaya was out of sight and presumably already in the garden, and the quartet left the wall together and angled directly towards the shrubbery in their haste to reach what little cover was available before the guards resumed their duties. Brann vaulted a knee-high hedge and caught his foot, tumbling and rolling onto short grass that muffled the sound of his fall but was not soft enough to prevent the flash of pain from his ribs. The hedge enclosed the grass on all four sides and, with a grunt, he gathered his legs under him and made for the side closest to the tower, stepping over it carefully this time and dropping to lie hard against it. He found Sophaya and Konall already doing the same, and the boy pushed a lock of his white-blond hair from his face as he looked at Brann.

'You never cease to entertain,' he said drily.

Sophaya looked up at the building, and Brann followed her eyes. Some of the windows were dark, some let light spill out, but one – on the second-top level – had a lantern sitting directly on the sill. Philippe had left his sign. The lamp was placed not only to signify the window that was their target, but also that the guards on the Duke's door had been lured away to tend a sudden and violently painful illness afflicting the captain and brought on by a powder supplied by Grakk and slipped into his goblet by Philippe. The two windows to the right of the lamplight were in darkness, lending credence to what Philippe claimed was common knowledge among the staff: that the Duke would retire religiously to the top floor at fall of darkness every evening, never to be disturbed and with only dire consequences awaiting any fool who risked doing so.

'No time like the present,' Sophaya murmured and rolled into a crouch, but Brann grabbed at her ankle.

'Wait,' he hissed.

She scowled at him, either from irritation at being stopped or from the insult to her professional judgement, but she slid back down to hide once more, her head close to his. Her voice was a whisper, barely more than a breath. 'The boy said that the guards are lazy, that they patrol only occasionally.'

Brann kept his words equally as quiet. 'But when would they be more likely to wander around than right after they have been disturbed from whatever they have been doing?'

She looked at him as she considered it, then nodded.

They waited.

It seemed at first as if he had been overcautious. Then they heard the voices. Two men rounded the corner at an amble, one grumbling at the sergeant always taking whatever benefits came their way, the other content that they had been treated to entertainment beyond the ordinary. The grumpy one stopped at the edge of the garden. Brann caught his breath, his hand moving to the hilt of his sword. He watched through the sparser branches in the lowest few inches of the hedge, slowly gathering his legs ready to roll and spring. He heard a soft scrape – Konall must be doing the same. He reached out a foot, feeling the boy's arm, and pressed against it in restraint. *Wait*, he thought, cautioning himself as much as the other boy. *Nerves erode judgement. Wait until you know you cannot wait.* He eased his head round with excruciating slowness to find Grakk and Gerens; the tribesman was curled behind a waist-high bush clipped into an onion shape, while the boy was kneeling behind a statue of a boar, his eyes flicking fast between Sophaya, Brann and the two guards. With Grakk and Gerens further away, Brann and Konall would have to deal with any discovery themselves, and swiftly.

Still grumbling to his companion, the guard turned to face them. Brann's fingers tightened on his sword, and his toes dug slightly into the surface of the soil. But the man did not peer in their direction; he did not call his colleague's attention to something unusual; he did not reach for his sword or ready his spear. The man reached only to loosen the front of his breeches, and he relieved himself beside a small bush.

Brann felt the tension release him from its iron grasp and fought instead to stifle laughter born as much of relief as of the ridiculous situation he found himself in. The guard finished and, spear tucked under one arm, fixed his clothing as he walked away. Not one of the hidden group dared to move until the two men had disappeared around the corner of the tower.

The instant they were out of sight, however, Sophaya rolled and rose, moving in one motion to a sprint to the wall of the tower. All of the others remained where they were, keeping to as much cover as was possible until they, too, would have to move – all but Gerens who, with sword drawn, was crouched beside the girl. While she faced the tower, he had his back to the rough stone, head swivelling constantly, eyes scanning for danger, ever the protector.

Sophaya settled a coil of rope, stained a similar colour to the stone blocks of the tower, more securely over one shoulder and down to the opposite hip, and without hesitation reached up and started to climb. Brann had witnessed her agility many times and knew of feats she had achieved in defeating every physical barrier that was placed before her, but this was the first time he had seen her in action, and he marvelled at her. He would have been amazed had a creature of the forest found purchase on such a surface, so his mind could barely grasp the way that Sophaya moved with sure and rapid grace up the wall: fingertips and toes – clad in soft tight-fitting boots barely thicker than hose – finding grip where he could conceive of none.

His wonder seemed to freeze time and his brain, and it was only when Konall's soft words broke his trance that he jerked his attention back to the surroundings to check for any danger that Gerens might have missed, however unlikely the baleful boy was to do that.

'Squared corners.' The Northern boy's voice was thick with scorn. 'A few flung boulders and that's knocked away, and then all above is coming down.'

Brann looked at it. 'I suppose they reckon it is far enough from the town walls that it is liable never to be a target for siege catapults. Squared corners mean more conveniently shaped rooms inside. This is built for comfort and prestige, not defence.'

Konall's disgust was undiminished. 'A whole town should be built for defence.'

Brann grinned. 'Not every populace is as well versed in siege architecture as yours, you know.'

'Cretins.'

Smiling, Brann looked back at the wall, Sophaya had closed on the window with the lamp. She reached the lip and, after a brief look over the edge, slipped inside in a fluid movement. The lamp receded until the glow grew instead in the windows to the right, growing brighter beside one opening as it was, presumably, set close. Moments later, the rope uncoiled down the side of the building, and the three joined Gerens as he grasped the end, tying it in a large loop.

His dark eyes locked on Brann's. 'Remember, this goes around you and under your arms. Do not attempt to pull yourself up – you are in no fit state. Konall and I will pull you up once Grakk has reached the room.'

Konall held the end of the rope steady to let Gerens start

to climb, walking his legs on the wall. The blond head turned to Brann. 'Konall may not bother. Konall is wondering why we let you insist on coming along in the state you are in.' His eyes turned to the bush still dripping at the edge of the garden. 'Although I suppose you do have your uses.'

'At least,' Grakk said, 'that incident did prove one thing.' They both looked at him, and found his calm eyes looking back impassively. 'They have no expectation that danger will visit them within these walls.'

Brann frowned. 'Because one guard has no respect for his superiors and is not afraid to talk about it?'

Grakk smiled. 'Because there is one part of a man's anatomy that he will never risk taking out if he thinks there is the slightest chance of sharp-edged objects being swung about at any point in the near future. And that was it.'

Brann was about to laugh at a rare Grakk joke when he saw the look in the tribesman's eyes. And, when he thought about it, Grakk was right. He looked up to see Sophaya help Gerens through the window and moved to let Konall grasp the rope to start his climb. That his ascent was slightly slower than that of Gerens owed more to physique than anything else – while Konall was lean and strong, Gerens's rangy build lent him an agility beyond Konall's assured but steady style, although when it came to Grakk, the man of the desert tribes scampered up the wall as if the rope were a bannister on a stairway and made Gerens look sluggish in comparison.

Brann looked around, suddenly very aware that he was alone. The area in sight was empty, which was good, but the bright light and the sense of danger made him want to shrink against the wall. Even though he knew the guards' rounds were seldom carried out, still he couldn't help looking back and forth, expecting at every moment to see armed figures appear. He felt at the loop of rope that Grakk had dropped over his head before he had left him, tucking it into place and patting him on the head with a wink. It was rough, the thickness of a finger, and seemed strong. He hoped it was. He nestled it more securely under his armpits and, just as he did so, he started as he felt the rope pull tight against him.

Grakk's head popped out of the window to satisfy himself that Brann was ready and, at a nod from the bald head, he felt the rope tighten and lift him from the ground. He started to spin and, alarmed, grabbed the rope with both hands, scrabbling with his feet at the wall to try to keep him facing the surface. His ribs and the wound on his left arm stung, but he managed to get into a rhythm, half-walking and half-bouncing with his feet as he was pulled upwards in rapid lurches. He was concentrating so much on maintaining his balance that the thought of discovery from below was forgotten. One step, then the other, he was jerked upwards. He looked up, and was surprised to see the window only the height of a man above him. He could just make out the sound of soft whispers, and grinned at the thought that he would soon be among his friends.

The whispers stopped. The movement of the rope stopped. Everything seemed to stop. In the silence and stillness, Brann became aware of the soft wind blowing his hair across his eyes, a breeze that would have been welcome at ground level but served here only to remind him how exposed he was. How vulnerable. He was at the mercy of others from above even more than below. Who would think to look up, much less launch any sort of missile almost six storeys upwards with any accuracy? On the other hand, any loosening of the rope above...

He hung, totally dependent on the rope. It was bearing his weight without even the slightest give; it could only be that it was tied off. But why? His mind raced. The whispered voices had stopped abruptly, but there had been no further noise. They must have heard something and be either trying to remain unnoticed or preparing to defend themselves. If it was the latter, it went against his nature not to help them. And in either case, he hated not knowing.

He flinched at the sound of a door crashing open. Shouts burst briefly, then a quiet voice spoke. Brann could not make out the words, but they were shortly followed by the clatter and clang of metal hitting stone: dropped weapons. His stomach knotted. His breath came loud in his ears. He started to haul himself up, hand over hand, his left side searing with pain, the agony overpowered by his urge to reach his friends. The rope creaked as he moved, but softly; he could only hope it was soft enough to merge with the noises of the town beyond. In any case, the consequence of it being heard, grave as it would be, was still preferable to being discovered a short distance below the window and a long drop above the ground.

And in any case, the idea of doing nothing while his friends were in danger had started his muscles moving even before his mind had debated the issue.

He reached the window undiscovered. He forced his heaving breath to be still and eased the last few inches that let his vision clear the sill. And he froze.

His friends stood unarmed, each with a lightly armoured guard on each arm and a blade at their throat; Sophaya closest to the window and just to its right, the rest extending away in a curved line. To the left, regarding them calmly across the room, was a well-dressed man, diminutive in height and almost unhealthily slender, who pulled thought-fully on a bottom lip that was as thin as his face was pinched and pale, features that merely emphasised the sunken depth of his eyes. He ran the hand through thin dark hair and sighed. 'But you are all so *ordinary*! How could you possibly think you could succeed?'

A door beyond him stood open and Philippe, his face wild with fear and marked with a swelling on one cheekbone, was dragged through by a lean guard with hard eyes, unarmoured but wearing a tunic that was black like the tabards of the other guards – in his case with a red stripe down the centre.

The small man smiled. 'Ah, you thought yourselves so clever, did you not? A man on the inside; a man with a potion.' He took a goblet from the guard holding Philippe. 'Thank you, captain.' He sniffed the dregs curiously. 'No odour. Instantly dissolved, I believe.' The captain nodded. 'Fast acting, too, I hear. Interesting. Most interesting. If any of you have more of this most effective powder on you, I will enjoy investigating it further in due course.' He looked at them. 'Yes, effective, though you see my captain standing here before you, most decidedly awake. You see, you thought you knew everything, I am sure, but you did not know *me*. You did not know that I have no interest in the minor issue of how my captain or anyone else sates their desires as long as they can still serve me as I require. My captain has no need to be secretive from me, and no fear of anything needing to be hidden from me. So when your pretty boy here did not hide well enough his inept attempt to slip powder into a drink, my good captain was able to subdue him and alert me that something must be afoot. The rest was simplicity, waiting to see if someone would come to me, as the boy is incapable of doing anything of any great importance himself. Waiting, moreover, to see who would come, how they would come, why they would come.' He chuckled with the contentment of a man who is more clever than all around. 'We have seen the if and the how – and soon we will hear the who and the why.'

Brann's arms were beginning to shake, but he forced his fingers tight around the rope. Now was not the time to give himself away. Or to fall, for that matter. The rope groaned as his weight rolled slightly to one side. He caught his movement and his breath in the same instant.

But the small man was pacing nonchalantly as he looked at the sullen faces staring at him, his footsteps loud enough to mask any small noise from across the room and outside the window. 'What, no conversation? Let me start it off, then. What was your purpose? Robbery? Or perhaps murder?' He raised an eyebrow. 'No answer?' He looked at one of the guards holding Sophaya, her eyes defiant and glaring. 'If these gentlemen remain so rudely unresponsive the next time I ask, please cut her throat. Keep the head unmarked, though, as I have plans for it.'

Gerens's eyes bulged, and his voice growled. 'You said she would not be harmed if we gave up our weapons.'

The Duke, as Brann assumed he could only be, smiled indulgently. 'Of course I did, and she was not harmed, was she? But that was then, and this is now. I have further use for this bargaining tool, do I not? Especially as it proved so effective the first time.' He pursed his lips in consideration. 'Maybe we should just slice her soft throat now as a statement of intent...'

Gerens roared and strained at his captors, managing a step forward. The Duke turned again to regard Sophaya, but Grakk's calm voice dragged his attention away once more.

'Strangely enough,' he said, 'it was actually a quick chat with yourself that brought us here. Perhaps we could dispense with the unnecessary gripping of arms and just pull up a chair.'

The Duke looked with intrigue at the precise speech and cultured tone, then laughed in delight. 'I think I will keep you till last. But unfortunately, you do not seem willing to give me a sensible answer, so...' He looked at Sophaya again. 'Kill her.'

Brann moved.

He yanked at the rope to fling himself forward, all of his senses focused on the scene before him and far from any pain in his wounds. In the instant between his hands leaving the rope and reaching for the inner edge of the windowsill, he felt a coldness settle over him, his eyes hungry for movement that made his choices for him. He pulled at the sill and his legs came up under him, bracing on the ledge. As he launched, he saw the Duke's eyes widen with the sharp surprise that hits hardest at a man who is convinced he has control, and then he was tumbling to roll on one shoulder. On the way down, his long knife slashed, parting, like thread, the rope as it tensed against the wall sconce it had been tethered to, and as he came out of his roll it sliced just as easily across the back of the knees of the guard lifting his blade to execute Sophaya.

The man screamed as his legs buckled and the girl wheeled, the soldier's knife in her hand. Almost faster than Brann's eyes could follow, she had cut across the back of the hand of the man to her right, his fingers spasming and releasing his sword and, as her second movement opened his throat, Brann came to his feet and battered his shoulder into the dying man, knocking him into the next guard along. The guard had let go of Konall and was turning towards them, but now found himself entangled in the arms and slipping in the blood of the body thrown against him. Brann's hand flicked his axe up from his belt and, with a roll of his wrist and a wild swing, cut the black metal through the dead man's arm and into the neck of the struggling soldier. It was not a time for finesse.

He wrenched the axe free and blood sprayed into the face of a man poised to stab a short spear at him. He dropped to a crouch, away from the line of the lunge, and thrust his axe forward, hooking the head behind the man's ankle. Jerking the axe as he stood, the man was upended and he continued the movement to swing the axe over and down to stop with a crunch in the centre of the man's forehead. It was quicker to draw his sword than drag the axe free, and he spun in a crouch, blade held ready, as he sought the next danger.

He saw carnage. It had been a natural reaction for the guards to turn towards unexpected danger, but it had also been a fatal reaction. As the captives were released, each had instantly reached for the closest weapon, either their own from the floor or whatever they could reach from the belt of the guard.

'Wait!' The Duke's voice cut across the room, and they stood, chests heaving, blood dripping, every guard lying dead. Every guard but one – a sound came from a man curled around his entrails, a low bubbling moan was all that could emerge from the half of his face that was left.

Gerens bent down, and now every guard lay dead. They faced the Duke, and saw the captain beside him, Philippe held in front with a knife at his throat. The captain grinned.

Brann's hand reached fast behind his neck for the throwing knife he kept strapped at the top of his spine, but Konall grabbed his wrist.

'Too risky a target for anyone, and I have seen you throw when you have time to think about it.'

He let out his breath, the cold fire of combat fading. The Northern boy was right. Brann's throwing *was* atrocious.

He flinched as a flash flickered past him, and the captain screamed in agony, his hand clutching at an eye suddenly gushing blood. Philippe stumbled and ran from him and, as the man swung wildly with his knife, Grakk neatly ducked under the swipe and finished him with a thrust of a sword up under his ribs and into his heart.

With a low growl, Gerens leapt for the Duke, but Grakk was quicker, placing himself in the way. 'Not just now, young Gerens.'

The boy's eyes burnt darkly still, but he halted and nodded, looking at the captain's corpse and then at Philippe. 'Well, at least that has saved us the bother of stopping in to visit that bastard for you on the way out.'

Philippe smiled weakly, but the relief in his eyes was strong.

The Duke glanced at the door, but saw Konall standing in its way, arms folded and a cold smile on his face.

Without taking his eyes from the Duke, the boy closed the door and, with exaggerated deliberateness, slid home the bolt.

The Duke's eyes lingered on the broken and bloody bodies of his guards but, rather than fear, his expression was lit by an excited fascination.

Grakk came to stand before him. 'Now,' the tribesman said, 'perhaps we could have that chat we mentioned.' He looked around the room. 'Although perhaps it might have been easier to have it when I first suggested it.'

The Duke's eyes were still alight. 'But then I would have missed your exhibition of such magnificently efficient brutality.' He turned his lascivious gaze on Brann. 'And this one – oh, I could find some wonderful uses for one such as he.'

Brann looked back impassively. He had seen this man's sort before, baying and slavering in the crowds at the pits of Sagia's depraved City Below. Such people meant nothing to him.

A noise came from behind them and all spun, weapons in hand. A small girl, aged no more than six years, stood at the bottom of a winding staircase, staring up at the group. Barefoot and dressed in just a simple shift, she looked around the room. With a cry, Sophaya rushed to her, sweeping the girl into her arms. She felt over the small figure quickly. 'Unharmed, I believe,' she said over her shoulder.

Brann looked at Grakk. 'And unmoved by the gore,' he said quietly.

Grakk nodded. 'Unhurt physically, perhaps, but...'

Sophaya took the girl to a chair at the far side of the room, sitting to cradle her and speak soothingly to her.

Brann turned to Gerens and Konall. 'I'll take a look up there with Grakk.'

'You will not dare!' the Duke screamed, fury filling the words. 'No one goes up there but me. *No one!*'

Brann looked at the sudden emotion with interest. He pointed at the girl in Sophaya's arms. 'She did. And now we will.' The Duke screamed in rage, his eyes bulging, and Brann looked at Konall and Gerens. 'You two keep an eye on him. If you have to ensure he stays still and quiet,' he gave a half-smile, 'please do it in a way that will still allow him to speak.'

The pair said nothing but turned to stand and stare at the Duke. His ranting continued, and Gerens punched him hard in the face. The man fell silent but still quivered and stared, his anger barely controlled.

Grakk followed Brann up the stairs, and they emerged into a room the same size as the one below. A lavish bed sat against the far wall and a desk strewn with documents lay between them and it, but it was the shelves around that drew their eyes. Jars contained organs and body parts, the former suspiciously human-looking and the latter definitely so, all floating in liquid. A trolley lay in front, the top lined neatly with an assortment of shining blades, saws, pincers, and other instruments that Brann had only seen before in the rooms of the top physicians in Sagia, those who tended the elite, and expensive, gladiators. His eyes moved past the trolley and came to a table of metal and...

His head swam. He felt his knees go from under him. He staggered to one side and retched onto the floor.

A boy – a boy's body – lay on the table. His face was untouched, revealing that he had been much the same age as the girl downstairs, but his torso had been sliced to allow the skin to be peeled back to either side. Ribs had been clipped away to allow complete access and for the organs to be exposed. Some of those organs had been removed and lay neatly to one side. The rest were still visible.

And the heart was still slowly beating.

'Oh by all the gods,' Brann whispered. 'What evil is this?'

A sheet of notes in neat and precise script lay beside the boy, and as Grakk moved to seek some clue from it, he noticed a small empty vial near the child's head, and sniffed it briefly. 'What little consolation there can be is in the fact that he has slept through this.'

Pain constricted Brann's throat, making his voice hoarse. 'But when he wakes?'

'He must not wake.' Grakk picked up a slender blade, its tip curved, from the trolley and deftly nicked a vein in the small boy's neck, dark blood swiftly pooling on the table top. 'He will not wake.' A single tear ran down his cheek, but the tribesman seemed unaware. 'The gods will have him now.' He moved beside Brann and put a hand on his shoulder. 'You wondered about the gods? This is where we need to believe they are there to care for those such as this poor soul.'

Brann nodded, but felt a fury building in him. He rose and reached for his knife.

Grakk's hand tightened on his shoulder. 'I know,' the man said. 'I know. But we are here for a purpose. We have seen the monstrosity of our enemy in the past, and for the sake of other children like this, we must not let further examples of the same divert us from our course.'

Brann nodded, and forced his breathing deep and slow. He looked away from the table. He would not look back. He gasped as his eyes lit on two cages, tall as a man's waist and narrow – in one, a small boy crouched. Brann almost slipped as he rushed to it, but as he drew close he saw his haste was wasted. The eyes were open but unseeing. The hands were missing several fingers, but still grasped the bars with what ability they had possessed. He had been cut and stitched with precision in multiple places, with some wounds having partially healed while others were clearly more recent. Again, a sheet lay alongside – a quick glance revealed a list of dates and notes, but a quick glance was all Brann could bring himself to give it. The body was stiff to the touch, but he still felt at the small neck for a pulse. He had never thought he would find himself glad to find a child to be dead.

Two similar cages sat alongside, both empty. On one, the latch was bent and the door ajar – it seemed most likely to have been the home of the little girl.

Grakk was at the desk, looking through the documents. 'Look here,' he said. 'This is what we seek.'

Brann moved across, averting his eyes from the boy on the table and glad of something to take his attention that did not involve the torture of children.

Grakk indicated piles of paper, one a map and the rest covered with text or diagrams. 'There is more here than we can peruse at this time.'

Brann shrugged. 'So we take it all.' He pulled a sheet from the bed and laid it by the desk, lifting the papers onto it. Grakk nodded and helped him, tying it into a bundle when they had finished. Brann looked back at the bed. 'To think he slept here, *chose* to sleep here, in the midst of all of this.'

They couldn't leave the room quickly enough, and wound their way back down the stair.

The scene was much as they'd left it, except that the Duke had acquired a swollen eye and was clutching one wrist to his chest. Brann stood in front of him, staring, and wondering what happened in the head of such a man that made him capable of such things.

'You saw my workroom, then?' the man said brightly, almost proudly. 'So much has been learnt in that room. So much has been discovered, such advances achieved, such help that will be brought to those who seek to progress the human condition. If you can grasp even a fraction of the enormity of what has been achieved in that room, you will thank your gods for the work wrought by such higher thought.' His eyes glittered, and he shook with excitement. 'If you will but permit me to share just some of my findings...'

Brann fought to control himself. 'Right now, I thank the gods that I am ordinary.' He looked past the Duke. 'Gerens, it is time for this man to answer our questions.'

Gerens nodded solemnly. 'The slow way or the quick way?'

'To be honest,' Brann said, 'I would love the slow way, but we are not blessed with time. Those who knew that something was amiss, I would expect, are all in this room, dead or alive, so we can do what we have to do. But I would rather we were on our way,' he thought of the scene in the room above, 'sooner rather than later.'

'The quick way, then.'

He marched the Duke to the window and pushed him backwards until he was lying on the sill. Grabbing an ankle in each hand, he tipped him until the man was hanging upside down above the drop.

'He's gone quite rigid, chief,' Gerens said. 'I think he's a bit frightened.'

Brann was sure he was. 'Are you sure you can hold on to him? Remember we need information.'

'He really is very light,' Gerens reassured him. 'There's actually nothing to him.' To demonstrate, he let go with one hand, then leant out of the window slightly. 'Now, don't wriggle. You might break free, don't you think?' He reached out and grabbed the free ankle again. 'There, we go. Don't want him to get too scared to speak, I suppose.'

'Good,' Brann said. 'Ask him about Loku.'

Gerens leant forward. 'My friend would like to know if you have encountered a man called Loku recently. Or maybe you know him as Taraloku-Bana?' There was a muffled sound from outside, and Gerens spoke over his shoulder. 'He knows him as Loku, and he was indeed here when we thought he was. It appears he is a colleague.'

'Ask him who he reports to.'

'My friend would like to know who your boss is in your affairs with Loku.' He turned his head again to Brann. 'He says Loku was arranging a meeting across the water with others like them, to report to he who controls them and receive instructions. This dangling man is to meet this boss for the first time at that meeting.'

'Ask him where Loku is now.'

'My friend would like to know where that bastard Loku has gone.' He relayed the message once again to the room. 'He says there is a camp near here, a day's ride to the east. He might still be there. Some have already been sent to the next stage of fulfilling their purpose, and he was to assess who would be ready to go next.'

Konall strolled across and looked with interest over the top of Gerens. 'I must say, this Duke is being fairly eager to help.'

'Would you not, in that position?' Brann asked.

Konall frowned. 'It would be impossible. I am too heavy for Gerens to hold for such a length of time.' He noticed something and eased partially past Gerens to peer out of the window at an angle. 'Excuse me,' he said politely to Gerens.

'Of course,' Gerens said, leaning flat on the sill to allow Konall to lean further. A moan came from outside the window.

Konall turned back to the room. 'Two guards have come round the corner. The fools are chatting enough that they are unlikely to look up here, but the man hanging from Gerens's hands will be able to see them very soon, and I'm pretty sure he will start shouting.'

Brann looked at the others, and saw that they were looking at him. He considered the options and the situation. 'We need to shut the Duke up, and we need to divert the attention away from the front door.'

Gerens turned from the window, empty-handed. 'That's easy. Anything else?'

The Duke's wail was cut short by an audible thump, precipitating shouts of alarm.

Brann shrugged. 'That should do it.'

'A quicker end than he deserved,' Konall reflected.

Brann kicked a stool, sending it careering across the room. 'You don't know the half of it. Let's go.' He looked at Sophaya. 'Ready?'

She nodded and stood, the waiflike figure still huddled in her arms. Grakk ripped a curtain from its hanging at the opening to the stairs leading upwards, and they wiped the worst of the blood from their faces and hands. They retrieved what weapons were still protruding from the various bodies lying around the room and cleaned them also, sliding them back into their sheaths. Grakk pulled the object from the captain's eye and wiped it on the curtain, turning it over curiously in his hand. It was a flat piece of metal, shaped into a star with barbed points, and the tribesman looked at Sophaya. 'An interesting weapon,' he observed. 'I have heard of such among some guilds of assassins in the Empire.'

She stroked the child's hair. 'You mix with all sorts when you work in certain sections of society in a big city. It pays to develop contacts, especially when you can learn from each other.'

Grakk was still examining the star, weighing it on his hand and turning it on his fingertips.

'Keep it.'

Grakk smiled. 'Thank you. You are kind.'

She shrugged. 'I have several.'

Brann sheathed his axe, eager to organise their exit. 'For the first few floors, at least, we will try to pass unobtrusively. Or, at least, as unobtrusively as can be managed by a group that looks like us.' He turned to Philippe. 'We need someone to lead us down.'

Konall looked at him askance. 'We just keep going down stairs, surely, until we reach ground level. How much leading does that need?'

'No,' Brann said, his eyes still on Philippe, 'we need someone to *look* like they are leading us down, at least for as long as we can manage before someone realises that something is wrong. Every step we don't have to fight for, hastens our departure.' He put his hand on Philippe's arm. 'Can you act a part?'

The young man smiled weakly. 'I may be useless at drugging someone, but I have spent so many years acting in one way or another that I'm not sure if I can do anything else. What do you want?'

Brann chewed his lip, gathering his thoughts. 'People in here recognise you. If you are directing us, explaining loudly about things as if we were guests of the Duke and you have

104

been asked to show us out, it would be good. The more you look to draw attention to yourself, the less people think you don't want them to look closely. They just get irritated and hope you go away quickly. Or at least, I hope they do.'

Sophaya grunted. 'Only one way to find out. Now can we go? There may not be much to this little one, but she's not made of feathers.'

Gerens made to reach for the snuggling girl, but she just pressed harder against Sophaya, who shook her head briefly. He nodded in acceptance, but stepped close, loosening a large knife in its sheath. No one would harm either girl while he could still move.

Brann took a deep breath. 'Yes, we should move, but one more thing, Philippe. Eloise is downstairs. In the guard room.'

His eyes widened. 'You only thought to tell me this now? Why have we dallied here?'

He made for the door in a rush, but Brann restrained him.

'I'm sorry, but we came for a purpose and could not leave without it. And to rush without thought would be to rush to death, and we cannot help her if we are lying bleeding on a stairwell.' He gripped him tighter. 'Can you do this?'

Philippe stared at him for a moment, before the actor returned to his eyes. He straightened. 'I can. But we do it now.'

No more words were needed. They followed his abrupt exit. No more words on that matter, but Philippe had already slipped into the overbearing conversation of one who looks to show off their petty importance. 'If you follow me, I'll show you the guard room, as the Duke requested of his most trusted servant.' He turned and said in a low voice.

'If people think you are going somewhere else inside, they won't think about you heading outside. Do you think that's right?'

Brann wasn't sure it was necessarily so, but nodded with a smile. It did no harm to encourage Philippe, and the main thing was that he kept talking. As Philippe continued his guided tour, each proclamation more strident and pompous than the last, Brann ran over in his mind the layout the young man had described to them. A single winding stairway ran from top to bottom, wide enough for three men abreast and with a landing at each level. Below the Duke's chambers on the top two floors were the late captain's rooms, and then the kitchens situated where they could serve those above and below equally as quickly. The next floor down housed storerooms: half for the cooking staff and half for the guards' equipment, while the level below that held sleeping quarters for guards and servants. At ground level were more sleeping rooms and the main guard room, and below was a cellar with half-a-dozen cells around a central area where prisoners could be questioned in view of those awaiting the same fate.

They passed the captain's level quickly, Philippe averting his eyes from the interior as they did so, and approached the kitchens. 'I will show you the guard room as agreed,' Philippe pronounced even more loudly than before, his words audible over the work of those servants preparing for the next day. 'But if you care to look into the kitchens on the way past, the Duke said that you would be welcome to do so.'

At the sound of the reference to the Duke, Brann noticed the heads of the servants stare down, every one wishing to avoid being noticed. That was fine, it suited them.

The store level was passed quickly, but, as they approached

the upper sleeping quarters, three drowsy guards stumbled into the stairwell, roused by the shouting outside.

'Quick!' Philippe yelled, his voice filled with panic and his hands grabbing the first soldier and propelling him down a few steps. 'There has been a most terrible accident! The Duke! A fall! The garden! Oh my, we must all help, we really must! Please hurry!'

Clearly dreading the consequences of not being on hand to help the Duke in his time of need, the men almost fell in their haste to run down. Brann and the others followed fast – who would question anyone rushing in the company of guardsmen?

They reached the ground level and Philippe cut past the front entrance and flung open a door with clearly no consideration of his own safety. They piled into the guard room behind him with weapons drawn – and stopped.

Alone in the room, Eloise crouched in a corner. She had managed to retrieve a shift from the pile of her clothes on the floor, but had dressed no more, as if she only had the energy for the minimum to cover herself. Her hands were pressed to her lap, where the pale material was stained red, and she turned a face to them that was swollen and cut beyond recognition of the girl who had left them on the street outside. It was her eyes that struck Brann hardest, though. As a child, he had been at a friend's house when old Rewan, who tended the ailments of villagers and animals alike, arrived to end the misery of a working dog that was too injured to recover. The animal had seemed to know Rewan's purpose, and Brann now saw the same look in Eloise's eyes: a cornered fear, a shrinking from the inescapable, a desperation for mercy.

Philippe cried out as he rushed to her. His arms wrapped

her into him, and he rocked, singing a soft tune into her ear, a melody Brann could only guess had seen the pair through times both hard and lonely. He looked up at them, his own eyes stricken, his voice a whisper of horror. 'How could you let her face this? How could you leave a girl to face them?'

Brann couldn't answer. He was asking himself the same questions.

Grakk knelt beside the pair. 'It was beyond our power,' he said softly. 'All we thought, all *she* thought, was that she would dally by them at the gate, turn their eyes to her. When they took her inside, when she went with them, what she did – it was bravery on a par with anything I have seen on a battlefield.' He put a hand on Philippe's shoulder. 'She did this that we might help you.'

Philippe looked again around them. 'Those last words do not exactly make me feel better.' But the anger left him in a long sigh, leaving abject acceptance in its place. 'We both knew something like this can happen; does happen. Everyone in our... our line of work knows that. You just have to think it will not happen to you or those you love, or you could not carry on.' He smiled weakly, humourlessly, grimly. 'I know, that sounds stupid.'

Brann walked over. 'Not to a fighting man, it doesn't.'

Philippe nodded, and drew strength into him with a slow breath. 'Eloise, my darling, we need to go.' He leant in close and spoke into her ear, and his words gradually had effect. She unwound her body to stand, leaning on her brother.

'Yes,' she said, her tone as flat as her eyes. 'Go. We must get go. Away from here. Far, far away.' She looked at him. 'Take me away.'

Konall lifted a cloak from a hook on the wall and wrapped

it around her as she passed, while Gerens took her free arm, supporting her at that side as well.

Brann glanced around the room. His attention had been so caught by Eloise that he hadn't noticed a large opening in the floor: a stout wooden hatch lying open and allowing him to peer cautiously over the edge. Steps led down and, as Brann moved to a better angle, he could see a wide square room, the central features a slab of a table with metal restraints set into the wooden top stained with blood old and new and, around the sides, barred cells.

Memories stirred at the sight of the cells, and he pushed them away. Approaching footsteps indicated that another room lay beyond his vision, and he held his breath, reaching for the hatch. When the three guards came into his vision, though, they walked across the way, never thinking to look up the stairway. It was the prisoner held between two of them that caught his attention and stayed his hand on the hatch. A young woman, her build athletic and strong, her hair the colour of the summer sun and framing a face golden of hue and heart-shaped, who moved as can only a dancer or a warrior. When pale blue eyes turned to meet his, he knew she was no dancer.

On impulse, he slid the knife from the sheath strapped to his right forearm, and reached down to set it on the step at the extent of his reach. A slight frown creased the space between her eyebrows, then a nod was the last he saw of her as the guards continued their way to a cell. He suspected that his knife would be put to use before long, but whenever it would be, they would be gone by that time. Still, it pleased him that it would be put to use by her.

His intention had been to close the hatch and bolt it to trap any guards below, but instead he rested it back open as he had found it. If events in the cells reached the conclusion he was sensing they would, there would be no guards able to exit in any case.

The others were already out of the guard room and he ran quietly to catch up. They moved as quickly as Eloise could manage, down the steps at the front of the tower and straight for the gate.

Brann looked around. The courtyard was empty – all must be around the rear of the tower, at the Duke's body. There was certainly enough noise and consternation echoing from that direction. He fixed his eyes on the gate.

Thirty paces. Twenty. Ten.

It was at five paces that two guards ran around the corner of the building. They saw the bedraggled group and veered away from the tower entrance to face them. They stared at each other.

'Philippe,' Grakk said from the corner of his mouth. 'How many guards are there here in total?'

'At least two dozen, maybe more,' he said, his voice starting to tremble.

'We can't engage these two without them raising the alarm,' Brann said. 'And we can't take on all of them without at least some of us dying.' He looked at Eloise. 'And we can't outrun them.' The men were coming towards them, shouting across questions. 'So maybe we need to wrong-foot them.'

He waved his arm frantically, urging the guards to hurry over. 'Please, hurry! There is someone else hurt. We need to get them to a healer.'

The guards stopped, one with his spear lowered, the other with a sword held warily. They both eyed the four armed men before them. 'What are you talking about?' one said.

110

Brann automatically ran his eyes over them. A spear thrust would come across the attack line of the swordsman, hampering his movement forward. Neither had a shield. The distance could be closed in moments. They were not even wearing helmets, dishevelled hair as if they had just woken all that lay between a blade and a blow to the skull. Their eyes moved nervously...

He paused. The faces seemed familiar. The hair... as if just out of...

They were two of the three men they had run into in the stairwell. They *had* just been roused from sleep. They knew nothing about Eloise's arrival at the tower. It opened up a possibility.

'It's this young woman,' he said, pleadingly, indicating the figure hanging between Philippe and Gerens. 'She seems to have been brought in for the Duke. We don't know what happened, but she is in a bad way. She needs help.'

The guards looked at each other, and one nodded at the other. 'Well, it's not as if the Duke has any need of her now.' The spear lowered and the sword was sheathed.

The older of the two, a bearded man, smiled slightly. 'Look, friend, I have no idea who you are, or what the Duke wanted of this girl, though I could come up with a few suggestions. But he's not in a position to want anything any more and some would say that's not a bad thing. Probably best for all if we open the gate to check the street outside and you just go about your business. Better for us, better for you and,' he looked at Eloise, 'best of all for her. Take her as far from this tower as you can.'

Brann relaxed. 'Thank you.'

The man shrugged, unbolting the gate and swinging one

half inwards. 'Sometimes straightforward is as complicated as life needs to get.'

They all breathed a little easier.

Then Eloise lifted her head. She did not see the faces. She had not heard the words. But she saw the tabards, and the Duke's insignia. She shrieked and hurled herself at the nearest guard, Gerens's knife in hand. Before he could react, she had sliced across his throat, blood spraying beneath a face frozen forever in disbelief. She launched herself at the other, who had stumbled back in shock, his spear coming up in defensive reflex. The point took her in the chest but her momentum took them both down, the spear ripped from his hands in the fall. Amid screams and snarls that turned to coughs, she stabbed three, four five times into his chest and throat and horrified face. She stabbed for the few short moments that she had left to live, then lay still in the shared mess of their blood.

Grakk and Brann reached her just as she stilled, Gerens and Konall casting around for danger with weapons drawn. Sophaya kept the child's head turned from the bloodbath. Grakk bent over Eloise and checked the obvious, then shook his head to confirm it. Philippe was on his knees, hands held in supplication, eyes struggling with comprehension, every part of his face straining, a silent scream tearing itself from his soul.

'So what now?' Konall said.

Brann took a last look at the scene, as Konall hauled Philippe to his feet.

'Now we run.'

Chapter 3

When he had ruled, the world came to the Emperor. Now it seemed that some things had relaxed.

Arrogance that relaxes standards will build complacency from indolence just as easily as it builds dismissiveness from pomposity. Either forms weakness, and weakness offers less resistance to pressure.

A cracked wall will never again be truly strong, no matter the patches. In some cases, a wall will, weakened, still serve its purpose, for the pressures it will face are less than even the reduced strength of the wall.

But when the wall faces strong and repeated pressure, even the smallest cracks will spread and widen and fracture and bring the wall to rubble. When even the first small cracks appear, one remedy alone will suffice: tear down the wall and build one anew; the only question being when, not if. But the new wall must be completed before the old is destroyed, for even a weakened wall is better than none.

Such is the wall of an Emperor's power.

He had known it, had maintained an Empire on it. Set

the minimum standard at the highest level, and tolerate no relaxation.

Those who ruled now did not know it. They governed for their pleasure, believing they governed efficiently, never knowing that they benefited from the decades that had come before. Place the running of the Empire before all, and the pleasure will come in its wake; rise each morning with the first thought of your own contentment, and the source of the contentment will be pulverised by inattention.

The wall will crack.

A guard's rap at his door heralded the entry of the current incumbent of the throne. He slumped in his chair and fixed a bland ghost of a smile to his lips a moment before the Emperor strode in.

He mumbled pleasant inanities in response to the eloquent and almost-believable claims of successes and assertions of wise rule that followed the cursory enquiry after his well-being and were intended, he was sure, to bolster the man's own self-belief as much as the ostensible purpose to reassure a venerated elderly relative that all was well with the world.

As soon as the door closed, renewed determination drew his posture straight once more. He moved to his desk and drew up rapid notes in handwriting that few could read and in a cypher that none but he could understand. To a reader, they were the scratchings of deranged senility; in reality, they formed architectural plans.

Plans for a new wall.

A wall already under construction.

The cracks were growing.

****

114

They ran.

Joceline saw them coming and started to ask, presumably about Eloise, but the question died on her lips at the sight of the stricken Philippe. Konall's handful of tunic propelled him and horror and disbelief filled his eyes. She glanced at the small girl, now in Gerens's arms, stronger as they were than those of Sophaya, but postponed any curiosity in favour of turning and lifting her skirts to allow her to match their pace, leading them through the winding streets with an assurance that defied the darkness of the hour.

Not for the first time, Brann tumbled on cobbles. Ignoring the pain, he glanced enviously at Gerens, the only one of them not to have fallen – a fortunate fact given his burden. Moonlight allowed the other boy to see his look.

'The slopes around my home were rock, not nice smooth grass. Rock teaches you early on how to keep your balance... and that you want to learn it.'

Streets blurred into one twisting, slipping, frantic journey. At first, their footsteps were the only sound but, before long, bells began to ring their message of alarm.

Joceline half turned, gasping at them. 'If we can stay ahead of their messengers, we should reach the gate you asked for before the various barracks near the walls know exactly why they are being roused.'

'Good.' Brann was panting as much as she was. 'As long as the messengers don't use horses, we should have enough of a start to stay ahead of the communication, and they won't know that they are to look for us, or in fact search at all.'

Joceline stopped at the edge of an open area that lay between the last of the houses and the town walls, a killing ground perfect for archers should an enemy breach the defences. She pointed at the base of the wall, where they could just make out the darker colour of a door.

'There,' she said. 'It bolts on this side, as does the door on the far side of the wall. As you wanted, the nearest gates in either direction are distant enough that you should be able to get enough of a start on any pursuers to see you away.'

Brann nodded. 'And the size of the tunnel? And doorways?'

'Small enough that nothing bigger than a man can fit through. Dogs, yes, but no horses.'

Sophaya frowned. 'Not much use as a gate. Not many options.'

'It will be a sally port, young lady,' Grakk said. 'Far enough from the gates that defenders may issue from it unseen to take unawares besiegers at those gates, or even sneak a messenger away to request help from elsewhere.'

'Right, so they can't chase us on horseback. Good,' Gerens said.

Shouts broke out in the distance to their left, spreading quickly through the streets behind them. The pattern was repeated shortly after from the right.

'It seems they can send messages on horseback, however. Maybe time to leave?'

Sophaya lifted the little girl from Gerens, and set her before Joceline. 'This is Antoinette. Do you think you could manage to find her parents?'

The woman nodded, but the girl looked up with eyes that were as dead as her voice proved to be. 'My mummy and daddy are dead. They shouted at the soldiers when they took us away.'

A tear started in Sophaya's eye, but Joceline merely

crouched and took the girl's hands in hers. 'Well, I will just have to take care of you, won't I? We will find you work to occupy you and train you in skills you never imagined you could learn.'

Brann was shocked. 'She is no more than six years! You don't mean to bring her up as a...?'

Joceline's glare cut him off. 'The seamstress across from the inn has need of an apprentice.'

He was glad the darkness would hide his blush. 'Good. Of course. We should go.' He looked at her. 'Thank you, for all of this.'

She shrugged. 'Just tell me this: does the Duke still govern?'

'Not in this world.'

'Then the thanks are mine to give to you.'

Shouts drew closer. Without a word or a look back, Joceline took Antoinette by the hand and ran for the shadows. Brann looked at Philippe, who looked after the receding pair, almost out of sight already, and then turned back. 'There is nothing here for me now but sorrow,' he said. 'If you will allow me, I would like—'

Brann's answer was to grab his tunic and drag him with him as, without further hesitation, he bolted for the wall. The others, impatient to leave, needed no encouragement to run with them.

To expect to reach the cover of the door without being seen would have been pushing optimism too far, but they almost made it. A score of paces from their target, a group of men rounded a distant corner. The open ground and full moon gave the guards a view that was sufficient to show several figures behaving suspiciously, and to men already enthused by the chase, anything questionable became prey.

The men began to shout and run in the same instant, although one lingered long enough to sound three blasts on a horn. Answering horns sent back single notes from at least four locations.

Brann thumped into the wall, his chest heaving, at the same time as the others. Gerens paused for nothing, hurling his shoulder at the door without missing a stride. The wood shattered inwards and the boy tumbled through, already back on his feet by the time the others piled in.

'It may have been open, you know,' Konall pointed out.

'It definitely is now,' Gerens said.

They hurried into the short corridor through the wall, barely more than a few hands of space to either side of their shoulders.

'I dare you to do the same to the next door,' Konall said.

Gerens grunted. 'I don't mind getting wet. Better than waiting to be stuck with a sword.'

Light penetrated no more than a few yards behind them into the passage, and they felt their way at a trot through the black, feet slipping on the damp stone of the floor. Brann strained his eyes for the slightest hint of light ahead but still discovered the door with his hands rather than his eyes. The others piled up behind him, then backed off slightly as his fingers found three large bolts and slid them free. He yanked at a handle, and old hinges groaned as he heaved it open at the second attempt. The moon was shining from the far side of the town, but outside was lighter than the tunnel and some little vision returned to them, the water of the moat a deeper black than what lay beyond. He knelt and felt in the darkness.

'There should be a plank lying at the side of the tunnel,' he called urgently. 'Run it across the moat and we are away.'

'I have it,' came Grakk's voice. 'But it will not be our bridge. Wet floors and wood are excellent for rot, but not for strength.'

Brann cursed. There was no option. 'Gerens, you will get your swim after all.'

The shouts behind were nearing the broken door behind them. Brann launched himself blindly into the moat, hitting the water and hearing the muffled splashes of the others doing likewise before he regained the surface. The distinctive taste in his mouth was expected – and welcome, under the circumstances – but had obviously come as a surprise to Konall.

'What in all the hells have we jumped into?' the boy spluttered.

Brann grinned. 'Just don't drink any of it.' At least it meant that the others were waiting for them.

Grakk called to him. Brann saw his dark silhouette crouched at the doorway and was handed the bundle of documents. He took them in one hand while his other kept his head above the water, then watched in alarm as the gangly figure leapt wildly past him in the general direction of the others.

'That was Grakk!' he yelled above the sound of the splash. 'Remember he can't swim.'

'Got him, chief,' came Gerens's voice. 'What are you doing back there?'

'I'm on my way.' An explanation seemed irrelevant. 'Just get him to the other side quickly.'

He heard the water thrash as they struck out and followed in their wake, swimming one-handed as fast as he could while carefully keeping the bundle of documents clear of the water. He made the far side as figures, lit by a torch, started to appear at the doorway. Cries from the guards increased in excitement as the splashing of Brann and his companions being helped from the water by strong arms from above told them how close their quarry was. A scrape of wood on stone was followed by a curse.

'Sounds like they have discovered the rot in the wood,' Brann said to Cannick as the man pulled him to the bank of the moat with an ease that belied his age, while Hakon and Breta could be heard helping the others. 'Is all prepared?' He received a nod. 'The horses?'

'It was too noticeable from the wall to have them waiting here. They'll be on their way soon.'

'They are not here?' There was panic in Philippe's voice, the alarm increasing as the splashes of men jumping into the water started to be heard in rapid and unceasing order. 'It doesn't matter how far we are from the nearest gate, if we are on foot they will ride us down with ease.'

Konall swept his wet hair from his face and reached to tie it behind his head, as he always did as a precursor to a fight. 'He has a point, if a little dramatically expressed. And we are fairly outnumbered by those already on their way.'

A soldier started to drag himself from the moat, and Gerens casually swatted him with his sword, looking across the water as the baying of hounds could now be heard from the tunnel. 'And then there is *that* development, too.'

Philippe grabbed Cannick by the arm. 'So when will the horses come? When?'

Cannick gently disengaged his grip. 'Just as soon as they see the fire.'

'Fire?' Philippe cast about wildly. 'What fire?'

Cannick lifted a lamp that was shuttered to send light only towards the empty land outside the town, and smashed it onto a towering pile of dry, brittle branches loaded into the back of the cart, now empty of its barrels of oil. The dry wood flared up in seconds.

'Ah,' said Konall. 'That fire.'

'Not quite,' Cannick said, as Breta and Hakon leapt forward to run the blazing cart at the moat and tip it head-long at the water. 'This fire.'

Fire arose from the water as if by magic. Swimmers screamed as much in shock as agony, and the men at the doorway, lit by the spreading flames, shrank back against those behind. The light gave them vision at their own side of the moat as well, revealing two large barrels lying at the side of the water, their tops staved in and contents gone.

Gerens grinned with cold humour. 'The oil.'

Brann nodded, remembering the trickle of oil in the rear yard of the inn the night before, when the idea had slipped into his head. He was glad it had worked; the still water of the moat letting the oil stay concentrated at that spot for the short time since it would have been poured there.

Two arrows flickered at the corner of his vision and thunked into the ground not far from Grakk.

The tribesman looked at him then raised his eyebrows. 'Shall we move?'

'In the gods' names yes,' Brann gasped, aghast at his complacency. The flames that kept men and beasts at the foot of the wall from following also made their little group perfect targets for archers at the top of it. In any case, he had no idea how long the fire on the water would last.

They had little to gather and less to entice them to delay, and were running into the darkness in seconds. As soon as they had stumbled beyond the range of an arrow, tripping and bumping each other in blindness, Konall stopped them.

'Squeeze your eyes shut, and count to ten,' he said. 'Your eyes still want to see in the firelight. So remind them what dark looks like.'

When they opened their eyes, the way was clear to them, even with the moon behind clouds. Brann looked at him approvingly, and Konall shrugged.

'Old hunting trick from where the winter nights would show you what real darkness is.'

They ran again, but this time faster.

Every thirty paces, Grakk gave a shrill whistle.

Sophaya moved alongside Brann. 'If he is trying to attract those who bring the horses, would he not be better advised to use light?'

'The source of light is easier to pinpoint over distance, such as from the town gates,' Brann panted. 'The direction of a sound is easier to find up close than from far away, so we give less away to our enemies pursuing than we do to our friends seeking us.'

She grunted, accepting his reasoning. He wondered, at first, at a girl of obvious intelligence not seeing this for herself, but remembered her background. When you spend your life, and make your living, in the confines of tightly packed buildings and narrow streets, the accepted wisdom is that light can be concealed by walls or even a cloak, but sound carries greater distances and around corners, and is the greater danger. Different circumstances, different lessons.

Brann's breath was loud in his head, but the growing sound of hoof beats was louder. They stopped, and Grakk whistled again, giving final confirmation. Despite reason telling him that only their own companions could have reached them so quickly, still Brann's heart quickened and his sword found its way into his hand as he watched the dark shapes gallop towards them.

Then a rider vaulted from his saddle, and Marlo's cheerful voice greeted them.

Brann relaxed, finding his horse and swinging onto its back, gratefully feeling the familiar power of the beast beneath him. Marlo was beside him, and he pointed at the dark shape of Philippe. 'We have brought an extra passenger for you.'

'Why me?'

'You are light enough that the horse will not mind as much taking the extra load.'

'Mongoose is lighter.'

'You are skinnier.'

'Sophaya is skinnier.'

'You want to suggest to Gerens that another man rides with Sophaya?'

A short pause ended with a flash of white teeth. 'Philippe, you may ride with me.'

Hakon guffawed. 'You might want to watch how you put that!'

Breta slapped the back of his head. 'Restrain your ribald comments in the presence of ladies, pig man.' She hawked and spat as hoof-kicked dust swirled and caught at her throat. 'Men!'

Hakon looked at her, but thought better of responding.

They rode as quickly as rows of vines would allow, until they reached a road.

Brann wheeled his horse. 'Konall? Hakon? East.'

Without hesitation, both pointed to where the road led to their left. He saw Philippe's quizzical look.

'Born as seafarers. Under the sun or the stars, they always know.'

The clouds had cleared and the moon lit the road to allow a gallop to be risked until they had crested three successive rises, after which Brann slowed them to a loping canter, being more concerned with ensuring the horses could last the pace as long as possible. He moved alongside Marlo's horse, looking at Philippe.

'You know the town,' he called above the noise of the hooves. 'Will he be mourned?' Thoughts of the Duke clearly brought back the reality of his sister's death and, as Philippe crumpled into himself, regret at having to seek information clenched his gut. Brann was on the verge of leaving him to his grief when the young man pulled himself tall in the saddle once more, drawing strength into himself with a long slow breath. Brann's remorse turned to a surge of emotion as he watched courage gather in Philippe's eyes.

'They will rejoice.' His voice was flat, controlled. 'They will rejoice, but they will do so behind the walls of their houses, for no one under the Duke's rule was safe from betrayal, and it takes time for trust to grow and feelings to be expressed openly.'

'And the loyalty of the soldiers?'

Philippe shrugged, having to grab at Marlo's waist to regain his hold as his hands moved with his shoulders. 'They are loyal to the job. Like every other job, some are in it for the money, some like to feel important; some are good men, others are bastards. And like everyone in that town, all were in fear of even the appearance of disobedience.'

'So what I'm wondering is, how much will they be inclined to follow us?' He paused as he thought of Philippe's background. 'I'm sorry, how could I expect you to know? You were not one of them.'

The level gaze never left him. 'But I do know people. And I know that when he,' his head nodded at Gerens, 'let loose his grip, he not only rid the town and these lands of a madman, but in one heartbeat he also created uncertainty. No one stood ready to step into his place, because he trusted no one to repress the ambition he would have held in their place. And the Captain of the Guard was also killed. They will not follow after they know the truth, and dawn is more than time enough for that.'

Brann bit on his lip as he considered it. Once the officers realised fully what had caused the alarm and that their leader was no more, and once those holding positions of power in the town – and those who would wish to do so – discovered that the Duke was dead, all concern would focus on the question of who would assume control, and any interest in the small group of unknown people would disappear along with the shapes into the dark of the surrounding countryside. Philippe was right. 'Thank you.'

The young man turned his face forward once more. Brann saw the glisten of tears start to shine in the moonlight, and was struck by a memory of a voice of feigned coarseness in a dark alley. *Remember me like this, my lover.* He fished in his coin pouch, fingers finding the button Eloise had handed him immediately before walking into the danger of the Duke's keep. Leaning across, he pressed it into Philippe's hand.

The young man stared at the button in silence, the tip of his thumb rubbing gently across it as if to confirm it was real. An object of such simplicity, but holding an enormity of sentiment. His chest constricted sharply as a violent intake of breath was prevented from becoming a sob only by a jaw clenched with fierce determination. His fingers closed tight over the button, and eyes drenched in conflicting emotions turned to meet Brann's. He nodded, once.

Brann steered his horse away, allowing him his sorrow.

They continued at a canter until light started to creep from above the horizon ahead. Brann slowed them to a trot, and then a walk and, when the sun was fully in sight, Mongoose spotted a brook not far from the road.

As the horses drank, they broke out dried meat and bread, noticing their hunger now that they had stopped. Brann untied the bag of documents and pulled out the map, spreading it on the ground before him. He called Cannick over.

'What have you there?' the old warrior said.

'A present from the Duke.' Brann grinned. 'I suppose it's now a bequest.'

Cannick smiled back. 'Very good of him. Is it any help?'

'That's what I want to know. You know this area – what do you think?'

The older man groaned slightly as he knelt beside Brann. 'I don't know these lands intimately, but enough to understand this easily enough. There is Belleville, and we are here.' He indicated a spot. 'See where the river runs in close to the road, just after the road bends sharply?'

Brann traced a finger across eastwards to a symbol marked onto the map in fresher ink than the main design. 'So this must be the camp the Duke said Loku headed for.' He frowned. 'There are three more of those symbols in the area around the town. I don't like the look of that.'

'There is much of this whole affair I don't like the look of,' Cannick growled. 'The sooner we have a chat with that bastard Loku, like we did with the Duke, the better.'

'You are right.' He called to the others and wrapped the map up once more with care. 'At least we know it is a single road to reach it, with just a fork near the camp.'

Cannick nodded. 'If I am picturing the distances right, we should reach it shortly after noon.'

As it transpired, they reached the fork late morning, though it proved to be less of a fork in the road than it had appeared when drawn on the map, and more a narrow offshoot of a track, overgrown with the bushes, thick and thorny of branch, that grew abundantly on both sides of the road.

Konall rode close, his hunter's eye drawing his curiosity. 'Someone has worked hard to make this look unused and unwelcoming. Look.' He leant to the side and cautiously grabbed the end of one branch, taking care to avoid the large curved thorns. As he nudged his horse to walk it away, the entire bush moved with him, opening the start of the track to allow easy passage.

'Very good, young lord,' said Grakk, and dismounted to lead his horse with care between the narrow path between reaching branches.

They followed him up a short but steep slope, eyeing the wicked barbs of the thorns and imagining easily the damage just one could cause if ripping the skin of a passer-by, whether human or animal.

On cresting the rise, they saw a dramatic transformation. Where the track was unable to be seen from the road, it had been cleared to allow easy movement, and was clearly well used.

Despite the caution that potential proximity brings, they moved with as much haste as they could manage. *Well used* meant the chance of meeting one of those well-users was high, and uncomfortable. The way ahead started to lead upwards again, though not as steeply as the stretch from the road. Brann saw a rocky outcrop a couple of bowshots to the right, and whistled softly to attract Grakk's attention. He pointed that way, and the man nodded, realising, as Brann had, that they did not know what lay over the crest of this small hill.

Mongoose pulled up alongside him. 'Don't fancy knocking on the front door, then? Pity, you lot had all the fun back at the town.'

'Don't worry,' Brann reassured her. 'I'm not ruling out any fun here too.'

They led their horses into the outcrop, great angular rocks jutting at angles but with space to pass easily between.

Brann looked around. 'We are far enough in to be hidden. Marlo, watch the horses while we have a look.'

For once, Marlo's face was missing his smile. 'Why am I always the one to stay behind?'

'You have a way with the horses, and it is important to keep them quiet.' He didn't want to say that the real reason was his reluctance to place the boy in any greater danger than was ever necessary, but relented at the disappointment written across Marlo's face. 'Fine. Gerens, show Philippe how to keep the horses quiet but ready for a quick departure if necessary.' He looked at Marlo. 'Grumpy, you come with us.' The smile returned.

They crept through the rocks, reaching the highest point of the small hill. They crawled the last few yards, rough ground scraping beneath them but otherwise silent. The whole group, bar the two at the horses, eased their heads in unison to look at what lay beyond.

Brann gasped slightly. The sight that greeted him was familiar, similar in so many ways to the village he had seen in the mountains of Konall's homeland. The squalor, the hovels, the impalement stakes that were almost like religious focal points and, most of all, the people, with their air of belligerence and degradation and, no doubt, the same dead eyes. Similar in so many ways, but different in one: here there were no women or children, leaving the scene both more tense and less horrific. For Brann, worse than any other aspect of the previous village had been the acceptance of casual brutality and torture as commonplace and routine by children who knew no other way of life.

They slid away from the edge and moved back to the horses before anyone spoke. Brann saw Konall, Hakon, Cannick, Grakk and Gerens, who had also travelled south with Einarr from Halveka, look at each other, the same grimness in each gaze.

Breta growled. 'What in the darkest hells was that?'

'We have seen such before,' Brann said, 'in the North.'

'Ach, shit.' Gerens spat in disgust. 'When that fool dangling from the window mentioned a camp, rather than town or village, I had suspected such but hoped for different.'

Brann realised that Breta, Mongoose, Sophaya, Marlo and Philippe were looking at him intently. He shook his head at the memories that filled it. 'In the mountains of Halveka, near the home town of Konall and Hakon, a camp had been secretly established by Loku, and populated by the worst in society: those who glorify in inflicting pain and torture, who feast on suffering; the scum of every society brought together and with their basest and cruellest features encouraged and fed.' He looked at Hakon and

Gerens, his eyes flitting from them to Grakk. 'Some of us were taken there and subjected to their degradation.'

Hakon stood from where he had been scratching meaninglessly in the dirt with a dagger, knuckles white where he gripped the hilt. 'And two of us went there voluntarily to bring the three imprisoned in it to safety.' He looked at Brann and Konall. 'Some things are not forgotten.' He sheathed the knife and slipped an axe from his belt. 'I also do not forget that we gave those bastards a beating, and we can do the same to their cousins here.'

'Easy, big man.' Cannick put a hand on Hakon's shoulder. 'No use in all of them and half of us getting killed.'

Brann nodded, thoughts competing as he weighed what he knew with what might be possible. 'If Loku is still here—'

'We net two fish on one hook,' Konall said. 'So we go in fast and hit them before they realise they are under attack.' Like Hakon, his weapon was drawn.

Brann held up a hand. 'You Northmen will be the death of me! Literally.'

Grakk said: 'What if Loku is killed in the confusion? Or is not there at all and we have wasted time when we could be on his trail?'

Brann paced, options being dismissed or compared. 'Indeed.'

'Still, if the bastard dies,' Hakon was not deterred, 'how is that in any way a bad thing?'

Konall sighed. 'They are right. His death will be a thing of great joy, but our vengeance, and the service such an occurrence will bring to the world in general, is secondary. First, we must determine the greater threat posed by the conspiracy he serves, whether it aims to sow discord, topple

130

rulers or anything in between, and he must be able to talk to lead us further on that path.'

'The young lord is correct, my friend,' Grakk said, patting Hakon on his broad back. 'We need to catch him, to learn what we can of this enterprise, of his superiors. If we know there is activity in the Green Islands, in Halveka and now here also, this is even more widespread than we envisaged. We *must* find Loku, and learn what he knows, whatever it takes to do both.'

Hakon grumbled and kicked a stone. 'Can we at least kill some of his little friends down there?'

'Actually,' Brann said, 'it would be a good idea, I think.' Hakon brightened immediately, and there were signs of enthusiasm from several of the others. 'We need to know if Loku is there or not, and quickly, for if he is not we can't afford any further distance growing between us. But we cannot live with any sort of conscience if we leave this nest of death behind us.'

Cannick walked across. 'So, what are you thinking?'

Brann saw every pair of eyes upon him and pushed aside the discomfort of wondering why his opinion should be decisive to let his thoughts gather. 'Well...' He spoke slowly as the leaves grew on the branches of the plan that was forming in his head. 'We cannot kill them all without sustaining casualties ourselves, and in the most practical sense, that would slow us down further. But we can disperse them. And such people tend to cowardice, so remove the bravado of the crowd and all they have is the life they lived before this. A cut-throat thief is not something I would wish on any community, but they exist already in every town and city, and better that than the slaughter and terror these are gathered to wreak, whether the murder of innocents we heard of in the South Island or the attempt to wipe out Konall's entire ruling family in Halveka.' He looked at Hakon. 'And we can kill a few of them in the process.'

'Fine,' said Konall. 'Kill a few, disperse the others, that's the idea. So how?'

'I always find,' Brann smiled, his confidence in his ideas growing as they flowed, 'that panic is an excellent weapon. Especially amongst those who enjoy the suffering of others but fear their own. So we make them think they are doomed. Sharp weapons and confusion should do the trick.' He pointed at Marlo and Philippe. 'You two take half the horses each: one of you to this side of the hill at the path into the settlement, and the other slightly further along this hill. Keep below the skyline and, at our signal, run them round in circles to make as much dust as you can. Feel free to shout a lot, too.'

'Sounds fun,' grinned Marlo. 'But what will the signal be?'

'Screams,' said Brann.

The rest of them were in place in minutes. Creeping close to the edge of the camp was not difficult when danger was not anticipated and standards were slovenly at best. He looked in both directions. They were in pairs – Gerens protectively beside him, Cannick with Grakk, Konall with Hakon, and Breta with Mongoose – spread wide to give the impression of a large attack. He glanced back where elements of the rocky outcrop broke out from the slope that led down towards the camp, and saw Sophaya with the vantage point she needed, placing arrows ready on the top of a slab.

He looked again into the camp. The sun was high and the air thick with heat, making for torpor and quiet; few moved among the basic huts of brittle-dry branches stacked into squat cones. Insects buzzed and birds called from on high. It would seem tranquil, if they didn't know what sort of people the inhabitants were. And then there was the tall slender stake not more than a score of paces from where he lay, a corpse with less than half its tissue remaining a third of the way from the top and a scattering of well-fed carrion birds close by. As they watched, a thin man clumsily speared one of the birds, pinning it to the ground while another threw rocks at the writhing creature until it eventually lay still.

'That's the way to do it,' the rock man snickered. 'Feed it till it trusts you, then it won't suspect when you come looking for dinner. Beats hunting any day.'

The first man jerked his spear free and jabbed it in the direction of his companion. 'Don't be thinking you get equal picks. It was my spear that did the business. It was me that pulled the bits of meat from her,' the spear tip jerked in the direction of the impaled corpse, 'to give to the bird. I get first pickings.'

'All right, all right.' The man held his hands up in acquiescence, and the other laid his spear close by his side as he knelt over the dead bird.

But Brann noticed that a rock was still in the standing man's hand, and that the first man never turned his back on him, feeling with his hands as he hacked chunks from the body, his eyes never dropping. With a squashed mass of dripping meat and feathers cradled in his arms and his spear awkwardly gripped in one hand, he scuttled towards the far side of the camp. As soon as he moved away, the other man seized the bird by the neck and made off with what remained, looking from one side to the other all the way as though expecting another to be attracted to his prize.

'No time like the present,' Brann muttered to Gerens once the pair were out of sight. At least there was none of the long waiting before action – time that bred nerves and ate at confidence.

Winding a rag across his face to cover nose and mouth, he stood and walked calmly past the first hut, finding a broad-shouldered man crouched over a cooking pot. The man's eyes widened and mouth opened to shout as he saw Brann, but in looking up he also left his throat exposed, and the keen edge of the black-bladed sword cut almost completely through his neck. Brann lifted a burning branch from the fire beneath the pot, and Gerens did likewise. He touched the flame to the man's hut, the dry wood accepting the fire with fervour, and the pair split left and right, walking behind the next hovels in line and setting each one alight as they went.

They had each fired two more huts before the screams and shouts started to rouse the camp; alarmed men running to determine the source of the noise but finding only gathering smoke and, within, swinging blades and death. Gerens had met up with Brann and he could only guess that the others had likewise reunited as he had instructed – each would fight as a pair, protecting each other from the unexpected attack that can see even the most skilled warrior felled by the most inept.

Brann emerged from the bank of smoke, sword in one hand, knife in the other and Gerens by his side. Sophaya's arrows flitted over them, every one finding a target. From her high position she would be able to see through the smoke as it dissipated and distinguish friend and foe. As the huts burned ever more fiercely, however, it would not be long before she could shoot with certainty no more. It seemed as if that time had arrived when no arrows fell for several breaths, until a screaming man came running at Gerens and a shaft took him square in the chest.

'Magnificent,' Gerens's admiring voice breathed.

Another man, naked but for a pair of ragged breeches, darted at Brann, a hatchet in each hand. Arms and legs swinging in ungainly wildness, the man hurled one of the axes with more clumsiness than efficiency, and Brann was able to watch its tumbling flight and lean to the side to let it pass. The man continued his run, remaining hatchet held high in his left hand and ready to strike, and Brann stepped towards him with three rapid paces, closing the distance quicker than his opponent had anticipated. A swing of the sword took the high hand off at the wrist, and the knife hand opened his throat before the man even knew he had been struck at all.

Brann stepped past the man as his sucking gurgles quickly faded, sweeping his eyes across the scene. Marlo and Philippe were undertaking their tasks with gusto, dust and shouts rising from beyond the hill in equal measure, and he stared to his left, trying to spot his companions stationed in that direction. He stumbled, knocked to the side, and turned with both weapons at the ready, but it was Gerens who had collided with him. The boy grabbed a thrust spear by the shaft, pulling the holder stumbling forward and yanking the weapon free, whirling in the same movement to stab the weapon into the back of the assailant. A good move, Brann thought with appreciation, and one worth remembering.

Pushing aside his annoyance at allowing a foe to approach so close unnoticed, he scanned the area properly. No one else was near enough to attack imminently. In fact, it looked as though no more attacks would come. Those arriving from the further parts of the camp were greeted with the sight of blazing fires and thick billowing smoke, dust rising from massing forces about to crest the hill and, emerging from it all, masked warriors with blood on their blades and bodies at their feet.

They fled.

Scrambling and careering, they ran for their lives in every direction but the one that promised death. They headed into the open countryside with thoughts of no one but themselves, scattering like seed from a farmer's hand.

The group converged and moved free of the smoke. Brann pulled the material from his lower face, glad to be able to breathe freely again, as Hakon slapped him heartily on the back.

'Thank you, my friend,' the boy said, gripping Brann's shoulders from behind and squeezing them affectionately. 'That was fun.'

'It was also most effective,' Grakk said, joining them. 'A highly efficient plan, young Brann.'

He smiled. 'Far more effective than I had even imagined. They ran sooner and faster than I thought they would.'

Cannick snorted. 'You underestimate the weakness of character of such as those. Even when they win they run away, just as soon as they have rifled your corpse for valuables.'

The smoke was lifting as the huts quickly burnt out, and Gerens was staring at the rocky outcrop with a frown. 'Where is Sophaya?' he said, worry forcing the words out abruptly.

Brann laid a calming hand on his arm and pointed to the end of the ridge that lay on the side of the camp where they had approached. The slight figure could be seen staring out across the open land beyond.

'As soon as she could no longer see to shoot, I told her to head there with Grakk's looking tube thing.' He looked at the tribesman. 'The...?'

'The oculens.' Grakk shook his head. 'You have a truly awful memory.'

'I do,' Brann nodded. He couldn't deny it. 'Anyway, she's been watching for Loku. With her sight aided, he could not escape her notice even if he left the moment we struck. She will remain there until we are sure he is not still here.'

'So now we search the site for him?' said Hakon.

'Now we search the site.'

They did, but with no sign of Loku or any of his effects. They met back at the horses and cleaned off their weapons.

'Not bad work for an hour or so,' said Mongoose, blood matting her hair, but presumably – hopefully, thought Brann – not her own.

'True,' said Brann. 'They are scattered, and we can still get a good half-day's travelling behind us yet.' He looked at Cannick. 'How far to the northern coast, do you reckon?'

The battle-worn face creased in brief thought. 'Five days. Maybe less if we push it.'

'Then let us push it.'

There had not been many horses in the corral at the settlement, but they found one of sufficient quality to take for Philippe. With proper feeding it would build its true strength in time, and it was young enough to keep up with the rest, though it looked exhausted each night and Brann felt guilt at the need to force it so much. Still, there was no choice, and they had been lucky with its character as it gamely forced itself to keep pace with the rest. Riding long each day and stopping only briefly, they found themselves approaching the port of Selaire during the afternoon of the fourth day. It was a compact port, and they dismounted to walk their horses through streets busy with the throng of thriving trade.

They headed straight for the docks, where boats of all sizes and purposes bumped in close confines, shouts of men, squeals of seabirds, and clanking and banging of cargoes being moved from quay to vessel and vessel to quay echoing the sounds of every port Brann had visited in his travels of the past years.

Brann looked around, a faint memory stirring.

Cannick noticed. 'We stopped here to pick up a cargo when you first, well, "joined" our crew. Remember now?'

Brann did remember. 'You know people here, then?'

'It was mainly Einarr who did, but I met the harbour master a few times. If there is a ship leaving for Cardallon soon, it is his job to know.' He nodded to a street that angled away from the docks. 'See there, between the fish market and that warehouse with the hoist bringing the crates to the upper floor? Head up that road for two minutes at the most and you'll see an inn with boxes of flowers above the door: The King's Lady. Strangers could always eat and drink there in relative safety in the past, so hopefully it's still the same.'

Brann nodded. He knew as well as Cannick did that their group could defend themselves, but trouble with drunk dockers or sailors, or fending off locals intent on relieving them of their valuables would, at best, waste time. 'I thought they didn't have kings around here.'

Cannick smiled. 'Drinkers like to reminisce, inns need drinkers, so innkeepers like history.'

He headed towards a brick building with external stairs

leading to a balcony and what looked like a busy office, from the number of people leaving and entering, and Brann caught up with his meandering companions just as Marlo caught at the sleeve of a passing stevedore.

The man turned aggressively, causing Brann's hand to drop to his knife – a safer weapon of choice in a crowded area, where innocents could be caught in the sweep of a sword blade – but Marlo's expression was bright and pleasant.

'Excuse me, sir, but do you know of a tavern where a group of travellers may satisfy their hunger?'

The man's expression changed at the question. He glanced around as if to check whether any other passer-by was listening, and smiled at Marlo with too much enthusiasm for Brann's liking. 'I don't know of any *taverna* any further north than near enough a month's riding to the south, but there are a few *inns* around, being that dock work is thirsty work.' He pointed. 'Head for the ship, right there, and you'll get taken care of all right.' He slapped Marlo on the shoulder and headed off in the direction of that same inn, and Marlo turned to the others enthusiastically.

'There,' he said proudly. 'I have found us somewhere perfect. Did you hear him say they would take care of us?'

Hakon took his arm and gently steered him away. 'I am sure they would, my trusting friend, but not in the way you are thinking.'

Brann inclined his head in the direction Cannick had indicated, and they followed.

Marlo, still guided by Hakon's unshakeable grip, wasn't happy. 'But...'

Hakon grinned and released his arm, instead wrapping an arm around the slight shoulders. 'Marlo, we will keep you alive and, in return, please do not ever change. Even in our darkest hours, you remind us that there is light.'

Marlo scowled. 'I was only trying to help.'

Konall spoke from behind. 'Hakon is right. Now shut up.'

A frown still wrinkled Marlo's brow, and he looked around at the others and the amusement in their eyes. He shrugged and grinned. 'Fair enough!'

Hakon ruffled his hair. 'That's what I mean.'

The King's Lady proved to be as normal and devoid of miscreants as any inn found in a port could be, and, from the approving smile Cannick bore as he met them at their table, it seemed that it was as he remembered it.

The grey-haired warrior lifted a leg of chicken from in front of Brann and savoured a large bite.

'Got us a ship with room enough for all of us and the horses,' he said around the meat.

'That's excellent,' Brann said. 'When does it leave?'

'On the evening tide.'

'Tonight?'

Cannick nodded, taking another bite and moving to the side as the innkeeper brought another platter filled with more meat, followed by another of bread and cheese. Hakon and Breta eyed the food appreciatively.

'Also excellent,' Brann said. 'When do we need to leave here?'

Cannick lifted another piece of chicken. 'Precisely?' Brann nodded. 'Now.'

Hakon eyed the food. 'Not excellent!' he said, aghast. 'Very, very far from excellent.'

The innkeeper glowered. 'Well, you paid for this. I'm not taking it back.'

Hakon looked horrified at the very thought. 'This will cover the cost of two new serving platters.' He placed a handful of coins on the table and, after a thought, added a couple more. 'And a jug.' He lifted the two platters, passing one to Breta, and the jug of ale and smiled beatifically at the others. 'Actually, now is fine.'

The captain took the agreed price from Cannick at the foot of the gangplank, and eyed Hakon and Breta dubiously. 'The amount does include feeding you, you know.'

Cannick smiled. 'Don't worry, they will still appreciate any meal you put their way.'

'Afternoon,' Hakon said cheerfully as he passed them, proffering the platter politely and towering over the man.

The captain declined the offer with a shake of his head and turned back to Cannick. 'I believe you.'

The wind was favourable as they rode the tide from the harbour, taking them quickly to sea. They were split over the two passenger cabins, and Brann was happy to settle in a bunk after the hard riding of the past few days. He watched as Grakk moved a lamp to a hook above the centre of the room and spread out the Duke's bedsheet and the documents within it on the floor, starting to sort them into piles.

'Do you want any help?' he said to the top of the tattooed scalp as the man already pored over them.

Grakk shook his head. 'Your offer is appreciated, young Brann, but my tribe has lived for centuries with a primary purpose of collecting, studying and archiving information. Perusing this and sorting the relevant minority from the irrelevant majority is what I learnt to do at the age that you were watching your first grain ground. My concentration is best when I work alone.'

Brann left him to it, but watched his quick movements and flitting eyes with interest until the rocking of the ship saw him drift into a doze. It had been a while since he had been on open water in the choppy Northern seas, but the familiarity was comforting.

He was roused when a sailor brought them supper late on, and noticed with astonishment the progress Grakk had made. Six or seven large piles lay to one side, while the man was sifting through one small set of papers that lay in front of his crossed legs.

'You were not wrong about being good at that,' Brann said, and received a shrug in reply. 'What have you found?'

'Three things: the first being that we will not have to carry this bundle around with us any more. This,' he tapped the pile in front of him, 'is all that is of use.'

Brann nodded. 'And the second?'

'That our friend Loku is one of several agents at his level in the organisation who are charged with generally sowing unrest, fear and confusion in key areas, on various scales – the establishing, populating and developing such camps as we have seen being a prime example of this. These agents tend to be strategically placed, but Loku is different in that he seems to have a roving commission, covering several separate territories, perhaps because his position with the Empire restricts the time he can spend away from Sagia. For that reason, he is often used to communicate and liaise with the others, such as at Belleville.'

'You said plots operate on different scales. We already know of anything from scattered atrocities to the attack on the ruling class at Konall's home. But are there other parts of this that are as big as what happened at Markethaven? That was an established army.'

'According to what we have here,' Grakk waved a hand over the papers, 'that was connected, but separate. Whoever is directing this whole strategy took advantage of an ambitious warlord to the east of there, and north of the Empire, and filled his head with ambition. A different tactic and outcome, but to the same ends: unrest, confusion, even regime change where possible. It is becoming ever clearer that we *must* find who is at the top of Loku's conspiracy, who is devising and coordinating it all, for if we only strike at those lower down the chain, other attacks will spring up like new shoots after the rain. The man, or woman, at the top must be removed for there to be any chance of stopping all of this. Finding that person is everything.'

Brann nodded grimly.

A gruff voice broke into the conversation. 'Was that the third thing you learnt?' Cannick had been listening from his bunk and sat up. 'About Markethaven? That was more than just a siege of an affluent town with plunder in mind, as they had pillaged and destroyed with determination on their way there and seemed intent on invading further had they been successful at that town.'

Grakk shook his head patiently. 'That was still part of the second.'

'So the third is...?' Brann said.

Grakk smiled. 'We know exactly where Loku is heading, and when.'

Brann was on his feet. 'The meeting across the water the Duke spoke about! Where they were to meet with the man controlling them. When is it?'

'Two days from now. At nightfall.'

'Where? The port where we land in the morning?'

'Waelclif? No. It is near Eabryg, a market town in the

lands of a minor lord. The lord's estate steward is Loku's fellow agent. He operates from the hunting lodge, and that is where they will meet.'

Cannick reached to the tray of food that the sailor had brought. 'I know that town, Eabryg. Einarr had trade links with a merchant in the next town, and sometimes we would stop over there.'

Brann looked at him. 'How far is it from Waelclif?'

Cannick grinned. 'If we push it, two days.'

They stepped onto the dock with a sharp wind plucking at their clothes and the dawn sun struggling to break through thick clouds.

'Welcome to the Green Islands,' Brann said.

Mongoose pulled her cloak tight around her. 'Feel good to be home?'

Brann stared around. 'This is not home. Gerens and I are from Alaria, the North Island. It's colder, and wetter.'

She huddled deeper in her cloak. 'This is bad enough. I don't know how the two of you survived in your village.'

'We didn't grow up together. Same island, different parts.'

She frowned. 'You didn't know each other? On the same island?'

'It's a big island. Two or three days' ride across, and a good couple of weeks from bottom to top, or so Einarr told me.' He thought of the Northern lord, Konall's uncle, and missed him. There was a calm assurance about the man that made a crisis less of, well, a crisis. He pulled out his own cloak. 'But you are right about one thing: having got used to the Southern climates, I am not sure myself how I got through the weather there. I suppose it never occurred to me that there was any other type of climate.'

They led the horses through the town to a farrier's workshop where a broken shoe on Sophaya's horse could be replaced, and the smell of porridge from the inn next door soon pulled them inside.

Brann smiled as Hakon asked for an extra portion in his bowl. 'Get enough to eat last night?' he asked.

Hakon nodded as he ate. 'Yes, thank you. Fortunately, the Sagian ones, Marlo and Philippe, were not used to the sea and allowed us their share of the food.'

'Not Sophaya?'

'She was fine. She seems to cope with anything, doesn't she?'

'Don't mention that to Gerens. I'm still not used to him waxing lyrical, though only he could do so with one word.'

Hakon grinned, and took another mouthful. 'Magnificent.'

Marlo popped his head through the doorway. 'That's us ready.' He smelt the food and a queasy look dropped over his face. 'I'll be outside.'

Hakon looked at his bowl, still a third filled, and fished for his purse. Brann stayed his hand. 'You cannot eat porridge on the back of a horse, and you can't just keep buying tableware. Finish it and I'll get your horse ready for you.'

'Truly,' Hakon said, his spoon a blur, 'you are the very best of friends.'

Brann couldn't help smiling as he lifted both of their packs and joined the others at the horses. He saddled his own first, settling his pack with his personal supplies, including his mail shirt, in a saddlebag on one side and confirming the equivalent, holding food and water, was balancing the weight on the other. His bow and quiver he stowed in a holster behind his right hip, and he checked that a long knife – more of a short sword, really, was settled behind his left, covered by the round shield that he hung over it. He was halfway through fixing Hakon's gear when the boy appeared behind him.

'Oh,' the Halvekan accent said over his shoulder. 'If I had known it would take you so long I could have had some more porridge. I'll see you in a few more minutes then.'

Brann whirled with a scowl, but was greeted with a grin and a wink. He punched Hakon with all the effect of punching a stone waymarker, and the big boy laughed in return.

'Thank you, Brann. I will finish it from here. You wouldn't do it the way I like it anyway.'

Brann was still massaging his wrist and decided not to punch him again.

The innkeeper stopped them as they were setting off, the first of them already heading up the street. He held a cloak aloft, and Brann reined up, seeing that it was Mongoose's, the young woman having taken it off when she had entered the warmth of the inn.

'Thank you,' he said to the innkeeper, leaning down to take the bundle. 'She has left already – I'll take it for when the cool air reminds her she has left it behind.'

He flicked his own cloak out of the way to let him wedge it beside his pack in the saddlebag, and the innkeeper's eyes locked onto it with interest.

'Your cloak has a distinctive repair,' he said.

Brann tensed. 'The cloak was my father's and the repair my mother's. Both are now dead, and this all I have left of them. What of it?'

The man held up his hands. 'I mean nothing sinister by

it, friend. There has been a man here describing one of your appearance and a black cloak with that shape of repair. I have heard talk of him asking in other hostelries, too. Just thought you should know.'

Gerens had moved his horse close, his hand on his knife.

Brann saw his feet slip from his stirrups, and raised a hand of his own to halt the boy's leap before it began. Without looking away from the man standing before them, he said: 'Gerens, it's fine. The inkeeper would have to be an incredible fool to mention this if he intended an ill outcome for us, considering he is unarmed and outnumbered. And should he intend to pass information to this person who hunts me, telling us first would serve his purpose little and his health less.'

Gerens's horse was as skittish as he was, its hooves loud on the flags of the yard. 'Unless he would demand payment for his silence.'

The man smiled disarmingly. 'How would that work? You are leaving anyway, and I know not where, so what could I tell him? And why would you pay me if you could not know that I would keep my word or not? The only way you could ensure I would keep my silence would be to ensure I was silent for evermore, so why would I invite that?'

'It makes sense.' But Brann frowned. 'You are very calm in the face of danger.'

The man shrugged. 'I run an establishment where men with hard lives drink. If I don't stay calm in the face of tension, then tension soon turns to a fight and a fight turns to a brawl. And I've never seen a brawl yet where anyone other than the innkeeper pays for the damage.'

'So why tell us?'

He looked back with a level gaze. 'Why not? You caused no harm, and came and went with no fuss. I saw the cloak and I had no reason not to tell you.'

Brann smiled. 'Thank you.'

The man waved as he walked back to the door.

They caught the others quickly and found Mongoose already shivering and feeling in her saddlebags for her cloak. Brann tossed it to her, and she caught it, rolling her eyes at her forgetfulness.

They left the port without further delay, passing guards more busy yawning and sheltering from a steady drizzle than scrutinising, and pausing only from rubbing sleep from their eyes to wave them through the gates of the walled inner town in cursory fashion. Double the number of buildings lay outside the walls than within them, and they clattered through streets where the only other movement came from the early risers who baked bread or prepared workshops or stalls.

Gerens nudged his horse beside Brann's. 'I couldn't help but notice, chief, a wince when you reached back with that cloak at the inn. Your wound bothering you?'

'A wince? I did not!'

Gerens shrugged. 'A wince, a slight tightening at your eyes, call it what you will.'

Brann laughed. 'Only you would notice that, Gerens. I'm fine, thank you. Grakk has an excellent honey-based concoction that is helping it to heal quicker than I thought it could. It just nips a bit sometimes, but then it would, wouldn't it?'

Gerens snorted and fell silent, but his eyes showed how little he was convinced.

They were soon in green countryside, Brann finding memories coming unbidden at the familiar sight of the lush vegetation of a landscape never short of water. He blanked his mind, then filled it instead with thoughts of what lay ahead. The first thing they should do would be to try to spy on the meeting, if they made it there in time. Then capture the man in charge, the one closer to the overall command. Once they had him, there was no longer any reason for Loku to remain alive.

The miles drifted by as they moved at a steady pace, stopping infrequently. Dusk had already fallen by the time they made camp, such was their desire to make use of every hour of travelling that they could. Brann ate sparingly, his stomach knotted with desire to get closer, sooner. While the others chatted, he sat apart, his back against a tree, his eyes on the patches of stars between the clouds.

'Gerens is keen for me to look at your wound,' Grakk's voice said beside him, 'and I have eventually succumbed to his pestering.'

He lifted Brann's arm and nodded almost immediately. 'It is fine. It was a clean cut, and is almost fully mended. Now the big one.' Brann said nothing but lifted his tunic to expose his side. Grakk's eyes and fingers probed in unison, gently and perceptively investigating. Brann suppressed any vocal reaction – the sensation was stinging more than sharp pain, and Grakk was clearly trying so intently to be tender that it would be a shame if he felt that he was not completely successful.

The tribesman grunted in approval and smeared more of the thick, sticky honey-based paste along the length of the cut. 'It heals quickly. We will have to forgo, still, our weapons practice to allow it to knit fully as soon as possible, but I will replace that with instruction in military history and tactics, which is an area where I feel you lack.' He ignored

Brann's look of distaste for sedentary learning, and gave the wound one last look. 'Oh for youth again, with the recuperation of young tissue. Enjoy it while you can.'

Brann felt his mouth smile despite himself. 'If I can be as youthful as you are when I am your age, Grakk, I will be overjoyed.'

The older man sighed. 'You do not see the old worries that hang over me, my boy.' He squatted in front of Brann. 'Although I believe worries hang over you, too. Gerens told me also of the words of the innkeeper.'

Brann nodded. 'It is not a nice feeling to have someone, maybe more than one, trying to track you, even though we were warned before we started this journey that this would be the case. I guess we all prefer to be the hunter than the prey. It's a bit ironic, isn't it, when we are chasing Loku? You know, funny that, while we are on his trail, he – and I can only think it is he, for who else? – has set others on mine.' He shook his head in annoyance. 'But what I can't work out is how he knew we were here.'

'Just a twist of fate – you may be Brann of the Arena, the undefeated champion of gladiators in the City Above and fabled vanquisher of all-comers in the dark pits of the City Below, renowned across the Sagian coast, but here you are just another traveller, and a fairly nondescript one at that, if you don't mind me saying.' Brann smiled and shrugged, and Grakk continued. 'I suspect Loku set these things in motion before we arrived in Sagia. He wanted revenge for what happened in Halveka, and he blamed you, we know as much. After all, he had put a huge amount of time and effort into his attempt to wipe out the ruling nobles and put his own man in place, only for you to not only discover his plot but then to fight and best him as he enacted his plan. Considering you were then widely acclaimed for saving those he sought to destroy, can you imagine his feelings towards you?' His finger reached out and lifted Brann's sleeve, showing the dragon tattoo. 'You have the acclamation of Einarr's people on you always, remember? He will have that episode etched as deeply in his memory.' He took a drink from a water skin. 'He will have thought you would return to these lands after leaving Halveka, heading home, so he will have set his dogs to try to pick up your scent across these islands.'

Brann nodded with a sigh. 'I suppose it is just something I have to bear.'

'We all have our burdens, and better to be aware of them. Better, then, to carry them, than to have them hanging over us from where their weight can drop upon us unexpectedly and crush us.' He stood with the fluid grace that marked his every movement and returned to the fire.

Grakk was right. If such a man found him, Brann would be better able to survive should he be expecting it. He followed Grakk to the company, and slept better that night for doing so.

The road the next day was similar to the previous one, quiet but with the occasional traveller or those toiling in fields only too happy to offer directions to mannered enquiries. This was the sort of civilisation, Brann mused, that Loku and his ilk sought most to disrupt, and its pleasant and welcoming nature made it the easiest of targets. He wondered why the deranged plans had not turned this direction already, but was glad they had not. These lands reminded him of a childhood that seemed that of another.

The rolling fields turned to the start of a forest. They

passed what few people they encountered with a wave of acknowledgement at most. Directions took second place to keeping quiet on who they sought, now that they drew close.

They had travelled for a mile, at least, into the trees when Konall looked around. 'Notice something? Plenty of game. Too much. This place is not hunted often.'

'I had been thinking the same thing, young lord,' Grakk said. 'I will scout ahead. We do not want to ride openly to the front door, and sentries can also hide with ease in these surroundings.'

He slipped from his horse, handing the reins to Breta, and within moments had disappeared into the undergrowth to the side of the track. They rode at a walk, Brann's impatience nagging at him but the sense in Grakk's caution holding him in check. It was a good half-hour before the tribesman returned, emerging silently from the trees on the opposite side of the trail from the one he had entered on leaving.

'We should leave this path,' he said.

Brann reined up his horse, reaching for his sword. 'Now?'

Grakk was calm. 'Not as urgently as that. My arrival would have been more hurried were that the case. This path leads directly past the lodge we seek, maybe a ten-minute ride, but there is a game trail not far ahead that will take us to the rear.'

'Any sentries between here and there?' Cannick said.

Grakk's impassive eyes turned his way. 'Not any more.'

No more needed to be said. They branched off along the trail, easily wide enough for the horses initially but causing them to dismount once they were further from the main path. They entered a small clearing, and Grakk stopped them.

'It would probably be best to leave the horses here,' he suggested. 'If needed, we could lie low in the saddle and risk riding from here at speed, but any further and that would not be possible.'

Brann nodded. 'Philippe?' he said, turning, but the actor was already dismounting.

'I know my limitations in even potential combat,' he said with a quiet smile. 'I will endeavour to be of benefit in other circumstances.'

Brann tethered his horse to a branch. 'You got us into and out of the Duke's tower,' he said. 'You have no obligation to prove your worth.'

Philippe's eyes saddened at the memory, but he nodded and tended to the horses.

Cannick looked at Brann. 'What are you thinking? All of us?'

Brann had been thinking of little else during the ride, as Cannick knew well. 'I think the fewer of us who go inside, the better. Maybe me, Grakk and Sophaya? There is more chance of remaining undetected, and I think we can inflict most casualties if they flee and we have most of us waiting outside to catch them doing so. People flee with speed, not caution.' He paused. 'At least, that is what seems best just now. It may change when we see the situation up close.'

Hakon grinned wolfishly. 'The *inflicting casualties* bit was enough to get my vote.'

'Sounds reasonable,' Cannick said. 'The plan, not Hakon's part.' He turned to the big boy. 'Not that I'm ruling out your contribution in that respect. You never disappoint there.'

Hakon happily took a large axe from his saddle, and the others nodded their agreement.

Brann turned to Philippe. 'Take the stakes from Breta's saddlebag and use them to tether the horses in a row. It is easiest for us to get going quickly from that. And if you hear the sound of rapid approach, set off yourself back the way we came as fast as you can. If it is us coming, you will be one less person in the way of the others, and if it is not us, you are better alive somewhere else than dead here.'

Philippe paled slightly at the thought, but without a word moved to Breta's horse.

Led by Grakk, they moved quickly through the trees. The tribesman moved unerringly forward, and a dozen paces after they had passed the corpse of a guard, the building started to come into sight. Moving from tree to tree, they slipped to the edge of a large man-made clearing, the lodge at its centre.

Clearly built for comfort rather than defence, there was no outer wall, but that also meant that there was little cover between the trees and the building itself. It was a two-storey wooden house, the size of a wayside inn, with a broad balcony running the full circumference. They were, as Grakk had predicted, at the rear, where a separate stable block at right angles to the main house offered the best chance of approaching unseen.

Brann gathered the others a few yards back into the trees. 'The plan, simple as it was, still stands. Grakk, Sophaya and I will go in; the rest of you work in pairs, as we did at the camp. Gerens, you go with Cannick. Marlo, you stick with them as a three.' Spread out to cover potential routes of exit.' He grinned at Hakon. 'And cause as much havoc as you can.'

They immediately split to find positions, and Brann was left with Grakk and Sophaya.

154

The girl looked again over the scene before them. 'Stables then up to the balcony?'

Brann smiled. 'I'm glad my thoughts match those of the expert. Let's go.'

They stopped by the treeline but, as far as was possible, could see no watching eyes. They waited, seeking sign of movement.

'There comes a point,' Sophaya said softly, 'when you just have to go, and put your faith in chance.'

'Fair enough,' Brann said, and went.

The others followed closely, flitting across the open glade, Brann feeling as exposed as he ever had in the Arena – although, as a gladiator, he had never feared the unseen flight of an arrow. The distance seemed twice as long when covering it by foot than by eye but, despite his strained nerves, cover it they did, and undetected.

They pressed against the wall of the stables, panting from nerves as much as effort, the smooth wood glorious to the touch. Brann flicked a look around the corner, spotting the main door to the building and an area before it empty of life. As he made to move for it, however, Sophaya grabbed his shoulder, and he looked at her in irritation. She winked and pointed upwards to an opening in the gable end at upper floor level: direct entry to the hayloft, with a pulley extending and a length of rope dangling a hook above their heads.

Her voice was a murmur. 'Why expose ourselves without cause?' She didn't wait for an answer but leapt to the top of a water butt and, from there, a spring took her fingertips to a horizontal beam running from front to back that protruded no more than the size of an arrowhead along its length. It was enough for her to scrabble up in a double jump that first brought her toes to the ledge in a squat with her hands flat on the surface above it, and then, as she started to tip away from the wall – causing Brann and Grakk to gasp in unison – saw her launch up and away at an angle. Her hands closed around the beam of the pulley and she let her legs swing out behind her, using the corresponding swing forwards to dive feet-first into the loft. Her grinning face reappeared over the edge a moment later.

'Gerens has his description of her right,' Brann said.

Grakk nodded. 'And now you see how she can manage to get into so much trouble if left to her own devices.'

Before his words had finished, the girl had lowered and secured the rope. The two quickly pulled themselves up, Brann noticing that his wound hurt less already than it had on the ascent to the Duke's tower, albeit this was a much shorter distance. When they stood beside her, Sophaya stripped the rope from the pulley, winding it instead between her hand and her elbow.

Brann moved cautiously, but Sophaya shook her head. 'Already checked. No people below, only horses.'

They trusted her: this was her domain. They ran the length of the loft, the hay muffling their steps and the horses barely responding to the noise. At the far end, Sophaya moved to where the roof sloped low enough for her to use her knife to prise loose two of the planks above, exposing the thatch. She parted the straw and stretched up for purchase. 'Come on, then,' she grinned, and disappeared upwards.

'She is enjoying herself far too much,' Brann grunted, but Grakk just reached up with a smile and hauled himself agilely through the gap.

As Brann stretched up to follow, two pairs of hands grabbed his wrists and he was hauled to the rooftop. Sophaya eased off her shoulders. 'You are heavier than you look,' she said. 'Next time, please come without a half-healed wound so we don't feel obliged to help you.'

Brann looked at her. 'Right now, I am really hoping there will not be a next time in this fashion.'

Sophaya merely smiled sweetly and bounded to the ridge of the roof. As they moved up more gingerly behind her, she unwound the rope and swung it back then forward, releasing it to send it sailing at the balcony. It cleared the railing and she gripped the rope, stopping it before the hook could strike the balcony floor. As it dangled, swinging, she drew the rope back to dig its point into the wood of the handrail. The eaves of the stable were formed by two great beams that crossed at the top, and she pulled the rope taut and tied it to the end of one of those beams.

'Neatly done,' said Grakk.

'Indeed,' said Brann.

'Naturally,' said Sophaya.

The balcony was lower than their perch and they were able to hold on with hands and crossed ankles, sliding themselves down fairly easily. Brann flexed his left arm and swung his elbow in a circle experimentally, and the wound in his side barely registered even the mildest of complaints. Not for the first time, he silently gave thanks to Grakk and his mysterious honey unguent.

They crouched in silence, taking in their surroundings. A series of doorways led from the lodge to the balcony, each with tall shutters lying wide to allow circulation of the early evening air, still warm in the late summer.

They listened. A murmur of voices was distant enough to be from the ground floor; the upper floor was quiet, though that was no guarantee of emptiness and safety.

Sophaya crept on the balls of her feet to the nearest doorway, lying flat to slide her knife blade past the edge of the opening and using the reflection of the blade at various angles to check for obvious signs of anyone within the room. Satisfied with her first inspection, she eased her head around the doorjamb.

She jumped lightly to her feet. '*Empty*,' she mouthed, and slipped inside.

They found themselves in a wide square hallway, several doors at the far side leading presumably to bedrooms that would look out on the front of the lodge, and a stairway near them leading downstairs. They crept to the bannister and crouched to peer through.

They saw a large open room, what appeared to be the general area of the lodge, with easy chairs and small tables before a large hearth. Seven men were rising from a long table that dominated the centre of the room, one of them Loku, his garb heavier than when Brann had last seen him in Sagia, in keeping with the more Northern weather but still with a distinct style of the South, much as he had worn when he had posed as an ambassador to Halveka. His black hair was, as ever, slicked back with oil above eyes that regarded all with cold calculation. Brann tensed, and felt Grakk's restraining hand upon him. Angry at himself for allowing the distraction, he patted the hand in reassurance and looked with a more methodical eye.

The men were splitting into small conversations, chatting quietly as if their meeting had finished. Brann cursed to himself. Had they been an hour earlier, or even less, they might have discovered much of the conspiracy's plans.

Something nagged at him, then he realised. No servants. It looked unusual where men of even minimal wealth gathered, and each of these men looked to be from a comfortable lifestyle. Five armed men stood silently at the far end of the room; Brann guessed that the sentries outside had been the estate manager's men, and wondered which one of the others had come without a bodyguard. Perhaps Loku, as he had travelled from abroad. He dismissed his musing, for it mattered not. The numbers were the numbers; what they could learn and what swords they would face thereafter were their considerations for now.

A tall man stood beneath the hidden trio, apart from the rest, his face unseen – distinctive dark red hair tied behind his head and extending past his wide shoulders to the small of his back. Loku moved from view but reappeared moments later, a decanter in one hand and two glass goblets in the other. He handed one to the red-haired man and poured wine into both.

'It appears our plans are moving apace,' the familiar voice said. 'Will you carry favourable reports to the High Master?'

A deep voice, harsh as a heavy grate drawn over stone, answered. 'You know I have no access to he who leads us all. I must, as we discussed tonight, now travel north to attend to matters there and then on to Alaria and Halveka, but the Council of Masters will meet soon and I will make haste to meet that appointment immediately after. The one who does speak to the High Master will hear our reports and convey what is necessary to him.'

Loku's voice was eager. 'But you will tell of our progress, Master? The campaign in the North, the camps around Belleville, the inroads in the North Island? Once we have subdued the Northern lands, we will turn our attention to the soft target that the South presents, and all will be in motion. We will rule in at least one kingdom and have seized some amount of territory in others. And despite being engaged in all of this activity, we have also sent on many men to the cause. You will remember to tell all of this, yes?'

The man had been staring across the room, but now turned to look directly into Loku's eyes from close range. He stood a good head taller, and the Empire's spymaster stepped back, clearly intimidated. 'There is an element in your questions, Taraloku-Bana, that extends beyond efficient reporting. A tinge of desperation. Why would that be, I wonder?'

Loku almost cringed. 'Halveka and Markethaven. I would not like the High Master to think I was capable only of failure.'

The tall man thought a long moment before answering. 'Halveka was, it cannot be denied, a failure. All you had built was wiped out; all you had planned was quashed. Any inroads your rebuilding makes there now is behind where it would have been had you conducted affairs there better. Markethaven, however, was not entirely a failure. You set it in motion with skill subtly and adeptly used over time. He who conducted it failed at the end, but the purpose was not conquest, as he thought, but the sowing of chaos and fear, as you intended. The High Master will already know of that success, and it will have redeemed you in his eyes for Halveka, I am sure.' He placed a hand on Loku's shoulder. 'I will ensure the news of the work done by you and your colleagues here is carried to the High Master's ears. He will know of your loyalty and dedication.'

The fawning gratitude in Loku's eyes was almost pathetic.

'There is one other thing, Taraloku-Bana, that I must discuss with you.' Wary fear replaced gratitude. 'The one who thwarted you in Halveka. He was instrumental at

Markethaven.' Loku's eyes widened, and Brann pushed back at the anger once more. 'You had the chance to make him dead in Sagia, but chose instead a slow agony that you thought would kill him. It did not.'

Loku paled. 'I thought him an irrelevance to our plans. His fate was personal to me, and still is. His most likely destination is these islands, and I had men seeking him here after Halveka, so they continue as we speak. Master, be assured that I have at all times endeavoured to keep my personal retribution second to my service to the High Master, however. The tasks of my duty have always been my priority.'

The voice was low. 'The death of this one is now part of that duty. Word has reached a member of the Council of a prophecy attached to this boy. He matters more as a danger than as the object of your petty retribution.' Loku could not stop his eyes from betraying his surprise, but he quickly hid it.

Brann felt his companions looking at him, but steadfastly pretended not to notice. Now was not the time for discussion.

'*When* you get the chance again, do not dally. Make it quick and make it final. Surety of death paramount over all as far as he is concerned.'

Loku lowered his head. 'So it shall be, Master.'

The man nodded curtly. 'That is all. I must be on my way.' He drained his goblet, and handed it to Loku, who took it with a small bow.

'We should go as well, Master. The less time we spend as one company, the less there is to connect us.' He turned to those filling the rest of the room. 'My friends, our business here is concluded and Master Daric must be to other affairs. We should return to our public lives, too, but before we do, I am sure you, like me, wish to express our thanks to the Master for his continued guidance.'

All turned to face the red-haired man, placing their right hands on their chests and bowing their heads. The man gave a cursory wave and turned for the door, lifting his cloak from where it lay on the back of a chair.

There was a general rumbling of movement from below, and Sophaya risked a quiet word. 'Now?'

Brann shook his head sharply. Should the red-haired man be among those who may spill from the lodge in flight, their companions waiting outside would not see him as different from any other target. 'Let him leave on his own,' he whispered. 'We need him alive. The others will not betray their cover until they see sufficient people running from here to make their attack worthwhile and effective.'

The Master swept from the building without a backward glance and headed for the stables. Within moments, he led his horse into view and mounted, before cantering to the edge of the clearing.

Brann stood. 'Now.'

He put one foot on top of the bannister and launched himself. A flash at the corner of his vision was most likely one of Sophaya's throwing stars, a cry from one of the agents as blood spouted from his neck lending weight to his guess. He landed knife in hand and feet first on the back of one of the men, hurling him forward to strike his face against the table edge. The knife across his throat ensured he would not rise.

Brann had his axe in hand as he turned in a crouch, ready to react. The axe was slower than his sword but, when swung, more fearsome to face and it was panicked flight that they were intending to induce. Sophaya landed lightly to his left, a second star already having found the chest of one of the agents, although this time the wound was not fatal. She had a short sword in one hand and a slim knife in the other, and was moving to complete the job her first star had begun, though whether she would reach the man while he still lived was uncertain. A guard was rushing Brann, his sword swinging, and he stepped to his left, holding the vertical axe at either end and blocking the sword's movement towards his right. He continued the axe's movement to cut the blade's edge across the back of the man's neck, slicing deep enough to sever everything less than an inch from the surface. A chop downwards finished what probably didn't need finishing, but you never leave *probably* behind you in a fight.

Grakk had made it halfway down the stairs before he had leapt the bannister, and his curved swords were making short work of a guard with a two-handed sword that was far too big for indoor work: apart from the clumsy movement, it also ensured that none of his colleagues could safely get close enough to support him. After stepping nimbly away from the massive swings, Grakk needed just three blurred movements to finish the contest.

The energy of combat was surging through him, and Brann felt an animal roar burst from his lungs. Those facing them were shaken from automatic attack by the noise, and seemed for the first time to take note of the bodies of their fellows and the blood-caked figures, dripping blades in hand, stepping towards them.

They ran, pushing and grabbing each other as they hurled themselves at the door.

'Well,' said Sophaya, retrieving her throwing stars. 'That seemed to work.'

'Flight always seems to be contagious,' Grakk observed as they made quickly for the door. 'We naturally attack as individuals, and have to be taught for it to be otherwise, but we flee as a herd. Interesting, is it not?'

Brann grunted, exiting the lodge at a run and jumping the few steps to the ground beyond. 'I am more interested in Loku and that Master of his.'

He cast around him. Mongoose and Breta were engaging three mailed guards and one agent, with Gerens, Cannick and Marlo running either to help them or head off the fleeing figures beyond them. A rider galloped straight for Konall but Hakon stepped in front of the horse, his axe taking away its front legs. It went down in a tumble with a horrific squeal and Konall was already moving to engage the unseated man.

Everywhere was shouting and screaming and running and brutal fighting, and as Grakk and Sophaya ran to give help, Brann caught sight of Loku breaking across an empty area beyond the stable and closing on the trees.

Brann sprinted. A bow lay under a dead guard, a Halvekan throwing axe embedded in his chest, and Brann dragged it free and grabbed at the quiver thrown loose to one side, his hand coming away with just two arrows in his haste. Two would have to be sufficient.

Loku had entered the trees but Brann kept his eyes on the spot where he had disappeared and tore after him. He heard the sound ahead of a man more intent on speed than silence and raced in its wake. In moments he saw movement, and angled to follow. The undergrowth was not thick in this part of the forest and he soon could clearly see Loku's wild run. He forced his legs faster. Just a little closer and...

He skidded to a halt on rain-soaked earth and leaves and

flung up the bow, the arrow loosed an instant after. It barely skiffed against a branch, but the touch was enough to divert it past the man and into a trunk in his path. It may have missed, but it was enough to shock him into stopping. Brann moved closer again as Loku slowly turned.

The man smiled. 'Of course,' he said between breaths. 'It would be you, would it not.'

Brann raised the bow.

Loku held up both hands. 'Wait.'

Their mission now had new prey. The waiting was over for this one.

He drew the bow.

And the wood snapped.

Brann ducked automatically as the shards of the bow flailed at his head. Whether it had been defective or had cracked when its owner had fallen was immaterial. All that mattered was what was possible now. His sword in his hand, his head came up with a glare and found Loku no more than a dozen paces away, and a mirror of him.

'So,' the man said, 'it has come to this. Two who are dedicated to the death of the other, alone and together.'

'I will take your head,' Brann growled.

Loku shrugged. 'Possibly. But consider this: you want my Master. And you want to kill me. And you will probably kill me. I saw you in the Arena. And in the City Below.'

'You put me in both.'

'And so I made you what you are. I am your creator, I suppose.'

'I am what I am in spite of you. You are nothing to me.'

'And yet,' Loku smiled, 'you chase me across countries.'

'I chase the truth of your work. Your death will be a bonus.'

'But the truth of my work is at present on a horse riding from here.'

Brann paused, and he could see in Loku's eyes that he had spotted the doubt.

'And there, dear boy, is your dilemma. Fight me and you will most likely kill me, but you are not so much better that it will be quick. And with every blow, that horse steps further from you. So you chase the horse, and the truth,' the smirk returned, 'or chase me.'

And with that, he turned and ran into the forest. Away from the road heading north.

Brann stared at his receding form, then back in the direction of Daric, then back at Loku. He roared at the sky. But he knew.

He turned and ran for his horse.

When he reached the clearing once more, the quiet after combat had fallen over all.

He counted the standing and the fallen. All of his companions were standing, but not all of the foe had fallen.

He ran to Cannick. 'The agents?'

'Three escaped. Loku?'

'He also.'

He looked at Brann's face through narrowed, appraising eyes. 'You had a choice to make.'

Brann felt like his his head would burst with the pressure of anguish. 'And that choice is riding north right now.'

'Then let us get to Philippe and be on our way.' Cannick rounded up the others as Grakk emerged from the lodge with folded paper in his hand.

'We have another map,' the tribesman said. 'Their meeting would appear to have been purely verbal unless this Master has taken with him any written records, but they did have this map of the Green Islands, presumably as reference. Unfortunately, they have not added any marks appertaining to their plans or resources, so it gives no clue to their plans and capabilities.'

Brann looked at it. 'But it does give us an overview of the islands, which is helpful since none of us knows our way around.'

Breta was looking over his shoulder. 'Really? I thought these islands were your homelands?'

Brann smiled sheepishly, reminded of how far his horizons had grown in the most recent part of his life. 'The North Island, yes, but until Einarr educated me, I didn't even know the name of anywhere further than the next town to my village. Your whole world is only as large or as small as your experiences, interests and needs, I suppose.'

Breta grunted non-committally. ''Spose.'

It was not long before they were thundering up the forest road that Daric had taken, but it quickly became clear that they were already too far behind their quarry to see even signs of his passage, never mind the man himself.

Brann had hoped that Daric had been far enough from the lodge for the sounds of conflict to be inaudible and unable to alert him, but it now seemed that he had either heard the clamour and taken to his heels, or had already been so far beyond the limit of the noise that his head start was too much. Either way, he appeared unlikely to bring him into sight any time soon.

Still, however, they pressed on, refusing not to try. It was only when both night and rain started to fall that they admitted that they would not find him that day.

Brann spoke to Konall as they set up camp for the night. 'You are the best hunter amongst us. Have you seen any signs of his trail?'

Konall shook his head. 'I can track beasts, and usually large ones where their trail is different from any other creatures moving over the same ground. This is a horse on the packed surface of an established road – a road that is well used by many other riders. This would be like trying to track a specific fish in a river.'

'It was worth a try,' Brann said.

The haughty face looked down at him. 'Only a farm boy would think so.'

Brann flushed. 'A mill b...' He saw the hint of amusement at the corner of one of Konall's eyes, the equivalent of a guffaw from Hakon. 'I think I'll see to my horse.'

Konall nodded. 'Good idea. Stick to your capabilities.'

He abandoned the battle already lost and took a bag of feed to his horse, checking at the same time the extra mounts they had acquired at the lodge: a better horse for Philippe than the one he had ridden since the attack on the settlement, and an extra horse to join Philippe's former horse as pack animals, carrying food for humans and beasts as well as tarpaulins they had requisitioned that would provide cover from the rain that they felt was inevitable at some point.

Marlo was picking a stone from the hoof of Hakon's horse, having groomed his own, as usual, to perfection. The animal was calm with the boy, allowing him to work efficiently and quickly. He was good with animals, Brann thought. Some people were just natural in certain ways. Perhaps the beasts just reacted as well to his pleasant disposition as humans did. Marlo looked over and nodded to him with a smile.

He thought of the boy he had first met, eager to help at the gladiator school, eager to help after it. He had broadened and there was a little less naivety to him – but only a little less. Brann hoped it stayed that way. It was good to have some innocence around so much hardened cynicism.

'That spot on your horse will be cleaner even than Marlo's,' Hakon's voice said behind him, causing him to jump enough to have to juggle the stiff brush he had been using. The big boy's booming laugh was filled with delight. 'Good to see I can still sneak up on the best.' He laughed again, a guffaw that startled the horses as much as Marlo pacified them. 'Seriously, though, you really should expand your effort to more than just the one patch you have been brushing since you started.'

Brann smiled. 'I was lost in thought. I am not trying to rival Marlo, believe me. That is a talent I could never hope to match.'

'And not his only talent, by the way.' Hakon looked over at the other boy. 'Hey Marlo, who taught you to fight?' Marlo grinned and winked, and Halon turned back to Brann. 'He took out a guard about to slice Konall from behind, not that Lord High and Mighty would ever admit it. A cut to the side to stop the blow and attract his attention, a deflection, a cut across the sword arm and a stab to the throat. All quick as you like, all shallow to keep them quick, all effective, and all dead in the blink of an eye.' He winked at Brann. 'It reminded me very much of someone, but I just can't think who.'

Brann tried to look innocent. 'I may have given him a few pointers every evening.' He grinned back. 'He grew up among skilled gladiators and under the wing of a genius former-general. He could hardly be anything other than a quick learner.'

'He does not have a killer's instinct, however,' Hakon said.

Brann grew solemn. 'And may we all help that to be preserved. He has enough killers around to protect him.'

Hakon clapped him on the shoulder. 'You are not wrong there.' His face became thoughtful. 'Talking of non-killers, what do you make of our new friend?'

'Philippe?'

Hakon nodded.

'He has been through a lot. His sister...'

Marlo had wandered over, and Hakon leant in close to the two of them, even though there was no one else close enough to hear anyway. 'I mean, can we really trust him? Because he is... you know...'

Brann frowned. 'Because he likes men like you like women?'

'Though not in the same quantities,' Marlo pointed out.

'No!' Hakon was dumbfounded. 'One of my best friends when I grew up was the son of a pig farmer, an esteemed man in a land where bacon is a welcome alternative to incessant fish at the dinner table. From time to time, Olaf would slip down to the pigs and slip in, if you see what I mean. Everyone knew it, and we didn't feel the urge to copy him, but to us he was just the friend who made us laugh easily.'

Marlo looked askance at him. 'Are you really comparing Philippe's inclinations to those of a pig-shagger?'

'Of course not!' Hakon said, hurt at the very thought. 'I mean, Olaf wasn't Olaf the Pig Shagger to us, he was just Olaf. So in the case of Philippe, who likes humans, just different humans from the ones I like, how could I think ill of him? He is just Philippe.'

'I think that kind of makes sense,' Marlo said slowly.

Brann grunted. 'It is Hakon-sense. You will get used to it eventually.' He looked up at the big boy. 'So what was your point about Philippe?'

Hakon looked uncomfortable. 'The things he had to do. He was forced into a life he would not really have chosen, I am sure. He said one night over a skin of wine, everything he did, he did to try to make life better for his sister. For all his pretence, and he is very good at pretending, I think he would have gladly taken a different way of earning the same coin.'

'I'm sure he would,' Brann said.

'What I mean is, he did all that for her, and then he had to watch a death that was... Well, from what you told us, it wasn't pleasant.'

Brann stared sightlessly. 'No. It was not,' he said flatly.

'So,' Hakon pressed on, 'I worry about him. He needs to live for himself now, but he is still living each day in sorrow for his sister.' The big earnest eyes turned to the other two. 'Do you think he would take it badly if I befriend him? If I try to help him? Brann, you were really mad for a while – a complete lunatic, if truth be told – and worse even than Philippe. Did you resent anyone trying to help you?'

Brann smiled softly. 'No I did not. And nor will he. You are a good man, Hakon.'

'And your tolerance for other inclinations is admirable,' Marlo said innocently. 'But not surprising, in retrospect, when we consider your friendship for Mongoose.'

Hakon grinned. 'My intentions for Mongoose go far beyond friendship.' His voice tailed off as realisation slowly crept upon him. He stared, his eyes widened and, almost as slowly, his jaw dropped. 'You mean... Mongoose... Like Philippe... But with women?'

The pair nodded.

'Women do that too? Just like...?'

'Well,' Brann said helpfully, 'for the avoidance of doubt, not with pigs. But with other women, some of them, yes.'

'Well I never,' Hakon said in astonishment.

'And you never will,' Marlo said, and Brann could restrain his mirth no longer, his laughter proving contagious and the other two soon doubling over as much as he was.

Cannick's voice cut though their amusement. 'When you children have quite finished your play, you might like to get something to eat and to bed. We have an early start tomorrow on the trail of that Lord High Bastard. Our new quarry awaits us.'

Brann was still wiping the tears from his eyes as they returned to the campfire. For a few moments, he had forgotten the dark nature of their quest. He would wake as determined as ever, the step closer to their ultimate quarry that Daric represented lending fresh impetus to his relentless urge to find the instigator of the ills that were afflicting so many people, but tonight, he had needed those moments. He missed his family more than he wanted to consider, and he needed the strength of friends at times like these. The true value of companions extended far beyond the strength of a sword arm.

Chapter 4

The sand laid a gossamer thin cover over the squared top of the balcony balustrade. He traced numbers in it, calculating days, distances, numbers of men.

She entered with a soft knock, followed by the other servants, those who changed his bed sheets, refilled his fruit bowl, rinsed his privy. Her demeanour reverential, she placed the fresh jug of cooled water on the table beside his outdoor chair.

At the clinking of the ice, he realised the extent of his thirst.

She bowed, breathing the word in her sand-dry voice. 'Excellency.'

He acknowledged the service without turning, a raising of one finger more than most in the palace granted a servant.

She maintained her bow as the door clicked softly shut behind the other servants.

She straightened. 'Oh, so you are on your feet today, old man. You must be feeling adventurous.'

'So must you, crone, to speak in such a way and expect to live.'

'Take a drink, the sun is high, the air is hot, and the words do not seem to leave your throat properly, as that sounded like a threat.'

'It was. And I will drink when I wish, not at your behest, witch.'

He turned, the pleasantries over.

'How goes it at the house.' He didn't have to say which house. There was only one ever discussed.

'Much the same. He recovers; she mollycoddles him. He grows restless; she mollycoddles him. He adapts to moving with one foot; she mollycoddles him. Basically, there is much mollycoddling.'

'Real men do not like mollycoddling.'

'He is a real man. He responds with respectful grumpiness, and pushes himself to a state of mobility where he can leave the house and roam for longer each day.'

His eyes narrowed. 'Which is why she does it.'

'Indeed.'

'You women are indeed mistresses of manipulation!'

'You men always need direction.'

'Devious!'

'Subtle.'

'Deceitful!'

'Intelligent.'

'You are not more clever, nor as much as you think!' he shouted, and his dry throat responded with a cough. He snatched up a tumbler of water and drained it.

She smiled. 'You drank. I am glad.'

He glared at the tumbler in fury. The trap had been laid, baited, and sprung to perfection. He clenched his fingers around it, forcing himself not to hurl it towards the desert. He would not give her that satisfaction, at least. He placed *it with exaggerated care on the table and turned back to the balustrade.*

Gods, he loved their exchanges.

His vigour revived, he lapsed into thought once more. She moved beside him, moving a hand above his tracings in the sand as she looked across them.

'You estimate.'

'It is all I can do. Gathering information is key, but it is tormenting when that is all you can do when others are acting.'

'But you cannot be there. They can. So they do all that they can do, and you do all that you can do. At this moment, you need them. But there will come a time when they need you, and what you do now ensures your readiness.'

'I know. But I still hate it. And I will need to be ready sooner than I thought. If they can complete their task sooner than we all thought.'

He drew a long line across the sand. 'Now is here.' His fingertip cut a short vertical line through it near the start. He lifted his finger and drew another line down through the long one an arm's length to the right. 'This is when we had to get to.'

'Had to?'

He nodded. The finger cut down through the long line a quarter of its length before the second mark. 'This is now when we had to get to.'

'Our time is shortened by as much?'

'By at least as much.'

'The one who gave you information is reliable?'

'The one is the highest one there is. Unreliable in many ways, but he has the greatest access to information in the Empire. After all, he is the Empire.'

Her eyebrows arched. 'He gave this information know-ingly?'

'Of course not. But he gave it all the same.'

'And it is?'

'Disruptions are rife across the free nations to the north of the Empire's boundary. Trade is dropping. Trade, more than all of the tributes, sustains the Empire; even he is aware of that. So he readies a force to help restore order. Two millens will march.'

'Two?' *The surprise was unconcealed.*

'The fool recalls one from the South, across the Great Water.'

'But that leaves decreased numbers in a region where dissent is growing.'

'Indeed. He is fooled easily and oft, and in this case his foolishness is to believe that low levels of rebellion signify a lack of threat. He should know that low levels of rebellion signify roots taking hold, and from roots come growth and strength.'

'So what will you do?'

'I need do nothing. He makes his own problems. My efforts are unnecessary.'

'And for those whose efforts we rely upon?'

'I can do nothing.' *His hand swept with venom through the sand, the designs and calculations lost to the air.* 'One I have sent to watch over him, where possible, from afar, when once I could have sent half a hundred to guard his every step. One who may not even find him. But essentially, I can do nothing.

'How I detest doing nothing.'

****

The first village they came to after leaving the edge of the forest was no more than a hamlet, sitting on a crossroads, and formed of the homes of woodcutters, and an inn that served the needs of residents and travellers in equal measure.

Small settlements were good: those passing through were more easily noticed. Their assumption that he would take the road leading north was confirmed, and they wasted little time in following. The road, they were told, led for two days' riding to the town of Benorthangeat. Sitting, as it did, equally from east and west coasts, with three rivers converging close to it and, most importantly, with several roads leading from the rolling farmlands they had already traversed and towards the more harsh and rising lands they were approaching, it was known as the Gateway to the North.

It was just the place that Daric would head for; given the many routes that spread like rivulets from its northern gate, it was just the place he could disappear from.

They stopped at a wayside inn less than a day short of the town. The horses were still fresh and they had not long broken their fast, but Brann was keen to ask questions.

Breta wasn't happy. 'If we had ridden over one more hill last night we could have slept in beds and eaten heartily.'

'If we could see over hills we could do more than eat and sleep well,' Brann heard Mongoose say as he gave his reins to Gerens and headed inside with Grakk.

The common room was empty but for a portly man sweeping the floor.

'Good morning,' Brann said cheerfully. 'Do you have a moment that we could ask after a friend of ours who might have passed this way?'

The man's attentions remained on his broom. 'I run a

business of sustenance and repose, not a repository of scuttlebutt.'

Grakk's eyebrows raised. 'A learned man,' he said appreciatively.

The innkeeper stopped and rested his weight on the broom, regarding them sourly. 'I have plenty of books for the quiet periods, and plenty of quiet periods of late since travel from the North diminished. I reserve my garrulous cheer for times of custom.'

Grakk beamed. 'I would be content to converse with this man for the entire day, had we the time.'

Brann grunted. 'We don't have the time, and he won't be conversing unless we give him something to do.' He walked to the door. 'Breta, the innkeeper has the need to prepare breakfast for someone. Might you oblige?'

She was inside in a heartbeat.

The innkeeper dropped his broom. 'How may I help you, madam?'

She looked at him as if she had never heard a more stupid question. 'Food. Whatever you've got.'

He shrugged. 'I can manage that.' He stopped just short of the door behind the bar. 'How many of your party might be inclined towards hunger?'

Brann was getting irritated. 'Look, I'll pay you double the price if you do it fast.'

He saw the man's eyes narrow at the impatience in his tone, and realised his mistake. The man smiled the smile of a cat with a vole in its grasp. 'How eager are you for this information? There have been few customers recently, but enough for your friend to perhaps have been one of them, and their paucity means merely that each becomes more memorable.'

Brann sighed. 'Hakon!' The Northern boy ducked through the door, and the innkeeper's eyes widened. 'He'll have the same.'

'I can rustle you up something in an instant, sir!' He disappeared in a rush and they could hear his shouts despite the shut door. 'Woman! Girl! Get this kitchen running now.'

They also heard the answers he received. Grakk looked at Brann solemnly. 'I am guessing that he does not exercise the total and respectful control of his establishment that he would seem to want to demonstrate.'

'As long as he is quick, I don't care about his domestic relationships,' Brann said. 'Whatever information he has, it had better be good.'

He *was* quick. In a remarkably short time, Breta and Hakon were served and the innkeeper moved to the bar where Brann and Grakk waited. The others, he had asked to wait outside – he didn't want the innkeeper to be tempted to ask for even more custom. The fleeting visit he had envisaged was already a thing of past whimsy.

'So,' Brann said. 'What can you tell us?'

The man frowned. 'Many things. But I am not aware of what you want to know.'

'Right, here it is. Tall man, red hair hanging to his waist. Heading north. Have you seen him?'

'Yes.' The man picked up a tankard and studiously blew dust out of it. 'Is that it?'

'Not for two breakfasts for the price of four, it's not,' Brann growled. He took out a pouch of coins and his long knife, and laid both on the counter. 'One way or another, you are going to be helpful, and quickly so. Enough of these games.'

The man pulled himself upright. 'I am not intimidated by you.'

Grakk leant in conspiratorially, and winked. 'You should be. Learn it from me, before you do from him.'

The innkeeper looked from the old soldier to Brann, to the knife and back to Brann. His eyes finally settled on the money. It seemed he decided against pushing his luck. 'A man such as you describe came in last night. Late on, it was. He declined my offer of a room; seemed excessively hurried. Wanted to know how much further Benorthangeat was and where he might find a bed at that time of night. Anyway, I managed to sell him a flagon of ale, and he watered his horse, which, incidentally, looked fairly lathered and done, though that didn't stop him pushing it hard as soon as he set off again.'

Brann patted him on the shoulder with an encouraging smile. 'There, that was much better. Just one thing. Did you recommend somewhere for him to stay?'

The man shrugged. 'Of course. The Gateway is always a busy place, but these days the traffic is mostly heading southwards. Still, people need a place to stay, no matter the direction they head or the reason for their journey, so competition between the innkeepers for the business is fierce. The busiest establishments are those near the North Gate – those that the travellers fleeing the North find first on entering the town. My brother's inn has the misfortune of being near the South Gate. If I send custom there, it may be in return that a stone has found its way into the hoof of one of their horses when southbound travellers leave from his inn, and they must stop to see to it at the first wayside inn they encounter.'

'Which happens to be this establishment,' Grakk said. 'Take it that we understand your commercial strategy. Please instead provide the name of this inn of your brother and the location.'

'After entering at the South Gate, direct yourselves towards the centre of the town. Before long, you will see a lane leading off to the right with a forge at the corner – The Griffin can be found directly across from it. Tell Walwyn that Norvin sent you, and that I said your onward journey should be trouble free.'

'In other words, no stones in horses' hooves,' Brann said.

'He will be very assiduous in checking them for you, to ensure healthy and unproblematic travel.' The man looked pointedly at the pouch of coins.

Brann looked at Hakon and Breta and flicked his head to the door. Both rose, Hakon the more reluctant of the two. 'Not even a short time available for another course?'

Breta slapped him on the back of the head. 'You'll get fat,' she scolded him. He shrugged and followed her, muttering, to the door.

The innkeeper was still flicking his eyes at the money on the counter. 'You can't fault a man for trying.'

Brann looked at him. 'You or my large friend?'

'Perhaps both.'

Brann picked up his knife, playing the point against the tip on one finger. 'Hakon was shown the error of trying by Breta. Do you need your lesson as well? Keeping an inn is hard enough work with all ten fingers.'

The man paled slightly. 'You have been more than generous in your assessment of the price.'

Brann considered this. 'You are right. *More* than generous.' He started to reach for the pouch.

The innkeeper's hand closed over the money, then darted away from it as the knife twirled in Brann's fingers. The man blustered in desperation. 'It may not be relevant, but in case it is useful enough to warrant payment in full, I can tell you more.' He was talking fast, lest the money disappear before he was finished, and his eloquence diminished with it. 'You are not the only person to visit here with questions. A man, not overly tall or,' he looked at Brann, 'less than average, but strong of shoulder and arm. He sought a boy or man,' he was still looking at Brann, 'of around your size and build, but of paler skin. Said he may have a black cloak, with a distinctive tear that has been carefully stitched where most men would have instead replaced the cloak.'

Brann's hand moved instinctively around his back to feel for his cloak, but remembered that he had left it stowed in a saddlebag as the early sun had been pleasant.

He sheathed his knife and turned, leaving the pouch on the counter. 'Thank you for your service.'

Grakk fell in beside him as he headed to the door.

'Thank you for your custom,' the innkeeper called. 'It will be welcome should you pass this way again, er... I did not hear your name.'

'No,' Grakk said over his shoulder. 'You did not.'

Thoughts of his cloak drove the sentimentality that saw his hand drift to pull it free and wrap it around his shoulders, fastening it with the black brooch they all wore; the brooch fashioned from the same metal as his weapons by an eccentric genius of a smith in the desert beyond Sagia. Between them, the cloak and the brooch sparked enough thoughts to occupy his mind during the short ride to the town, and before long they passed through the gate in the low walls – more a token than a defence – without question, the main flow of traffic heading outwards. Konall had hardly passed comment on the paltry – almost non-existent – defences indicating a naïve lack of expectation

182

of any danger, before they found The Griffin exactly where it had been described.

Walwyn greeted them warmly. More rotund than the man who had sent them there, the difference between the brothers was even more marked in his demeanour: he was jovial and bursting with cheer. Too much, for Brann's liking. If a man works over-hard to seem a certain way, then truth is seldom what you see.

But the man could project whatever character he liked. All that concerned Brann was finding Daric but, on enquiring, his heart sank at the shake of the innkeeper's head.

'I am sorry to say, you have missed your friend. He purchased a new horse, leaving his own as part payment, from a trader near here, and left as dawn broke. He will be well on his way now, but where I cannot say, as many roads lead north from this town.' He looked around the large group. 'If your party would like to be accommodated here in the hope he will stop by on his return from the North, I can certainly allocate you rooms.'

Brann looked around the common room, filled to half its capacity with merchants and tradesmen taking a break as the day reached its mid-point, and with not a traveller in sight. The nature of the normal clientele was clear, and he was sure the inn did have plenty of rooms available.

'Thank you, but we must decline,' he said, his voice as flat as his spirits. 'The man does not intend to make a return journey in this direction.' Still, the atmosphere in the room was pleasant and the smell of food enticing. He took off his cloak. 'We will, however, eat as we consider our options. And if our horses could be fed and watered also…?'

Walwyn beamed. 'I shall oversee your sustenance myself, and my sons will see to that of the horses.'

Brann looked at him flatly. 'Make sure to tell them to check that there are no stones in the hooves.'

The innkeeper was a picture of innocence. 'But, of course, good sir. I would envisage no other scenario.'

Brann stared at him still. 'Keep envisaging.'

The others were already around a table and he settled on the empty stool at its near end, folding his cloak and sitting it on the end of a bench where there was a small space beside Sophaya. He was never totally comfortable with his back to a room, but it had its advantages: for one, it allowed him more freedom to react to danger than he would have if he had any of his companions in his way or sitting tight beside him. They sat in silence, the others as deflated as Brann at the news that Daric could have headed in any one of a dozen directions.

Brann sighed. 'This moping is getting us nowhere. Let us look at what we know.'

Cannick nodded. 'He is heading north, where there is trouble. Trouble instigated, we believe, by those of his ilk.'

'But,' Konall said, '*north* covers a fair bit of ground, full of people who would probably try to kill us. After torture.'

Mongoose looked at him. 'You are scared of people who want to kill you?'

Konall's expression would have withered most people, but she stared back calmly. He said, 'I refer to the difficulty in tracing one man in that amount of people and disorder.'

She nodded. 'That is true.' She looked at Brann. 'He has a point.'

Brann thought on it, but before he could speak, Sophaya did so. 'Remember, in the hunting lodge. He said after he had met people in the North, he was going to Alaria, wherever that town is.'

Brann stirred. 'It is still further in the same direction, and it is not a town. Alaria is an island. The North Island.' He looked at Gerens. 'Our island.' He felt himself become animated. 'We do not know where he goes next, but we do know where he will be after that.'

Cannick frowned. 'The whole of the North Island is not much less in size than the whole of the South Island. If we can't find him in just the northern area of *this* island…'

'That is true,' Brann said, undeterred. His appetite returning, he broke off a hunk of bread and dipped it in his stew. 'But if we can get ahead of him, we can start gathering news of the activities of this cult, or whatever it is, and have a better guess at where he might be heading than we would in the north of this country where we would always be chasing a faint trail and asking for information from people who are either frightened victims, nervous soldiers or vicious degenerate lunatics.'

Hakon grinned. 'Now you put it that way, it might be more fun.'

Laughter rippled across the surface of their tension, and familiar smiles returned. Brann glanced fondly around the group, faces now so familiar that he felt uncomfortable if any were absent for a length of time. He had endured some hard times, but a burden is lighter the more shoulders that bear it.

He felt himself become wary, his breathing caught and his muscles on alert. Why? He looked down, realising his hand had moved to the hilt of the knife in a sheath strapped to his left forearm. He frowned, looking back to his companions. Conversation had stopped; tension was strung taut across them. Gerens and Grakk had slipped their knives free and were holding them subtly ready. All eyes were focused behind him. His own hands had noticed the drawn weapons, even if his eyes had not.

He remained ready, but slowly held up a hand in restraint.

Gerens looked ready to be unleashed. 'A man approaches.' His voice was low but every word was clipped with urgency and barely-restrained violence. 'Medium height, strong shoulders. Eyes on you.' There was a slight inflection of worry, something Brann had never heard before. 'Eyes on your back.'

Brann had already prepared his move: spinning low to his left with the leading arm sweeping in the hope of warding off any blow and the knife following ready in his right. It would be effective and would minimise stretching the wound in his side – despite the moment of combat tending to close his mind to any message from the injury, still it made sense in the longer term to avoid aggravating it and counteracting the rapid effects that Grakk's assiduously applied unguent had been producing.

But for now he sat still.

He looked only at Gerens, but spoke quietly to them all in what little time must remain. 'If he means to attack me, he must know it means death, with all of you here already. And if his life means nothing to him and he only wishes to take mine, he would most likely have rushed me already, heedless of all else. But... be ready. In case.'

His back felt so exposed, as if he were inviting a blade. He wished he was wearing his mail shirt, as inappropriate as it would have been to arrive at the table in an inn dressed as such. The knife now drawn, his left hand dropped to grip the stool beneath him. He could swing that as he moved to divert a weapon.

He twitched as footsteps scuffed slightly, heightened

awareness catching the sound over the hubbub of the room. The sound stopped.

'You could have run.' The voice was hoarse, but his insides crumbled at its sound. 'You could have run. But you didn't.'

His eyes, wide, stared at the table top, seeing nothing. His breathing sucked in with a violent stuttering gasp that stayed within. The room swayed momentarily, as if he were back on the ship. The knife dropped to the floor.

He stood, slowly. His legs seemed distant, unresponsive, awkward.

He couldn't turn. He couldn't turn. He couldn't make himself turn.

Again, the hoarse voice. This time cracking, the words barely managing to be said. 'You could have run. You could have, but you... you...'

He turned.

'Father?'

The man before him shuddered, his mouth working soundlessly. His legs collapsed beneath him and he dropped to his knees, arms outstretched.

Brann fell into those arms, and they grasped him ferociously.

He felt the emotion surge in a judder through the chest his own arms enveloped. His father, his implacable father, his stern, forbidding, unyielding, formidable father, his father sobbed. A great racking groan that dragged years of suppressed emotion with it. And at the sound, Brann's own emotion released, and he sobbed with him. Hurt and pain and loss and fear and sorrow long held at bay poured forth, his chest aching with the effort.

The sobs gradually eased, and Brann felt the arms around

him ease with them. The large familiar hands moved to each side of his head and held him at a distance that let the same eyes as he saw in every mirror he had encountered regard him.

The voice was even more hoarse now. 'My boy.' The head shook in disbelief. 'You could have run.'

'I did run,' Brann whispered. 'You told me to go, and I ran.' His eyes moved from those of his father in shame.

But the hands raised his head again. 'No. Not then. When they killed your brother, you could have run. You should have run. Run to live. But you didn't. You brought him back. You loved your brother so much, even in death he meant more to you than your own life. When I saw you do that...' He shook again, fighting to resist the sobs again. He took a breath, long and slow, in and out. 'When I saw you do that, in that moment, I loved you more than I have ever loved anyone or anything.'

Brann gave his head a shake, trying to rethink memories into a new shape. 'But you sent me away.'

'To live.' The hands on his head strengthened, the importance of the words transmitted through the grip. 'I had lost one son. I knew those who had killed him must be close. All I could think was that I could not bear to lose both.'

Brann's mind whirled. 'All this time, I thought you rejected me. You hated me.'

A look close to horror swept across his father's face. 'I could not stop loving you. I tried. I told myself every night that you must be dead, that I followed a fool's errand. But I could not make myself believe it. I thought you lost. But what is only lost is not gone, it can still be found.' He shook his head again, his eyes never leaving Brann. 'I thought you lost.'

'And I thought you dead.' Confusion brought a frown. Of course, his father would not have known what Brann had seen. 'I was captured, by those who killed Callan, but it was other raiders who attacked the village. But the one who killed Callan was different from the rest, and he's now dead, in fact I killed him, and the others – the ones who captured me – are actually now my friends, and...' He realised he was babbling. 'Anyway, before I was captured, I looked back, and you were fighting, and then you were forced inside the mill, and it burnt, and you were trapped. And you and Mother and... and...' Tears filled his eyes again and he brushed his sleeve across his eyes in irritation at the interruption. 'You and Mother and the twins, you all *died.*'

His father looked at him, and raised his eyebrows. 'Well *I* clearly didn't, did I? And you will be glad to know that Mother and the twins are alive and well, too. They awaited me in our boat on the river, at the back of the mill. When the timbers collapsed in the fire, I was rendered unconscious, but Kyla held the boat while Mother and Tavin managed to drag me to it. They saved my life.'

Brann sat back, his shoulders hitting the table leg. His family was alive. *His family was alive.* He rubbed the heels of his hands against his temples, trying to absorb the thought, trying to reject the belief that had become a part of him. He grinned. His family was alive.

He flew again into his father's arms once more, but this time with joy. He laughed, and his father laughed with him, a sound as rare in his memory as the tears already seen and awkward in the man's throat – and all the more touching for it.

He felt a hand fall gently on his shoulder and looked up

to find Breta's concerned face. Her voice was unusually soft. 'You will speak better with your father, I think, if you sit up with us at the table.'

Brann looked around the surrounding clientele in growing horror. 'Oh gods, what must they think?'

Breta shrugged. 'Oh, don't worry. It's fine. They just thought you a pair of drunks and ignored you.'

Brann laughed, and helped his father to his feet. Cannick had shifted along everyone on his bench to leave space at the end, and Brann righted his stool and quickly ran through the names as his father eased himself down beside the veteran warrior with a nod of thanks.

'So,' his father said, 'this life you say I saved: you must tell me what has become of it since last we saw each other.'

Cannick barked a laugh. 'We may need another round of drinks or two if we are to do that.'

Hakon was halfway to the innkeeper. 'Already in hand,' he called. 'And food, of course.'

Brann watched his father sit in silence as the story was told, different people chipping in as their part in the tale became relevant. He said little himself, almost every part of his journey having been witnessed by someone in the group.

Instead he took the chance to look at his father. The dark hair was now streaked with grey, his build was as strong as ever and his face carried a few more lines than he remembered, as well as a small scar on one side of his forehead. But it was in his eyes that there was change. Where he remembered grim assurance, he now saw the effects of a man haunted over time by desperation and despair. He thought back to the father who had raised him – what the boy had thought cheerless repression, the young man now recognised as having been principled determination to instil values and standards for the years when his life became his own. That period had been thrust upon him sooner than had been expected, but it was only in this moment that he realised how much he owed his survival to the lessons once resented.

His father had been waiting to meet him all these years, and it had taken the troubles of nations to open his eyes to the man before him. But he saw him now. And Brann smiled.

'So, Garryk,' Hakon said, 'what do you think of your son's tale?'

Brann felt his father's gaze land heavy and long upon him. 'I sent away a boy with signs of the man, and have found a man with the best of the boy.'

Brann's finger traced a circle in spilt ale on the table. 'There is a side to me you will not know.'

His father was unperturbed. 'There is a side to all of us, and many of us do not know it of ourselves. You may be fortunate to know yourself more fully than most.' He paused, then: 'Is it evil?'

Brann almost smiled at that. His father never had been reticent about saying what needed to be said. Almost smiled, but the question itself killed any humour at its birth. He could feel the heat grow on his face as he answered. 'Some may say so.'

Grakk cut in. 'Some may say so, but only those who would say a cornered boar is evil, or a wolf with a spear point in its face. It is nature, and there is no good or evil in possessing talent, only in the way that it is used.'

'And the way it is used?'

Grakk met his gaze. 'For good. In our opinion.'

'As it was your opinion I sought, then that is sufficient for me.'

He took a long draught of his ale, and Brann's eyes widened. 'When did you start to drink ale?'

The grim face – though now Brann would have it no other way, he realised – regarded him over the tankard. 'Since before you were born.' He set it down on the table, but toyed with it as he spoke. 'Just because you never saw me influenced, does not mean I abstained completely, merely that I wished to be fully myself around you. In any case, the feeling of not being in control of myself does not sit comfortably with me.' He stared around the room. 'Though I admit to taking more of it than I am accustomed to do in the past year or so. Men are more inclined to accept questions if asked over a mug of ale or cider.'

'That is true.' Cannick took a swig of his own drink. 'And we had heard that you were seeking Brann, but just didn't know it was you.'

Garryk looked at Brann. 'You know there are others seeking you, as I was, but for their own ends.'

Brann nodded. 'We know their ends, but not their faces.'

His father's voice was grim. 'I heard of several, though came across but a few.'

Brann's interest rose. 'You met some of them? Do you know where they are now?'

'I do.' He took another drink. 'They are where I buried them.'

Brann nearly dropped his drink. 'You killed? You?'

The eyes that met his were implacable. 'I did what had to be done.'

Gerens stared with his dark eyes. 'I can see the family resemblance already.'

But Brann just stared at his father. He could not imagine the man he had known killing in cold blood. His thoughts must have been plain on his face, because his father sighed, and said, 'I have done many things for the first time. I lasted no more than a month after the mill was rebuilt before I left the village and came to the South Island. I, who had never been further than the nearest market town since my birth. I have travelled its villages and towns since, chasing news of the son taken from me.'

'But I could have been anywhere.'

'But I couldn't be everywhere. If a net is cast in the sea, you will catch fish but perhaps never the type you want; cast in just one small pond, and you quickly exhaust the stock; but cast in a lake, and you will eventually find what you seek. So I decided on the South Island, and tried to cover as much as I could.'

'But the mill was your life!'

The head shook. 'The family within were my life. Are my life.'

'But you left them.'

'They are safe, and cared for. And I will return to them. I can now return to them.'

Brann frowned. 'But you left them not knowing if I was even alive.'

'I had no choice.' The eyes were still locked on his. 'When you are a parent, then you will understand.'

Konall leant forward. 'You are not a parent, so can we leave that for now?' He looked at Garryk. 'Have you travelled north of here? Or close enough to know what is happening there? In particular, the best route to your island?'

Brann saw his father's eyebrows raise, and heard Marlo start to apologise for Konall. He held up a hand to placate the boy. 'It is fine, Marlo. My father appreciates bluntly honest speech.'

Garryk shrugged. 'Words are just words. Why use time saying those that are unnecessary, when you could be saying those that are needed?'

Konall looked at Brann. 'I like him better than you.' He turned to Garryk. 'So?'

'So,' his father said, 'you can abandon your idea of travelling through them.'

Cannick looked at him. 'How so?'

'There is fighting from Hamm to Marbury.'

Breta frowned. 'From where to where?'

Garryk saw her lack of comprehension replicated on every other face. He sighed, and started to move platters and cups around on the table. 'I'll do my best to explain, but it won't be as clear as a map.'

Grakk looked at Brann with a twinkle in his eye. 'Actually...'

Brann grinned. 'But perhaps best not here, in full view. Sophaya, I know you have the funds secreted away, but do you have sufficient on your person to negotiate with our host for rooms for the night?' She nodded and slipped away. 'We should finish eating and adjourn upstairs once Sophaya has secured the rooms. We have planning to do.'

Konall gestured to Garryk with a chunk of meat skewered on the tip of his knife. 'He likes his planning, does your son.'

The man nodded. 'Just like his mother.'

'If it helps,' said Hakon cheerfully, 'he's also a right wee devil in a fight.'

Brann's father looked at him with a face that never changed expression. 'As I said...'

Grakk snorted as he moved past them, his shoulders shaking. He clapped Garryk on the shoulder and pointed at the door. 'Map,' was all that the mirth permitted him to say.

Brann shrugged. 'It is true.'

Sophaya returned with news of three rooms, and Brann looked at Hakon, Breta, Marlo and Philippe. 'The stables have a secure room so the saddles and tack will be fine there, and handy for the horses in the morning, but we'd probably all feel more comfortable if the packs and the weapons we don't have on us were up in the rooms. Would you mind?'

The four left without a murmur, and Sophaya led the way upstairs, Brann falling in beside his father at the back.

'They seem to like you,' his father said. 'Not that I think they shouldn't, but... it is good to see.'

Brann smiled. 'We have been through much together. Adversity does that, I suppose.'

'Good people do that. Adversity can breed animosity as much as comradeship.' He looked at the figures disappearing through the door. 'The girl with the rooms, the four who go for the packs – they do as you bid.'

He shrugged. 'I just say the obvious thing, and if it makes sense, why would they not?'

Grakk's voice came from behind. 'He does himself an injustice, father of Brann. A man's words carry weight if he has a history of making sense while others still ponder or, just as perilously, act rashly.'

'I know he does,' his father said. 'I did not speak falsely when I said that he was in his mother's image.'

Grakk took his arm, turning him to face him. 'And now you do yourself the injustice. Your image is in him also.'

The man frowned, his face settling into it as if to its natural expression. 'Him?' He looked at Brann. 'Like me? Not in any way.'

Grakk shook his head. 'More than you think. Consider: when you searched, month after month, you must have encountered setback after setback. And yet you never gave up.'

The broad shoulders shrugged. 'Where is the sense in that. Hard times are like a fight against adversity. If a man knocks you down, you get up or you invite him to finish you.'

'And how often do you get up?'

Garryk was perplexed at the question. 'Every time, of course.'

Grakk grinned and slapped him on the back enthusiastically. 'And there we have it. With the son as with the father. What his mother gave him, the ability to think when all around cannot or will not, has kept all of us alive. But what you gave him, more than anything else, has kept *him* alive when any other I have met would have died a dozen deaths.'

Brann looked at his father as the man took in the thought, and saw the magnitude of it take root. He wasn't ready for a show of emotion twice in one night. 'Right now, however, it is my mother's desire to plan that is calling to me, so if we could leave the talking and continue the walking, it would be helpful.'

They found the others congregating in the biggest of the three rooms they had been allocated and, without ceremony, Grakk spread the map out on the floor. Hakon had brought a jug of ale and passed around tumblers, although Brann noticed that his father took instead water. He did the same.

Garryk knelt by the map and talked them through a lesson first of geography and then of the turmoil filling those lands. 'You can see Cardallon, here: broader at the lower parts, where you have travelled roughly along the border

196

between the kingdoms of Saria and Westland, and tapering slightly towards the top. The Northern kingdom, Ragalan, spans the width of the island, from the ports of Hamm and Marbury that I mentioned before, and begins just north of Benorthangeat. Where Cardallon reaches its north coast, the land spreads wide, jutting into the sea east and west and matching the wide southern coast of Alaria. Some say that, before the time of man, this was all one island, and that an irritated god smashed a divide and let it be filled by the sea to separate two relentlessly squabbling tribes of giants.' He shrugged. 'Whatever the truth of it, crossing The Break from one island to the other can be treacherous from the fierce currents entering and meeting and fighting within it, but the distance is short even at its longest point, perhaps just more than half a day's sailing, and those living on either side became skilled generations ago in navigating its waters.'

Breta held out her flagon to Hakon and let him fill it while her eyes remained on Garryk. 'So what is the problem? Surely we just ride to the coast and find one of these expert boatmen?'

'The problem,' Brann's father said, 'is here, and here, and here, and here.' His finger stabbed at places along the northern end of the kingdom of Ragalan. 'Devil men, riders with masks, have gathered bands of men, depraved and mad, but mad enough to be heedless of danger in combat and dangerous even to trained soldiers as a result. Mostly they terrorise villages, killing and torturing and leaving only embers behind. When the king's soldiers are sent to engage them, sometimes they fight and sometimes they run, but the pertinent truth for us is that, if a stranger ventures anywhere into that area, from one coast to the other, they are as likely to be killed by crazed lunatics, terrified villagers, or desperate troops – basically, anyone you come across. It is a hell of chaos, terror and death.'

'Precisely what Loku and his associates aspire to,' Grakk said thoughtfully. 'But why?'

Garryk looked at him in enquiry, but Brann held up a hand. 'That matter is an explanation for another time. What we need to know now is how we can pass them by?'

His father shook his head. 'We cannot. The danger is fluid; in many spots at any one time and with those spots always moving, so you cannot hope to avoid it.'

Mongoose frowned. 'But we must try to slip through. We cannot fly over it, can we?'

'We cannot indeed,' said Garryk. He placed a broad finger south of the east-coast port of Marbury. 'But we can...'

Brann smiled. 'Sail around it.'

'Indeed,' said his father.

Mongoose groaned. 'Not again. I think I'd rather face the lunatics.'

They made good progress, leaving at dawn the next day and following the course of the River Cayd until it angled south-east. They camped for the night at that bend in the great river and, as the sun rose behind heavy clouds, struck out on a direct line for the coast, sighting the sea as the cloud-masked sun threatened to dim its light on the second day.

Brann squinted and thought he could make out lights glinting.

His father confirmed it. 'There is a small fishing town there, more of a village really, but large enough that we should be able to find a boat to take us north if we pay enough. We should press on and make it there tonight.'

'For a man who had never travelled beyond Millhaven for the market, Father, you certainly know your way around.'

The man grimaced. 'When you spend your time searching three kingdoms for your misplaced son, you tend to remember where you can find a bed under a roof and not under the stars. Especially during the rainy months.'

Marlo looked over his shoulder. 'Which are the rainy months?'

'All but one,' came Gerens's sour response from behind.

Brann laughed. 'True. And that's in a good year.'

It was dark by the time they reached the village – it could not be described accurately as anything more – and they let the horses walk at their own pace down the last slope. A cluster of houses gathered in a curved huddle, as if protectively, around a similar cluster of fishing boats, the light spilt from windows shining from swaying masts and gently rocking hulls.

Garryk headed for one building, bigger than the rest, that proved to be a tavern, and they left the horses with a lad in the yard at the rear and gratefully eased muscles aching from two days of hard riding onto seats around two tables.

Brann was beside his father. 'What is the name of this village?'

'Don't know.' He waved to attract the attention of an older woman, thin but with the wiry strength that is formed from years of relentless work. 'Never needed to know. As long as I know what a place offers and how to find it...'

The woman reached them and whipped a rag from her shoulder to wipe the table. 'And how can I help you good people?' Her eyes fell on Garryk and she straightened with a smile. 'Well, look who it is!'

Eleven pairs of eyes turned on Brann's father. He shrugged. 'One of the few places I was never thrown out of for asking too many questions.'

The woman laughed. 'Only because we like a good story here. So tell me, did you ever find your...' Her eyes landed on Brann beside his father and flicked back and forth, from one to the other. 'Don't tell me...'

Garryk nodded.

She beamed. 'Well, this calls for a celebration. First drink is on the house.'

Hakon grinned. 'How many nights are we staying here?'

Brann ignored him. 'Can I ask, er...?'

She spread her arms wide. 'Of course, ask anything! You are like a figure of legend to me, I have heard so much about you. And it is Cwen, by the way.'

Brann smiled. 'Brann.'

'I know!' she laughed, pointing at Garryk. 'Him, remember? So, what would you like to ask?'

'We are looking for a boat to take us north, to Alaria. Would there be any men here who would consider it? We would pay generously, of course.'

'I know just the man.' She turned to face across the room. 'Ormod!'

A face with what appeared to be as many creases as years, and both were copious, looked up. Grey eyes in sockets sunken more even than the cheeks below them looked at her with resentment. 'What?'

'These ladies and gentlemen would like a lift to Alaria.'

He looked sourly at the group. 'Piss off. I'm at my dinner.'

'Not now, you old fool. Tomorrow.' She looked at Brann enquiringly, and he nodded confirmation.

'Where in Alaria?'

She looked at Brann again. 'Anywhere suitable in the South,' he said.

'First bit you come to that's safe,' she told Ormod.

'They can pay?'

'Of course!'

'One hour after dawn.'

She turned back to Brann. 'Don't mind Ormod – he might be a grumpy old sod, but no one knows these waters better than he, and his sons and grandsons handle the boat the way you would expect a family of sailors to do. So, now you can enjoy your meal.'

'And that first round of drinks,' Hakon pointed out.

Marlo's voice piped up. 'Cwen?'

She noticed him. 'Oh, aren't you a darling? What can I do for you, my pet?'

He blushed. 'Will we maybe need two boats? They did not look over big, and we have horses.'

'Oh, pet, you won't be taking your horses. These are boats built for men and fish, and nothing bigger. We can keep them for your return, or I can buy them from you. There is a trader in Hamm who is making a very good living at the moment selling horses to the king's soldiers, and there is a regular need for replacements these days.'

Marlo looked crestfallen, but Konall kicked him under the table and snorted in disdain. 'Grow up. They are just a means of getting from one place to another.'

Marlo was about to respond, but Brann cut in. 'If we can't take them, we can't take them.' He turned back to Cwen. 'We will pay you to care for them, but if we have not returned in the course of one moon, you may sell them. We do not know if we will return this way.'

She frowned. 'You lose out twice that way. I shall buy

them from you now, and if I see you within that time, you may buy them back for the same price plus the cost of the feed.'

Cannick swivelled in his seat at the other table to face Brann. 'I never thought I'd find myself hungry because my meal is delayed by horse trading in a tavern in a fishing village, but here we are. You won't get a fairer deal than that, lad. Take it and let the lady do her job.'

Brann nodded. 'Seems fair. We will include the saddles and tack, but will take the saddlebags and weapons holsters, as they are personal to each rider.'

'Excellent,' she beamed. 'I will deduct the cost of your food and lodgings, and give you the rest before you retire, once we agree a price.'

And so they found themselves on a slick and cold stone quay in the early morning, looking at the only boat that had been left in the harbour when the rest of the fleet left just as the sun breached the horizon. Ormod sat on a barrel, watching and shouting critically as what must be his two sons and three grandsons busied themselves in readying the boat, working in the unison of a well-practised team.

The old man held out a gnarled hand without a word as Brann approached, and he placed a purse of coins on a leathery palm creased with ancient rope scars.

'Is that enough, Captain?' Brann asked respectfully.

The hand weighed the purse for several seconds. 'It'll do.'

The wind remained favourable throughout the day, and there was still a good hour before sunset when a fishing village, almost identical to the one they had left, came into sight, and Mongoose hauled herself up to peer at it through bleary eyes.

'Please tell me we have not returned to our journey's origin and must start it all again,' she groaned.

Garryk took a rag and wiped her face. 'The fisher folk spend so much time at sea, they do not consider boundaries on land as much as we do. Over generations, individuals move and visit along the coasts of this sea, mingling with those in other villages and never seeing a difference between a harbour on the north island and one on the south. They see more in common with each community set on this coast than with those of us who live off the land, and marriages and families among those villages probably have formed a breed apart. They have their own songs and stories, their own customs, and their own attitude to building a town or village: it is just a place to rest your head before you sail again. Every settlement looks the same, which can be as comforting in a way as it can be confusing to those as us.'

Mongoose grunted. 'I don't care. Just tell me we are ending this journey of hell.'

Garryk put the cloth in her hand and stood. 'We are ending this journey of hell, girl.'

'Good.'

As the hull bumped gently against a quay, two of the grandsons were already leaping ashore to help the passengers and their baggage from the boat. Not a second was wasted when the task was complete; with a smile and a nod, the pair stepped back aboard and pushed against the quay in one smooth movement. Without any further backward glance, the boat was heading back the way it had come.

'What now?' Konall said, feeling in a pocket on his pack to check his bowstrings for dampness.

'Now,' said Brann, 'we find an inn for rumours or news on goings on that sound like the work of the likes of Loku,

Daric and the rest of them, and we find horses for sale.' He looked at his father. 'And what now for you? Home?'

His father nodded. 'Home. Though, first, I would share this part of your quest with you, if you would allow it.'

Brann took a step back in astonishment. 'You are the father, and I the son. I ask permission from you, not you from me.'

His father's face was hard, but there was pride in his eyes. 'In this, I do.'

The inn proved fruitful as they found the fishermen, on returning from the day's work, were eager to swallow ale and spout stories gleaned from crews they had encountered from other harbours. Merchants who had waited for the uncertain time of return of the boats were also eager to pass the time and added news from inland to the mix.

It appeared that the efforts of those under Daric on the North Island had proved less successful than on its southern neighbour; the widespread communities and the hardy people, bred into a harsher climate, making for greater resistance for smaller gain.

'He will need more men up here,' Grakk had observed. 'Once they have their objective on the other side of The Break, they will either try to sweep quickly through the softer targets of the more southerly two kingdoms and then flood this place with men, or will head here first to leave the easy target down south as a final loose end to be tidied up.'

Brann had agreed. 'Either way, he can do nothing while there is so much activity in Ragalan, and all he does on this trip is to gather facts to present to this Council of Masters, probably with the next move to be decided at that point.

If we can work out where their activity here is, then we can seek to intercept him.'

The merchants had directed them to the farm of a horse breeder who had been delighted with the unexpected sale of fourteen animals without having to take them to market. Perhaps of even greater value, he was also able to pass on tales of atrocities committed by bands of men with the faces of demons, and knew the names of several villages and hamlets that had been attacked. The towns, for now, seemed too large to be under threat. Brann had produced the map and the man had been happy to mark the positions of the affected settlements.

'If you and your friends could send these demons back to their hell, I am happy to help you find them,' he had said, his fingers tracing a symbol in the air.

'They are not demons, but merely men with masks,' Brann had corrected him. 'Nevertheless, they deserve a hell all to themselves, and we are more than happy ourselves to put them there.'

'Good enough for me,' the horse famer had said with a smile reflecting the grimness in his voice.

At their camp that night, Brann hung a small lantern on a branch and spread the map beneath it. His father, Konall and Grakk moved to look at it also when they noticed. Brann looked up at them. 'I am seeing a pattern in these attacks,' he said.

Grakk nodded. 'The same thought had occurred to me when the farmer marked them. All a similar distance from a central point?'

'You would attack their camp?' his father said. 'Is that wise?'

Konall looked at him askance. 'You fear to attack them?'

The response was familiar in its lack of patience for being challenged. 'I care for my son, fool. My own safety is secondary.'

Konall bristled. 'Your son has followed a path often treacherous for some time without a nervous mother hen.'

'If you are willing to accept his death when an alternative course could have been taken, then you are as callous as you are stupid. Typical Halvekan.'

Konall leapt to his feet, eyes flashing and hand reaching for his knife. Brann and Grakk hurled themselves between the two men as Garryk roared, 'They will not kill my son, noble boy, and neither will you!'

The others stirred quickly around the fire. Brann felt sick in the pit of his guts at the sight of the two facing off, but Grakk maintained a stillness and placed a hand on the heaving chest of each man.

'You are both right,' he said. 'We are not afraid to attack them, but there may be better ground than that chosen by them.' He looked at Brann. 'Is that not so?'

Brann found himself struggling to collect his thoughts, as though they were butterflies in a breeze, but forced his brain to work. 'Yes,' he stammered. 'Yes.' He took a breath, letting logic take hold. 'These men here are different from those we found in the camp near Belleville. These seem to be a vanguard, fewer but more redoubtable and organised. Perhaps the officers who will control the wild troops, if they can be compared to anything organised. So their camp will be better defended and they will be less inclined to surprised flight. But the priority is not killing them, but getting to Daric and finding where this Council of Masters will meet.' He looked pointedly at Konall. 'We can kill them all later, but have to be patient.'

In the time his words had taken to say, the tension had lessened slightly. He looked from one wild face to the other, and saw the tightness start to ease there also. 'If we can look at the possibilities?'

Both nodded, and slowly squatted once more by the map. Brann and Grakk did likewise, between them. 'He said he was coming from Ragalan to here and then on to Halveka. So if the camp *is* there, we can look at his options for heading for the east coast. Let's start with that.'

As Brann finished his meal, he heard several of the horses snicker. Marlo was ahead of him in moving to settle them, but he waved the boy back and told him to take the chance to rest. Sometimes, he needed to think, and he did that best alone.

He heard footsteps before Konall's voice, so he was surprised less by the presence behind him than the identity of the speaker. 'Happier with horses more your size?'

Brann smiled. 'These are what I thought all riding horses looked like until your uncle took me away from this. We also have pulling horses, which are massive, but I didn't realise there was a size in the middle more suited to the long distances and flatter land of the big land outside these islands. But then those horses wouldn't cope as well as these little fellows with the hard ground and slopes we have here.'

'I know.' Konall sighed. 'We have the same small ones as you, just for getting to a fight, mind you. Real fighting is done on a man's own legs.'

'Real fighting is done in whatever way wins. Congratulate a man for dying well, and do you think he hears you?'

The blond head nodded. 'You have taught me that, amongst other things.' He stroked the neck of the horse before him. 'We have none of these really big ones. I would like to see one, they must be an impressive sight. Hakon horses.' He laughed awkwardly.

Brann looked up at him for a long moment. 'Why are you being nice with me, Konall? I don't feel any more comfortable with it than you do.' Realisation dawned as he spoke. 'You are apologising!'

'I am not! Did you hear me say the words?'

'You don't have to.'

'I know.'

'So you are apologising.'

'I am.'

Brann smiled. 'Thank you. But you should really apologise to my father.'

Konall turned and looked into the darkness. 'I did.'

'You did?'

'Are you deaf? I offered to let him hit me.'

'And did he?'

'No.' Konall spat in the dirt. 'He apologised to me, for his words. Except he did it with dignity.' He shook his head. 'Your weirdness is obviously a family trait.'

He turned and walked back to the fire. Before he had gone three paces, and without turning, he said, 'Sorry,' violently hawked and spat, and punched a tree branch.

Brann smiled.

He sought out his father, and found him sitting against a tree, a short hunting spear propped against the trunk, a broadsword, whetstone, and oil-damp rag neatly laid on a cloth by his side. A buckler sat on his lap, and he was working intently with a needle and thread on a leather strap that looked so well kept that it could have been crafted that morning. 'Meticulous as ever,' Brann thought, nostalgia stabbing through him.

He slid down to rest his back on the trunk also. 'Want a hand?' He pointed at the sword.

'If you like.' The man grunted. 'Seems like yesterday I had to force you to do the slightest thing around the mill. Now you're offering to work.'

Brann started tending to the sword's edge. As he had expected, it could be used to shave before he even started. He grinned. 'I might have worked more in those days if you had offered me a sword to work on. Sharp weapons are always more exciting to young boys than sacks of flour.'

'Those who have never used a weapon see the shiny blade; those who have, see the butchered flesh. Not so exciting then.'

Brann nodded. 'There is truth in that.'

He father's hands stopped but he still stared down at the small shield. 'I wasn't there. You have seen so much you should not have seen, and had to endure what you should never have faced. A father should be there for his son. I was not.'

Brann's voice was equally low. 'You *could* not. It was what it was. I am lucky.'

His father looked at him sharply. 'Lucky?'

'Yes.' He ran a finger gently along the edge of the blade. 'I had something that let me survive. It was in me. Others built on it, but it was in there already, and I played no part in putting it there. Someone else in my place might not have had that, and would have died. I was lucky.'

'I could be there now, though. But I return home. I was not there for you, but I can be there for my other children, and I must. The stories I heard, they tell me you can take care of yourself in the world you now inhabit, but I have to ensure the twins can be ready for the world they will find. Can you understand why I must fail you again?'

Brann grabbed his father's arm urgently. 'You are not failing me! You have given up how many months of your life on the barest whisper of a chance of finding me, and you achieved it. And now if you go home, I have a family there I thought were gone. You have given me something to return to. I have survived times where all I thought I had of my own was my life, and I fought hard, so hard, to keep that. Think of the urge to survive when I have the four of you in my mind.'

The man grunted. 'You are right. Sometimes the right choice is the one that hurts the least people. Not much fun for the "least people", though.'

Brann smiled. 'I'll survive.'

'You'd better,' his father growled.

Brann sighted down the blade, more than satisfied with its condition. 'This is a nice weapon. Good balance.' He laid it back on the cloth between them. 'Seems strange to picture you with a sword, though.'

'If I had wandered the open roads alone without learning how to use one, my search wouldn't have lasted very long. What we are planning here is different, though. I have always reacted to a situation, never had to sit and think about it beforehand.'

Brann sighed. 'They say the waiting is the worst, but it's not true. The sewing up afterwards beats it every time.' He smiled. 'But the waiting isn't great. Want to practise? See if I can help.'

His father looked at him, his face as hard as ever. 'Do you know how ironic that sounds from a child?'

'I'm not a child any more, Father.'

'You are to me. Always will be, and never you forget it.' He stood. 'But in the meantime, I am not too proud to accept some pointers if it helps me to watch your back.'

Brann rose also. 'I work with Marlo most nights, so we can include him.' He whistled over to the boy and nodded in the direction of a space the other side of some bushes, and Marlo jumped to his feet immediately, sword in hand.

Brann faced his father first. The man was tentative, never having faced anyone in practice before, let alone his own son and with an edged weapon in hand. Brann parried and moved carefully, letting the strokes build in assurance as his father grew more confident that he would not kill his boy.

Brann felt the power held back and, mixed with a basic aptitude learnt through necessity, it would compensate for the lack of teaching against a certain level of foe. In fact, he was surprised at the level his father had brought himself to, for although the blows lacked anything close to skill or fluidity, each movement was deliberately intended and efficient as a result.

He paused, stepping back and holding up a hand. 'Apologies, Marlo. I did not ask you over to watch. You two practise, and I can watch more closely from the side.'

The pair proved to be fairly evenly matched. Brute strength and a practical style met a careful grounding in technique and years of watching masters at work. More than once, Marlo's nimble footwork or deft parry avoided a shoulder to the chest or a pommel to the jaw, and Garryk's buckler or braced blade absorbed the full force of an overhead swing or knocked a thrust wide.

'Stop,' Brann said. 'Catch your breath or one of you will make a mistake and someone will get hurt.'

Marlo rested his hands on his knees, his chest heaving.

He looked across at Brann once he could speak. 'He uses his strength like you do, but needs to learn to use an opponent's attack movement against him to gain an angle or unbalance him.'

Garryk grunted. 'No chance of that. I am what I am. My feet are rooted into the ground for strength, and I will never be described as graceful.' He glanced at Brann. 'Your mother, though, that is a different manner. Remember how she dances?'

Marlo grinned, slapping Brann on the back. 'You see, you are a perfect combination of both of your parents. You can take absolutely no credit for any of your success.'

Brann grunted. 'That has sealed your fate the next time we practise, cheeky brat.' He grinned. 'But the two of you can show me some more of how good you are.'

Blades clashed once more, and Marlo's laughter rang out along with the sound. 'I will beat you, old man. You do not even know the basics!'

'You know your weakness, little boy?' Garryk grunted in time to the thumping of his blows. As Marlo looked at him in curiosity, feinting and thrusting with smooth speed, the man's sword rose high in an ungainly but mighty overhead swing. Marlo raised his own weapon, two hands on the weapon to ensure strength and the rising blade at a perfect angle to deflect the downward swipe in just the right direction to leave the sword arm flailing away and open the body for a winning thrust.

Brann winced in anticipation of what was to come. And what came was not the downward swing of Garryk's sword, but the punch of Garryk's buckler straight between the boy's raised elbows and into the centre of his face.

By the time Marlo's eyes returned to focus, he saw a man

212

standing astride him with his sword tip resting on his chest. 'Your weakness,' said Garryk, 'is that you are a slave to the basics. Not everyone you fight will have learnt the *right* way.'

Brann offered Marlo a rag to stem the blood from his nose. 'A valuable lesson. There is no right or wrong in a fight, only winning and losing. Winners earn the ability to be right or wrong afterwards; losers can do nothing but rot.'

Marlo smiled ruefully. 'A lesson I am eager to learn, for I have plans for the foreseeable future that do not include rotting.' He gave Garryk a slight bow. 'Thank you, Brann's father.'

Garryk watched the boy's receding back. 'And I thought you were cheerful. What does it take to wipe the smile from that boy's face?'

Brann's mouth twitched up at one side into a half smile, one of affection. 'I hope I never find out. He is our light when we are in the darkness.'

'Then keep him close.'

'For his light?'

'For his own protection. Leave him alone in a fight and your light will be extinguished.'

Brann nodded. 'I know. Why do you think I train him every night, as Grakk trains me after I finish with Marlo? I am given military history one night, which is actually fairly fascinating, and weapons practice the next, which is fun and useful. I hope to give to Marlo a better chance of life.'

His father looked at him. 'All of that can be useful. You never know what you will need to draw upon when life is unpredictable – which we have certainly learnt it is.' He gestured in the direction Marlo had gone. 'And, by the way, train him all you like, but the best gift you can give him is your sword guarding his back.' He nodded at Brann's weapon. 'Talking of which, that is a fancy black blade.'

Brann drew his sword, then offered his axe and knife to his father's hands in turn. Garryk turned them over, examined them in the glow of the lamplight, tested their edges and swung the bigger weapons. He whistled softly. 'I think I have just proved that I am no expert in weaponry, but someone must think highly of you to give you these.'

Brann replaced them on his belt. 'He seems to, though I never worked out why.' He thought back to Alam, the former Emperor now content to let others think him a doddery old man while he plotted and schemed – the man who had sent them on this pursuit of Loku. Brann was certain Alam's objectives were his alone, and that Brann and his companions (and all others employed by Alam) were tools he used in achieving them, but he was more than happy to undertake this mission if it uncovered the people behind what was looking more and more a bid to control power in the Northern states outwith the Empire... and if it let him bring Loku within the length of a sword thrust.

'I am sure you will find out some day.' Brann was rolling down the sleeves he had folded up for the practice, but his father's finger stopped the material. 'Two sheaths on your forearms, one filled and the other empty.'

'I lent one to someone.'

'Lent? As in hoping for it to be returned?'

'Unlikely.' He thought of the recipient, and the mystery she had radiated. She had aroused a curiosity that he could not shake off. He shrugged. 'I am so used to the feel of them on my arms, I have to wear the pair. I will see it returned or find another to fit the sheath.'

'Handy place to have them.' His father paused to regard him, his look searching. 'Any others?'

'Possibly,' Brann admitted. 'One in each boot, one across the back of my belt for my left hand to reach and,' he stretched behind his neck to pull the throwing knife from between his shoulder blades, 'this one. That's the lot.'

'Sure you've got enough?'

'Well,' Brann said, 'it's always good to have…' He stopped. Memories hit him in rapid succession: the extra couple of bags of flour kept back from market in case of a neighbour's unexpected need; the extra purse hidden under the seat of the cart, just in case; the extra horse in the barn; the extra hammer beside the tools; the extra millstone in the corner. 'It's always good to have something more in reserve.' He stared. 'You always… And, in these past times, I have so often…'

Garryk's face did not move, but there was a smile somewhere in his eyes. 'I'm glad I actually managed to teach you something.'

Brann threw his arms around his neck. 'You taught me everything that matters.'

His father winced, working himself gently free of Brann's arms. 'With care, boy. Your friend hits harder than I will ever admit to him. I need to ease these shoulders before what is coming in the days before us.'

'Then come and we will see Grakk. He has magic fingers for the relaxing of muscles.'

They walked slowly towards the firelight, Brann swinging the lantern at his side.

His father broke the silence. 'A throwing knife? Throwing? You?'

'On the odd occasion, I get lucky and hit someone.

Sometimes the right person. If I'm really lucky, with the right end of the knife.'

'Sounds about right.'

There was another long silence.

'Still can't catch either?'

'Still can't catch.'

A contented sigh. 'Comforting.'

Brann found his side was pressing close to that of his father. 'It is.'

They lay on the top of a low rise, the grass damp under them, overlooking the dark packed earth of the road as it wound, the height of two men below them, around the base of the hill.

Konall eased his sword free for the inspection he had given it every dozen breaths since they had settled there. 'You are certain they come this way?' His voice was a whisper.

Brann gritted his teeth and hissed his reply. 'As I told you every other time you asked that very same question, there are only two roads coming this direction in this area: this low road and the high road. Grakk scouted a score of riders on the low road, all with demon masks under their dark hoods, and one at the van with red hair to his waist. They come this way.'

Konall stared at the road. 'Just want to make sure.'

Brann stared at it also, but felt the grass and the soft earth under his fingers. The familiarity was welcome; he felt like he belonged. But... he felt something else, too.

He realised. The last time he had lain on grass like this, his brother had died in front of him, mid-conversation, mid-smile. His chest constricted, sucking in a breath sharply.

His father looked at him. 'What is it?' he murmured.

He didn't want to talk about it right now. 'Nothing.'

The eyes narrowed. 'I know that look. I have seen it many times. I have caused it more than a few times.'

'I told you, it's nothing. And we should be quiet.'

'Why? They are not close.' But his voice had dropped to a whisper nonetheless.

'Exactly. We need to listen. We can see a fair bit down the road, but to know of their approach further in advance, we will hear them before we see them. It is the opposite of seeing the dust in the desert.'

His father rolled on his side to let him look at Brann more easily. 'I'm sorry, in the what?'

'The desert. Surely you...' He stopped. How would his father know of the desert any more than one of the camel-riding Deruul, the tribe who led caravans across the sea of sand beyond Sagia, would have heard of snow? He continued, his voice soft and low and his eyes fixed on the road below. 'It is a land of emptiness, like a sea of sand. No respite from the heat during the day, no comfort in the cold at night, no trees, barely no animals, and definitely no water. And the slightest movement kicks up dust, meaning you see the signs of riders before you hear them.' He grinned. 'About as much the opposite of this place as you can imagine.'

His father grunted. 'Doesn't sound the most appealing of places. This place here will do me fine, I think.'

'It will do me fine, as well, to know you are here. Assuming we can get rid of those we meet today, and their ilk.'

Garryk nodded. 'Better get listening then.'

As they waited for the sound of horses, Brann's eyes wandered to the positions where various members of their band waited to play their part. He would have felt more comfortable were he able to check their readiness personally, but the circumstances dictated, as they often did, that he had to trust them. Still, he could find no people he would trust more.

The rumble of the horses came; a hint on the breeze, at first, but growing to an unmistakable sound of hooves drumming on the hard-packed surface. He didn't have to look at those beside him to know the tension that had swept through them all – he could feel it. The riders came around the far corner, and he dug his fingers and toes into the ground, ready to burst forward. But he held himself now, forcing patience into his straining muscles. They must wait. He hoped the others would. All he could do was hope. He reminded himself to breathe.

And, in seconds, the first rider, his hood thrown back to let his long red braid swing and bounce behind him, was at the mark: the twig they had laid against the slope of the hill. Hakon and Breta jumped in front of the party, their size and roars as much as their sudden appearance startling the leading horses into rearing and milling. The others bunched behind, becoming easy targets for the arrows of Sophaya and Marlo, stationed uphill to the fore and the rear of their prey respectively.

Before order could set in, Brann rose, sword and axe in hand, and saw Gerens and Mongoose do likewise on the other flank, while Grakk and Cannick closed in at the rear.

He charged, knowing the two with him would be at his side. Every way the riders turned, they saw warriors bearing down on them. Brann counted five of them downed by the arrows already, and a sixth standing by his dying horse. Two broke to meet his trio head on, and Brann took on the first, sliding feet first down the last of the slope to pass under a spear point and reaching with his axe at the underside of the horse as its momentum took it past. The fine edge of the blade cut across the animal's belly but also across his target, the wide leather of the girth that parted like silk. As the horse reared with the pain and fright, the saddle fell loose. When the horse fell on its side, the prone man watched with a scream of horror as its full weight toppled towards him. Brann was already on his feet and turned in a crouch to see his father holding his spear in the side of the other rider, as Konall fell upon him from the other side and finished him off. He moved to his father. He was not about to lose him again.

A man on foot, his hooded cloak tattered and fluttering but his dark demonic mask still in place, came at his father, a sword and shield held ready. Brann's chest constricted as he realised the assailant would reach his father before he could, but Garryk stood calmly and turned the sword's swing deftly with his spear, thrusting in return and forcing the man to lose his momentum. As the two traded blows, Brann closed with them, but saw a second foe run at his father from the other side. By now, however, he was on them and he hurtled past his father, launching himself and crashing his shoulder into the man's shield, knocking him at an angle and into a stagger. The man recovered in an instant, though, and swung with an axe at Brann's head. Brann's own axe came up, knocking the weapon high and locking the axe heads together. The assailant's shield came up to protect the head and chest, and Brann instead cut his sword at the knee, the black metal slicing clean through the limb and into the other leg. The man's scream as he flipped to the side was cut short as Brann's axe hacked into his neck.

He was already sweeping around one knee, and the back of his axe head smashed against the ankle of the man fighting his father. Garryk's spear did the rest.

He didn't have the time to ask, nor did he need to – his eyes told him that his father was uninjured. He cast about sharply, all seeming clear and instant as it always did in combat. All of the foe were down but one: his red hair flying, he was digging his heels hard as he wrenched his horse's head towards an opening to the road ahead.

Brann pointed, screaming, 'We need him alive!'

As the horse gathered its back legs beneath it, Grakk leapt with a whoop, landing on its haunches behind the rider. The horse leapt forward and Grakk started to topple backwards, but grabbed the long braid to pull the man with him.

The braid, and the hair, went with him as the man, his cropped black hair exposed and his mask falling loose, urged his horse away.

'It's not him!' Hakon cried, and less than a heartbeat later, Sophaya's arrow took the man through his throat.

Brann's eyes flitted about wildly. A decoy! Had Daric known they stalked him, or was it always his practice? But what did it matter? Catching him or missing him, that was all that mattered.

His sight fell upon the ridge, where a lone rider galloped along the high road. He grabbed Konall's arm, pointing. 'There!' He started dragging the boy. 'The horses.'

The pair sprinted, sheathing their weapons as they went and Konall casting aside his shield. They rounded the bend ahead to find Philippe waiting with their mounts, and ignored the man's startled questions to grab the first two available and drag themselves onto their backs.

Their horses started to gain immediately, heading fast towards the point a half a mile ahead where they could branch up towards the higher route. They had to get ahead of him to cope with the slower climb towards his road, and they inched their way into a lead, Brann finding himself watching the other rider more than the road ahead and trusting his horse to merely follow Konall's. The thundering of the hooves filled their heads, and the damp air and mud from the horse in front hit Brann's face, but still they urged their horses on, bending low on their necks.

They reached the track leading up, a straight diagonal up the hillside to the high road. Brann stared at Daric and at the point they would meet his path. They could make it. He willed his horse ahead, feeling the inevitable labouring along the rising ground.

Daric reached the junction ahead of them. They wheeled their horses in pursuit but, whether it was the effect of the climb or that he had a superior quality of animal, he started to pull away. He knew it, and turned, a look of triumph plain on his face.

'He cannot get away,' Brann yelled in despair.

Hakon drew up his horse and, before it had stopped, was already leaping from the saddle, longbow and an arrow in hand. His feet hit the ground with the surety of a tumbler Brann had seen in a southern village and, with grace and balance he drew and loosed in a single motion as Brann passed him, his horse's gallop unabated.

The arrow streaked away and took the horse high on a back leg. It stumbled and started to fall, throwing Daric from the saddle. Brann raced his horse up to him as he started to rise and threw himself from its back, sword drawn.

Daric's leg buckled beneath him, the broken bone clearly

pushing against the cloth of his breeches. He ripped the demon mask, identical to those worn by the others, from his face and glared in hatred. If he felt pain, it was not evident. He grabbed at a large knife and held it before him.

His eyes lit on the black blade of Brann's sword, and widened. 'You? The miller's son?'

'Proud to be.' It was a snarl. 'And a miller's son now has you.'

'No,' said Daric. 'You don't.' His knife sliced across his own throat in one swift movement, spraying Brann with blood to add to that of man and beast already slick on his face and clothes.

'No!' Brann screamed, but as the man coughed and choked his last seconds, there was triumph in his eyes. Then they dimmed.

Brann sank to his knees as Konall cantered up.

'Oh,' the tall boy said. 'That's unfortunate.'

Brann looked at him in despair. 'What do we do now?'

'You do what you always do. You think about it, form a plan, and tell us.'

They relieved Daric's horse of its pain, and although they searched the corpse fruitlessly, they found a satchel of papers on his saddle.

It was a sombre pair that returned to the others.

Grakk looked at the satchel Brann passed to him. 'I take it he is lying up there somewhere.'

Brann nodded. 'All of this,' he swept and arm across the scene, 'was for nothing.'

Grakk frowned. 'Not so. We suffered not one injury other than a cut to Mongoose's forehead, which she believes will add to her rakish appearance, and these despicable men will not be undertaking any more of their loathsome endeavours. That is not an outcome to be dismissed.' He held up the satchel. 'And considering the identity of the bearer of this, I am sure its contents are not inconsequential.'

Brann nodded. 'I hope so. The havoc wrought by this organisation Loku is part of is worse than we ever thought. We must find that bastard's superiors, and soon. Every day their scheme continues, more people who should be ploughing fields are dying in them; more towns are being laid waste. If they take power in one of these countries...' He shook his head and sought out his father, who was already coming to him.

'You are unhurt, Father?'

The man nodded. 'I would do that any day to save my son from danger, but I hope you understand if I say I would rather not do it ever again.'

Brann found himself smiling wearily. 'Be very certain, I wish very hard that you never do that again. I don't know if my nerves could take it.'

His father snorted. 'Now who is the mother hen?' He stared at Brann, then at the ground, as if trying to find words for a feeling of great strength. He looked up. 'You wondered, when you showed me your weapons, why someone thought so highly of you, remember? That,' he jerked his thumb to where Brann had fought, 'that,' he tapped a finger on Brann's forehead, 'and that,' he patted Brann's chest over his heart, 'that combination: that is why. This someone places great store in you.' He frowned. 'But whatever he thinks, he is not more proud of you, nor does he love you, like I do. You are my son.' His glower was fierce. 'But don't you ever tell your brother and sister I said anything as soft as that.'

Brann's hug was as strong as his father's words.

Grakk coughed gently.

Brann turned to face him, seeing the papers in his hand. He smiled. 'You haven't wasted any time in getting started.'

'I didn't know if we had time available to waste. And my curiosity was exceeding my patience.'

'And...?' Brann raised his eyebrows. 'Can I assume, as you are bringing this up, that you have discovered something already?'

Grakk became animated. 'Of course. Come here.' He crouched, placing the satchel on the ground. He leafed through the papers in his hand until he found one, stuffing the rest in the bag. 'This!' His face was lit with triumph, his eyes with anticipation.

'Are you going to tell me or do I have to read it myself?'

'This,' said Grakk, 'is the letter inviting our friend Daric to Halveka. So we know who he is meeting, where they are meeting and when they are meeting.' He grinned at Brann's dumbfounded expression. 'And there is more.'

'More?' Brann's voice was weak with the disbelief at the opportunity handed to them. 'What more could there be?'

'It says...' Grakk cackled with glee and danced in a circle. 'It says, "We look forward to finally making your acquaintance."'

Brann stared. 'They have never met him.' His voice was a whisper. 'They have never set eyes upon him.'

'Indeed,' said Grakk. 'And we have this.'

In his hand was the red wig worn by the decoy they had ambushed.

Brann smiled darkly. 'I can enjoy his death after all.'

Hakon draped a heavy arm around Brann's neck in brotherly fashion. 'That's the spirit. And while we are there, you could tell my sister all about it.'

Brann felt himself blush. 'We will not have time for idle chatter,' he said. But Hakon's grin proved he had seen the hope that had lit in Brann's heart.

His good humour fell away as his father walked over, leading his horse. He could see the man's expression. Brann knew. 'You are leaving.' All of a sudden, his mission, the driving passion that had given him purpose, seemed immaterial, unwanted. The thought of climbing into the saddle and riding home beside his father was overwhelming in its allure.

His father saw it. He nodded to the east. 'Your path lies that way. Mine to the north-east. No point in me doing two sides of a triangle.'

Brann's voice was rough in his throat. 'I have just found you.' He meant it in more than one respect, and he saw in the man's eyes that he understood.

'And you will again, now you know to look.' Brann felt his father's iron grip on his shoulders. 'If you turn from your path, you would wake tomorrow and feel the emptiness in your day.' He glanced at the others around the road, fixing their horses after Philippe had brought them over. 'They need you to do this. You need you to do this. So do it, and then come and tell your family the story.'

Brann nodded. But still, the image of his family, his village, his world for most of his life pulled at him. His heart wanted nothing other than to ride north at his father's side, and without a moment's pause, and a father's instinct must have seen it painted across Brann's face. The big hands turned him to face away. 'Go,' he heard his father's voice say softly. 'Go away. Now. Go. Away. From. Here.'

He was right. Again.

Brann reached behind him, finding his father's hand. Squeezed it. And walked away.

Chapter 5

They shuffled through streets caked in dirt, just two more old people in dark clothes and darker shadows.

A figure stepped from an alley. Barely any moonlight seeped through the clouds, but enough to show the knife in the man's hand.

'I'll take what you have now.' The voice was grim, but there was the telltale quaver of the slave to the dream smoke. The fact that he would see two elderly members of the poor as targets for his thievery had already betrayed his desperation. 'Now.'

He turned slowly to the thief, his hands still tucked into the opposite sleeves of his robe, the cheaply made garment showing signs of careful maintenance and the cleanliness of self-respect. The man was shaking, but whether from irritation or the amount of time since his last smoke was unclear. What was clear, however, was the impatient unpredictability in his eyes.

'What do you think two people of our years, in this quarter, might have of value?' His voice was dry with age, *but held the firmness of an adult talking to a slow child. 'Did you look before you spoke?'*

The thief shuffled, uncertainly. 'I don't care how little you have on you, it is more than nothing and that makes it something.' Anger started to push down his hesitation. Eyes that were old enough to water slightly in the cool air of the night were not too old to notice the fingers tighten on the hilt. 'Now, I'll take what you have from your willing hand or I'll take it from your dead one. Either way...'

He opened his eyes wide in shock. 'You would murder us? At our age?'

Impatience now brought a snarl. 'What of it? I should not because you are old? The opposite: time will bring death soon enough anyway; I would steal a year or so from you, no more. What loss is that?'

'Little to you, but much to me. You will find, should you manage to live long enough, that the fewer years you have ahead of you, the more you cling to each one that lies before you.'

'Enough of this!' The knife drew back, the arm tensing for the blow. Rusted and pitted the blade may be, but it would cut flesh all the same.

'Wait, wait.' His voice was pleading, frightened. 'All I have is this.'

His right hand started to pull from the sleeve, and he stepped closer to the thief, more easily to pass his meagre possessions.

The knife lowered and the thief's other hand reached forward eagerly.

The old mind smiled and old muscles felt young for a heartbeat as his own blade came from his sleeve and slashed across the proffered wrist. The thief's weapon clattered on the ground as the hand was used instead to grasp the wound. The man dropped to his knees beside the forgotten knife, his eyes wide with horror at the thick blood seeping through his grasping fingers.

'You have killed me!'

'If you are talking, you're not dead.'

The eyes looked up. 'I will be soon.'

'Take your tunic, wrap it tight around it and instead of cowering on your knees in the dirt, use the time to find someone who can fix it. If you go now, you have a chance.'

The man staggered to his feet clumsily, then looked in confusion at his tunic, its grubbiness testament to his priorities in life, but less caring about its hygiene at this moment than about the difficulty of removing it without letting go of this wrist.

'Here.' The old woman stepped forward, taking her companion's knife to cut the tunic from him, the fabric parting as easily as the skin had. She wound the rags compactly around his wrist, allowing him to pull away the other hand, and placed that hand back up on it.

He watched her work, seeing a new side in someone he thought he had come to know.

His voice was as dry as Death's well of compassion. 'You were right, boy: I may have only a year or two left to me. But keep living your life in smoke and I will outlive you. The gods know there is nothing more certain.'

The wounded man merely stared at him, then ran stumbling into the lane he had emerged from.

She looked at him. 'Will he find someone in time who can fix that?'

'Of course. Do you think there are more knife wounds in the rich parts of the city or the poorer? The two most *busy professions here in the Pastures are those who sell temporary escape from reality and those who deal with the consequences. He will know of several and find one close.'*

They resumed walking. She broke the silence a short distance later. 'In years past, you could have cut his throat, not his wrist.'

'That is the thing about the past and the future: they are not now. And you are the person you are now, not the one you are or will be.'

'But you are the product of what you were.'

'Exactly. The product, not the image.'

They had arrived at a nondescript door in a nondescript building. She knocked with a deliberate rhythm, and the shutter over a window opened a crack; an eye and the glint of metal all that was visible. Bolts were heard moving and the door opened to reveal an armed man who gestured that they should enter. It was closed the instant they were inside, the heavy bolts being slid home once more.

A man rose at their entrance, offering the female visitor his chair by the fire, waving away the offer of help from the attendant warrior to move swiftly to fetch two more chairs, a crutch compensating for a missing foot.

His old eyes watched the crippled man's movements carefully. Some people reacted to a setback with self-pity, others with practical and relentless determination; it was clear which category he saw here.

His companion initially disregarded the offered chair and moved to the other seated at the fireside, a lady whose age made him feel as though he were once again a young man.

'Mother,' she said, the love evident in the word. 'My apologies, it has been too long.'

Eyes crinkled and smiled back at her. 'It has been barely longer than a week, Cirtequine, barely that. Talk with sense.'

'Still, I miss you. I should be here more often.'

'Be here more often, and you would not miss me so much, so you would not. You would not miss me at all.'

Cirtequine smiled and took the chair. She looked across at the man accompanying. 'Mother, you know—'

A raised hand from the older woman stopped her words. The gold charms on the chain across her forehead tinkled as cloudy eyes turned his way.

'Of course I know Alam. I knew him as a boy; why would I not know the man?' She pointed at the one empty chair, the one-footed man having sunk into one of the two he had brought over. 'Please, boy, sit. We have much to talk about, so we do. Much to discuss.'

He sat, feeling younger than a young man. 'If you would excuse my bluntness, Lady Aldis, I did not come for chatter and pleasant reminiscence. I would speak of fate and destiny.'

The pale eyes locked on his, and he felt – knew – they saw more, so much more, than what simply lay before them.

'What else do those such as we discuss?'

****

Brann stood near the prow, spray in his face and his eyes on the approaching coastline, visible in the soft light of early morning. Daric had booked passage in advance on a ship sailing from the port of Thiel, and Cannick had been sent ahead to negotiate an increase in the travelling party to eleven rather than the six that had been originally agreed. The captain had been dubious at first, both about having room for the extra passengers and the fact that Daric's intermediary had changed identity, but it was soon proved that, in almost any such situation, money alleviates all concerns. The conversation also revealed one other useful fact: that Daric had never travelled this way previously, so his absence would not be noticed.

The crossing had taken the best part of a week, winds not being favourable and, indeed, blowing them south of their intended course. Brann had Cannick considerately suggest to the captain that he take them to a port a half-day's sailing to the south of their original destination. This time, the captain was only too happy to accommodate the change as it would save him a full day on the next leg of his journey, delivering a cargo to Selaire.

Konall knew the area well – it belonged to a warlord, not his uncle but a neighbouring one and, while no two warlords were friendly, there was a mutual respect and, mostly, peace between the two. Consequently, Konall had visited the region on many an occasion and was able to confirm that their point of landing was well-suited to their plan to get into character once on dry land and move to the meeting from there. To meet Daric's contact as they left the ship would reveal too much of their company to scrutiny and, what was more, would reduce their options. To avoid both was preferable.

Hakon joined Brann, his contentment obvious at feeling his hair blown by the sea air. 'It will feel almost like home,' he beamed. 'And interesting to see this part of the country, too.'

Brann looked at him with curiosity. 'You don't know this area as intimately as Konall does, then?'

Hakon's big laugh boomed as far as the gulls above. 'I know it hard to believe, Brann, but Konall and I are slightly different. He is the son of a lord, and nephew of a warlord, while I am just the son of a warrior, albeit a senior one.' He frowned. 'Senior warrior, that is, not senior son, although since my brother is only ten years old and my sister is, well, a sister, I suppose I *am* a senior son. But that was not the point.'

'No,' Brann smiled, 'it was not. Please continue.'

'Anyway, he travelled places with his father on official trips and I, well, I didn't. A page was not necessary for official trips, only for chores and tasks at home and more chores and tasks on hunting. Furthest I got from the town was either official hunts or leisure ones with my friends, and all hunts went inland, not along the coast. I never got any further away until, that is, we all had our wee adventure in the mountains.' He laughed again. 'Now I'm coming back from the deserts of the Empire to a place in my own homeland that I grew up thinking was too far away, even though it was the next settlement of significance along the coast from Ravensrest. How ironic is that?'

Brann slapped him on the back. 'See? Stick with me and you get experiences you never envisaged!'

'Aye, but experiences that are going to turn me into an old man before long.' He ruffled Brann's hair with a force that almost took his head from his shoulders. 'But a happy old man.'

The port was close now and, for the first time in the journey, the wind was perfect for them, whipping them directly towards the harbour mouth.

They disembarked into a small port that was busy enough for no one to take any notice of them, and quiet enough that they passed from it and into the countryside without hindrance. The ship had been a reasonable size and – despite the captain's protestations of difficulty to Cannick when a higher price was sought for their passage – with sufficient spare capacity that they had been able to bring their horses with them. It would not have been a terrible hindrance had they not been able to do so, but Brann was now glad that they could mount up and set off as soon as they were on the harbourside. He felt pulled towards their target.

They stopped a mile from the town and gathered at the side of the road. Hakon looked around the landscape, bleaker and more windswept than the one they had left and with ground that made unrewarding toil of farming, with a beatific smile on his face. Konall knelt and drew his fingers through the sparse and hardy grass, then rested his hand flat as if trying to feel the essence of the ground. Brann knew their feelings. He, too, had been surprised at the strength of the sensation that had struck him on returning to the ground of his birth.

'How far?' he asked Konall.

The boy looked up, his reverie broken. 'No more than half a day.'

Grakk was surprised. 'Two ports in such close proximity?'

Hakon laid a friendly hand on his shoulder. 'This is not your Empire now, friend Grakk, this is our dear land. Most people live on the coast, because the sea is more giving than the land. You'll do well to find a cove without dwellings of some sort and boats moored, and everything above the size of a hamlet calls itself a port.'

'Interesting,' Grakk mused. He had appropriated Daric's satchel and its contents, and he pulled forth a sheet of paper and scratched some notes on it.

Marlo laughed. 'You are turning into a proper little Scribe, Grakk.'

Grakk drew himself to his full height and looked down on Marlo from a distance of no more than a hand's breadth. His glare, however, would have had its effect from a hundred times that distance. 'Little? And you think only those of that slave caste are interested in recording information of value?' Marlo paled, and Grakk grinned and patted his head. 'Relax, young Marlo. I jest.'

For once, Marlo had no reply.

Brann looked at the road ahead, matching the coast as far as they could see. 'This the best way?' he asked Konall.

The boy stood, brushing dirt from his hand. 'All the most direct roads link the coastal settlements, because of what Hakon told you.'

'Then let us know when we draw close, and we will ready ourselves.'

Konall nodded, and they moved off. His estimate of the journey time was proved accurate, as they expected from his precise approach to all in life, and on sighting the smoke of cooking fires he called them to a halt.

'This is the distance you requested,' he said to Brann.

'Good.' He wheeled his horse to face the others.

Marlo was already pulling the cloaks and masks they had taken from the riders they had ambushed, and Hakon was checking the straps on his horse for a ride ahead. Brann reached up to pat the large boy on his shoulder.

'Remind me, how long could it take you to reach Ravensrest, and your father?'

Hakon grinned. 'Normally, a good couple of hours, but after being away from home for so long, much less than that.' His smile faded as he looked past Brann. 'Oh dear. This is not going to work, I am afraid.'

Brann frowned and turned. Marlo had passed the outfit

they had taken from the fake Daric to Konall, and the tall boy, the member of their party with the closest physical build to Daric, had the red wig on his head and was swinging the heavy cloak around his shoulders.

'What isn't going to work?' Normally the sight would have been comical, but Hakon's words had killed any humour before it could even begin.

'That. No one will believe it.'

'Why not? They have never met Daric. All they could have is a rough physical description of a tall man with long red hair, and an air of authority. And if ever a situation was made for Konall's perfected approach to life of aloof disdain, this is it.'

Hakon shook his head. 'It is because it is Konall. These are local people he is meeting. At some point, he will have to remove his mask, and as soon as he does, no wig in the world is going to stop anyone within a hundred miles of Ravensrest from recognising that face in the instant they see it.'

Brann's heart sank. 'But everything rests on us luring them from the town. We have no idea of their strength in the town, here, and cannot risk taking them on in a place that is their stronghold. We have no one else but Konall, given – as I said – that physical description is all they will base their recognition on.'

'Well, almost no one else.' They turned in surprise at Philippe's voice. The boy shrugged. 'I am a match for Konall in height.'

Brann shook his head. 'Philippe, it is far too dangerous for you.'

The boy frowned. 'This is more of an acting job than a fighting one. Have you forgotten…?'

Cannick spoke softly. 'The boy has a point.'

Philippe pressed on. 'Look, it only fits with difficulty over Konall's hair anyway, and my hair is much shorter.' He moved forward entreatingly. 'You have all taken me in without question, and when the opportunity to repay you in some measure through the very skill I have that you all do not, do you think I would rather be watching picketed horses for you?'

Brann shook his head. 'I am still not happy about it. If something happens to you and I could have protected you from it...'

Grakk moved closer also. 'It perhaps is Philippe's decision as to whether he wishes protection. We could all say the same about Marlo, or even you, at times.'

Brann frowned, but he could feel his resolve faltering. 'Gerens does feel the need to protect me.'

Cannick nodded. 'But he still allows you to do what you feel you must. He protects by watching your back. You can do the same today for Philippe.'

'There comes a time for everyone,' Grakk added, 'when they have to do what they think they should, if they are to be the person they can be. You of all people must know that.'

Brann nodded. 'Fine.' He faced Philippe. 'But I will never be more than an arm's length from you.'

Philippe smiled weakly. 'I wouldn't be going if I thought you weren't. I'm not that brave.'

'Yes,' said Brann. 'You are. It's one thing going into something where you may have to fight your way out, but a whole different thing where you know you cannot.' He sighed. 'You'd better try on the wig, then.'

Konall tossed it to him, and it slipped onto his head as if it had been made for him.

He took the cloak and swirled it into place, spinning dramatically through a full turn. When he faced them once more, his appearance drew a gasp from every throat. His posture had pulled straight and haughty, matching his face. His eyes were even no longer his own, staring with casual scorn around the group. His voice had deepened and acquired the assurance brought by expected obedience when he spoke. 'Which of you fools must I take with me?'

Breta laughed delightedly. 'By the balls of the gods, that is good!'

Philippe grinned awkwardly and shrugged, the pretence dropping as quickly as if he had flung away the cloak and wig. 'It is what I do, my dear. Or at least, used to. I had not realised how much I missed it.'

'Well,' grunted Cannick, 'from the look of that, we should have no fears about you down in the town.' He looked across pointedly. 'Should we, Brann.'

Brann was still unable to shake off the nerves about placing Philippe in such a situation, but forced a smile. 'Of course not. Now we should look at hanging a couple of weapons on you to complete the image.'

Philippe nodded. 'Of course. Just don't let me try to draw a sword or they'll realise I don't know which end to hold.'

'Leave that side of it to us.' He turned as a thought hit him. 'This does open up another possibility, however. Konall, you could accompany Hakon, which means you can go straight to your father, rather than Hakon having to explain it all to Ulfar and asking him to speak to Lord Ragnarr.'

Konall was at his horse. 'Do you honestly think I was

going to stay with you halfwits instead of seeing my family now that we have a real actor to play the role?'

Brann grinned. 'I expect you would have stayed if you had thought it necessary.'

The tall boy paused in the action of climbing into the saddle. 'You are probably right, but you have made the offer now and there is no going back on it.' He kicked his horse into movement.

'I could always change my mind.'

Konall's back was to him as his horse walked away, so his voice was drifting back already. 'I can't hear you.'

Brann noticed, though, the crestfallen look that Hakon was wearing. He raised his eyebrows in question.

'It was the "straight to Ragnarr" bit,' the boy said, miserably, seeming even more enormous than usual when on horseback and viewed from the ground. 'I have missed my family.'

Brann punched his ankle affectionately. 'Do you think I would do that to you?' Hakon looked at him, not fully comprehending. 'Do you think Konall wants you to hold his hand while he speaks to his father? I would wager he will be happier if you leave that to him on his own.'

Hakon's big grin burst across his face. He made to speak, but instead just beamed at length, nodded, and shook his horse into life. He cantered past Konall, his booming voice carrying back to them. 'Don't worry, my lord, your page will remind you of the route. And of the pace required.'

Konall's gesture at the broad back was obscene, but still he gave his own horse its head and let it match Hakon's, stride for stride.

Cannick laughed. 'I love a man who can be made happy so easily.'

Brann smiled. 'Me too.' He turned to the rest. 'Right, let's get organised.'

They sat on their horses near the outskirts of the town, masks in place, and sinister in their stillness under the trees on the grass verge just beyond a bend in the road. Residents would not spot them but anyone led to them would find the sight imposing, if not unsettling. And Cannick had been sent as intermediary once more in the hope that those meeting them would indeed be led to them – surely, they would come to Daric's summons, rather than expect Daric to come to them? Still, they would deal with whatever came their way.

Brann glanced at the others through the eyeholes, his breathing loud in his ears and hot in his face behind the thin metal. Philippe sat slightly ahead of them, he and Grakk sat immediately behind, and Gerens and Breta were silent behind them. Marlo, Mongoose and Sophaya were hidden a short ride further back on the road they had travelled along, in case they needed archery cover while making a fast retreat.

He returned his attention to Philippe. From the moment he had mounted his horse, he had remained in his character to the extent that Brann had found himself almost believing the ruse. It was chilling to see the look from those eyes, and he was glad to have the cloaked back to look at most of the time. Even now, Philippe sat straight and tall, mask on, long red braid brought forward over his shoulder to accommodate the raised hood and hanging down the right side of his chest. He stared relentlessly at the road ahead, imperious and silent.

The silence let them hear the hoof beats: a canter

approaching the bend ahead, quietening to the walk that brought the party into sight. Cannick led a group of eight horsemen, all of them brawny and not one on the decent side of reputable.

He halted in front of Philippe, and inclined his head. 'Lord, I can present your emissary in this land, Ove, son of Ingvar. Ove, this is—'

A man rode from among the bruisers: small weasel eyes matching pinched weasel face matching thin weasel body. Brann's attention flicked back to the eyes: they were the giveaway. Darting, cunning, suspicious, calculating, probing. But when Philippe removed his mask, they also became fearful.

'This is Master Daric?' the thin voice whined. 'How could I not know?'

Philippe slowly pushed back his hood and slipped the long braid back over his shoulder. His gaze bored into the weasel.

'It is always better to be sure, in everything,' he said, his tone deep and heavy with power. 'Is it not, Ove, son of Ingvar?'

The man nodded nervously. 'It is that, Master, it is that.' He looked around nervously. 'We have a camp further inland, where we have prepared a welcome. If that would please you?' Philippe stared at him. 'Or do you have other plans? We are, of course, at your bidding.'

Philippe stared still. Ove squirmed. Eventually, Philippe nodded. 'We will see your camp.'

Brann breathed in relief. Only this road led inland from the town, initially, splitting later, so they would soon pass by the spot where their three archers lay in wait.

'While we ride,' Philippe continued, 'you can start briefing me on your situation here.'

'You would not rather wait until the comfort of the camp?' Ove said. A glare turned his whine to a stammer. 'As you wish, Master. Of course.'

'I have travelled far. I wish to waste no more time.'

Ove indicated the road ahead, and Philippe moved his horse to walk it alongside him. Brann and his three companions moved in immediately behind, with Cannick respectfully to one side; it was more than uncomfortable leaving Ove's bodyguards at their unguarded rear, but there was no way he was letting Philippe be separated from him, and it also allowed him to hear their words.

'You lead here?' Philippe asked.

'I have that honour, Master. Following Lord Loku's absence, it has fallen to me to rebuild our work in these lands.'

'Ah, Loku, yes. His plan here came to nothing. His men were routed by slaves.'

'They were indeed, Master, but not for nothing. The people of this land had a danger living hidden among them. They are no longer unaware of that danger, and look in every shadow for a repeat. And so we sow rumours and stories, feeding that fear, while at the same time we rebuild. We have three camps hidden, and we gather recruits where and when we can.'

'Such as the camp we ride for now?'

'No, Master. This is a temporary camp, set for your arrival and to avoid delaying your departure, for I am aware you have important business elsewhere. The other camps are in the mountains and the wilderness, to avoid detection.'

Darkness filled Philippe's voice. 'What do you know of my plans elsewhere?'

'Only what we were briefed in Lord Loku's communications.' Ove's voice mixed panic with appeasement. 'He has been most helpful in aiding our work to rebuild here. If you were not able to visit us within the next month, we were to dispatch a delegate to report to the Council ourselves, but thankfully we have been honoured enough to receive your presence instead. A report from you of our endeavours will carry so much more weight, don't you think?'

'Naturally. You will be hoping, therefore, that the weight of my opinion reflects favourably on what I discover here. And what do you know of the location of the Council's meeting?'

The man shrugged. 'Only as little as anyone knows, Master?'

There was an edge to Philippe's voice. 'Which is? When I ask, you answer without evasion.'

Even from behind, Brann could see the small man swallow nervously. 'Only that it is in the Kiss of the Two Seas, as it always is. Were we needed to send someone there ourselves, Lord Loku would have notified me of the identity of the agent there, and he would have taken our report and presented it to the Council.' He looked up at the imposing figure at his side. 'That will not now be necessary, of course, with your presence gracing us, Master.'

Philippe ignored him, and Brann resisted the temptation to glance at Grakk. *The Kiss of the Two Seas*? If anyone knew of the place, it would be the tribesman with a childhood of education and adult years filled with travel and a thirst for knowledge. He forced his eyes forward. If Philippe could maintain such a pretence without pause, he could surely manage to stay in character himself when the only requirement was to keep in line, be silent, and stare straight ahead.

Philippe jerked a thumb back over his shoulder. 'These your men?'

'A few of the more robust that we have. Most of those in the camps are not so well developed, but we keep the best as our elite guard, and,' he preened himself, 'brought the best of those for your escort. More of these are in the town, in case of need, but the majority of the force is split over the camps.'

'For training?'

'For gathering, Master. The training, as ever, comprises the usual consumption of narcotic herbs. Lord Loku's instructions have always been clear that a trained man is long to prepare and hard to replace, but a man frenzied on the right herbs can be sent into battle in an instant, and an entire army can be readied in this way in the time it takes to train a single soldier to hold a sword. Some have gained practice through raids that spread a certain level of unease at least, and terror at most, but many have been sent on to serve as instructed, and many more will be ready to go soon.'

Philippe nodded sagely. 'It pleases me that you hold so true to our principles.'

Ove swelled with pride.

The larger man began to speak again, but stopped himself as a thought seemed to occur to him. 'The Council. You mentioned leaving at the end of the month to reach the city.' Ove nodded enthusiastically. 'You are certain there is sufficient time? When do you believe the Council is scheduled to be held?'

Brann smiled. Cleverly put.

Ove seemed flustered once more. 'Why, Lord Loku was quite clear with the date in his most recent missive. It—'

244

They were distracted by the rumble of hooves from behind. A great many hooves.

The air was filled with the ring of steel as all present drew their weapons, turning their horses' heads towards the rear.

A band of horsemen thundered into view, at least a score of them. Unease grew in Brann's stomach, but Ove smiled, waving a reassuring hand in the direction of Philippe and his men.

'There is no danger, Master. My cousin has brought the remainder of our men from the town.' He frowned. 'Though why, I cannot think. If you will excuse me?'

Philippe nodded slightly, and Ove rode to meet a man only marginally different in appearance from himself. The rest of the men, chests as burly and eyes as hard as those with Ove, passed them by and reined in ahead of the group. Most likely, these men were there to protect them from a threat to Daric but, regardless, Brann felt uncomfortable: it was bad enough having potential foes at your back, but in front as well... His sword remained in his hand, as did those of his companions. He glanced at the road ahead. If they had only passed around the next bend, they would have been in sight of their companions and their arrows. And if they had only done so before these visitors had arrived.

But considering *if only* ahead of *what is* can only leave you unprepared. And he hated to be unprepared. He let his horse wheel slightly back and forth, as if restless, to view the situation through the mask.

Ove nodded to his cousin and smiled. Brann relaxed slightly. The cousin trotted his horse to Philippe, who sat impassively watching.

'My profound apologies for the interruption, Master,' he said, drawing close. 'If I could have a word in confidence?'

Philippe nodded, and the man drew alongside, leaning in.

'I have to let you know that—'

His hand shot forward and grabbed the long braid of hair. One sharp yank and the wig flew from Philippe's head, the man's other hand holding a broad knife at the young man's throat. He moved it up slightly to pat against Philippe's jaw.

'You can close that, if you wish. What you should be concerned about having opened for you is your throat.' He smiled, clearly enjoying himself. 'I don't know who you are, but I know you are not Master Daric. And you may not know me but, more importantly, given this situation, is what I was before this new calling: a cut-throat, and a highly effective one at that.' He glanced at Brann and the cloaked riders beside him, all of whom were edging their horses close with muscles tensed to attack. 'You, who accompany this imposter, should understand that most who specialise in cutting throats prefer a slender blade for ease of conceal-ment, but I always favoured this heavy blade for the one very effective reason that just the slightest twitch of my wrist will open the gullet in the beat of a gnat's wing.'

They froze.

'And now,' he was almost crowing by this stage, 'you will all lay down your weapons.'

Brann's head swam. To disarm themselves would be a momentary prelude to the death of them all. *But* to watch Philippe die would only buy them time to take as many of these men with them before they were overwhelmed. *But* Philippe would die anyway. *But* to watch him die and not to act...

Grakk clearly shared his last thought. A flash of silver

streaked past the edge of Brann's vision and, before the throwing star had even lodged in the side of the man's face, Brann had hammered his heels into the flanks of his horse, jumping it forward. The cousin's hands had no sooner clutched at his face in shocked surprise, knife and Philippe forgotten, before Brann's black sword speared his neck. Blood spilled from his mouth and nose, before spraying over a horrified Philippe as Brann wrenched the black blade free.

'Better his than yours,' Brann said, hoping to snap the boy from his paralysis. 'Get behind me.'

The five clustered around Philippe. Brann pushed back his own hood, ripping off his mask to give him the vision he was used to. He lifted his round shield from his saddle and slipped his arm into place, never taking his eyes from those in front. The men facing them had been momentarily stunned at the sight of the sudden death, but now steadied themselves, spreading wide at front and rear to offer as many blades as possible to a single attack. There was no rush, however. The numbers so heavily favoured them that no one wanted to be the first to charge onto a sword, preferring to wait for several to go together.

Brann glanced at the others. 'Take it to them?' Universal agreement. He looked at Philippe. 'Stay close. See a gap, take it and run.'

Without waiting for a reply, he launched his horse forward, aiming to the edge of those ahead, where the road met the verge. Hit at the end of their line, and the rest could only swing round on one of their flanks. If they could punch through before they could be closed in at the side and the rear, they might have a chance at flight.

The five battered as a tight unit at the wall of horse and man, sharp edges hacking and throats snarling with bared teeth. Their move was unexpected and they made headway, but only enough to enable Philippe to break away; his anguished look over his shoulder at those he left behind all that they saw of him before he rounded the far bend. They were forced back, and Brann turned to face those he knew would be there.

Three men cried out among the foe, falling with arrow shafts protruding. More arrows followed but it would not be enough before they were overwhelmed and the remainder of the force could turn their combined attention on the vulnerable archers. It did, however, give a moment to regroup.

'Tight circle!' Brann yelled, but realised the command was already unnecessary. The others, as experienced as he – or more so – were already moving to do just that. They would not fall cheaply. Defiance roared from him in a sound more animal than man, but he could already feel the icy calm of combat spreading through his mind, stilling his emotions and sharpening his thoughts.

Movement in an unexpected direction caught his attention, and he jerked his head to see Ove wheel his horse and head up the opposite verge, where he could circle through open land to either a town or inland. Frustration lanced through him at the thought of losing vital information, but his attention was drawn back to the more immediate danger as men closed on all sides. Sword hacked and thrust, shield deflected and battered, horse twisted and turned in terror as he reacted and reacted and reacted and reacted.

There was a roar.

It was not from those they faced.

Those they faced turned in confusion. Brann took the chance to gut a man, then looked up.

Above the heads of their enemy, a party of riders, around fifty in number and with Philippe at their head, crested the rise that Ove had just climbed. The weasel-man's horse reared and threw him, and the men and women facing him likewise leapt from their horses, but in their case with intent. Mailed and with sword or axe in hand, they charged.

It was finished in the time that Brann managed to assess the health of his companions. All were fine, thanks to the arrival of their succour so soon after their desperate last stand had begun. Their foes, however, had fared otherwise. Not a man of Ove's band, save the man himself, still drew breath. And each breath that Ove took was one of terror. His hands had already been bound before him, and he knelt, shuddering and staring at the ground, between two warriors with bright blades in their hands and loathing in their eyes.

Chest heaving, Brann looked past him to see an enormous man, as tall as Hakon, but broader of shoulder, and with Hakon's face, but with the lines of greater years partially covered by a great shaggy beard. A huge battle axe was cradled in his arms as if it were a toy, and the man stared at the scene below, his eyes attentive to all. His eyes landed on Brann, and he nodded his greeting. Brann smiled back and waved, his sword still in his hand and the movement seeming more like a salute. He didn't mind. Considering he had saved their lives, if anyone deserved a salute, Hakon's father did.

At the thought of Hakon, Brann looked around the scene before him. He breathed his relief into the cool air on seeing the large form of the boy using the cloak of a dead enemy to wipe clean the blade of an axe similar to the one his father held, chatting cheerfully to Konall despite the blond boy paying no attention whatsoever to him and instead eyeing the corpses suspiciously, as if daring any to rise up and seek a last strike.

Brann moved to them, but barely managed three paces before a blur of movement from his right ended with a body thumping into his. He tensed in fear for the few heartbeats it took for a sword to drop at his feet and a shield to the ground at his heels. Arms and legs wrapped around him and a voice in his ear was so familiar that it seemed only hours since he had heard it last.

'You stand and breathe!' Valdis said delightedly.

'Not for much longer on both counts,' Brann gasped, 'unless you ease up your grip.'

She ignored his words. 'And not much of the blood on you is your own, so that's a good sign, too.' She disengaged her various limbs and stood before him, frowning critically as her hands felt and prodded at him as if he was a potential purchase at a livestock market. 'Have you put on weight?'

'It's muscle,' he said, defensively, and more than a little put out.

She smiled with contentment. 'Of course it is. I would expect nothing less from my dragon warrior. But you did give me a fright when we saw all those men around you. If you could not place yourself against quite so unfavourable odds in future, it will give our relationship more chance of longevity.'

The floundering he was feeling in his head was even greater when words attempted to emerge. 'The odds...? I did not choose... I... Longevity...? Relationship...? I...' He gave up.

Mongoose's laughter burst over him from behind. 'I liked this girl when I saw her fight, and I like her now more even than then.'

Brann turned, finding himself pleased at the interruption.

Breta was nodding sagely. 'Indeed. You see? I did tell you there were places other than the land of your birth where woman behave properly, with sword in hand and blood on the blade rather than a needle in the fingers and a pot on the stove.'

'Oh, I can sew and cook as well,' Valdis said brightly. 'It's just that there's a lot of fighting goes on here. It is better to know how to swing a sword if you are likely to face one.'

Mongoose couldn't have looked happier. 'If this place was warmer, I might never leave.'

Valdis dug Brann in the ribs. 'So?' He looked at her in confusion. She nodded at the two women, and raised her eyebrows. 'Your friends are...?'

'Oh, yes, of course.' His composure was still far from intact, as he now remembered was all too often the case around the girl. 'This is Mongoose and Breta. Mongoose and Breta, this is Valdis, Hakon's sister.'

'And, to you, more than just Hakon's sister,' Mongoose said pointedly, with a smile filled with mischief glowing in her eyes. 'Which makes it useful, I think, that she does not share her height with her brother, for you might find it harder to fight in boots with soles as thick as your legs are long.'

Brann felt the only way he could stop blushing was to leave the conversation. 'Talking of Hakon, I really must speak to him. If you could excuse me?'

Before he had even turned, however, the voice of that very person boomed behind him.

'Little sister! You have met some of my friends already. Excellent!'

Valdis wheeled and punched him in the stomach, a blow that appeared to barely register with her brother. 'What is not excellent, is that you were not here watching over his safety! You run off to visit your family, and leave him here to face these savages.'

'Dead savages,' Hakon protested.

'Dead *now*.' Her glare had a far greater effect than her punch had achieved. '*Not* when they started trying to carve him up. At least *Gerens* stayed to protect him. *He* knows how to be a good friend.'

Brann felt obliged to speak. 'I can defend myself a bit, you know.'

She scowled, facing him. 'Don't you start. And that's not the point. It is my dolt of a brother not doing the one thing his sister asked of him. How am I to let you wander around the world if he is not to do that single simple thing? How, I ask you? Eh?'

Despite having her back to Hakon, she still managed to emphasis the final word with an unerring stamp onto the top of his foot. This time, she did elicit a yelp of pain.

'Oh my,' Mongoose said with joy. She had found a tree stump beside them and was seated, arms folded, clearly soaking up the entertainment. 'I actually did think I could not love this girl any more. If you don't appreciate her, Brann, just let me know.'

Valdis looked ready to resume her rant when a voice deeper than the sky rumbled across them.

'Children! Cease your squabbling. You are not yet too big for me to take you over my knee.'

Brann seriously doubted whether that day would ever actually come while the big man still drew breath.

'Especially you, boy,' he said to Hakon. 'Your sister cannot grow a beard, but why you should choose to keep your face as smooth as a girl's is beyond me. You have been absent for too long, I see.' Hakon's beardless face coloured and, for once, he had no answer. 'And you, boy,' he said to Brann. 'It is a good day when I can greet you again. I am pleased to see you have put on a little strength, if not any greater height.'

Brann smiled. 'It is good to see you too, Ulfar. And it was even better to see you a short time ago, when we were otherwise engaged. I am grateful for the haste you made to reach here.'

The eyes, a matching pair for Hakon's, creased in a smile. 'My two older children may tax a man's nerves, but they do have their redeeming factors. You have my son's eagerness and my daughter's incessant nagging to thank for the speed of our travel.'

'Still,' Brann said, 'you lead the lord's warriors and you decide where and when they go. You have my thanks.'

The wide shoulders shrugged. 'If you insist. Now, however, we have talked enough. We have bodies to burn. We have you to get back to a welcoming hearth for what time you have available. We have plans to lay to attend to camps that I learn these savages have established once more. My son has a beard to grow. And,' his baleful gaze turned to the man kneeling on the grassy bank, 'we have a prisoner to question.'

The hearth was indeed welcome. The ride to Ravensrest had been short and seemed even shorter with Valdis chattering brightly at his side. He was glad of the distraction for more than passing the time – a group of warriors had remained at the site of the fighting to dispose of the bodies, and Brann had found himself suppressing a shudder at the thought of his own awakening amongst corpses. It was just one of several memories that relentlessly invaded his dreams but, if they were to cling to him through time, he preferred they kept themselves to his times of sleep; he had enough to occupy him in his waking hours. And now fatigue was reeling him in, like a fisherman when a battle with a catch has reached the inevitable end moments. The hearth was welcome.

The party, missing only Konall and Hakon, was grouped around the fire, awaiting their time to brief the lord. On returning to the town's keep, Valdis had left him with a squeeze of the hand and a smile that brought back memories of the way she had entered his heart what seemed a lifetime ago, when they first met as he masqueraded, poorly, as Einarr's page. She took her leave to wash and attend to her kitchen duties with a song on her lips and a lightness in her demeanour as though battling with sword in hand was all part of her day's chores. He knew it wasn't – most of the routine soldiering was undertaken by the regular warriors – but he also knew that combat was second nature to every citizen of a Halvekan town. Their training and architecture were the two reasons that no one could remember a town in that land ever having been successfully attacked. He smiled, thinking of how unsurprising it was to see Mongoose's liking for this place. He glanced across at the girl, seeing her sleeping on a divan built for three, her head resting on Breta who was in the same position over a very much awake and very much alarmed Marlo. Brann's smile turned to a grin.

Cannick stood and moved to pour himself water. He caught Brann's eye. 'Want one?'

'Please.' The older man handed him a wooden beaker, and Brann waited until he had seated himself once more before carrying on. 'Did you notice Sigurr's ship in the harbour when we rode in?'

Cannick nodded. 'I'm guessing the Warlord's presence is why we are waiting while the lords talk. They have much to consider before we come into the equation.'

Grakk opened an eye. 'Indeed. Ruling is many-faceted, and every facet must be considered as a part of the whole.' He sat up straighter as voices could be heard approaching, one of them being particularly loud. 'And light is about to shine upon our facet, I believe.'

The door was flung open and their host, Lord Ragnarr, filled the frame, holding a flagon of what Brann presumed was mead. He had never seen him drink anything else. He stepped inside, allowing his older brother to enter. All awake leapt to their feet at the sight of the two men, and those asleep were roused by the sound.

'My lords!' Brann said. 'We must have missed your summons, or we would have attended you.'

'There was no summons,' Ragnarr said, frowning. 'Why would there be?'

Cannick smiled. 'It is customary in most lands for the lords to have those who would speak with them, come to them.'

Sigurr smiled, and the similarity to Einarr became clear in that one expression. 'In most lands, then, lords must waste a great deal of time when they need to speak to someone.' He spread his hands wide. 'Welcome back. From your previous service to us here, you will always find an open door and a smile whenever you visit, but on this occasion your information is also welcome. Please, be seated.'

He drew a chair over beside them, and Ragnarr perched upon a large table to one side, his face serious. 'If you would indulge me first, however, I would ask after my son.'

Brann drew a breath. 'He was wounded. He—'

The warlord nodded solemnly. 'Konall told me of his wound, and the treatment. It is not ideal, but better for a warrior to lose an extremity at the ankle than at the neck. I am more concerned with his mind.'

Cannick leant forward. 'If I may, my lord, I was the last to see him before we left.' Sigurr nodded for him to continue. 'He was pragmatic, positive even. His full determination was focused on recovery and an understanding of how he would approach as much of life as possible with as little change as possible. I would guess he would travel home as soon as he was able.'

Ragnarr's grunt was similar enough to that of a bull eyeing an intruder to its field to cause several of them to jump. He stood to stretch his back. 'Unless his sense of duty takes him elsewhere first, knowing my nephew.'

'It seems that *my* nephew possesses much of the same philosophy,' Sigurr observed. 'Konall is already packing to continue his journey when his companions leave once more.'

Brann brightened. 'Konall is not staying here?'

Ragnarr's eyebrows, as shaggy as his beard, shot up to hide in his hair. 'You want him to stay or want him to travel?'

'Travel!' said Brann, Marlo and Mongoose as one. The others nodded in the moment after.

The heavy wood of the table creaked in protest as Ragnarr sat back in astonishment. 'Well, blow me down. It seems my boy may have changed a little in his travels.'

'He has his moments,' Gerens said drily.

'And you want more of them?'

'I think we can endure them. It is what friends do.'

'Good enough for me.' Ragnarr's beard was split by a grin as huge as the rest of him. 'He's all yours. You do seem a good influence.' He shook his head and took a long draught from his flagon. His mumble rumbled into his drink. 'Friends. Well I never.'

Sigurr cleared his throat. 'If we could proceed?' He looked around the group. 'Maybe one of you would like to fill me in?'

Brann could feel the crestfallen look that must be written across his face. 'I fear that we may not have the full information we may have been able to acquire, had Ove's cousin not caught up with us so quickly. Philippe,' he indicated the young man, 'was skilfully eliciting it from Ove, but we do not know where the camps in your territory are located, their numbers or the date of the meeting of their Council that we must try to reach.'

Sigurr smiled. 'Fret not, youngster. Your friend Grakk was good enough to answer Konall's questions on the ride here, and the man Ove has been... encouraged to furnish us with the missing details. What we need from you is the story of everything that has happened since you sailed away from here.' He rested his elbows on the arms of the deep chair, and steepled his fingers in front of his mouth. 'Just don't take too long.'

'You have other business?' Brann resolved to ensure they covered everything as quickly as possible.

'No, you do. That Council meeting you are so keen to find at the Kiss of the Seas? The one with the date you were so eager to discover? If you sail tomorrow, you might just make it in time.'

257

It was well into the night, but not as late as it could have been thanks to the rehearsal the story had undergone with his father, when a young page boy led Brann to the small room allocated to him for the night. The memory of that time with his father took his thoughts across the sea, imagining the man's return to the family Brann had thought dead, with news of the son they had thought dead. Further nostalgia hit him as he saw he had been given the same chamber as he had occupied on his last stay here.

The page boy's eyes had been wide when he had been told who he was to guide through the corridors of the keep, had widened when Brann had consented to lift his sleeve and show him the dragon tattoo that was this people's highest mark of honour, and were still wide when he left Brann at the door to the room. Brann smiled at the small figure retreating down the passageway. The days of such innocence and wonder seemed so distant that he felt as though he should be an old man. The gods knew he felt it tonight. Candlelight from within leaked from the crack of the ajar door, and he pushed it open, lifting one leg to pull at his boot as he went and hopping in a crouched stagger to cling onto his balance.

He froze.

Valdis was bending over a small table, laying clothing upon it. She looked up. 'I see your adventures have not endowed you with any grace of movement.' She laughed, a sound of wonder. 'You can move, you know.' She patted the bed. 'Set yourself here, and I will help the young hero with his boots.'

Brann grimaced. 'Not much of a hero. Never mind stopping the man behind our troubles, we don't even know his identity.'

She sat by his side, resting her hand upon his arm. The movement of the mattress beneath him stirred his stomach, and the feel of her fingers stirred it more. Her voice was as calm as he was not. 'You are getting there, though, I believe. A ladder has rungs for a reason – you must climb them in turn to reach what is too high for a single jump.'

He stared at the floor. 'I know. Because of that, I had to let Loku go. I had him, Valdis, and he got away again. He was before my sword in these lands when I was here last, and in the woods in Cardallon shortly before we travelled here, and both times he escaped.'

She smiled softly. 'Look at it from his point of view: every time he thinks he has escaped you, still you hunt him. He even tried to have you killed several times, I hear, and you only came back stronger.'

'I came back broken.'

The way that her brows drew together melted his heart. 'Stronger. You, what is *you*,' she tapped his chest, 'is always in there. You may be added to, but that is a problem for others; it is you who I see when I look in your eyes now, and that is all I want to find.'

An awkwardness of guilt surged through him. He could not look at her in return. 'Valdis, there is something I have to tell you. There was… there…'

She frowned, puzzled. 'The princess?'

His eyes went wide as the shock thumped into him. 'You know?'

She smiled. 'You think brothers and sisters do not talk?'

'Hakon told you? And still you came here to see me?'

She laid her hand on his arm again. 'Brann, our people are warriors. We have been for more generations that even our elders can remember. We live from birth knowing how

259

fragile the thread of our life is, and how unpredictable the breaking of that thread can be. Those who have never faced a blade held by one with death in his eyes cannot comprehend the way we think, the way we feel, the way we cope, the way we survive. And I do not just mean the way we survive to retain life, but also the way our minds survive to retain ourselves.' She sighed. 'I have seen my share of fighting, but I have seen nothing compared with my father and brother, and I see the toll it can take at times. In the face of horror and tension, we grasp what comfort is there, what goodness can keep us sane, whatever form that takes. Some may not like that, but it is the way it is and seeking to wish it otherwise is like seeking to turn back the wind with a shout.' She smiled impishly. 'Anyway, it is not who you are with first that matters, but who you are with last. If you have no one to compare me with, how will you know I am the best of them all?'

Brann stared at her. 'I feel like I have given a complete confession without saying a single word.'

'Then,' she said, drawing him to her, 'the time for talking is over.'

Chapter 6

She stood, her aged body swaying before the hearth in his chambers; the sparks of a thousand colours dancing in the flames from the powder she had thrown among them. The heady aroma drifting into the room caused his head to swim, but she breathed it deep into her chest, head thrown back and arms hanging limply by her sides.

She snapped erect, face swinging towards him, eyes blank but still boring into his. Her voice, as hoarse and soft as ever, was made ethereal by a monotone, distant and detached, as though she spoke from another plane.

'The elements start to align.'

'What elements?'

'Duty, he has ever possessed. The will to live, he has ever possessed. Love, now, will drive him with greater force in each. Old love and new love. And more.'

'What more?'

'The factors must meet. The forces must collide.'

'And will they?'

'They move to converge.'

'How long? When?'

'It *will* happen when it happens. Fate regards time like man does not. Destiny knows no when, but only what.'

'But it will happen?'

'It must. Or all is lost.'

He paused. The one question above all he must have answered. The one question above all he was terrified to ask.

'He will prevail?'

'He alone can answer that. And only in his deeds.'

She collapsed.

He shuffled to her. Placed a cushion under her head. Drew a blanket gently over her.

It was ever thus.

He sat.

He stared into the flames.

He thought.

****

A dozen days' sailing, normally a pleasure to Brann, dragged to seem a dozen weeks. Coming after a ride of four days to the east coast through the domain of the neighbouring, and helpfully friendly, warlord, the time to their destination stretched interminably. The ship they had boarded – one of several retained by Einarr in his ally's port for eastern travel – was different from the bigger vessels Brann was accustomed to when travelling on the open seas. This was shallower and open, the more traditional longship of the Northern peoples, and better suited to travel that could involve the varied environments of sea and river, of ports and shallow beaches. It was not so suitable for the transport of horses, but in a city their own legs were all they required; should they have to ride from the city, enough of their funds remained to facilitate it.

They had sailed south-east to where the sea cut into the land like a giant estuary, so wide that they were three days into it before land could be seen to either side, and even then, at the limit of their vision, it narrowed no more in the leagues they passed. At its head, the great saltwater River Den – more really a narrow (if a width of a half-day's sail could be described as such) and gently winding section of the sea – led to the strip of land known as the Kiss of the Two Seas, where the similar, but shorter, River Der led from the opposite side of the Kiss to the Inner Sea, an offshoot to the north of the Sea of Life on whose encircling shores sat most of the lands of the ul-Taratac Empire. Upon the Kiss stood the city of Derden, the northernmost city of the Empire and their destination, and they could not arrive soon enough.

Brann stood, as he had done every hour of the past few days, at the prow. Half of his thoughts filled by a face in the candlelight of a small stone room, the other half willing into sight the city he knew lay ahead. Today he saw it, a smudge on the horizon ahead.

Grakk came to stand beside him as the favourable wind filled the square sail, the sleek hull slicing through the water and the ship feeling as though the city pulled them towards it ever faster. The sensation suited Brann's mood.

The pair watched as the smudge became shapes, and the shapes resolved themselves into buildings.

And what buildings they were.

The first they could discern were the dockside structures, sturdy and functional in any other port but here they arched and angled with a beauty crafted with an artist's eye, reaching into the water on curving piers of pale stone as if giant fingers offered a welcome grasp of safety to approaching vessels. As they neared further and saw deeper into the city, wonder after wonder competed for attention, slender spires soaring to needle-points or magnificent towers standing in grandeur of ornate solidity, arches and buttresses curving in breathtaking arcs or curving amongst each other in intricate complexity. And domes: everywhere mighty domes vied each to outdo all others in awesome size, or vivid colour, or inventive architecture. It was a fraction of the size of mighty Sagia, the beating heart of the Empire, but Derden was its superior in grace and beauty.

'The Mirror City,' breathed Grakk.

Brann frowned, but was unable to tear his eyes away from the scene to let his companion see his puzzlement. 'The what?'

He could hear the grin in Grakk's voice. 'It is two cities that are one.'

'So is Sagia. The City Above and the City Below.'

'This is different. This is the way they meant it to be.'

Brann groaned. 'Enough fragments of truth! Just tell me, please.'

'The impatience of youth,' Grakk lamented. 'Very well, it is thus: the Kiss can be ridden in one half of an hour and, on this side, sits the city you see, while on the opposite sits one identical, where our meeting, we are told, will be held. From the first building to the last, every time a structure is built in one, its likeness must be built in the other. One city, in two parts, each the mirror of the other.'

'Why?'

The edge of his vision caught Grakk's shrug. 'Because it is the way this place has been built.'

'But why start doing it?'

'The story is that in the dawn of time, before man took his first breath, twin gods set up home here, each building on the opposite coast of the Kiss. It was only when their palaces had been completed that each saw the other's and saw that the structures were as identical as the builders themselves. The palaces are long gone, if they were ever here at all, but the tradition has remained. After all this time, no one wants to be the one to break it, so everyone builds twice over.'

Brann shook his head in wonder. 'The beauty! It is easy to imagine the hands of gods in this.'

Grakk laughed. 'The beauty springs from the hands of men or, rather, their purses. The Der and the Den link the lands on the east side of the Sea of Life with the lands of the North, saving the journey west through the length of that sea and then north and around the Vine Duchies. Time and distance govern profit and loss, so a vast amount of trade passes through this city, with merchants keeping boats in both ports, and the Carter's Guild here, who control the passage of goods and people from one coast to the other, being among the richest families in the Empire. Where the passage of trade is beholden to a single location, then that is where wealth abounds, and wealth seems to carry an obligation of ostentation. Thus, the beauty of the buildings before you.'

Brann whistled. 'It is indeed remarkable, and all the more so for the fact that we only see but one half of it.' His eyes roved across the scene once more. 'And the domes?'

Grakk's hand fell on his shoulder as the man faced him. 'You can always tell the wealth of a city by the number of men who try to buy their way to heaven. This city has more temples than any other. Never mind the priests, there are clerics and acolytes here who live better than royal families in other parts of the Empire.'

Brann shook his head in disbelief. 'And Sagia is happy with such wealth in another city?'

Grakk smiled. 'The Empire is happy with the taxes from such wealth. Even just such as those the merchants declare.'

Sail down and oars dipping into flat water, they slid between the piers and towards a gap in a wall, its top twice the height of any ship's mast, that curved away, left and right. The opening was wide enough to allow the passage of four ships abreast so one longship glided through with ease, dwarfed not only by the walls but the space between them.

But scale was redefined by the sight that greeted them. The walls formed a great oval; the basin within the size of a small lake, with berths around its edge for more than a hundred ships.

'The mooring place of the elite.' Grakk's tone was impressed. 'Our Lord Einarr has influence indeed.'

Brann stood in silence, absorbing the scene surrounding him. Masts swayed around the edge of the vast walled basin, like a tranquil clearing in the centre of a private copse. Nowhere was there the raucous racket inherent to every dockside he had visited before; here, instead, busy purpose was lent an effortless air by calm efficiency.

'This is a place of wonder,' Brann breathed. 'It is like a heaven.'

Grakk turned to him and Brann found gravity in the eyes that looked into his. 'Did you learn nothing in Sagia, young Brann?'

Brann frowned. He stared back, beyond the rowing men,

into the open water, as if his sight sought the past. 'I learnt many things,' he said softly. 'Only some of them I care to remember.'

Grakk was patient. 'What built this place?'

'Trade.'

The head shook. 'Trade brought that which it is built upon.'

Brann nodded slowly. 'Wealth.'

Grakk smiled. 'So think of those you saw with wealth.'

'Power. Levels of power.'

'Correct. And wealth and power bring comfort and pleasure in some—'

Brann's words came slowly as his mind worked through Grakk's prompting. 'And in others, it breeds fear, suspicion, excess, arrogance.' He thought back to the fighting pits of the City Below, and to those baying in the crowd. 'And a desperation for something with more of an edge than pampered luxury.'

'So while this may appear idyllic...?'

Brann nodded. 'All is not what it seems.'

'*May* not be what it seems. Some handle well a life of wealth, some not so well. But when something may not be all it seems, what is it that we do, young Brann?'

Brann's gaze returned to the city. 'We stay wary.'

Grakk frowned slightly. 'We stay wary at *all* times. At times like this, we repel the deception that seeks to smother our wariness. Look not at the ornate veil, and not at the face behind, but into the eyes in that face. Therein lies the truth.'

Brann smiled softly. 'Still, I am eager to see at close hand such marvels of architecture.' As Grakk rolled his eyes in exasperation, Brann laughed. 'Fear not, my walking font of wisdom. I may like to look at a sword of exquisite beauty, but I will always choose the one best able to keep me alive and others dead.'

Grakk looked ahead, and sighed. 'There may be hope for you yet, youngster. And that hope is about to be tested.'

The hull bumped against a quay of perfectly dressed stone.

It was a quiet group who sat in two carriages on the journey from one city to the other, and an even quieter one that sat in a noisy tavern a short while after reaching the far city, which astonishingly did exactly mirror the first. Or did the first mirror this one? Or did they mirror each other? Brann was finding it hard to think. The faces around confirmed to him that the others had been as overwhelmed as he by the soaring structures of vivid colour or blinding white; the great squares of monuments and fountains; the wide streets of smooth blocks and teeming flowerbeds; the exotic spices and incense and perfumes that wafted from buildings and stalls and passers-by alike, and the people, the breathing embodiment of the affluence of the city, clothed in fashions and gems designed to display value, and carrying themselves with the assurance brought by opulence and authority as they leisurely moved or were carried or lounged in outdoor eateries where being seen seemed more important than consumption.

Mongoose set down her drink, the silver tankard more suited to a great lord's hall than a run-of-the-mill inn. 'It's too much. I hope we achieve our aim and can move on soon, for I am not sure how long I can endure this.'

Brann understood; the relentless assault of wealth on every sense almost overpowered him. 'An abundance of what is good makes it commonplace to those accustomed to it and overwhelming to those unfamiliar.'

Philippe smiled. 'I must say, dear boy, I wouldn't mind finding out whether I could become comfortable in such finery.'

Hakon dropped the clean bone of a fowl he had never before heard of onto his platter and wiped a sleeve across his face to remove the grease from his stubble. 'I could tolerate such food, also.'

Sophaya cleared her throat. 'It has other advantages also.' She smiled innocently at the questioning looks. 'All I will say is that our coffers have benefited remarkably from the walk from the quayside. In fact, a particularly smug gentleman would revise his attitude were he to realise he has more than paid for this meal that Hakon is enjoying so much.'

Brann waited for Hakon's guffaw to subside before continuing. 'Not one of you is under any obligation.' He met all of their eyes earnestly. 'I mean it. I am honoured that you choose to travel with me, but choice it is: you need never feel obligated to stay on this course should you wish otherwise.'

Hakon burped. 'And miss your terrible jokes? I didn't say the food was that good.' He reached forward and tore a leg from one of the several roasted and glazed birds on the table before him. 'In the meantime, however...'

Brann looked at Mongoose. 'In any case, you should get your wish. We have one day's grace before the Council meeting. Whether we meet with success or otherwise, the need to stay in this place will be no more.'

Cannick took a long drink. 'So, do we know what we are doing yet?'

Brann shook his head. 'All we know is that the venue is a temple, and where to find it. Grakk and I will scout it out in the morning. Then we can all discuss our course of action.' Laughter burst from all. 'What?'

Breta clapped him on the shoulder, almost knocking him face-first into his food. 'Even those of us who have not travelled with you for so long are well aware that the "we can all discuss" bit will comprise you explaining our tasks and us all nodding sagely in agreement.'

Brann saw agreement in each face. 'Oh, right. Er, thanks.'

The conversation turned, mainly prompted by Marlo and Hakon's bright chatter, to lighter matters, but Brann's mood refused to settle. He ate a little more, then forced cheer into his voice to excuse himself to bed before the long day ahead on the morrow. Their chambers lay two floors above in the five-storey building, and his eyes fixed themselves on the top of the next step on each of the first of the four flights of stairs he had to climb to get there, as his thoughts were pulled far ahead of what might occur over the following two days.

One floor up, he froze. A pair of boots filling his sight was all the knowledge he had of a man before him. He cursed, reaching for the knife on his forearm. Before he could even lift his head, a sword-tip flicked up to rest beneath his chin, the metal cold against his skin and the sharp point tickling at this throat. The blade pressed up, lifting his head.

Konall stood before him, eyebrows raised and head cocked to one side in silent question. His voice was cold. 'You were just given an indication of a small part of the esteem your companions hold for you, and you count it so little that you would let your life be taken with such ease.' In one smooth motion, his sword was sheathed. 'We need you to think, but not to let your mind close your eyes. You have more to offer than your ideas.' His arm extended and a hand rested on his shoulder. 'Look, I was trained from birth to fight, but still I should not be able to last a heartbeat against you. Yet I could have opened your throat before you even knew I was there, despite standing in plain view in your path.'

Brann shook his head. 'I am sorry, Konall. I just cannot help thinking of Loku.'

Konall was puzzled. 'Why? He is not a problem. After we have found our way to the top of this conspiracy, we will need a way to occupy our time. We will find him.'

'It is not that.' He took a breath, gathering the thoughts that had been swirling and building. 'It is the thought that when we first exposed Loku, then discovered his influence with the Emperor, we were stunned at the extent of his power, at what we thought he planned. But all we have learnt since is that he was just a small part of it; like a junior officer in one of the Empire's millens and not the general we thought. He is as far from the top of this conspiracy, as you put it, as a fish is from the top of a mountain. Every further rung on the ladder that we discover proves this more.' He gripped Konall's arm and his eyes locked on those of the taller boy. 'So all I can think is: just exactly how big is all of this?'

Konall stared at him, absorbing the words, then shrugged. 'All the more reason to keep finding the rungs on the ladder, until we move from the fish to the top of the mountain.' He frowned. 'Although I understand your reasoning, the fact that you cannot climb a mountain using a ladder, and that a fish would die long before it had cleared the foothills, shows that you are overthinking all of this. Too many thoughts become like a crowd in panic, running in all directions and into each other. See not the vastness of what we face, but only the next few steps. Before you know it, your fish will be at the top of the mountain.'

Brann remembered an old general in the streets of Sagia. 'I met a man once that you would like.' He sighed. 'Sometimes it is hard, though, to stop thinking about the vastness of what we face.'

Konall nodded with serious consideration. 'Then we turn to my other solution.' He produced a flagon from inside his tunic. 'The wine they serve in these southern lands is a feeble apology for a drink. Fortunately, in a city where the trade routes of a hundred countries meet, it is possible to acquire a particularly decent mead. At times like this, you need to clear the shit from your head. And the best way to do that is to retire to your room and have a friendly drink.'

Brann smiled and hurried to catch up as Konall turned without waiting for him and started up the next flight of stairs. 'Friendly?'

Konall grunted. 'I said the drink was friendly, not the company. Don't get overexcited. There is a limit to how much you deserve.'

Brann smiled and clapped the back in front of him. 'I already receive more than I thought I deserve.'

'Oh, shut up,' said Konall.

The morning still held a chill as Brann and Grakk approached the location for the Council meeting that Ragnarr's men had drawn from Ove. Brann was glad of the sharpness in the air, his head still pounding from Konall's prescribed treatment.

Grakk glanced sideways, smiling. 'Konall successfully cleared the shit from your head, then.'

'He told you what he said to me?'

'No, you told me. Or at least, you garbled that small part of it to me shortly before you passed out. The boy had it right, though. Whatever else he told you, that was what most needed to be said.' He stopped and fished a small vial from a pocket and unstoppered it. 'Here, sniff this. Deeply.'

In the instant Brann did so, his eyes widened and filled with tears and he coughed violently. But his head also cleared.

Grakk's grin was gleeful. 'It is not as effective as a whole-body cure as the Lady Tyrala's drinking concoction, but it will let you observe with clarity and assimilate what you see.'

They entered a wide square, empty of any of the array of features that assaulted the eyes in many of the other open spaces they had passed on the way. At the far side stood a great cube of a temple, its massive black dome all the more impressive for the lack of distraction before it. It was the symbol above the tall double doors that drew Grakk's attention, however.

He whistled slowly. 'Of course. An ideal meeting place for them.' Brann looked at him in question, and received a wry smile in return. 'The temple of the order of Akat-Mul.'

Brann frowned, wiping excess tears from his eyes. 'He who guides and guards souls on the path to the afterlife?'

'He also who seeks to preserve life. The priests of this order are the foremost adepts in the study of healing, and the most widespread teachers of those who would wish to practise the craft.'

'And yet they deal in death?'

'Not in the causing of it, but in attending to the aftermath.'

'I had heard that they also hasten it on occasion.'

Grakk smiled. 'Not so. You have heard the tales of sailors

and warriors who know a little about a lot and address the deficit with imagination born of a suspicious fear of the unknown and an unquenchable taste for the salacious. There are men enough of the sort to be willing to take a coin to take a life without priests having to get involved. And those men and their ilk keep these priests busy enough in their existing activities without adding new duties.' He looked at Brann. 'Whatever your beliefs may be on higher powers and a life beyond our comprehension, there is no doubt that the attachment of gods to aspects of our lives not only creates a worship of those gods, but a devotion to what they represent. The greatest minds known to history, and the greatest advances in knowledge, have been within the temples dedicated to healing, cultivation, commerce, even engineering, to name only a few.' He nodded at the temple before them. 'Everything has its successes and its irredeemable situations, but by nature of it dealing exclusively with the sick and injured, this order has had to address death as the result of the inevitable irredemption of a proportion of cases. They have therefore also become skilled in the passing of the body after the passing of the spirit.'

Brann understood. 'So that is why this Council of Masters would choose to meet here? Because of the association with death?'

Grakk's head shook. 'This is an order of discretion and tact, and so this is an order of mutes. Every priest below the more senior levels takes a vow of silence – even their teaching is conducted through demonstration and display. Someone senior within this temple, perhaps the most senior, will be in league with the Council to enable this meeting to be held in this place, even if its true nature is concealed, but what they seek here above all is the silence of those around them.' He started forward. 'Come, see for yourself.'

Brann felt the wariness that had been absent when Konall had surprised him the night before return with force. 'We are just going to walk in?'

'Of course,' Grakk said brightly. 'Do you think they build these great edifices and not want anyone to come in and witness their magnificence? All are open to the devout to enter and pray at any time, which is fairly useful to the less-than-devout snoopers as well.'

He moved off at a brisk walk, and Brann had to trot to catch him. He grinned as he tapped the tribesman's arm. 'Wait a moment. Did you say *irredemption*? Is that even a word?'

Grakk didn't miss a step. 'Did you understand what I meant?'

'Yes.'

'Then it is a word now.'

They reached the doors, one of which – despite being solid wood and three times the height of either of them – swung open silently and with ease at Grakk's touch. They slipped inside and Brann found himself squinting as he was assaulted by colour and light. Noise, too, abounded: chimes set in high windows and catching the slightest breeze; voices muttering in fervent prayer, chattering in animated conversation or lifting in song, and even the strains of an instrument or two in distant corners or alcoves.

His astonishment must have been clear, for Grakk grinned. 'You expected a pious hush? Remember, the Order of Akat-Mul is dedicated to life, and their dealings with death are a consequence rather than their prime concern. Sure, some come here to end their lives, but while that is not unknown it is far from frequent; and while the priests will attend to the aftermath, they will always attempt to prevent it should they discover such intent.' He gestured around. 'The priests may be silent to maintain constant thought, awareness and consideration, but life is colour and noise, and the absence of each is a characteristic of the absence of life. So they encourage both. This temple is a celebration of life, and its perpetuation.'

It was true. More startling even than the noise was what greeted his eyes. They had entered directly into a huge circular chamber, the walls and floor faced with smooth tiles reminiscent of the chambers of healers or cooks he had seen in Sagia – easily cleaned, and kept clean. Huge chandeliers, each of at least a score of large lamps, hung in a wide spiral that drew the eye all the way to the apex of the dome a dizzying height above, their light reflecting on the tiles, on images and scenes and patterns and words, all picked out in myriad colours after colours after colours. Brann turned slowly, craning his neck, and staggered slightly.

He gasped. 'All you see is that there is more yet to see than has been seen. And so your eyes cannot stop.'

Grakk caught his arm. 'Look at your feet, regain your senses. It is much to absorb.' He tilted Brann's head back down. 'Then, once your world has stopped spinning, look at the people, and keep your head on the level. And focus – we have a job to do.'

The reminder of their purpose sobered Brann's thoughts. He scanned the area, and the plenitude of activity started to resolve itself into groups and individuals. Some prayed quietly, seated on pews that formed concentric rings around an effigy of the god, tall as a two-storey building and of slender grace, with one hand holding herb and threaded needle to symbolise remedy and the other resting on the head of a child to indicate care, all in the shining white of marble in striking contrast to the otherwise universal variety of vivid colour. Others stood in small clusters, singing bright songs of praise to, and appreciation of, life. Some small groups gathered to talk and laugh; Brann was close enough to one such group to be able to hear those involved swapping jests with delight.

Grakk smiled as he saw where he looked. 'The followers of this god believe that humour is the essence of a healthy outlook on life.'

Brann watched the rosy face of a silent priest beam and nod as he listened to the side of the group. 'There is a lot to be said for that.'

Around the perimeter, seats and divans allowed minor diagnoses and treatments to be carried out, while the open curtains on some of the alcoves behind revealed stone benches for more serious surgery. As he watched, four porters walked quickly and quietly to an alcove, the stretcher between them bearing a man emitting blood and groans in equal measure; an acolyte moved efficiently behind, cleaning spilt blood from the tiles in their wake. Above – Brann was more careful with his gaze as he lifted his eyes again – balconies in ring after ring rose high towards the great domed ceiling, the lower levels visible enough to show figures in the order's rainbow-hued robes, some with hoods up and some down, as they moved between openings in the wall behind, their intent unknown but exuding an air of consuming and urgent purpose.

Brann finally looked at Grakk. 'It is certainly a busy place.'

'The body is a complex entity. There is always something that can go wrong... or be made to do so.'

He nodded. 'That's the truth.' He looked about. 'So what

are we looking for? I've seen routes and escape routes; I've seen tight areas where we could be cornered and tight areas where we could form a defence; I've seen open areas where we have room to fight and open areas where we could be surrounded and overwhelmed. What else is there?'

Grakk shook his head. 'Always the fighting mind. You will have seen all that in the first moments after you regained your balance. But since you know the place, now look at the people. Look properly, with your mind as well as your eyes.'

Brann started to stare around but Grakk caught at his arm and steered him to the side of the hall, behind a lustily singing group and before an empty alcove. The tribesman's penetrating eyes rolled in mock dismay. 'You could not be more obvious if I gave you my oculens to look at them.' He sighed. 'I knew I should have brought Sophaya. By now, she would have been able to describe any given person and be more wealthy to the tune of at least a couple of purses and several rings.' His head wagged in sorrow. 'But I have you, so I must make the best of this sorry situation.' He grasped Brann's shoulders from behind and pointed him to face past the group.

'Pretend you are singing, and look past them to see the people.' The fingers gripped tighter. '*Pretend* – just mouth words. I have heard you sing. We are trying to remain unobtrusive.'

Feeling self-conscious, Brann worked his mouth, letting his eyes scan slowly across the crowded area before him. It was as he had seen, the activities he had witnessed, the people... He frowned. His eyes tracked back: something had seemed wrong, different. He tried to catch what it might have been.

278

That was it. A man stood, unobtrusively minding his own business. And that was exactly it. He was not singing, or jesting. He was not praying, or marvelling at the wonder of the temple. He was not tending to the sick, or being sick. He was unobtrusive. He was nondescript. He was forgettable. And he was determinedly so.

Grakk saw the direction of his gaze. 'Exactly,' he said softly. 'He also looks. He also examines. And, unlike you until this point, he looks at people.'

'The Council?'

Grakk nodded slightly. 'Most likely. Were he a religious newcomer or one here to witness the wonders of this city, he would look up and around, much as you did. A thief would have watched the people, but would already be in action – they do not loiter too long in one place. An official would be busy and, moreover, in a priest's robes. He who scans faces so intently has a distinct purpose, and as we know of the meeting tomorrow, we would surmise, with a fair chance of success, that he is a scout, if you will. He checks for any signs of danger ahead of the arrival of his superiors, for anyone in the least suspicious, for anything out of the ordinary.'

'Just as well you pulled me over here, then,' Brann said.

Grakk's eyes pierced him. 'I do have my moments of sense, you know.'

Brann smiled. 'So what now?'

'Now we leave. As surreptitiously as possible. And, to that end, separately, I would suggest.'

Brann nodded. The swish of a curtain turned his attention to an alcove close to his left. His nerves on alert, he jumped slightly, but an elderly lady emerged with a heavy limp. It was too good an opportunity to pass up.

He moved to her side, smiling what he hoped was disarmingly and offering his arm. She returned the smile and added her thanks, and together they moved slowly towards the entrance, chatting brightly. Brann forced his eyes to remain with her, straining against the temptation to flick a glance at the watching man.

They reached the tall doors, the sunlight dazzling as they stepped past an entering group. Brann shook his head slightly as it struck him that it was almost quieter outside the temple, despite the bustle of the street, than it was within. At the sight of the lady, four bearers moved smoothly to the foot of the steps with a palanquin. She turned to Brann, reaching within her robe to produce a purse of pearl-studded silk. 'My mother always said that manners and kindness should be rewarded above all else. I agree with her, and you have shown me both, young man.'

Brann flushed and drew away. 'I sought no profit, my lady.'

She smiled gently. 'Not in monetary terms, perhaps, but I am the fourth generation of my family to breathe the air of this city, and the lungs of this city gasp for trade and commerce. Everyone in this place seeks profit.' She winked, startling him. 'The years may have slowed my body and,' she glanced at her ankle, 'made brittle twigs of once strong bones, but those same years have also shown me enough of life to teach me to read people as well as ledgers. You sought to profit from this in your own way, and you have done so. But so have I, in gaining the arm of a handsome young man.'

Brann smiled. 'You seek to persuade me with flattery?'

Her laugh was as soft as her touch as she stroked a finger down his cheek. 'I seek with flattery merely to demonstrate that I also gained from this experience. You think an old lady enjoys such a pleasant experience every day?' He could feel himself blush, and her laugh strengthened to a chuckle as her fingers reached carefully into the purse. Her face remained bright as she continued, but her tone grew darker. 'Should you wish to continue to avoid attracting certain eyes, you should take this coin. I can see kindness in you, and for this I seek to repay you with counsel, but even the caring souls in this city would not consider holding a door for another without recompense, so you would be advised to take this coin.'

He smiled and lifted it from her palm. 'Thank you.'

She turned and a servant came to take her hand, while another opened a small door in the side of the palanquin, but she turned back as she reached it. 'I ask only one more favour in return, if my coin and my advice are sufficient to purchase this extra service.' He raised his eyebrows in question. 'Do not harm this temple, nor those who serve its ethos, I entreat you. Within those walls are those who stray from the self-aggrandisement that suffuses this city. Its existence is an essential respite for those of us who grow weary of a life of verbal skirmishes.'

Brann inclined his head. 'I assure you, my lady, I intend no harm to any of those who hold dear its values.'

'I believe you, and I thank you.' She waved a hand airily. 'But much as I may have wished to be three-quarters of a lifetime ago and more, I am not your lady. I am Calantha, of the House Psomas. Should you ever need succour in either of the twin cities, remember that name.' She winked again. 'I shall not ask yours, as I prefer not to be lied to, particularly by those I find myself liking.'

A raised finger raised the palanquin, and she stared calmly

ahead as she was borne into the throng beginning to fill the square before the temple.

Grakk walked past him, his voice a murmur. 'Meet at the far side.'

Brann walked in what he hoped was a casual amble from the steps and took a meandering path across the square. He was almost across when Grakk appeared at his elbow.

'Becoming quite the ladies' man, aren't we?'

Brann bristled. 'She was a harmless old lady. And very nice with it.'

'Not one person who achieves any measure of success in this city can be classed as "harmless", young Brann.'

Brann grunted. 'That's what she said.'

Grakk grinned. 'Then that was indeed nice of her.' His voice became firm. 'But we have plans to lay, so let us walk as we talk to allow you, on our return, to explain tasks and have your companions nod sagely in agreement.'

Brann laughed. 'We had better not waste time, then.'

By their arrival at the inn, all aspects but one had been addressed.

Grakk shook his head in exasperation. 'How to get close? It is such a well-chosen location, inaccessible without discovery and easily defended by a few.'

Brann caught his arm in excitement. 'Perhaps too well chosen. We can use the characteristics of that location against them. Sometimes to be obvious is a better disguise when subtle would be expected.' Grakk's look urged him to waste no time in explaining. 'It is something you said in the temple: an official would be in a priest's robes.'

Shortly before sundown, four priests of Akat-Mul sat huddled in their smallclothes in a basement storeroom, bound, gagged and terrified despite Hakon's earnest reassurances of their safety.

Brann pulled on a priest's many-hued robe and watched as Grakk, Gerens and Sophaya did the same. That this religion venerated life in all its forms placed it amongst those that admitted women to the clergy – in fact, although the god himself was male, the reverence for maternity was so great that the highest position in the clergy was always filled by a priestess – so Brann had been able to include Sophaya amongst the three who would accompany him; the three best suited to dealing with a tight situation, should one occur.

Hakon nodded to them and slipped through the door to return to the main public area where he would join Konall, Breta, Mongoose and Philippe in scattered positions and various activities but all ready to move instantly to the source of any outbreak of violence that they heard. Brann wasn't sure how useful Philippe might be should fighting break out, but the young man had been so keen to be involved that he had allowed it and, in the meantime, his acting ability and speed of calm thought in tense situations might be useful should any of the other pretend devotees encounter a challenge to their cover.

Outside, a slumbering drunkard in the shape of Cannick sat slumped against a wall at one side of the square, while at the side across from him sat Marlo, returning to his days as a street urchin to sit begging from the evening passers-by; no one would leave through the main entrance without being seen by one or both. During the afternoon, Brann had sent Marlo and Sophaya to circle the building and they had reported no apparent entrances other than the huge main doors. There could, of course, be doorways hidden from sight, but with his limited resources Brann was forced to prioritise support within the building where any action was most likely to occur.

The old soldier in Cannick was amused by Brann's irritation at the restriction on his plans. 'Any officer, from the highest general to the lowliest subaltern, can find a use for more swords and will moan at their lack,' he had pointed out. 'Plans are all about priorities.'

'And about what to do when things don't pan out as expected,' Brann had replied.

The broad face had split into a loud bark of a laugh. 'As is always the case, young Brann, as is *always* the case.'

Brann thought back to the exchange as he curbed his impatience and gave Hakon a minute or so to be well clear of them before easing open the door. The time when plans may have to be adapted – discarded, even – ran from the first moment to the last, and his stomach churned at the thought. He almost wished for the fighting calm that would settle over him when the self that he had grown to suppress as naturally as breathing was released by the threat of violence. *Almost* wished. Violence was not part of the plan.

His hand moved to the sword at his side, tied to his thigh to prevent it from shifting and revealing its presence under his priest's robe. Violence had a tendency to *make* itself part of the plan.

They moved, unmet, through the dim corridor. On close inspection, the thick dust on the floor would reveal their passing, but what had been more important to them was the indication it had given of how seldom the passage was used. The bound priests would hopefully remain undiscovered until an anonymous message alerted their colleagues, at dawn the next day, if all went to plan.

Brann forced his thoughts back to the present. To dwell on the unexpected would make him too distracted to deal with it should it occur. They climbed the short spiral staircase that let them emerge in the main hall area. Immediately, Philippe happened to stumble upon them, clutching his ribs and limping.

'May I prevail upon your good selves to aid me in my need,' he implored.

Grakk nodded benignly and took him by the arm, leading him to the nearest empty alcove. Sophaya drew the curtain as soon as they were all inside, but left the slightest gap to allow her to peer outwards.

Brann smiled. 'You don't feel that you overacted at all there, Philippe? The limp was a touch dramatic.'

Sophaya snorted. 'I think it was just right. Have you seen the way men suffer?'

Grakk regarded her disapprovingly. 'Now, young lady, that is perhaps an exaggeration. Should we observe how all women cry and scream at the sight of combat, when we have the evidence to the contrary before us provided by our friends Breta, Mongoose and even your good self?'

Sophaya's large eyes rolled. 'It was only a...' she began, but stopped, seeing the lack of comprehension in Grakk's face, and remembering Grakk's logical approach to humour – an approach with extremely narrow boundaries. 'Never mind.' Her smile was winning. 'My apologies, dear Grakk.'

He beamed and nodded.

The cold burning of Gerens's eyes turned to Brann. 'What now?'

'Now we wait.'

The wild hair shook like black flames as Gerens shook his head in disapproval. Gerens disapproved of many things, but waiting was high on that list. He wouldn't pace; he wouldn't fidget; he would sit still, statue-like, and stare. But the stare conveyed more impatience than any movement. Brann hated waiting also – everyone did – but Gerens made him seem like a meditating monk.

Time dragged by, slowed further by tension. Brann moved behind Sophaya, peering through the crack in the curtain. The sky through the high windows was noticeably darker, and the throng in the main hall had thinned. The temple would grow gradually quieter, although it never closed: neither illness, injury nor death had respect for human routine and, while the worship of the devoted tended to be a daytime activity, healers were required to be on hand in the darkness as much as the light – often more so, thanks to the work of miscreants in the city's alleys and shadows.

'They won't check this alcove?' Sophaya's voice in the silence, despite its murmur, made him jump.

Grakk answered. 'The closed curtain is sacrosanct. The work of the priests here is respected beyond exceptions.'

She wasn't totally satisfied. 'Even if it seems to be taking a while, and some helpful healer wants to offer help?'

The bald head was shaken. 'They are consummate professionals. Should they need assistance, they will seek it. So, conversely, should they not ask for help, they will be left in peace to concentrate as necessary.'

Philippe snored slightly. Brann's head jerked round, seeing the young man stretched out on a waist-high leather bench, a white blanket crumpled beneath him. 'Oh, gods, I had forgotten he was there. How can he sleep?'

Gerens shrugged. 'He seems to inhabit a role like we would a garment. He makes his head believe he is poorly, and his body follows.' He grunted. 'At this time, it seems a desirable lesson to learn.'

They fell back into silence. Philippe's gentle snoring was infectious, and Brann felt his eyes grow heavy. He yawned.

Sophaya stiffened as a shadow passed the space at the edge of the curtain. 'Mongoose,' she breathed to the faces bright with tension.

There was the sound of something small dropped to the tiled floor. A small stone was kicked under the curtain. Then another. And another. *Three suspected as being Masters had arrived.* Soft footsteps scuffed as Mongoose moved away.

'I see them,' Sophaya hissed.

His heart quickening, Brann moved to join her at the curtain, but Grakk waved him back. 'Allow no chance for suspicion to be aroused. It is in the nature of the young thief to remain unnoticed; your skills lie in other areas.'

They all looked at Sophaya. 'Each is cloaked and hooded,' she whispered. 'Two men, one woman.'

Philippe surprised them by sitting up. 'How can you tell, if they are hooded?'

Gerens frowned. 'Because she is magnificent, obviously.'

'And also,' Grakk said, 'because her livelihood depends on discerning such things.'

Brann waved them to silence. 'Where do they go?'

'I will tell you when they go somewhere. Calm yourself, they are walking slowly across the hall.' She adjusted her angle slightly, like a reed swaying in the breeze. 'Ah, good. A doorway, not the one we came from, but the next one along. They entered there.' She turned to look at Brann. 'Do we follow or wait?'

Brann smiled, looking at Gerens. 'We have waited enough.' Gerens brightened and shot to his feet. 'Why hide any longer, now that we know where to head? We are four priests, after all. Why would priests not walk about their temple?' He fixed his robe and pulled up his hood. 'You ready, Philippe?'

A glance at the young man told him that his question had been unnecessary. Philippe was already back in character. He had lost his limp and walked straighter, but in the tentative fashion of one still nervous that the pain would not worsen again in an instant. He reached for the curtain.

'Wait.' Grakk stepped in front of Philippe and passed him a handful of small coins. 'There are offering buckets placed strategically around the hall area. Priests are always more amenable to your presence if you make a donation in gratitude for your treatment, and the noise of several small coins attracts more attention than the sound of one. Should you then find a seat to pray, you are unlikely to be disturbed, even should you stay most of the night. Discouraging those who pay is not good for business.' He looked around the others. 'And remember, my priests: we do not talk. At all. You may not think you can be heard, but your body will give it away. The loquacious face each other in a different manner to the mute.'

Philippe nodded to Brann, and this time he did open the curtain, smoothly and without fuss. The others had their hoods raised also, and they left without a backwards glance at Philippe. The moment the alcove was empty, an acolyte entered and wiped the leather bench, replacing the blanket and taking the used one in a sack. Brann sighed slightly in relief that their patient had made use of it.

They moved with purpose to the arched opening and found stairs spiralling upwards, similar to those that had led to the basement but wider, able to let users pass easily in both directions. The first level they reached was too busy for Brann to think it could host a secret meeting, as was the second, but the third was quiet enough to sow doubt as to whether they should continue their climb. They moved onto the balcony to gather their thoughts; a treatment alcove with the curtain open to reveal it to be vacant beckoned them but, before they could move into it, Brann was jerked as Gerens gave his robe a surreptitious tug. Brann followed the boy's stare, and saw a single hooded figure move unhurriedly across the floor beneath them.

Too unhurriedly, unnaturally so.

The person headed for the wall directly beneath them, and did not reappear. Either they had entered a treatment alcove without a priest in attendance, which would be pointless for someone with a valid reason to be in the temple, or they would be climbing the stairs.

He glanced around. No one else walked this balcony at the moment. He stood with his back to the hall below and risked a whisper. 'Get ready to follow, whether this one comes out on the balcony or continues up the stairs.'

Sophaya shook her head slightly. Her head was down, her face lost in her deep hood, but they heard her whisper. 'Too obvious. Back down the stairs slightly, then climb. Slowly. Old trick: let the person pass you, then they will not be suspicious that you follow for they know you are behind them.'

It made too much sense for any reply, and they moved quickly to do as she had said. Footsteps hurried from below, and before long approached behind. In single file they moved as one to the side, their left shoulders brushing the wall and their heads down as if the figure passing them was of no importance. The dark cloak, clutched tight at the front by a man's calloused hand to prevent it from tripping him on the stairs, caught the edge of Brann's vision and then it was gone, the occupant of the cloak paying them as little attention as they had appeared to pay him.

The sound of boots on steps continued past the floor they had stopped on, and they quickened their pace. Each time they passed a floor, they glanced out, but though they saw movement on many, all were of the holy order and none in the black cloak that was the one colour that never clothed a cleric of Akat-Mul.

Brann glanced at Grakk, and saw the sharp eyes return his look. The eyes flicked up and Brann nodded. It looked like they were headed as high as the levels reached. It made sense: a highly secret meeting would tend to be held as distant from the activity of normal life as possible.

They came to the top of the stairway abruptly, finding themselves in a windowless corridor that curved with the shape of the dome. Six priests in robes identical to those of Brann's companions stood in file before a shut door, still as statues, and hoods rendering them creatures without identity.

Footsteps climbed behind them, the soft steps of priests, not the boots of those heading for the meeting, or so his logic hoped. It was a chance – slim, but a chance nonetheless. He inclined his head and the others followed him back down. Almost immediately, they came across six figures in the ubiquitous clerical robes. Brann, eyes down and hood up, paid them no heed as he made to pass them and received the same lack of interest in return. As he reached the last in the line, however, he turned. His knife, reversed to strike with the pommel, knocked two of the priests unconscious before his companions moved with a warrior's instinctive reaction to deal similarly with the other four.

ence brought encouragement that the priests were there only as subservient minions, too lowly to warrant even a passing glance. Brann let out a quiet sigh at the thought that this meeting was so deep within the organisation's walls of secrecy that it lent those attending a sense of safety. A false sense, fortunately.

The priests in front moved along the wall and slipped into an alcove each, and Brann followed suit as his turn arrived. It was not high enough for even him to stand upright, but he discovered a small stone stool carved as part of the architecture and perched himself upon it. It was set far enough back that he could see behind the pillars left and right, and was relieved to see that he sat the same as the legitimate priests to his right and his fellow imposters to his left.

He stared at the backs of the cloaked figures, his hand almost shaking with the force of his grip on his sword hilt. But he knew, for it was he who had impressed it on the others, that the most valuable prize tonight would be information, not assassination. Everything they had done in the past months had led them to almost the highest echelon of this mysterious and loathsome organisation – but almost the highest, not *the* highest. They had come so close to the one real goal they had. To indulge themselves in the slaughter of a great evil and lose the opportunity of reaching the greater evil was a thought that filled him with a shuddering horror. But if they could gain enough information and even seize the Messenger with the Masters still within the reach of a sword...

The door at the opposite end of the room opened and three men were led in by the same nondescript man that Brann and Grakk had spotted scouting out the temple earlier that day. He bowed to the Masters and indicated to the trio, their faces uniformly taut with tension, that they should stand with their backs to the ledge. Each of them clearly noticed the dizzying drop so close behind them, with one man visibly paling at the sight before he turned to face the Masters. The line of black cloaks stood stock still for long moments, the silence in the room growing more heavy with each pounding heartbeat.

One Master near the centre of the line took one pace forward. A harsh voice grated from his hood. 'You seek to serve. You seek to rise from the mass. You seek to lead men under our guidance.'

The three nodded, nerves jerking their movements.

'Some seek to harm us. Some seek to betray us. Some seek to infiltrate us.'

Brann's breath stopped in his throat at the last, but the focus remained on the three men who shook their heads in desperately emphatic unison.

'The word of man is fickle. The word of man is fragile. The word of man is meaningless.' He let the words hang, then looked at the tall priestess. 'The spirit of a god is true. The spirit of the god of life and death perceives the soul. The spirit of this god is among us.' He nodded to the priestess.

She stepped to a small table to the side of the room and, from a delicate stand, fetched a small golden ball, its upper side pierced by small holes that let escape a dense white smoke. She let it swing gently on a golden chain, the movement letting a cloyingly sweet and yet acrid smell drift as far as Brann's nose. His eyes watered slightly, but curiously there was no urge to cough – the smoke seemed to settle on the throat, leaving a taste, rather than irritate it.

The nondescript man indicated to the three men to face the ledge. 'On it,' he said bluntly. 'Kneeling.'

Each of the three looked at him as if he were mad, but the man merely stared at them. One shrugged and gingerly climbed onto the stone sill, and the others followed. One, he who was at the left of the three, swayed and lurched at the sight of the drop so close, and grabbed at the inside of the sill to catch himself. The others controlled themselves more, but they too rested their hands on the stone.

The blunt voice spoke again. 'Kneel up.' The man who had swayed looked at him in horror, but again was met with only a stare of unblinking eyes. He gave a slight groan and the man beside him took his elbow, assisting him to maintain what little steadiness he could muster as he pulled himself erect. Brann noticed, however, that the helping man held his companion, but did not let the other hold him. If the man should succumb to his teetering balance, he would be let go and would not drag the one beside him with him.

The priestess moved to the first man, the most nervous one. The smoking ball swayed, releasing increased clouds of smoke as it moved. She was tall enough to swing it slowly right around the man, encasing him in the haze. She stood a long moment behind him.

She pushed him.

With a scream that escalated from shock to terror to despair, the man plummeted. A sickening cracking squelching thud was audible even at this height, and there was a single shriek, though more of surprise than horror, from an unseen woman, then silence.

The priestess moved to the next man. He now was visibly shuddering as the golden ball swung around him, the smoke

295

as thick as ever. Again the wait. Longer this time. As no push came, his shoulders relaxed slightly.

She pushed.

He twisted as he went, a desperate hand reaching back for the ledge that was already beyond his grasp. Again the scream, again the sound of impact.

She moved to the third man. Somehow, he kept himself still, but as the smoke swung in front of him his breeches stained darker, the fear running from him and pooling on the stone floor at the inside of the ledge. She stood behind him, carefully placing her feet. He swayed, but managed to catch himself.

Her hand shot forward. She grasped the back of his tunic and dragged him back into the room. He fell backwards from the ledge, lying in his own piss like an animal frozen in fear.

The nondescript man grovelled as the Master stepped forward to loom above the man on the ground. 'You are found worthy. You shall lead. You shall serve.'

He walked back to his place in the line, and the nondescript man nudged the figure at his feet with one boot. 'The door you came in by. Now. You will be shown where to clean yourself and given your instructions.'

Brann was closest of the priests to them, and the priestess pointed to him. He rose, uncertain, but saw her finger move to indicate the table with the empty stand for the ball of smoke and he saw beneath it a basin with a cloth.

He smiled inwardly, and grimly. This was not the activity he had envisaged for himself for this meeting, but what must be, must be. He fetched the bowl and cleaned the floor where the man had lain. In doing so, however, he found himself in earshot of a low conversation between the nondescript man and the priestess.

'You can really read their souls?' he said.

Disdain. 'Of course not.'

'Then you knew already of the treachery of the first two?'

'I knew nothing of the sort. For all I knew, they were as loyal as you.'

'But...?'

'But now I know that the third man will serve with a loyalty bordering on fanaticism. Even the passing hint of a disloyal thought will fill him with this memory of terror.'

'And no eyebrows will be raised below at the two examples you made? This is, remember, a secret meeting.'

Her smile was as cold as her eyes. 'Most come here to celebrate life, or seek to prolong it, but some come to bring it to an end. It is not unknown, and so will not create consternation or suspicion. By now, the acolytes will have tidied and cleaned. There will be no sign remaining.'

The man nodded. Brann finished and moved back, returning to his seat, keen to avoid attention. There was no doubt in his mind why the priests were trusted not to speak of what transpired in such a meeting when any transgressors could meet an end similar to what he had just witnessed.

The nondescript man's subservient manner dropped from him like a shabby scabbard pulled away from a gleaming and keen blade. His voice became sharp. 'Colleagues. To business.'

He placed himself at the head of the table, and the Masters pushed back their hoods and sat three to each side of it, while the priestess sat at the vacant end. Brann let his eyes drift over the Masters. Four were men, two women and, in the moments before they sat, he had seen one common feature: eyes cold and unfeeling. The maniacs who did their bidding may revel in, and even thirst for, the pain and suffering of others, but these were different creatures. These felt nothing, and could inflict pain and suffering all the more easily, and effectively.

Am I so different? he asked himself. *When I fight, I am as cold and effective as they.* But he answered himself. *No. When I am not fighting, I make different choices to these people. It is not so much what you do, but why you start it and to what end. A knife can be pushed into a heart just as easily by the hand of a good man or bad; the difference is in the motive. The people seated around that table seek to sow evil and misery; I seek to stop it.*

The nondescript man spoke, snapping Brann's attention awake once more. The man exuded authority now, staring around the table with a calm assurance; sitting erect with both arms extended to rest calloused hands on the polished wood of the table top. 'Colleagues, welcome. The High Master awaits news of your progress and sends his wishes which you will, of course, treat as directives. As you are aware, I also possess his authority over all but the most critical decisions and permissions, should you seek them.' Brann sucked in his breath. The Messenger! The man continued. 'But, first: we seem to be short of one Master. This would be the first news we seek.'

A broad man cleared his throat. 'Daric was attending to affairs in Cardallon. He was due then to cross the sea before coming here. Things are somewhat chaotic in Ragalan, and while this chaos is admittedly of our doing and what we wish, still it does carry with it the potential for complications and even danger. It would not be unlikely that he has been delayed.'

A hard-faced woman grunted. 'From what I hear, the situation is such that it is not unlikely that he has been delayed permanently.'

The Messenger shrugged. 'Either way, it does not affect our actions. The fighting in Ragalan needs little direction from above to achieve the discord that we wish, and should we need them to divert their attentions south, one of you can take the message.' He looked around the table. 'Long-term, it does not matter, for there is now no long-term. The High Master is drawing this to an end. The millens have been sent north. The Emperor has reacted, so now the High Master can act.'

A stir of interest rippled through those before him.

A tall man with the face of a bird of prey – the Master who had spoken to the three applicants – said: 'And what would you require of us at this time?'

The priestess leant forward. 'I, too, am naturally eager to serve with whatever is needed in this most auspicious of stages.'

The Messenger looked at her. 'And the Mother-of-All? She would not be a problem?'

The woman snorted. 'She knows little and understands less. Age has robbed her of the facility for either. Her ear is held by a select few, and the others are concerned with matters internal at the Order. She will believe what I tell her and hear only what I choose to tell her.'

The Messenger regarded her coldly. 'That is what Taraloku-Bana told us of the sway he held with the Emperor. Such influence is fine until a personal agenda worms its way into the situation.'

She maintained her aloof poise, but Brann noticed she had to work to do so. Those who are accustomed to universal obedience are so easily unsettled by superior power. 'My only concern is for the cause,' she said.

'The High Master hopes always that this is the case.' He glanced at the balcony, and the implication was clear.

She nodded, but clearly paled as she did so.

The Messenger smiled. 'You will all have your parts to play, for that which you have so successfully set in motion in lands varied and widespread needs no more of your guidance to continue. Your talents will be found a use, fear not.' He spread his arms expansively. 'But who wants to hear instructions on an empty stomach? First, we refresh ourselves.' He raised his eyebrows at the priestess, and she took the opportunity to regain her composure.

Her hand flicked casually at the two priests at the end of the line, and the pair immediately rose to disappear through the far door, returning with two trolleys loaded with food. A second trip brought more trolleys, one more with food and the other with drink, and at their arrival, the other priests rose. Brann inwardly groaned as he and his companions followed suit, but if they had to wait while the Masters ate before they could hear the plans, then so be it.

They moved to the trolleys and copied the priests, lifting the platters and distributing them across the table. Sophaya lifted a tray bearing a decanter of wine and several goblets and moved to the table, leaning her legs against the edge to brace herself as she leant to lay the heavy load towards the middle of the surface.

The Master to her side leant back to admire the way her robe clung to her as she stretched forward. As she straightened, he caught her arm with one hand and pulled her hood back with the other, approval clear in his expression as he saw her large dark eyes and oval face with the soft fringe of her deep brown hair framing it.

Brann saw Gerens stiffen and tried to shoot the boy a warning look, but his friend only had eyes for the Master holding the girl he loved. Her arm remained gripped, and the man faced the rest of the group.

'I like the look of the dessert course,' he said, 'but I think I will save my enjoyment of it until after our meeting has closed.' He looked directly at the priestess. 'You are an Order that celebrates life, are you not? What better way to revere it than the act that creates it?'

She shrugged, no hint of any objection in her face.

Brann stared at Gerens, willing the boy's eyes to turn his way, but to no avail. Gerens was like a primed crossbow, barely balancing the straining force and the restraint.

The Master's mouth twisted into a form of smile, his eyes back on Sophaya, whose own expression revealed nothing of her thoughts. 'With all previously untried delicacies, of course, it is always wise to take a small taste of what the whole may be like.'

He bent and rose, his free hand slipping under the hem of her robe and up her leg to cup her buttocks.

Gerens sprang with a feral growl and a slender knife.

It was unclear which action from a priest surprised the Masters more: the violent lunge or the uttering of a sound. Either way, the astonishment shackled their reactions and Gerens was on the man, wrenching his offending arm so hard that they heard the pop as it left his shoulder socket. Brann groaned inwardly in frustration as he reached for his sword, his other hand grabbing his robe and whirling it up and over his head.

It was then that the Master made his biggest mistake: his uninjured arm reaching for the long serving knife that lay beside a steaming haunch of lamb. Gerens's arm was a blur, his slim blade ramming down and through the man's hand to pin it to the table. A scream of shock and widened eyes were all that time allowed the man before Gerens brought up his other hand, a second knife plunging through the front of the Master's throat and almost vertically into his head.

Both knives were pulled free in sprays of blood as the corpse crumpled to the floor. In the space of only a few heartbeats, everything had changed. In the time it took Brann to suck in a breath, it all changed again.

The scant seconds it took the Masters to react had passed. Weapons were drawn around the room. The priestess backed to the door. A priest screamed. He and his fellow clerics scrambled for the door in panic. The sound of boots running on the tiles far below told Brann his own companions had responded to the scream. The Masters whirled, their backs to the table, assessing the danger. The door at the far end of the room burst open and four men-at-arms barrelled in, knocking the fleeing priests back into the room before they managed to push past the soldiers and make their escape.

The Messenger's eyes lighted on Brann's black sword. Brann saw the man look him up and down. 'You!' he growled. He turned to the Masters, pointing at Brann. 'Kill him first. Then the rest.'

Brann looked at his own companions, the familiar coldness flowing through him. 'Kill them all,' he growled, and lifted his sword towards the Messenger. 'But keep that one alive.'

The Masters had thrown off their cloaks, freeing themselves to fight. Most had swords but one woman, sinuous and with a face that would have been taken to be kind until the cruelty in her eyes was seen, drew a pair of wickedly curved knives, a green gem set in the pommel of each hilt. Grakk shouted, 'Beware those blades: poison coats them. If she draws blood…'

The woman's smile was gleeful. 'One cut is always all it needs.'

Sophaya's throwing star took her in the throat, and the knives dropped to the floor. 'I hate poison,' she spat.

The Masters came at them. Two made for Brann. His axe had been left at the inn, being of a shape impractical for hiding beneath a priest's robes, but his sword and knife would easily suffice. Two men would not be easy, but they were not an insurmountable problem – three leopards in the fighting pits below Sagia had taught him that. The energy of his fighting self flowed through him, brightening his sight, heightening his senses, forming quick simple thoughts. There had to be an overall aim – manoeuvre them, position them, tire them, finish them quickly: whatever the situation demanded – but the actions to get there changed in every instant, and when he felt the repressed Brann rise, he found that what seemed in the moment to be right, usually was.

The pair came fast, but not rushing, spreading slightly with calculation in their eyes, working as a pair. They knew what they were doing.

But so did Brann.

He faked to his left but, as the man to his right struck at what should have been an unprotected back, Brann shifted instead and dropped, sliding to his right and under the blow. His sword swung at the man's ankles as he went but his opponent's reactions were quick and experienced, and the feet jumped just enough to clear the cut of the blade.

But no man can hover. As the feet returned to the ground, Brann's left hand was already moving, and the black-bladed knife sliced across the front of both ankles. The man screamed as his legs jerked back in unison, muscles reacting to flee the source of pain before his head even knew of the action. He flipped to the ground, chest and face striking the stone flags hard.

The second man sought to catch Brann before he set himself, and leapt over the dazed man on the floor. Brann expected it and moved in a backwards and sideways motion, allowing him to rise with sword extended. He kept it forward and the man saw his chance, swiping hard with his weapon to knock it wide. Now his own weapon was inside Brann's sword, allowing him an unopposed backhand cut at the head and neck.

Except that Brann's knife drove through his neck, the tip emerging on the far side. The razor edge cut forward, opening the throat in a shower of blood that almost blinded him, and before the movement had finished he had reversed his grip on his sword and driven the point down through the back of the neck of the groggy man attempting to rise from the floor.

Two men-at-arms and a Master lay dead across the room, and Grakk and Gerens were engaging the remainder, including the Messenger who fought with a level of skill that always allowed one of his companions to be in more danger than he was. Brann cast around for Sophaya, just in time to see her nimbly duck under a wild swipe by the priestess with what looked like a sacrificial knife and deftly grab an ankle to flip the screaming woman over the balcony to follow the two men she had murdered earlier. Brann was sure the irony was entirely intentional.

He was moving to join Gerens and Grakk when the door behind him crashed open. He whirled to find his other companions pouring into the room. The balance of power shifted in that moment, and Brann could see the recognition in the Messenger's eyes. As the remaining foes grouped with fanatical determination, the Messenger slipped back towards the door.

'He's getting away!' Brann shouted.

'Protect his departure,' one Master yelled. 'He must reach the High Master.'

The Messenger flung himself through the door and disappeared. Brann howled in fury and threw himself at the group, followed by their reinforcements. The groups clashed in a cacophony of crashing metal and snarling roars. But Brann did not seek to win a fight. They had a surfeit of numbers and ability for that. He sought a way through the bodies locked in straining combat, and almost immediately he saw a chance. A gap opened as their foes' number already started to dwindle and he dived and rolled, coming up in the same movement and launching himself at the door.

He found a corridor curving round the shape of the dome and hurtled along it, sheathing his sword and, after wiping it hurriedly on his sleeve, his knife. There were steps behind him: he heard Konall and Grakk following, with perhaps some more. A door leading to downwards-spiralling stairs was on his right, and he paused, straining to hear over the sound of his own heaving breathing. Feet on stone. Moving away. It must be him. 'Down here!' he shouted to those closing behind him and plunged ahead.

He flew down the stairway, right hand trailing on the wall to steady himself, though not enough to stop him almost falling several times. The risk was secondary. *They must not lose the Messenger.*

He was nearing the bottom when his attention was caught. He flung himself to a halt and backtracked. There it was. His fingers had snagged it as he had passed: the edge of a door not closed flush. As if someone had not quite had time to shut it securely. A secret door, formed from the smooth stone blocks of the wall and positioned precisely where the light from the spaced lamps did not exactly meet. He pushed it, and silent hinges let it swing smoothly away from him. An unlit torch sat in a sconce and a narrow stairway led straight down to his right, disappearing in the space of a few scant feet into darkness. He listened, but could hear nothing. But this *must* be his trail. 'In the wall!' he yelled back up the stairs to his companions.

He grabbed at the closing door and took the torch, jamming it lengthways between the jamb and the edge of the door. His friends could not fail to see it.

He took a deep breath and plunged into the darkness. He kept both hands on the walls, the stone not as caringly dressed as in the public areas of the temple but welcome to the touch nonetheless, and forced his feet to keep moving. He waited with every step for the blade that could come in the opposite direction and tried to concentrate his thoughts on his feet and away from the peril.

But it seemed that the Messenger knew not that Brann was alone and chose speed over the chance to rid himself of his closest pursuer. The stairs led down in a straight line, no turns, no switches – they had started well below the level of the dome and must follow the line of the flat outside wall.

His senses detected a change and instinct slowed him just enough to hit the unseen wall in front of him only mildly hard. He felt around, ignoring the pain in his knee that had been the first to impact, and the wall to his left moved at his touch. He pushed and it opened: another door. Moonlight seemed as bright as day after the pitch-black of the passage.

He breathed deeply again, and dived low through the

opening, turning in a crouch with knife in hand, facing back towards the doorway. No one awaited. His back was against something hard and big, and he glanced up to see the dark bulk of a broad statue, more than big enough and close enough to the wall to hide from eyes outside any use of the unorthodox doorway.

He cast to each side and saw a shadow move to his left. He was closer than he had thought, and set his legs to pumping once more, sheathing his knife once more. It would not do to fall upon his own blade.

There was scuffling and grunting behind as his companions burst from the doorway with less caution than he had employed. 'Here!' was all his bursting lungs could manage, but the noises behind and the turn from the dark figure ahead was evidence enough that it had been audible.

They appeared to be running along the roof of some sort of portico projecting from the side of the temple at the height of a single storey. As Brann strained his eyes for what little information he could gather, the Messenger – for he had to hope it was he – disappeared. He had not strayed to the temple wall, so it could only be that he had come to the end of the roof. With luck, he had fallen in the darkness and broken enough bones to end his running.

He slowed, unwilling to suffer the fate he wished upon his quarry, peering for the lip of the roof and finding it against the varied shades of dark beyond. The man was running down the street towards the front of the temple at not quite a full sprint. Either he had hurt himself in his flight or his destination was far enough away to make him want to conserve some energy. Brann suspected the latter. He had no such need – the sooner he caught him, the better – so he could afford to devote all his strength to a shorter chase.

He lowered himself to the extent of his arms and let his fingertips free themselves from the roof, jarring his whole body as he slightly misjudged the length of the drop. Ignoring the discomfort, he pounded after him. He had no time to warn the others; he would have to trust they were paying attention.

The Messenger reached the square and turned away from the temple, heading down a street to the side. As Brann reached the corner, he saw Marlo standing anxiously, having seen the running figure but clearly unsure if it was a person of importance or a worshipper fleeing the uproar that could be heard from inside and the alarm in the shouts of those already tumbling from the great front door.

'Marlo!' he shouted. 'This way!'

The boy immediately started after him and, as he set off, Brann saw Cannick follow. Marlo caught Brann before he had gone another dozen paces.

'You always were quick,' Brann panted.

'You always were slow,' Marlo grinned. He nodded ahead. 'The Messenger.'

'Yes.'

'The Masters?'

'Dead. Most, if not all.'

'Our friends?'

'Following. Not far.'

'All good then.'

'As long as we get this bastard.'

Marlo peered ahead. 'We are gaining.'

'We need to catch, not just gain.'

'Then we should run faster.'

Brann pushed himself on, and Marlo matched him. The man ahead glanced back, seeing them close. He redoubled his efforts towards a corner, the road turning right and left as it met a low building ahead.

'Quick,' gasped Brann. 'Run ahead of me if you can. We need to see if he turns again, and where, after the corner.'

But the man did not turn. He attacked the wall, scrambling up cracked masonry as if it were a ladder.

'Gods, he's like a squirrel,' Brann gasped.

'What do we do?'

Brann looked at him. 'All we can do. Follow.'

They reached the wall and scrambled up with greater effort and less speed than the Messenger. They reached a flat roof and saw the man already leaping to the next building. Scrabbling behind made them turn, only to see Sophaya slipping onto the rooftop almost as nimbly as the Messenger had done. Grakk was close behind, with Konall and Gerens in close attendance. 'A long reach has its advantages,' the noble said drily.

Hakon's voice drifted up from below. 'I'm not sure I can make it.'

Grakk narrowed his eyes after the running figure. 'Make for the docks,' he called down.

'I don't know the way.'

Mongoose's voice drifted up. 'Follow me, daft boy. Whenever the road slopes, we go downwards.'

The group on the roof were already moving, finding the gap that the Messenger had leapt to the next roof to be short and easily crossed. The next building was long and flat, and the bright moon and lack of building-thrown shadows let them keep their prey in sight. They started to gain.

'As long as we can see him, we should catch him and before the docks at this rate,' Brann puffed.

The next few seconds proved the error of his judgement. The building that directly abutted this one, was a full storey higher, with a wall at the top making it even higher. A chimney breast was one of the few objects that broke out from the smooth surface and the only one that reached all the way to the top, but it was all that the man needed. He leapt in three bounds: first, right onto a rain barrel, then left to a gargoyle with an open mouth to eject water from indoors, and finally right again to grasp the chimney. He scampered up the protrusion as though it were horizontal rather than vertical and flipped in a somersault over the top of the wall. With only the merest of backward glances as he reached the higher level, he was off.

They reached the obstacle and Sophaya was onto and up the chimney in a few short breaths, leaving the others panting at its base. Brann looked at it dubiously, then glanced at the others and saw matching expressions. 'Go,' he said to Sophaya's waiting face. 'Only you can follow him on this route. Keep him in sight until we catch up.' He didn't dare look at what he knew would be Gerens's disapproving glower.

She didn't waste time on a reply and disappeared. By the time they had managed to haul themselves up, both had left their sight.

Grakk nodded ahead. 'Keep going that way. The docks are not too far ahead.'

It was a frustrating run. They reached the edge of this stretch of buildings, glimpsing the solid darkness of water at the edge of their vision and lowered themselves to the street, running faster on the more familiar surface. As they broke cover onto the dockside, Sophaya dropped noiselessly to land beside them, startling all but Gerens who merely looked relieved.

'This way,' she said softly, leading them at a swift lope onto one of the curving piers. Ships of all sizes and styles bumped hulls, some in darkness and silence, others lit and with the muffled sound of chatter, laughter and music emanating from within.

At the end of the pier two identical vessels sat, the same insignia on each: one starting to push off and with oars being made ready, while the other was in advanced preparation to follow suit.

'The Messenger,' Sophaya said. 'He is on the first.'

Brann looked at it in despair as the gap from pier to hull widened with every thumping heartbeat. His eyes jumped to the matching colours flown from the second ship. 'We have to gamble,' he said. 'Or we lose all.'

To his surprise, no questions or comments came his way. The others nodded in acceptance and made ready to move, but at a thought, Brann caught Sophaya by the arm. 'The others know nothing of this. You need to let them know. You are the only one among us capable of finding them.'

'I won't make it back in time,' she said.

Grakk's voice was urgent. 'We won't make it aboard in time if we linger any longer.'

'I know,' Brann said to both. He looked at the girl. 'Tell the others to head for the house in Sagia where Einarr stays. It is the only place in that direction,' he jerked a thumb out to sea, 'that we all know.'

She looked crestfallen, but accepted the truth of the situation, reaching into her tunic and placing two pouches of coins in Brann's hand. She placed a quick kiss on Gerens's cheek, ignoring the anguish in his eyes at the unavoidable situation, and wordlessly ran with her effortless grace back towards the city.

The second ship was being cast off, and the four ran and jumped, startling a sailor as they thumped past him and thundered onto the deck. Within seconds, they were surrounded by sharp steel and suspicious faces. A well-dressed man with the bearing of the ship's master stepped between the sailors.

'What have we here? Stowaways? Thieving raiders?'

Brann looked up. 'If we are, we are not overly skilled at the stowing part,' he looked around at the assembled weaponry pointing its sharp ends towards them, 'or the raiding part. We seek passage.'

The captain laughed. 'I believe you do, and urgently so.'

He believed them fleeing the city. It was as good a reason as any.

'You would ask no questions?'

'Not if you have the fare.'

Brann held up one purse, bulging and heavy. 'Where can you take us.'

The captain grinned. 'For that, anywhere you like as long as it is where I am going, if you see what I mean.' He nodded at his cargo hold. 'Even though you have in your hand more than enough for hitching a ride, I have been paid many times more for delivering this cargo, so where it goes, you go.'

'And if we don't want to go there?'

'You are welcome to swim to your chosen destination.'

Brann shrugged. 'Not a hard choice.'

'And where do you go?'

The captain pulled himself up in pride. 'The Sea Stallion and our sister ship ahead, we are owned by a very important trading corporation, but one strangely shrouded in mystery as to its management, which makes it all the more impressive, don't you think? We sail in tandem to the south coast of the Sea of Life.'

Brann smiled. 'That will do us nicely.'

Chapter 7

'It is time for you to assume a role.'

He saw it in her eyes, but only because he had come to know her so well, had studied her as he had done over the many long years with each one of the select few who had held his trust. Her expression never changed, but he saw it in her eyes: excitement, and a little pride. That pleased him, for the drive to succeed and impress was a strong motivator to achieve results. And results were all that mattered.

'I am honoured, lord.' She bowed her head, conscious that her eyes might betray her emotion. He was pleased again. She was learning, and few, if any would have noticed the sign.

'You are satisfied, more like. You have wanted this for some time.'

She looked up, her young face startled, flushed. He fought to hide his own smile. It was good to know that he still had it in him to provoke a reaction.

She quickly controlled the stammer that started her words.

'*I mean no offence and harbour no disloyal ambition. I merely seek to serve you to the utmost of my ability, and ever more than before.*'

'*Calm yourself, girl. I want no one working for me who is comfortable with previous achievements, but only those who look to better them. You have shown this.*'

Her composure had returned. '*I have tried, lord, and I have learnt, but I was not certain I was ready.*'

'*Nor should you be,*' he snapped. '*That assessment is mine alone to make.*' He looked at her for a long moment, stretching the silence. Her face remained impassive. Even now, she learnt. '*And as I told you, it is time.*'

'*You know your thoughts are my guide, lord. I shall serve.*'

'*You shall. I had one who served closest of all; one who performed the tasks only he and I were aware of. He died.*'

'*I heard.*'

'*You are now that person.*'

She drew herself up, her height accentuated by her slender build. '*And you have a task for me.*' A statement, not a question. '*You would not tell me this news for my own pride.*'

He let the impudence pass. The thought process was more important. '*The pieces are moving in this game. We are moving towards a conclusion, but we are not there yet and we know not what form it will take, but we must be ready.*'

She nodded, her attention rapt.

'*You are aware of those who serve our cause from further afield, I know. There is a chance they may find their way to this city and, should that come to pass, we must be ready. There are those within this city whose services may be necessary, even vital. The three, of who only two are ever*

*seen. You know of whom I speak?' He paused and raised
his eyebrows and she nodded her understanding. 'We have
an understanding, I and they, based on mutual benefit from
time to time, but I cannot be seen to be in contact with
them, and they themselves shun contact with all but few
enough to be counted on one of your young hands.
Nonetheless, I need you to meet with them. I need the pieces
we are able to move, to be in place. I need you to tell them
that I wish them to be prepared to offer their assistance.
Can you do that?'*

Her voice was strong. 'I will do that.'

*'I know you will. I would not have put you in this
position were it otherwise.' He looked at her coolly. 'I
may not be as pretty as the last you served, and I may
not take you to buy fine dresses, but I will keep you more
busy.'*

'I would not have it any other way, lord.'

*'I know that also. Return tomorrow morning to change
my bedsheets, and I will give you names and instructions.'
He indicated the door.*

She nodded and turned.

*Before she lifted the latch, he stopped her. 'And
Persione—'*

*She turned immediately, her balance perfect and her stance
able to take her in any direction; a person distant from the
gawky ungainly servant he had first met. The training with
the Bringers of Darkness had been absorbed with enthusiasm, he had heard, and her movement was a direct
consequence.*

'Lord?'

*'I am trusting that personal feelings will not cloud any
of your decisions in the coming months.'*

'*My feelings are concerned only with earning your approval, lord.*'

This time, he did smile.

'*I know.*'

****

Brann learnt quickly that being accustomed to sea travel did not equate to being accustomed to all sea travel. His voyages before had followed the coast and, even when land was out of sight, there was always the comforting knowledge that it sat just beyond the horizon. Even the journey from Cardallon to Halveka had taken no more than a few days, so they had never been more than a day and a bit from the land either behind or before.

But the Sea of Life was more than a week of sailing from north to south and, when looking across the blue expanse, Brann found the knowledge that land was so far was disquieting. The vista, overwhelmingly empty but for the speck ahead that was the sister ship, made him feel that they sat unmoving in the centre of a great vastness, as if nothing he had ever known or seen still existed. Many was the time when he would shake his head to try to rid himself of the crushing sensation of insignificance, only for it to return the instant his eyes caught the view once more. And it was the only view there was.

The winds were fair, however, and the sailors had told them a couple of days after leaving port that the journey would be a quick one: a week at most if conditions stayed the same. They proved a friendly lot, despite appearing to have been drawn from the less scrupulous elements of several societies, but then an easy voyage tended to make sailors cheerful. The captain, too, was congenial, but Brann suspected that in his case his good humour was more the result of the handsome price he had been handed for little more than providing a few extra rations. Brann knew that he had paid well over the going rate for such a journey, but it suited him for the captain to believe that they were fleeing the consequences of some nefarious activity in Durden rather than pursuing the man in the ship ahead. The captain might say that he knew nothing of those who owned his ship, but the fact that he had the slightest connection with those they sought and who sought them was enough to make Brann even more cautious than normal.

Days without a change in the scenery distorted time and it seemed more like double the week that had been estimate when a cry from the man on the platform at the top of the mast raised even more cheer. 'Our destination,' a passing sailor confided, and Brann moved with the others to the bows, eager for the sight of something solid other than the ship that had become their world. They waited quietly until their patience was rewarded, but it was not a city that first greeted their eyes, but a landscape. Peaks, five in all, soared in stark clarity against otherwise fairly even surroundings.

Grakk nodded ahead. 'I have not visited here since the travels of my youth, when I first ventured into the wider world to seek knowledge.'

'It doesn't look up to much,' Gerens said sourly. They were among the very few words he had spoken since having had to leave behind Sophaya.

'It doesn't,' Grakk acknowledged, 'from here. This is an inhospitable land, with an even more inhospitable coastline. Settlements are widespread and further inland and, because of the difficulty in travelling from one to another, they tend to be autonomous.'

Gerens looked at him questioningly, as did Brann, but Konall cut in. 'Each rules itself and the surrounding land, like city states.'

Grakk beamed. 'Excellent, young lord. That is exactly how they operate.'

Konall shrugged. 'A childhood of education aimed at preparation for ruling even just part of a warlord's territory has its uses.'

Brann's eyes narrowed as he considered the information. 'Not much use for trade, however, and a trip of little gain for two ships of a trading corporation.'

Captain Rodrigo had joined them, and picked up Brann's comment. 'Very true, my young friend. We trade only in a few essential supplies and, in return, there is a particularly desirable type of wool from creatures hardy enough to thrive in this place. And,' he winked, 'they do have even more desirable gold mines, which is the reason the Empire extends its benevolent arm of care around this otherwise uninviting region. The Emperor's troops ensure that the flow of gold is strictly controlled and specifically directed, but a little can make its way to those who take the trouble to come here to trade, if you know what I mean.'

Grakk frowned. 'But two ships for such little interaction?'

The captain laughed. 'I know, but we only stop off here before doing our main business on the east coast of the Sea. It would make more commercial sense to send only one ship to divert here and the other straight to the main destination, but these days it is always wise to travel in numbers. We are quick enough to be able to be at each other's side before any other approaches, and two ships of this size are enough to deter most of the raiders who seem to have disrupted trade in increasing frequency in recent times.' He stared back over the blue expanse. 'We have been lucky, so far. Since I started sailing under these colours, we have not encountered any trouble.'

Konall glanced at the others and grunted. 'I am sure that will continue.'

The captain nodded enthusiastically. 'Indeed, indeed. I make sure we offer to the gods every morning and night, and I tell the men that as long as we do so, we shall be fine.'

'Absolutely,' smiled Grakk. 'However, would it not make even more commercial sense not to come here at all? The gold, you say, is little and its acquisition carries danger from higher authorities, and the rest is wool. The markets you head for in the East are more lucrative by far.'

'You are a man after my own heart,' the captain said heartily. 'I have often put forward this opinion, but, apparently, the corporation we serve has a trader's head for business but also a priest's heart of kindness. We must always visit here and the two ports close along this coast to do this token trade, and occasionally with a passenger or two to take one way or the other.' He beamed. 'They are not as good company as you, however. I must say, it has been a pleasure having some aboard with conversation as cordial as yours, almost making me feel as if you could have paid for some of your passage with companionship.'

Konall looked at him, raising his eyebrows. 'In that case...?'

'Absolutely not,' the captain said with a smile that was as wide as it was genial. 'Business is sacrosanct, even amongst friends, or where are we, other than lost?'

Konall's blond brows drew together, but Grakk's hand on his arm stopped him before he could speak. 'That is a conversation for another day. I am just surprised you bring passengers here at all. It is not the most enticing of destinations and was certainly not of our choice.'

The captain nodded. 'It is true, and they are few and seldom. Although I do believe there is one on the ship ahead. He is the most familiar of any who travel here and is a native of these parts, so I assume he cannot settle elsewhere in the world, no matter how hard he tries.'

Grakk looked at Brann, and Brann gave him a small nod before speaking himself. 'There must be something that draws him back. If you don't mind, would it be possible for us to travel ashore with the trading party to see something of this land for ourselves? Maybe we will choose to stay for a small while.'

The captain gave him a searching look. 'I know what you are about.'

They all froze, Brann's hand drifting towards his knife as he caught Gerens's similar movement.

The captain guffawed. 'All I can ask is that, if you survive your visit to the gold mines, you seek a different captain and a different ship as your transport away? The Empire's soldiers guard the mines with legendary brutality, but they are as kittens compared with the natives of these parts, should they be angered.'

Grakk clapped him on the shoulder with a smile. 'Your discretion is so much appreciated that, of course, we will do so.'

Accustomed as he was to coming ashore at well-crafted piers or docksides, or even the occasional sandy beach, Brann found the experience of landing from a longboat in a surging and pulling swell onto dark rocks that were as deadly slick as they were deadly jagged to be a disquieting one. His nerves were increased, rather than settled, by the casual indifference shown by the sailors towards the apparently impending doom, and it was with surprise as much as relief that he found himself still alive when he stood on dry land.

The situation had brought one benefit, however. The journey across difficult terrain was easy, indeed welcome, by comparison. They had helped the sailors to trek with their goods a short distance inland, where they found a small trading camp had been set up. There, the captain – for a small fee – had helped them to hire the mules that were the most appropriate, perhaps the only appropriate, mounts for the terrain they would traverse, and had pointed them along the one track leading inland.

Rutted and never sloping the same way for more than a score of paces, the track told Brann all he needed to know about the suitability of the mules, though the swaying beneath him let him understand the misery Mongoose endured at sea. He focused on the view in an attempt to divert his thoughts from his heaving stomach.

The trail wound through a dry land, though not the sand of the desert nor the endless black rock around Grakk's homeland. Here, dry stony ground bore hardy scrub and hardier trees, twisted and gnarled as if convulsed in their effort to push through the unyielding earth. The heat at sea level had been oppressive, beating on them as if the air were a hammer that somehow wrapped around the shape of their bodies, but as the track took them higher in altitude the temperature eased and became almost pleasant, despite the sun closing on its zenith. An eerie stillness surrounded them, though, the cries of high-circling birds and the staccato whistle of crickets the only audible signs of animal life.

Ahead, the five mountains on the skyline did remind him of Grakk's home, all with the same flat tops as the multitude that surrounded the secret city of Khardorul and one, the nearest, with a wisp of smoke drifting lazily from its peak.

Brann pulled out a strip of dried meat and looked at Grakk as he tore a piece with his teeth. 'No wonder you visited here. Do you feel at home?'

Grakk smiled quietly, almost sadly. 'This is far from my home, and very different. Look at the ground. Where I am from, the ground was made by the mountains, hard and unforgiving, sharp rock ever underfoot. Here, the mountains of fire burst from the ground in the days when the gods were children, and then fell silent.' He looked ahead at the closest peak, concern plain on his face. 'Fell silent until now, I fear.'

Brann frowned, in puzzlement more than the worry Grakk projected. 'But near your city, I saw clouds rising from the ground and they did not worry you unduly.'

'From the ground, yes, and those clouds were of steam. Water underground heated by the fires of the earth. But what you see ahead is the mountain itself awakening. That is not steam, but smoke. And the mountain was not breathing forth that cloud the last time I was here, merely a score of years ago and five more.'

Gerens was listening. 'Twenty-five years is a long time, Grakk.'

The tribesman's eyes swivelled his way, then back to the scene ahead. 'Not for a mountain.'

The track led them along the steep side of a valley, the vegetation more lush around the silver thread of the river glimpsed far below as the sun caught fragments of it through the thick foliage.

'They call it "jungle",' Grakk said. 'There are trees and plants more strange and wonderful than any you have imagined, and creatures that exist nowhere else, more strange and wonderful than any you could imagine. And deadly, in many cases.'

Konall looked down with interest. 'The plants or the animals?'

'Both.' Grakk kicked his mule forward to hurry it along, but the animal studiously ignored him. 'Some of the cities in this land are within great basins of the land, some so big you could ride for a full day to travel their length. There, the air is so thick with water that you can taste it, and the jungle fills everywhere. It is not a comfortable place for anyone other than those born there and knowing no other.'

'I think,' said Marlo, 'this is a land where one should finish their business quickly and leave quicker.'

'You think correctly, young Marlo.'

A roaring ahead spoke of a waterfall, and they rounded a bend to see the water dropping in a stunning show of power, as though a river poured without cease in a vertical torrent from the top of the cliff to their right, landing to the side of the road. There it collected in a deep and wide trench cut from the rock, disappearing under the trail and emerging in a thousand streams launching themselves over great steps cut into the slope below, each one brimming with crops.

They pulled their mules to a halt as the sight stunned them, the animals reacting instantly to the only command that pleased them. Brann looked closer at the levels below them, seeing smaller channels collecting water on the top step and distributing it along its length before dropping the excess to the next step where the process was repeated.

'These people are certainly no savages,' he breathed. 'Far from it. Who could think to design such a thing? Who could harness nature in such power to this effect?'

Grakk said, 'Only those with the capacity to innovate can survive in a land as harsh as this. And when the alternative is extinction, you will find it astounding what the mind is capable of conceiving.' He urged his reluctant mule forward. 'Come, dawdling is not helpful to our cause. Their farmlands will, in all conjecture, not be far from the city, but not so close that we can afford to waste time.'

Konall frowned. 'You surmise this? You do not know? I thought you had visited here before.'

'I do; I do not for sure; and I did but to a different city from this one. Does that address your points, young lord?'

'It does, as a matter of fact.'

They moved on, dropping back into silence in the face of a sight of such wonder. Brann shivered slightly, and the cool air was not the only reason. Such levels of alien intelligence were unsettling. He wondered what lay ahead. Or rather, who.

The track had become broader and had been rendered even, in keeping with the need for carts to carry produce along the route. At one corner, a wide dent in the rock face rising to their right presented a sensation of shelter and, with the sun dipping, they took the invitation and hobbled the mules, looping a rope around a small but sturdy tree for extra security; the plant's neighbour provided enough fuel for a small fire and they huddled around it, staring into the flames with cloaks and blankets drawn close as they ate, none in the mood for words.

Shortly after they resumed their journey, the light of the barely risen sun offering scant respite from the chill that had seeped from their rocky rest overnight; the track curved away from the valley and gradually the terrain opened up before them to reveal, before the five mountains but beyond a relatively-short area of flatter ground, a series of sharp ridges that cut across the landscape below them at varying angles though all very roughly parallel. Below them, indeed, for he saw that the gradual nature of the climb to this point had led him to underestimate the magnitude of the height they had reached, even though the ridges ahead were each greater in size than the hills surrounding the village of his childhood.

Brann's eye was caught by a curious shape ahead, one that proved to be a vast round hole cut into the ground. As the track wound back and forth on itself to allow them to descend rapidly, he saw the opening to be wide enough to require four shots to let an arrow cross its diameter, with a series of circular ledges stepping down from top to distant bottom. 'Similar to the ledges in the valley,' he mused quietly.

Grakk heard, and saw the line of his gaze. 'Similar construction, but in construction it holds a different and even more ingenious purpose. Before, we saw advantage taken of a spot where nature had provided an abundance of water, but here we see an understanding of nature and man's ability to use that understanding. They create great pits such as this as artificial climates.'

Brann frowned. 'Artificial what?' He stared at the distant pit, almost expecting a magical shimmer.

Grakk, however, leant across and plucked at Brann's cloak. 'You have this pulled tight around you.'

A shrug. 'Obviously. It's colder up here.'

Grakk pointed at the short plain before them. 'And down there?'

'In this sunshine? Hot, I would say, like before we climbed from the coast.'

'So higher is colder than lower?'

Brann looked at him. 'Of course. So?'

'So plants notice temperature more than you and I do. The heat is different at even small changes in height, and though we may not notice it, nature does.' He indicated the pit. 'Each level in that circle has more warmth than the one above, and different crops grow in different temperatures. Nature can also be fooled into thinking it is later or earlier in the seasons by being planted at a certain level.'

Brann felt slightly overwhelmed. 'People have thought this out, and calculated this so precisely?'

Grakk nodded. 'The mind responds well to challenge, especially where empty bellies are at stake.' He swept his arm across the vista before them. 'There are twelve such great pits, spaced around this plain, supplemented by extra farms such as the one we passed at the waterfall. Thus is a city fed.'

Brann pondered in silence the people who could produce such advanced thinking. In Sagia, the engineering of the great buildings and the sanitation and water-supply tunnels that served them had been impressive, but while the sights were awe-inspiring at first, they were almost expected of such a city of massive size and greater reputation. Here, however, in a harsh land that was inaccessible and largely unknown to outsiders, the discovery of even just what he had already seen was stunning.

And, he thought, chastening. Prejudging was all too often based upon no more than a meagre smattering of knowledge.

He turned his attention to the mountains beyond the sharp ridges. The nearest, the smoking one, seemed not a huge distance away. He managed to coax his mule close again to Grakk's. 'The mountains? Are they far?'

Grakk narrowed his eyes for a short moment, estimating. 'The closest, maybe a half ride of half a day.' He looked disparagingly at the mule beneath him. 'On a proper steed, that is.'

Brann grinned. 'Although perhaps longer than that if your proper steed fell off one of those mountain tracks.'

Grakk smiled. 'Of course, you are correct, young Brann.' He patted the neck of his mule, which in turn twisted round its head to regard him with a baleful eye. 'Sincere apologies, my sure-footed friend.'

Brann smiled and looked ahead again. 'But if that mountain is so close, the city we seek must also be very near.'

Grakk relaxed, comfortable again that he could be the logical one. 'It does make sense to place your food sources no further away than they need to be. The city of Tucumala lies in a long valley at the foot of that first mountain.'

'The smoking one?'

'The very same.'

'Was that a wise choice of location?'

'It was not smoking when the choice was made.'

Brann grunted. 'And now that it is, I am guessing there will be some consternation.'

'More than you might think, young Brann. Those five mountains, it is believed in these parts, are home to their five gods, each one with the body of a giant man and the head and wings of one of the fantastically plumed birds of the forests – birds that they feel are the messengers and the many eyes of those gods whose image they mimic. This is a highly devout people, and if one mountain is showing activity, there will be many interpretations of the mood, intentions, and requirements of the resident god.'

'From what I have seen of priests, not many of those interpretations will be of the happy variety,' Brann said darkly.

Grakk beamed. 'You are certainly the observant boy still, it gladdens me to see.'

They reached the more level ground of the plain, and were soon passing close enough to the crop-growing pit for Brann to be further astounded at the scale, far greater even than it had appeared from afar. Farmworkers – men and women alike wearing simple tunics decorated in wide angular bands of bright colours over bodies stocky and strong, and with broad hats shading universally black hair and equally dark eyes – toiled in unhurried silence and regarded the small party with glances that were as brief as they were indifferent, as did the occasional carter who passed them on the widening and well-tended road formed from precisely carved stone blocks. The mules and the sights around them, while unremarkable in both cases, still managed to eat up the distance to the edge of the plain.

Movement caught the edge of Brann's vision and he noticed carts moving along other routes, each as undeviating as the one they travelled and all converging on one point where the land began to rise to the ridges.

'From the other farming pits?' he said in Grakk's direction, receiving a nod in reply.

They entered the foothills on a road wide enough for more than four carts abreast; the route cutting through the landscape with the clear aim of ease of passage rather than winding and climbing through the hard rock. Bridges with clever struts or sturdy arches took them over slight dips and dizzying caverns alike, and where nature provided a barrier, it had been cut through as cleanly as if the gods themselves had carved the gap; in some sections, the rock too high above to remove completely, short tunnels continued their direct passage. Occasionally they saw habitation and the occupants close to it, but these were dwellings cut into the rock face or perhaps using natural caves, with building facades seeming to cling to the cliff face itself and ledges or cut steps linking the homes. Nothing sat at the edge of the road, however: nothing, it seemed, would be allowed to interfere in even the slightest respect with the clear passage.

Konall spoke from behind, his voice echoing as the mules trudged through the gloom of a tunnel. 'They do not seem to consider problems, only solutions.'

'Precisely, young lord,' Grakk said. 'As should we all.'

Konall looked at the smooth walls above and around them. 'They seem particularly skilled at executing those solutions. If Loku is in league with some of their greater minds...'

Brann grunted. 'He may be; he may not be. We will have to find out. And if he is—'

'We kill them also,' Gerens said flatly.

Brann made to speak, but realised there was little argument to the contrary. Some things were best explained through Gerens's simple outlook, as much a solution-seeking approach as the feats of engineering around them.

They emerged from the tunnel to see a valley open before them. They stopped.

Any wonder they had felt at the stepped farm in the mountains seemed as nothing now. The valley floor, a short distance lower than them, extended into the distance, where stood the smoking mountain. On each side, nature had stopped or angled the ridges to form steep walls of rock, dotted with more of the cliff-homes they had seen before. But it was what filled the valley itself that stopped their breath.

A mass of low buildings filled the floor of the valley like a carpet of white stone, similar in single-storey simplistic style to the structures of the lost city of the ancients, ul-Detina, the City of Ghosts on the border where the desert Deadlands north of Sagia met the rock of the lifeless Blacklands. The city where Grakk had taken them through a hidden portal to the secrets of his homeland, and a city of ordered beauty, of breathtaking creations whose construction was beyond understanding. But where the buildings of ul-Detina were laid out in a precision that spoke of flowing beauty in itself, those of Tucumala were a jumble, no road lasting more than a hundred paces, many of them less, before it was turned by a blocking structure, creating a haphazard maze of bewildering complexity. And where ul-Detina held statues of a size and crafting beyond comprehension in temple caverns of divine magnitude, Tucumala had pyramids.

And what pyramids! Five great structures that dwarfed the largest buildings of the Empire's capital or the greatest temples of Durden, they stood in a line from one end of the valley to the other, at varying angles and distances, erupting from the mass of habitation like…

'Like mountains,' Brann breathed.

'Indeed,' Grakk said quietly, reverently. 'Those I spoke to in other cities of this land spoke of this place, but their words were unable to do it justice. The Tucumalan people believe the mountains give homes to the gods, and so those mountains are forbidden to the feet of man. If they are to honour those gods and let their worship being them close in spirit to them, they must create their own homage to the mountains.'

Gerens stared with his dark eyes. 'So the king of these lands lives here.'

Grakk shook his head. 'They have no king. All the people of these lands share one culture, the same gods, the same traditions, the same technology, and a similar outlook on life. But each city holds its own fate, has an identity according to its surroundings: a home of the gods, a port, a provider of timber and so on. One people, ruled separately in a dozen cities.'

Konall's eyes narrowed and he lifted a finger of each hand, peering past them and changing their angles. 'That last pyramid, the furthest one: it is the biggest, just as the closest mountain, the smoking one, is the largest peak. The next pyramid is at the same angle as the next mountain, and the next pyramid to the next mountain, and so on, until the pyramid closest to us is a representation of the furthest mountain. They are as a mirror to the mountains, albeit smaller, of course.'

Brann studied them. It was true, what Konall said. What was more, the pyramids were built in great circular steps to give the same conical form as the mountains and, in further imitation, their tops were flat, forming huge platforms open to the sky, the smallest larger than the area covered by the great Arena of Sagia. In contrast to the mountains, however, these were most certainly open to the feet of the devout. Great ramps angled to the summits, with buildings their entire length, their purpose at this distance unknown. Movement teemed on the ramps, heading for and from peaks too lofty to reveal their secrets, but busy enough to suggest much was happening on top, and perhaps within, the edifices.

'If they are temples, they are busy ones,' Brann said.

Grakk shrugged. 'I told you before, they are devout.' He nodded at the smoking mountain. 'At times like these, even more so.'

'That also is mimicked.' Marlo pointed at the pyramid closest to the mountain. A haze of smoke, too indistinct to have caught their attention initially, drifted at the temple's top.

Grakk produced his oculens. He gasped. 'They have burnt the buildings on the top, I believe. That smoke is the remnants of a great fire, and only a conflagration on the scale of all that sat atop that pyramid could generate a lingering cloud of that magnitude.'

Brann frowned in confusion. 'Why would they destroy one of their holy places?'

Grakk looked at him, stowing his far-seeing tube. 'Their most holy place, young Brann. That temple, as master Konall surmised, relates to the largest and nearest mountain. It is where the father of their gods resides, and is the spirit of this city.' He stared back at the temple. 'Why indeed?'

'Something else I wonder,' Brann said, drawing four questioning looks. 'For a people with such organised minds and skills in construction, why the mess of a layout? It is out of character with everything else we have seen. It is chaos.'

'It is organised chaos,' Grakk said.

'Of course,' said Gerens. 'There are no walls. Yet the captain indicated that these can be a savagely violent people when brought to anger, and so they must be wary of attack. In streets like those, an outsider could become lost or misled, cornered or tricked, and all the while attacked from all and any sides by those intimate with the layout. The city is itself its defence.'

Brann and Konall looked at each other, eyes wide. 'Like the towns in Halveka,' Konall said in astonishment.

Brann grabbed him by the arm. 'And the keep. Your home. Look!' He pointed at the nearest pyramid.

'Of course,' the Northern boy gasped. 'Conical, entered close to the top, probably levels within. These are bigger, I grant you, but...' He looked back and forth between the pyramids and the jumbled streets, shaking his head in disbelief. All eyes turned to Grakk.

The tribesman shrugged. 'One thing I have learnt in my travels is that there are buildings, or gods, or words, or customs that can be found in places separated by half the world, populated by peoples who are not even aware that the other exists. There is much from the days before our history begins that we may never know.'

'Then,' said Brann, 'let us find out what we can know. The Messenger cannot be far ahead.' He kicked his mule into an amble, and the others followed.

The path switched back on itself in three long stretches to reach the level of the city, and the brief stretch to the edge of the buildings prompted them to dismount and ease their legs. On entering the first street they came to, however, they realised a problem. Marlo put it into words. 'Where do we go? Everywhere else has a central square to head to, or a main road lined with establishments. This is just a maze of houses.'

Grakk shrugged. 'First rule of travelling: when in doubt, ask a local.'

A man in a long white tunic above bare legs and looking much more appropriately dressed for the heat than they were with their heavier tunics, breeches, and boots, sat before one of a row of identical dwellings, freshly coated in white, with narrow windows empty of glass. He looked up from mending a leather strap at Grakk's approach, an open smile upon his face.

'Good day, my friend,' Grakk said, returning the smile. 'Could you perhaps direct us to an inn?'

A frown of confusion coloured the smile. 'An inn?'

Grakk nodded. 'A hostelry? A guesthouse?'

'A taverna?' Marlo offered.

The man shook his head. 'My apologies, I wish I could help you, but...'

Konall was astounded. 'You don't know where the nearest inn is?'

The man shrugged. 'I don't know what an inn is. If you could perhaps be more descriptive?'

Grakk pointed to his mule. 'We seek a place where we can rest, refresh ourselves, eat and have our animals tended.'

'Ah,' the man beamed. 'You seek a temple!'

Gerens, to Brann's accustomed ear, was barely controlling his patience. 'Praying was not on the list.'

'Indeed,' the man said. 'But those requirements that were on your list can all be accommodated at the largesse of the great god.' He stood, gold at his wrists and throat clinking as he moved and catching the eyes of all in Brann's party. 'Allow me to guide you.'

Without another word, he led them around a remarkable number of corners for the relatively short distance to their destination. The door lay open to a building slightly larger than the rest but otherwise alike, and the man gestured towards it.

'You are very kind,' Grakk smiled. 'How much do we owe you for your assistance?'

'How much of what?'

'Coin? Payment?'

The man shook his head again. 'I can only apologise again at my further confusion at your foreign terms. I merely told you of something I knew and you did not. If that is all you require…?'

Grakk nodded and patted him encouragingly on the arm. 'Thank you. You have been most helpful.'

'Helpful, maybe, but I feel most is somewhat an exaggeration. Still, I am glad that you have found what you sought. Good day.' He ambled back around a corner and was gone.

'There are some places we travel to,' said Brann, 'where things are new but just a different form of what we know. Here, however…'

'It is perhaps my fault,' Grakk said. 'I had forgotten that the peoples of these parts have no concept of money. Food and livestock are communal, and the products of each are freely distributed in exchange for the labour provided in service of the gods, most of which involves building and maintaining pyramids and houses. Their gold has only decorative value to them but they are acutely aware of its desirability in other cultures and trade very shrewdly and successfully in it – a fact that causes them no end of amusement at the joke they feel they play on the rest of the world.'

They stabled their mules and stowed their cloaks and larger weapons with the assistance of a priestess as accommodating as their impromptu guide had been, receiving simple food and something similar to goat's milk, accompanied by an attitude that suggested that the gods would not look kindly on those who neglected to distribute aught that was available and was needed. Indeed, with most of the population at work, she was grateful for the opportunity to perform a service at this routinely empty part of the day, she said with a slight bow, the rainbow feathers in her hair and forming the short cape around her shoulders waving softly as she did so. Nothing they offered in return was of any use to the priestess, so was politely declined. Feeling awkward, they thanked the woman profusely and left at the first opportunity.

'This seems an idyll,' Brann said as they were struck once more by the heat.

They stood before the unexceptional temple in a small square, no more than the size of a courtyard between buildings, and with a burbling fountain in the centre, where the few local people they saw stopped to water both themselves and their animals as they passed quietly by, acknowledging the strangers with a respectful nod.

'Don't get too comfortable,' Konall said. 'We have a job to do and still a fair amount of the afternoon to do it in.'

'Indeed,' said Grakk. 'Finding the Messenger might not be easy in this warren.'

Brann nodded. 'No point in all of us searching the same areas, asking questions of the same people. We should split up, and meet back at this temple at sundown. It should be the easiest place to find as we can just head back to this end of the valley. The house of the man who showed us the way is easily seen on the edge of the city, and this is the closest temple to that – anyone should be able to direct us if we forget the way.'

They nodded. Grakk cleared his throat. 'As we are five in number, I am at ease with allowing you four to be two pairs. In matters of gathering information in unfamiliar places, I am more accustomed to working alone.'

Gerens shrugged and moved towards Brann, but Marlo piped up. 'I would be happy to pair with Brann.'

Gerens looked at Brann, questioningly, his protective urge clear on his face, but Brann realised that Marlo, who had never in all of his years left the city of Sagia until he accompanied this party, had done so purely because of the friendship that had grown between the two of them in Cassian's school of gladiators. 'That's fine,' he said to Marlo but nodding at Gerens. 'You and Konall pair up and Marlo can come with me.'

Gerens almost looked as unhappy as he had at leaving Sophaya at the docks of Durden, but again merely shrugged, accepting Brann's word without question. Not for the first time, Brann wondered at the regard the boy held for him, but he suspected he may never find the reason. Certainly, now was not the time to investigate it.

'Let's use the temples,' he suggested. 'We can spread as far from each other as we can and request a drink of water at any we find. If these are the places most communal in this city, then someone, somewhere, may have heard of another foreigner arriving recently.'

The urgency felt by all was reflected in the quick agreement and the speed of their departure. Marlo led the way, bouncing ahead like an excited puppy, turning every few steps with his infectious grin. 'This is a place of wonder,' he enthused, walking backwards and sweeping his arm to encompass the surroundings. 'We are having such an adventure.'

It took only two corners before the city became far less idyllic.

A burly man, with the same features of the others they had met and the same white tunic, but none of the friendliness, stepped from a doorway into Marlo's path, the boy's back bumping into his unyielding chest.

Marlo whirled in surprise, already apologising for not watching where he was walking, only to find hard eyes staring into his and a broad blade at his throat, its edge already drawing a trickle of blood.

Brann's fingers snatched at the hilt of his long knife, the quickest weapon to draw, but a strong hand closed about his from behind, arresting the movement, and his own throat felt the touch of sharp metal. He tensed, automatically starting the movement that would free his neck and hand alike and turn the threat instead on the man behind, but the one ahead had already turned Marlo to him, pressing the blade more firmly up under the boy's chin and cocking his head enquiringly at Brann.

Brann froze. He knew he could free himself, but he was equally aware that Marlo would be dead before he had completed the move. He let go of his knife.

He heard footsteps behind and, while the blade was held against his throat and his head was pulled back by the hair, a third man yanked his arms behind him and bound his wrists with quick and blood-stopping efficiency. Once he had been secured, the man moved to Marlo and lashed together his wrists similarly.

The Messenger stepped from the same doorway that had held the first man. He ignored Marlo, staring at Brann in curiosity rather than animosity, much like a cat with a mouse pinned by its claws. 'Your naivety,' he said in an emotionless monotone, 'is astonishing.'

He nodded at the men, and a thick bag was pulled over Brann's head. His breathing became loud and laboured in his ears, and his mind jumped back to a hillside above his village, when he had first been abducted. Then, his brother had died. Now, he would do anything to prevent the same fate for Marlo.

A hand grasped his wrists and pulled him to stumble backwards at a pace where all his attention was on staying upright. He still tumbled in a painful heap several times, and heard Marlo do the same several times more. On each occasion, he was roughly dragged back upright before he could even have a thought of how to use the fall to his advantage. His entire mind became consumed with the process of lifting and moving his feet effectively as he was moved in a haphazard zig-zag, preventing him from ever settling into a rhythm of motion and keeping his thoughts from straying.

They stopped without warning, and he fell against the man pulling him; a hand grabbing his arm to halt him, dangling him at an angle and wrenching his shoulder, then righting him with what seemed like casual ease.

He was dragged again into cooler air and the hood went darker: inside a building. A door banged shut behind, heavy wood from the sound. The same noise of wood on stone, but in front of him, and then a hand between his shoulder blades pushed him forwards this time, a lurch of panic searing through him as his foot met only space and he pitched forward. The hand slid down his back and caught the rope where his wrists met, holding him precariously for a moment to remind him of his utter helplessness. Both arms pulled and twisted and threatened to pop from the sockets but this time he welcomed it: anything but falling helpless, blind and head first.

He breathed again, the air hot against his face as the hood confined it. He was pulled upright and felt gingerly for the step he hoped was there. His toes found it and he tottered his way down, needing no prompting from behind. He had long since abandoned any notion that he might have a say in where he was going.

His feet found level ground and he was turned and led a dozen paces. He was stopped. Held. Nothing happened until he heard several sandals scuffing as their owners moved around him, then the frustratingly general sound of something indeterminate being arranged and the clank of metal.

The front of the hood lifted slightly and his eyes, straining down to catch a glimpse of something, anything, after the darkness, saw the flash of light on metal an instant before the edge lay against his throat. A few swift slashes of a blade cut his tunic from him before his various weapons were unstrapped and lifted from their many locations about his body. Coldness touched the inside of one arm – more metal – before three jerks saw his hands come apart from each other, the severed cord hitting his heels as it dropped to the floor. He flexed his fingers, feeling the pain as the blood flowed again into his hands, and rubbed his palms together for an instant before his arms were grabbed again. He was dragged to one side and his hands were raised above his head, hard wood pressing against them as cuffs clamped around his wrists with a heavy snap. His legs were kicked apart and a hand pushed each back in turn until his ankles were secured in the same fashion.

The bag was pulled from his head.

Reflex sucked in a deep breath as his eyes blinked, blinded even by the dim lamplight. He jerked his head one way then the other, seeking his bindings. Two stout posts led from stone floor to stone ceiling, and were embedded in each. A wrist and ankle were manacled to each one, a heavy pin holding shut the clamps. He pulled at them, muscles straining as instinct moved him to test them. As expected, though, they were solid.

He looked across the room. Marlo was similarly secured, facing him, terror in his eyes but the flexing of his jaw hinting at the determination that was fighting a fluctuating battle with the fear.

Brann could understand the fear. He could feel it. There was little more terrifying than utter helplessness.

He forced his breathing to slow and deepen. However unlikely it seemed that a chance would present itself, he would not be caught unready if it did. He nodded at Marlo, hoping he appeared reassuring, but doubting he achieved anything like it. Marlo nodded back, his movements jerking. He never took his eyes from Brann.

Soft, unhurried footsteps descended the stairs, and the Messenger came into view. He looked from one to the other, his eyes settling on Brann. 'In an ironic way,' he said, his voice soft and even, 'you are a success. You sought me, chased me, followed me across the width of a sea, all to try to find the High Master. And now you will meet him. You should rejoice.'

Irony indeed.

A murmur sounded from above and the three men who had brought them followed the Messenger in, dropping to their knees, holding themselves straight but with heads bowed. The room resonated with a deep hum from the four men as they swayed slowly from side to side. A man descended from above: a cloak around his shoulders of long feathers of countless hues descending past his ribs, brushing the steps as he came. As his head came into view, Brann could see it was covered with the mask of an exotic bird:

a slender beak, the length of a child's arm, curving forward and more plumage encasing his head and lying flat to hang to the nape of his neck.

He reached the floor and moved to the centre of the room. A single raised finger stopped the humming, and when the rest of the fingers on that hand lifted as well, the men regained their feet.

The beak turned to Brann, then Marlo, then back to Brann. Eyes glittered behind the mask.

Both hands lifted to the mask, his head leaning forward to ease it free. The Messenger came to take it from him, standing in front of him to receive it, blocking Brann's view.

The Messenger stepped away. The head rose.

The eyes met Brann's.

Brann's eyes widened.

A wordless shout of shock, of rage, of disbelief burst from him.

It was Loku.

Brann strained at his bonds, every natural urge forcing him towards the man. His muscles heaved; his skin bled against metal; his eyes felt ready to pop from his head. He wheezed with the effort and the emotion, pulled by an irresistible compulsion – swamping reason and fact – to somehow reach the man and tear his throat from his body.

Loku stood calmly, waiting for the fury to subside.

Subside it did. The struggle fading from determined to desperate to despairing; the grunted gasping becoming heaving breaths that slowed and softened.

He stared at the man before him.

Loku sighed, his expression relaxed. 'It is sad to see such anger in one so young, but passion is always to be admired. You quite obviously believe deeply in your cause.'

'As do you,' Brann growled, his voice raw in his throat.

Loku smiled sadly. 'More than you know.'

Brann glared. 'Tell me, then. I am clearly not going anywhere soon.'

'Actually, you are, soon but briefly, but that is another matter and there is time to talk. For that is the reason you are here: to talk to me, or to my associates, whichever you choose. I will try to persuade you, but should you decline the chance, I will leave the messier activities to those with more stomach for such things.'

'No stomach?' Brann was appalled at the gall of the statement. 'You, who have brought about mass murder, who have made the infliction of torture and pain a leisure activity and cruelty an addiction, who have set people to wiping out entire villages and sacking cities across countries: you have no stomach for such things?'

Loku nodded slowly. 'An evil, I must agree, but sometimes an evil is unavoidable if an end is to be achieved.'

'An end? What end could justify that?'

'The end of a people. The extinction of a race. The snuffing of some goodness from this world. My people are threatened with doom, and if I can save them, then is my obligation not clear? If I question what I must do, I will falter, and if I falter, I fail the very people who I serve.' He stared at the floor, fingering a feather on his cloak, his voice uncharacteristically thick with emotion. 'I cannot fail them.'

He looked at Brann. 'I see you do not understand.' He gestured to the Messenger, who immediately gathered the men. 'I must show you. If you understand, you will aid me, I know it.'

One man immediately lifted a blade to Marlo's neck while the boy was unfastened. When he stood secured, this time

344

with iron manacles at hands and feet, the edge of the blade remained against his neck but the eyes of the man holding it fixed on Brann. The message was clear.

Despite the threat through Marlo, Brann still felt sharp metal press against his own neck. His hands were released first, and clasped in the metal cuffs linked by a short chain. He could see the logic: his hands were more dangerous than his feet, but even in the short space of time between restraints, they were useless if his ankles were still fixed to the poles.

A chain also linked his ankles, restricting all but the minimum movement needed to shuffle forwards and up the stairs, as they were prompted to do. The room above was bare but, along one wall, more steps rose to an open hatch in the ceiling. At the top of these, they found themselves on a flat roof with a waist-high parapet, the final pyramid of the valley rising in front of them and the first mountain looming immediately behind. The sun was beginning to set, and the red smudges it smeared across the darkening blue of the sky seemed to mimic the smoke drifting from the top of the mountain.

Loku noted Brann's eyes resting on the smoking peak. 'And so you behold our doom. Texacotl is angry, and we know not why. We prayed, but it brought Him no peace. We made offerings, but still He was not calmed. We sent priests, anointed for the journey – as dictated by our lore – to climb to the lip of His home and look within; those who returned spoke of His ire, so strong that the rock inside had melted to pool like a lake; His rage burning with such power that every hair on their heads, from their scalps to their eyes, was burnt and lost. Some offended Him so greatly that He took their sight with the heat. Still we prayed, more we offered, not merely the prized possessions and precious food of before but now sacrifices strong with the power of life: our animals, their essence released with their blood to send our love and homage to Him. Still His anger did not ease but, worse, it grew. So priests again were anointed and dared to look into the face of His anger. The very air of his home now poisoned them: just two returned to us, and one lived long enough to tell of the lake of boiling rock, now risen half the distance to the peak and bubbling and spitting its searing essence towards them as they dared to gaze upon His fury.' He sighed. '*The Second Annals of the Gods* describe similar anger from the other four gods, a hundred generations and more in the past, when the power of their fury flowed as rivers of death and destroyed men and women and all their works. Each time the people fled and a new city was built in the shadow of a more benign god, four times in all as, in time, each god became angered for reasons beyond the understanding of His mere subjects.'

Brann shrugged. 'So move again.'

'If only it were so simple. But man has no right to defy the will of a god and restore a city He or She has chosen to end. And there are no more gods from whom to seek succour; since the five crossed the sea to us in time long forgotten, all five will now have spoken. Every man, woman, and child of all the cities of this land bows to these gods, and if those chosen to live in the glow of Their magnificence were to abandon Them, all in these lands will be lost; without them, we are nothing. Their lore is our lore, teaching the knowledge of how we can live in these lands and encouraging the discovery of new methods. Some are required elsewhere, but here the remainder will stay, placing ourselves at the mercy of the greatest god of all.'

Brann grunted. 'And here you will die. Magnificence or

not, you won't exist. The others here I might mourn; you, however...'

The Messenger's face contorted and only a wave of Loku's hand stopped his vicious blow.

Loku stared at the peak. 'We must survive. And so we make the greatest offering of all.'

He moved to the edge of the roof closest to the pyramid, and Brann and Marlo were shunted in his wake. Before them lay a square, the ramp to the pyramid's top starting slightly off-centre while, in the other half of the area, a temple sat, no more ornate in design than any other building but set apart by the multitude of colours that swathed its walls, bold geometric shapes on a rainbow background of broad horizontal bands. Before the building was a low wall, no more than the height of a man's knee, marking an area square in shape and containing only two identical blocks of finely dressed stone, embossed with designs similar to those on the walls of the temple and picked out in matching bright colours. They were waist high and the length of an average table: altars, Brann assumed, in the sight of the mountain and its resident god. Behind them stood a glowing brazier.

A crowd of worshippers were starting to fill the square, filtering in silently and standing, facing the temple and side-on to Brann. They stood silent, without moving, presumably in obedience to religious custom as no priests were evident.

The Messenger moved close behind Brann, calm menace in his every word. 'You are in the presence of a great one. Shout to them and you will achieve nothing but the loss of your tongue.'

Brann stilled that very impulse. He was used to risking

injury, but not for no possible gain. Had it not been for Marlo's presence, he would have taken the opportunity to launch himself without hesitation over the parapet to the ground below. The drop was not substantial; if he rolled as he landed, he might avoid serious injury and his chances would be better than where he was at the moment. But with Marlo there... He subdued both his voice and his instincts.

Perhaps the crowd could see no priests, but those alongside Brann could: five of them on the roof of the temple garbed for the gods in long feathered robes and plumed bird masks, together with a young man and woman, each clad in a simple shift of deep crimson.

Brann looked at the garb of the priests and back at Loku. 'You are a priest!'

The Messenger growled in violence confined only by Loku's previously signalled restraint, his breath hot on the back of Brann's neck. 'Show respect, dog. You speak to the High Master of the servants of Texacotl. He is the priest of all priests.'

Brann ignored him, staring still at his nemesis, forcing his voice even despite the harshness that raked his throat. 'Hence your responsibility to your people.'

Loku's eyes remained on the scene on the roof before them, the group moving as if in a private performance for them. 'Naturally. If not I, then who?' He nodded at the rooftop. 'Watch. Understand our peril. Understand our fear. Understand our commitment. Understand our devotion. Understand the depth of our yearning that Texacotl should understand. Understand.'

The young couple faced each other, taking hands and locking eyes. They swayed slightly as the priests began to chant and, at the sound, the unseeing crowd began the same low hum that the men had emitted at Loku's arrival in the cellar.

Loku smiled, as a father might, protectively and with affection, over his young children. 'The great and the respected from each area of the city. They will return and relate.'

'Relate what?'

'The message we send to the god. The power of our devotion.'

A priest stepped up behind the young woman and raised a slender, almost needle-like, blade shining black, seeming to be some sort of stone. Brann and Marlo gasped in unison as he slipped it smoothly through the shift into the unprotected area below her ribs, but the woman gave no cry of pain, no flinch, no reaction, no awareness even, despite the dark blood that pooled about her feet as the knife was withdrawn in as swift a motion as it had entered.

The priest moved behind the man and slid the knife into him in identical fashion. Again there was no reaction other than to blink, once. All five clerics turned their gaze across to Loku without a break in their chanting. Loku nodded and lifted a finger, and a priestess, her gender evident in her build and movement, stepped forward with a golden goblet and lifted it to the man's lips. He drained it in a single draught as she tilted it, and almost immediately the priest with the dripping knife repeated his action, this time to the other side of the man's spine.

There was not even a flicker. Loku smiled.

Five times, the priests circled the pair, who swayed in time to the chanting, hands still held, eyes still locked. The clerics lined up two each side of the couple, and the fifth – the woman who had served the goblet – loosely looped a short length of cord the same hue as their shifts around the nearest wrists of the pair. She led them to an external stair at the rear of the temple and the group descended serenely, moving from Brann's view to reappear around the front of the building. At the sight of them, the crowd's humming grew stronger and, as one, they fell to their knees, swaying from side to side, eyes intent on the scene before them.

The couple were led to the front of the small enclosure, facing the assembled throng. The priestess untied the shifts at the rear of the neck for first the woman, then the man, letting the material drop to the ground. Neither the couple nor the crowd showed any surprise at the nakedness, nor the arousal of the man.

Brann, however, must have shown surprise.

Loku glanced sideways at him. 'The drink has several useful qualities for a ceremony such as this.'

The couple were led to the altars, each of which had a small step placed at its side by a priest. The man climbed atop one and lay flat. The woman was guided to the same block, priests holding each of her hands as she stepped up, standing over her companion then lowering herself to straddle him, the trails of her blood drying on her back and legs evident as she did so. The humming of the crowd increased with the pair's movements, building in intensity until the woman threw her head back and the man half raised himself, both shuddering in unison.

Brann glanced at Marlo, seeing in the boy the same discomfort he felt himself. Seeking refuge in flippancy, he raised an eyebrow at Loku. 'The numbing seems to be wearing off.'

'On the contrary. In greater quantities, the tincture will induce unconsciousness and, should the donor be careless, death, but in the first doses numb sensation and awareness but enhance the feeling of pleasure to produce certain reactions. We find it helpful in the rites that bring fertility to our mothers and to the soil, where the participant must be suffused with the rapture of the gods but must also be able to, shall we say, enact the ceremony.'

'You have just held a fertility ceremony? Now?'

'Not the ceremony, but the rite has been enacted for another purpose. It is a part of the whole of what we do here for the great god.'

His eyes, Brann noticed, were glittering. An uneasiness crept over him at the sight, and he turned back to the scene below, willing the pair not to be harmed, though he suspected the blood spilt already would not be the last they would donate. He hoped with a desperate fervour that whatever the pair lost in the sacrifice, it would be something relatively immaterial: a finger, or even a hand, rather than their sight; a scarring to the back rather than disfigurement of the face; perhaps just the mingling of their blood. Whatever the outcome, he prayed that they would be cared for throughout their lives for the sacrifice they would have made for their peers. Horror trapped his eyes on the young couple.

The woman had been led to the vacant altar, and both sat on the stone, legs straight before them and torsos upright, faces slack and eyes unblinking. The four male priests brought a golden goblet each and, as they were held to their lips, the man and women drained two apiece without pause. Within moments they sagged and were caught by the waiting arms that laid them gently on the smooth stone. Chests rose and fell gently, but otherwise they were dead to the ceremony. Fortunately so, Brann thought.

The light was dimming; the brazier was stoked and fed

351

with dry wood, its flames casting a dancing eeriness over the prone figures. At the sight, the humming from the crowd began again, although this time with a fervour that spoke of rising anticipation. Two male priests stepped to the altars holding long-handled tools, hinged near their gleaming blades of the same black stone that he had seen before, their sharp points curving to meet at the tip. The clerics stood on the steps to the side of the altars and raised the clippers high, prompting the humming to surge louder. The priestess stood behind, turning to the mountain and raising her arms aloft. She chanted, louder and faster, louder and faster, louder and faster. Her arms dropped and, with them, the tools in the hands of the priests did likewise, the separate points of the blades cutting effortlessly into the skin on the chests of the young man and woman. The handles were worked, and a rib was clipped as if it were no more than a brittle twig.

'No!' The word burst with horror from Brann, drowned by the drone from a thousand throats. 'No!' came with each rapid and coldly efficient snap of the clippers. He felt his eyes wide, his breath catching, his legs weak. He had seen barbarity, had caused much of it himself, but this...

They were still alive.

The four priests stepped one to each side of the young pair and, in the sharp proficiency of practised movements, the ribs were hauled upright, like the rotted hull of a boat Brann had seen wrecked on a beach while he sailed with Einarr. But these were no boats, those were no timbers.

The priestess swayed, arms on high but this time her right hand reflected the firelight. Shaped black stone wrapped around her closed fist, fingers linked through the grip on the back of a blade with the contours of the new moon.

She stepped forward, staring at the crowd from her mask

of a snarling big cat. Her blade swept first into the chest of the woman, and then the man, swift cuts made with deft precision. She stepped back and handed the knife to a priest. The flames on the brazier were coaxed higher by another priest, bathing her in dark yellow. She reached into each chest of the young man and woman and stepped towards the crowd.

When her hands swept aloft, blood streaming red down her bare arms, she held their hearts. Brann felt he could see them beat yet.

Violently, bent double by the force of the spasm, he vomited.

Marlo was already slumped on the ground, vacant shock in his eyes. Brann was wrenched upright. The last he saw was the two hearts cast upon the brazier, the flames leaping high, before he was dragged below, the humming reaching a crescendo as he staggered from it, tripping on the chain at his feet.

He was a third of the way from the bottom of the stairs when he fell. His mind was too numb to care, but unconscious reflexes turned his body to strike the stone floor at an angle and in a tumble. It did not prevent the back of his head from striking a wall, however.

He opened his eyes, gasping, as icy water dripped from his face. He could feel his wrists and ankles manacled once again to the wooden posts. He blinked while his eyes focused, as much trying to hasten the process as shake water from his lashes. The Messenger stood before him, a wet bucket in his hand.

Loku was behind the man. 'He is injured?' The Messenger shook his head. 'I am glad.' He stepped forward to Brann. 'I would rather this was resolved with no harm done.'

Brann shook water from his head in a spray of droplets, and his vision began to swim again. He let it settle, snarling, 'No harm? What about those two people out there, or what's left of them?'

Loku shook his head sadly. 'Sometimes, to save a body you must cut off a finger. They were that finger.'

'They were people. With lives. With families.'

'They were, they were, it is true. But their sacrifice was intended to save a population.'

'Why them?'

Loku stooped to pick up a stray feather from the floor. He stared at its detail as he spoke. 'The sacrifice was powerful. Two, not one. Young, not old. In love, which itself has great power. That love consummated for the god, which holds even greater power. The vessel of their souls, holding all of that power and still beating with life, given to fire, the very element that envelops Texacotl. It is the strongest of all sacrifices.' He turned his eyes to Brann, crushing the feather abruptly and dropping it casually behind him.

Brann was aghast. 'And you honestly believe that this will calm the fury of your god, or hold back the contents of that mountain?'

Loku chuckled. 'Of course not.' He shook his head in amusement. 'What you witnessed was the final resort of a desperate people who have tried everything less than this. They would never contemplate such an act under any normal circumstances.' He looked directly at Brann. 'Do you now see the extent of the desperation here? Can you understand why I must do what I must to save them? Will you help me save them?'

'Me? You hate me. You have tried to kill me.'

'Of course you.' Loku smiled gently. 'I know I developed a dislike for you, based upon the difficulties you caused me. And I did, as we know, place you in positions where it was likely that others would kill you. But they did not.' He stroked the front of his cloak, aligning feathers precisely. 'When I returned here to my home, when I immersed myself once more in my faith, I saw things more clearly. If the gods did not want you dead, then They must have a purpose for you. And if They think you can help me in saving my people, I will gladly follow Their will.'

Brann spat on the floor. 'How could I help someone who butchers two innocent people and rips the hearts from their living bodies, in the name of pleasing an angry god?'

Loku shrugged. 'I do not believe it will give a god even a moment's pause for thought. But what is important is that the people believe it will help. We are a highly religious people – our priests have spent centuries ensuring that this is the case – and so, as their leaders, we must show them we have taken the ultimate step, we have given the god the most potent offering there is. And they must see that it has failed. That it was not enough.'

Brann stared at him wild-eyed. 'What atrocity greater than that could you perform? Although I notice that you didn't have the stomach for the work you ordained in that square tonight.'

Loku carefully picked up his bird mask, tucking it under one arm. 'Would you expect a general to hack in the front rank or to direct the battle? Would you expect the king to cook the hog for the feast or the high priest to delve in the chest of a sacrifice?' He laughed, a merry sound. 'Of course not, and neither would a god. A god would see the value of the sacrifice, not the simple act that makes it, and so do the believers who witness it, and those who are told of it.'

'And those who are the meat of your sacrifice? What do they see?'

'They are told they must be a part of a rite, but not the form that rite will take. Once the draught takes effect, they know nothing at all. We are not savages, after all.'

'You are not...?'

Loku continued, talking over Brann with an amused smile and a sigh. 'Look, being the High Master of a religion has several advantages other than the ability to decide that I must travel abroad in my duties and represent my people. To these people, I am their leader and their ambassador. To the Emperor, I am his trusted Source of Information, having travelled to Sagia as a young man and giving two decades of my life to proving worthy of that role, my stature in the priesthood rising on the back of my accruing power at the Empire's courts, and the Emperor's opinion of my value increasing with my growing influence in the priesthood of the lands that supplied the gold that underpins his administration; each feeding on the other. And latterly, to the network of terror that I orchestrate, I am a simple agent of the cause, and who would suspect one so lowly to be a danger?'

'And yet you control them all.'

'Of course. In every case I am at the heart of the activity, while still placing the pieces on the boards of all three games. And soon the three boards will become one, and the pieces will link. It is what I must do, for my people.' He looked thoughtfully at Brann. 'I did notice that you also did not have the stomach for it. Which is surprising considering what acts you have managed yourself when your next breath is at stake.'

Brann's eyes flared with fury. 'Only because I had to. And never... that.'

Loku shrugged. 'Regardless, I would have you contemplate my invitation.'

Brann shook his head in disbelief. 'Work with you? You are insane.'

A strand of Loku's oil-slicked dark hair had dropped over his face, and he swept it back, sighing with regret. 'It seems that the gods must merely have meant you to supply me with answers. There are certain things I would know.' He ticked off questions on his fingers. 'I would know who is my enemy, the one who sent you, the one at the Imperial Palace who dictates your actions? What you wanted with the Tribe of the Desert? And what is known of my plans?' He leant forward, and Brann saw something in his eyes, something he had not seen there before, something he never expected to see. Sincerity. Tenderness. Loku spoke softly. 'The gods are everything to us. They have given us everything we have. But all my people have now is me. I do not know why the Great God threatens us with His doom, and I do not know what He wants from us to avert it. Our scriptures say we must face His judgement face on, and not falter in our adoration as we redeem ourselves in His eyes, else we will pass from the gaze of the gods, and our culture, our time in this land where we are privileged to live in the shadow of the gods, will wither and die.' He paused, his breath catching in his throat. 'I do not know what Texacotl wants from us, and I cannot lead my people from His shadow and condemn all in these lands where our very essence is rooted centuries deep. And so I have failed them. I have failed them, unless I can find the truth; unless I can find the source of the truth. And I know the truth is kept safe, hidden, protected. I will have it, and I will take it with all I can muster, for this one last hope is all I have. Is all my people have. I cannot fail them again. I will save them. I must save them. I have hated you; I have wanted you dead. But for this, I can love you. If you can so powerfully stand in my way, time after time, the gods have put a power within you. Stand with me, and bring that power to save these lives. Men's lives, women's lives, children's lives: innocents all. Can you not see this? Help me save my people. Please.'

Brann was taken aback by the earnestness that extended from Loku's voice to the man's eyes. He allowed his gaze to slowly drift around the room as if assessing the situation, trying to hide the fact that he bought time to assess instead Loku's questions. That Loku would guess someone influential at the palace was involved was expected: too much had been influenced contrary to Loku's plotting during Brann's time in Sagia for there to be anyone behind it less than highly placed in the Empire. Loku knew that Brann and his companions had travelled the desert for he had sent men after them, but he would wonder what had made the band go there instead fleeing to their homelands: they must have had a compelling reason. And the most obvious question was the last: *what is known of my plans?*

There was little that was surprising there, and even less that was likely to be answered. His eyes caught Marlo's; the boy's shock at their situation and the scene they had witnessed outside was clear in the frozen face, drained of colour. He knew Marlo must have one thought foremost in his head, pounding with increasing terror: if they can do that to their own...

He also knew what would follow when Brann had done

what he would do next. But there was nothing else he could do.

Loku cleared his throat. 'At times, we all must do things we never before contemplated, if there is a greater good.' He smiled encouragingly. 'The Royal? The Tribe? The plans?'

Brann spat at his feet. 'There are some things no man should ever do. There are things no man should see, or has a right to see. There are limits to what a man can justify.' He looked into Loku's eyes. 'Go fuck yourself.'

Loku shook his head sadly. 'You may not see the error of your thoughts, but you must see that we will have the answers soon enough, one way or another. And that the other way is not so unpleasant for you.'

Brann glared at him, trying to cover his fear with aggression. The image of Marlo's face slipped through his mind. Pure, innocent Marlo. He spat again. 'You are insane, the lot of you,' he snarled. 'A pox on you all, and a pox on your Texacotl. I don't know what's worse: a shit of a god who would destroy the only people who worship him, or the thick-as-shit people who would let him destroy them and praise him as he does it.'

Loku's composure faltered for the merest instant, fury flitting behind his benign facade like a shadow behind gauze. But he smiled coldly, and nodded. He looked at the Messenger, flicking a finger at Brann. 'Start with him.'

Brann sighed imperceptibly. The longer they were concerned with him, the longer before Marlo, who was less accustomed to pain, would be introduced to it. Still, as two of the men lifted a table to sit it in view of both captives and the Messenger unrolled a cloth bundle to reveal a gleaming array of instruments designed clearly for cutting, piercing, clamping, and striking, and several small vials of liquid, he couldn't help wondering at his decision, guilty as the thought made him. He swallowed, his stomach knotting, as the Messenger calmly lifted a rod bearing several lengths of differently coloured cord with an assortment of knots on each. He placed the ends of the rod on two hooks set into the wall close to the table and peered at one of the cords, tracing a finger down it as a clerk might when searching for a passage on a page.

Loku pulled a small chair back to the wall and swept his robe around him to sit. He smiled at the Messenger, and the man carefully selected a long-handled blade, much like a healer's scalpel.

The Messenger faced Brann, his voice as even and devoid of emotion as his face. 'Pain is, of course, the objective. Reaching the point when you would rather say the things you would rather not say than feel the sensations you would rather not feel. But you know what is the biggest influence here?' He stepped close and tapped the tip of the instrument on Brann's head. Despite himself, Brann felt his breath catch. 'Your own imagination is your greatest enemy in this, and the one you cannot avoid. Pain is bad, but worse is the anticipation. Knowing it is coming, knowing what is coming, and that you cannot prevent it. Even worse is knowing what is coming, but not where, nor when.' Brann was already acutely aware of this himself.

The Messenger held the blade before Brann's face, then traced it down his chest. He felt his muscles tensing at the touch. The metal moved to his left side, then up to his arm. 'Recent injuries, tended well and healed better. They may be useful.' The blade moved to his stomach. Without warning or pause, it pressed into and sliced the skin, sliding in just the depth of a fingernail but enough to make Brann clench his teeth and set sweat seeping as he fought not to shout. 'A sweet spot of pain,' the Messenger said, 'and a taster. Texacotl sends his regards.' He moved behind Brann. 'And now the anticipation. There are several such spots.'

Brann was so tense that he started to shudder. Control taught by combat stilled it after the briefest moment, but the edge of his vision caught Loku leaning forward in interest. Sick bastard, just as when the young sacrifices had been butchered.

Pain lanced from his shoulder and down his back as the blade was pushed into the top of his shoulder. 'A most helpful spot,' the Messenger explained calmly. 'A place where pain is more keenly felt, and generously distributed. There are several such spots around your body, as you will learn.'

Brann forced long slow breaths, his fists clenched. He knew he would scream at some point, but would make them wait as long as his will could manage.

The Messenger spoke softly. 'The Royal? The Tribe? The plans?'

Brann stared at the ceiling in silence.

The blade trailed across his back again. It lifted. Paused. The Messenger was right: he could not stop his mind wondering where, when.

But Loku cleared his throat. 'I am thinking. He could take a while.'

Brann cursed his misreading of the man's reaction. It has not been his fear that had piqued Loku's interest, but his control of it.

'It is possible to bring suffering without actually touching.' He flicked a diffident hand towards Marlo. 'Let us move your attention to our young friend over here. He may know less of value, but his worth to us is in the nature of what

361

our more knowledgeable guest will be able to bear. Let us test what he will be willing to let his dear companion suffer. Let the brave one see if he can be brave for his friend.'

Brann's eyes widened in horror, as Marlo's did in animal fear. 'No!' Brann shouted, but realised his mistake as he did so.

Loku smiled.

The Messenger gestured to one of the men and a large mirror was carried behind Marlo, propped against the wall and angled to let Brann have an unimpeded view should the Messenger stand directly behind the boy. The Messenger himself moved to Marlo and without preamble stabbed the blade into the big muscle at the front of his thigh. Marlo managed to half-stifle a shout of pain and shock.

'The Royal? The Tribe? The plans?' the Messenger asked the boy.

Marlo whimpered involuntarily, stopping it almost as soon as it came. He made no more response.

Loku shrugged. 'The watching one will know more than he, I am sure. Apply the incentive.'

The Messenger nodded simply and stepped behind Marlo. He laid the edge of the instrument on one shoulder blade.

Marlo shook, but stared at Brann, his voice weak, but audible. 'Say nothing.'

Brann stared at him, but as the Messenger's hand moved, Brann found himself unable to stop his eyes from moving to the mirror. The blade sliced a long slow line down at a slight angle, then returned to the spot and cut another, creating a narrow inverted 'V'. Marlo shuddered, head thrown back, and a low moan followed every inch of the cutting.

The Messenger examined his work. Apparently satisfied,

he moved to the table and selected slender pincers similar to, but larger than, those that would be used by maids to pluck errant hairs from a noble lady's eyebrows, and a new cutting instrument, this one with a longer, broader blade. He returned to Marlo's back and used the pincers to grasp the point of the shape he had cut and pulled, the blade sliding underneath and following the movement downwards. The skin peeled away and hung, revealing the raw flesh beneath. Marlo screamed, a juddering noise that lasted beyond the Messenger's action.

Brann stared at the ceiling, the pain he felt inside as keen as that he had endured on his back. He snarled at his weakness, forcing his eyes down to meet Marlo's. To abandon the boy completely now would be selfishness before compassion, and compassion was all he had in his power to give.

The Messenger turned to the mirror, his reflection looking at Brann. 'The Royal? The Tribe? The plans?'

Brann looked at Marlo. The boy opened his eyes. The movement trembling, he shook his head. Brann strained at his shackles, roaring in impotent fury. To watch Marlo suffer was beyond comprehension. But to help Loku with the information he needed would bring death and suffering beyond death, as they had seen from his minions already, to thousands, maybe thousands upon thousands. But Marlo was here, now. He could end it. They would die either way – why force such suffering on the boy? He looked again into Marlo's eyes. The boy's lips moved, sound refusing to come. He coughed, and tried again. Six words, hoarse. 'Give life meaning; give death meaning.' The words carved above the entrance to the sleeping quarters at Cassian's school, where their friendship had been forged.

That was why. To give in now seemed a betrayal to Marlo.

Loku must have seen the thought cross Brann's face. He sighed regretfully and gestured to the Messenger. The man calmly, as if he were doing no more than delicately filleting a fish, cut and peeled a second long flap from Marlo's back, the boy's scream filling the oppressive room. As the noise subsided and Marlo hung limply in his bonds, heaving chest the only movement, the Messenger again turned to the mirror. 'The Royal? The Tribe? The plans?'

Brann shook his head, hatred in his eyes but resolve weakening in his heart. He pulled on his suppressed self: the Brann born in the depravity of the fighting pits of the City Below; the Brann who emerged to fight; the Brann who could look on this. But that Brann was his to suppress, but not to summon, it seemed. That Brann rose when he chose, and the only conscious choice was to allow or deny that rise. He despaired. He looked at Marlo, ready to say he was sorry, that he could take no more. He locked his eyes with his friend, expecting fear.

But finding strength.

Astounded and ashamed once more, he ignored all but Marlo.

The Messenger gave no reaction but walked to his table, placing the bloody instruments on a rag laid to the side of the selection before him. His hands paused, moving to a large knife as the hatch above opened. The men assisting him moved before Loku, their broad blades held ready, but the tension relaxed as a local man hurried down the steps. Ignoring the scene of torture, he knelt before Loku until a light tap on his head raised him to his feet and allowed him to deliver his message in a low tone.

Loku turned to Brann. 'It seems our demonstration of the inadequacy of all we can do here to appease the god, has achieved success. The time has come to address the people, who are now ready to accept that I must seek the greater knowledge we need elsewhere. Even the highest priest needs the support of the people for the greatest of religious ventures. If you could be so good as to be helpful before I leave to join those who have been made ready for the fulfilment of my plans, it would be appreciated. If that helpfulness comes after I leave,' he looked at the Messenger, 'follow and enlighten me. I trust you to know what to do, in the meantime, to obtain it.'

The Messenger bowed his head. 'As ever, High Master.'

Loku nodded, picked up his bird mask, and left.

As if he had never been interrupted, the Messenger walked to the knotted cord and the wall and ran his fingers across them and, finding one, following it down as he looked at the knots with eyes and fingertips both, once more as if reading them. He nodded with satisfaction and turned back to his table, looking evenly across his precisely assembled equipment and tapping his fingers across the small vials of liquid until he selected one with a small grunt of recognition.

He unstoppered it as he moved to Marlo and, with no pause, delicately poured the contents into the top of each great wound on the boy's back, letting the liquid run down the exposed flesh.

Marlo's eyes went as wide as his mouth, his body arching forward in a spasm of agony as a sound, beyond a scream, a primeval noise of madness, burst from his core.

The Messenger waited patiently for Marlo to lose the strength to scream. He moved to the side of him to stare directly at Brann. 'The Royal? The Tribe? The plans?'

Brann filled his mind with the look in Marlo's eyes. His voice was a snarl of hatred. 'Fuck you.'

The man shrugged. 'We have had pain. Now we add loss. Remember, when we stop is your decision.'

Brann fixed his eyes on Marlo. Marlo looked back. 'Stay on me, Marlo. Only me.'

The boy nodded, though his body still shook without cease. Brann could hear the Messenger at the table, replacing the vial and picking up something else. He moved in front of Marlo, blocking Brann's view. His right hand lifted, and Marlo gasped, a high moan slipping from his lips. Brann started shaking, but it was nothing to the judder that convulsed Marlo as the Messenger reached towards his face.

Marlo croaked what sounded like two words, and the Messenger paused. 'I did not catch that,' he said evenly. 'You will have to repeat it.'

Marlo forcibly cleared his throat. 'Prince Kadmos,' he said, his voice a rough whisper.

'Good, good,' the Messenger said. He nodded to one of the men, who mounted the stairs in three bounds and ran from the house. 'The Royal. Now you see what is possible? However, your back would have thanked you for an earlier answer.'

He looked at Brann, and Brann stared back. The metal cuffs restraining him seemed ever more solid as he strained against them. If he could have one act left in his life, it would be to kill this man before he touched Marlo again.

The Messenger looked at Marlo from up close, his head cocked to one side as if assessing the bloodied boy. 'I am afraid, however, there were three questions.'

His right hand lifted. His left hand twisted itself into Marlo's hair to stop the violent trembling. The screaming started even before the instrument made contact.

When the Messenger stepped back, Marlo's head dropped,

but not before showing a face of awful contrast: the right side untouched, the Marlo he knew, the features familiar albeit slack with shock; but the left side... the left side drenched in a mass of blood and gore, the greatest concentration where, until scant moments before, his eye had sat.

The other Brann burst free. He felt coldness settle over him, a calm analysis unencumbered by emotion or convention. He was still himself, with his thoughts and memories and knowledge and opinions, but everything was more... straightforward.

The Messenger walked slowly to Brann, his impassive expression at odds with the blood and the gods only knew what else thick from the instrument in his hand to his elbow, dripping a macabre trail from Marlo to Brann, a connection of blood.

A connection of blood.

He understood that. And he understood that this man had to die. The uncertainty was how and when, but the certainty was that it must happen.

The Messenger stopped in front of him, staring into his eyes. Brann no longer strained at his bonds. It was obvious they would not break, so it would be pointless and a waste of strength. He looked back with equal calm and, in that moment, saw the first seed of surprise, perhaps even doubt, in the Messenger's eyes.

'The Tribe?' the man said. 'The plans?'

Brann frowned. 'Why would I tell you after what you have done to my friend?'

'So I will do no more? Believe me, this is only the beginning.'

Brann shook his head. 'You are already hurting him. You will kill us now, or you will hurt him more and then kill us. Or you will hurt him more, and then me more, and then kill us. When you kill us, the pain will be meaningless.'

'But when it is happening, it will be meaningful.'

Brann looked past him at Marlo. 'There is little more you can do. More of the same. Other pain. But it can only last so long. Tomorrow, and next week, and next year, and after that, it will be nothing, as if it never happened. But if I tell you, it will make it worthwhile. Why would I make this worthwhile?'

'And if I take his other eye?'

Brann nodded thoughtfully. 'Painful, yes. Horror to his mind, yes.' He looked at the man. 'But, truthfully, what difference if you have two eyes, or one eye, or no eyes when you are dead?'

The Messenger shrugged. 'We will see if you think the same when I bring forth his guts. When I take his arms and legs, bone by bone. When I turn him into a living monstrosity. When I keep him on the edge of death, denying him the release he begs for, with one pain after another. I need not take it slowly from pleasure nor hurry from distaste, I will just do what it takes. It is just a job.'

'I can understand that.' Brann looked deep into the man's gaze. 'Which is why I will kill you.'

The Messenger looked pointedly at the stout metal encasing Brann's wrists and ankles. 'You may be mistaken there.'

Brann looked deeper. His voice was a whisper, conspiratorial. 'I know it.'

He did not know it. He had no idea how it could possibly be accomplished. But he saw fear.

He smiled.

The Messenger composed himself in the space of a heartbeat. 'We will—'

The man across the room gave a strange gurgling sound. The Messenger started to turn, irritated at the disturbance. The movement brought him closer to Brann. Very slightly closer, but enough. Brann took the chance. He lurched as far as his arms would allow, his teeth closing on the man's throat. Closing and biting and clenching, holding tight, arterial blood seeping then flowing then spraying on his face, filling his mouth with the taste, threatening to choke him, snorting from his own nose as his own body tried to breathe, ignoring it all as he worried and pulled and shook and grunted like a fighting dog finishing its opponent. And the Messenger was finished, the fact masked from him only by his desperation. Trapped by the grip of the teeth he stabbed at Brann with the instrument in his hand, but it was designed for a purpose other than piercing; his other hand pulled and punched and grabbed and gouged but Brann gripped unyielding. An indiscernible shape flitted beyond his clear sight and, above the noise of his own grunts of effort and the frenzied gurgled gasps of the Messenger, sounds reached his ears of struggle, but he had only one thought, only one purpose. The Messenger's movements had quickly weakened and slowed and it was only a short time before the man fell limp. As his body sagged and Brann's teeth began to take his weight, he at last let go. The man fell at his feet. Brann spat blood and sweat and lost the taste of neither.

The room fell silent. Footsteps approached from behind. He tensed. Lamplight flashed on a blade stabbing down. His muscles tensed automatically, uselessly. A knife thunked into the wooden post to his right, embedding itself below his hand, level with his head. His knife, from the forearm sheath.

'Thought I'd never get the chance to return it,' a woman's voice said, low and with the slightest hint of hoarseness. And amused.

He shot a look at his weapons in a bundle at the wall. On the top were his arm sheaths, the last to have been removed from him. One was still filled.

The woman walked to the front of him. *Her build was athletic and strong, her hair the colour of the summer sun and framing a face of golden of hue and heart-shaped, who moved as only can a dancer or a warrior. When pale blue eyes turned to meet his, he knew she was no dancer.*

The coldness slipped from him. 'You,' he breathed, still panting. 'You?' The surprise and confusion lasted as long as it took for urgency to explode through his veins and into his head. 'Please!' He flicked his head at the restraints.

She nodded and slipped the pin from the cuff at one hand. He immediately reached for the other while she freed his feet. He stumbled as awkward stiffness stiffened his legs, but he ignored it and forced his legs to move, pushing past her in a frantic rush to Marlo.

'Oh sweet heaven,' she gasped as her eyes followed his movement. 'I was focused on the guard and then on you. The poor, poor boy. Does he live?'

'He had better.' The emotion growled from Brann. 'He will, or the gods will know my fury.'

He made to grasp Marlo around the chest to support him, but remembered the terrible wounds on his back and gripped him at the armpits. 'Release him.'

She did so and he took Marlo's weight. She helped him gently lay the boy on his front, and the injuries to his back became apparent. She gasped and made to lift the flaps of skin back into place.

Brann stopped her. 'He poured something into them, for pain.' His eyes darkened. 'For *more* pain. They need to be rinsed clean, I would guess.'

She looked across at the Messenger. 'That death was too good for him.'

Despite everything, Brann felt embarrassment. He wiped his hands at his face, hoping it would remove the blood – and whatever else – remained there. 'I... I had no other way to kill him.'

She shrugged. 'When you have to kill someone and there is only one way, that becomes a good way.'

'It was not the first time I have done that.' He didn't know why he felt the urge to explain. He wasn't even sure what he was explaining. He was just letting thoughts become words.

She stood. 'Then you must have had only that one way before now. You don't seem the sort to seek enjoyment in biting people to death.'

Brann frowned. 'I'm not, but how would you know? It is the only thing you have seen me do other than lay a knife on a step.'

She smiled a dark smile. 'And I thank you for that. But I have seen much more. From afar, but it has still been seen.' Brann tensed. 'Don't panic, I was sent by a friend, one with your best interests at heart. Most of my efforts were, however, in keeping up with your trail. It is fortunate that this occasion was one of those when I was close, although for you and, especially this boy, it would have been better to have been closer.'

Brann looked at her sharply 'You were sent to follow us? Who sent you? What do you know?'

Before she could answer, the sound of a door crashing

open in the room above sent the pair hurtling across the room, the woman to the stairs, a short sword appearing in one hand and a knife in the other, and Brann to the nearest dead guard, reaching for the broad-bladed weapon at his side. Before either could reach where they intended, however, Gerens hurtled down from above.

'Wait!' Brann shouted at the woman. 'He is a friend.'

She lowered her weapons. 'I know.' She looked at him. 'Trailing, watching: remember?'

Gerens reached halfway down the stairs, his eyes taking in the scene, and jumped from the side of them into the room. Grakk and Konall followed.

Relief showed clear in their faces as they saw Brann, but then their eyes fell upon Marlo. Grakk was first to him, kneeling over the boy, his fingers probing quickly. 'He is alive?'

The woman nodded. 'Barely.'

Grakk registered no surprise at her presence, absorbed in Marlo's state.

The woman walked to the table, picking up the one empty vial. She tossed it to Grakk. 'This was poured into the wounds on his back, I believe.'

Grakk sniffed it and nodded. 'Pain, but not damage. Though enough damage has been done.' He looked at Konall. 'Find water.' And at Gerens. 'Get what you can that is unbloodied on the tunics of those men. I need rags for cleaning and strips for bandaging.'

Both complied without wasting time on an answer.

Now that Marlo was receiving more expert attention than he could have offered, Brann started to feel naked without his weapons. The closest was the knife stuck in the wooden post.

A man rushed down through the hatch, his features marking him as a local. Brann snatched the knife but, as he threw, Gerens hurtled into his side, knocking his arm askew and sending the blade to clatter against the wall further down the stairs.

'He is with us, chief,' Gerens said.

The man was frozen in shock, staring at the knife. He looked hesitantly at Brann. 'My home is across the street. I was on the roof, wondering at the commotion in the temple square, and saw you two foreigners on this roof with the High Master and the others. Then I heard noises, noises that were not good.' He shuddered. 'Not good at all. I remembered talk at my temple – not that temple, where they did that... that thing – a different temple. A temple where we do not interpret the lore of our gods to as brutal effect as the High Master preaches. And when I heard talk of newcomers from lands afar, asking questions, I followed the whispers and sought them out. I sought to trade my knowledge of their friends for their knowledge that I thought may help us.' He paused, looking at Marlo with a sudden intake of breath. 'What I see here makes me regret that I did not find them sooner.'

Brann frowned. 'Why would you seek to help strangers? Why act against the High Master who seeks to save your people?'

The man made to step down, but hesitated and looked at Gerens. The wild black hair shook as the boy nodded that it was safe to proceed and the man walked forward, stopping to pick up the knife gingerly and hand it to Brann.

'Not all who worship are fanatics. Not all agree with what we are told. Not all want what we see. But to speak out at this time of fear is not a safe thing to do. Better to leave quietly, which is what my family are doing – have prepared to do every night, without the opportunity presenting itself.' He hesitated, dropping his gaze in embarrassment. 'This is not an easy place to leave at the moment, and a small family is no match for a squad of the High Temple's guards. I guessed that your party would be wishing to leave also, and thought that if I offered to guide you, then maybe you would help us if we need a more… physical approach.'

Brann nodded. 'Then we are fortunate indeed that there is one good man here.'

The man's eyes were sad. 'There are many who are good here, but many are afraid and that proves fertile ground for those who would sway their thoughts. We are fortunate, we have family in another city. I would hope that others would follow, but hope is all I have. I must see to my own family.'

'Certainly you must,' Brann said. 'Please, go, be with your family.'

The man nodded. 'My name is Matala-Kitu. I will pray for you.'

'As will I for you and your family.'

The man smiled and moved towards Grakk. 'First, I will check if there is anything needed from my home to help your injured friend.'

Konall had returned, a large ewer in his hands. 'Talking of names…' He nodded at the woman, who was cleaning her weapons on what Gerens had left of the tunic of one of the guards.

She looked up. 'Xamira,' she said. 'It means *diamond* in the old language of my people.'

Brann faced her. 'Brann,' he said. 'I think it just means Brann.'

'Gerens. The same.'

'Konall. After my mother's grandfather.'

'Guarak-ul-Karluan. It means *Soul of the Rock* to my people.' Grakk noticed the others' amused looks. 'My mother was a little overdramatic, I feel.'

Grakk had cleaned Marlo's wounds and spread them with his salve, and was finishing binding the skin on his back tightly in place with the bandages since he lacked needle and thread. He came to Brann and, without a word, turned him and quickly examined him, looking closely at the puncture on his shoulder.

'I will wager that was nippy,' he said.

'Somewhat,' Brann conceded. 'But nothing to what Marlo endured.'

'*Less than* does not mean *insignificant*,' Grakk pointed out.

He cleaned it and the wound on his stomach, smearing both with salve and pressing it into the cuts. Brann winced but said nothing. Being fixed was always better than receiving what needed to be fixed. If there was fixing going on, you were alive. Practised fingers quickly bound the wounds in strips of tunic, and Grakk returned to Marlo.

Gerens tossed a white tunic to Brann. 'I have enough material from the others and the owner of this one had his neck broken, so no blood or rips.' He nodded approvingly at Xamira.

Brann pulled it on and moved to gather his weapons. He saw the approving expression have replicated on Xamira's face when he assembled his extensive collection of blades. As he slipped the second forearm knife into its long-empty sheath, he smiled at her. She winked.

He looked at Marlo. Grakk was winding a bandage carefully around his head. He flexed his arm, feeling the bandages pull tight around his shoulder and around his torso. They would hold.

Konall looked at him. 'Now what?'

Brann looked at Grakk, who nodded and started to lift the still unconscious Marlo to a sitting position. 'The ship was putting into the next port along the coast after it had finished its business where it dropped us. So now, we run.'

Matala-Kitu was near the top of the stairs, but stopped at his words. He smiled broadly. 'Then there is something more I can help with after all.'

Chapter 8

The girl left the room with the softest of clicks as the door shut behind her. He stared into the fire as the old figure moved from sweeping sand from the floor to sit in the high-backed chair beside him.

'She has done well,' her dry voice whispered.

He could tell she was tired. Her voice always was the first to show it. 'She has accomplished what was asked.'

'Which is good, is it not?'

'Nothing is good or bad until we have information. When we do, we can act according to good or bad. In my experience, it is usually some of both.'

'In my experience also. You are prepared?'

His irritation rose. 'You think I would be content to sit idle?' He knew he was more annoyed at the waiting than at her. He snorted, the closest she would get to an apology.

'I would expect nothing otherwise.'

He could hear the smile in her voice, which was the closest she would go towards acknowledging an apology.

'And the one we cannot control? He in his throne room above us?'

'He will be the ruin of us all.' He thumped the arm of his chair in anger. 'Two millens. Two! It is like watching strategy in a child's game of war. But at least a child would listen to those who know. How can one who listens to no one but those who seek favour ever hope to learn?'

'He will learn,' she said flatly, 'but through failure.'

'Perhaps. Perhaps not even then. Some believe even their own excuses. And, in any case, by then the situation could be irretrievable by him.'

They sat in silence, the crackling fire fighting the chill of the dark evening as the heat of the day was lost to the clear sky of night.

'I have a bad feeling,' she said.

'Now you know my life,' he said.

****

They moved quickly, but not fast enough to draw attention, through streets busy for the hours of darkness.

'People may wish to sleep, but their needs do not,' Matala-Kitu explained, noting their surprise. 'Bakers need flour, carts need wheels, cooks need ingredients, craftsmen need materials and mended tools. All these and many more must be ready for the new day. Most people work during that day, but some are allocated to ensuring that they can do so. Everyone is of use, especially in these times when many have been conscripted for martial service: it is the way. Is that not so where you come from?'

Grakk looked at the scene they were passing through. 'Not on this scale of organisation.' He was clearly impressed.

The local man shrugged. 'Each has their own approach to life, I suppose.'

'Nothing truer than that,' Konall grunted.

Matala-Kitu nodded. 'In our case tonight, it serves us to be taking stores to the mines. Thus is explained the cart, which my family need for the few belongings we take with us.'

Brann frowned. 'You need to hide your travel?'

The man looked at him with a level gaze. 'Normally, no.'

Brann looked up at the cart, drawn through the winding streets by two mules made remarkably obedient at the deft touch of Matala-Kitu's wife, Lita. She and their child, a boy of some fourteen years, sat with a semi-conscious Marlo propped between them. He had been dressed in one of the ubiquitous white tunics and his dark hair had been slicked back with oil in accordance with the local custom; with his sallow skin, he could pass as a slightly older son. It was fortunate, Brann thought, that neither he, Konall nor Gerens, with their pale Northern features, nor Grakk, with his tattooed scalp, had been injured – and immediately guilt ran through him. What Marlo had endured...

Matala-Kitu walked with the four of them, carrying baskets on their shoulders with a selection of mining tools, worn but workable. 'My skill,' he had explained, 'is not in making them, but in repairing them. It too, is important.'

Grakk had nodded. 'Everyone is of use.'

'It is the way,' Matala-Kitu agreed.

They walked a short distance behind the cart, as if unconnected, but close enough should they be needed. Their foreign appearance, even under the shifting lamplight in the streets, had worried Brann but it was not long before he began to notice that a small, but significant, number of those they passed were clearly not from these lands.

Grakk noticed his head turning to follow a large red-headed man who looked as if he would be more at home in Cardallon. 'People travel for many reasons,' he said, 'and settle for many more. Where they go, they must work to live.'

Matala-Kitu spoke from behind. 'It is indeed so. The only place a foreigner may not work is within the mine, otherwise they can, and must, as everyone else must, contribute to the life of the city. It is the way. Although, as there is no direct link in them to the land and therefore the gods, they cannot offend Texacotl by fleeing in the face of his anger, as a fair number have done since his discontent began.'

'Thankfully not all,' Brann said as they approached the start of the road from the city and leading to the mine, several armed men impassively eyeing all who left the city.

The moment passed without incident, however. Marlo's bandaged head and dazed state drew their attention, but Lita's rehearsed explanation of an accident with a hoe at a farm and their inability to leave him unattended while they made the essential delivery to the mine was accepted. The continued flow of work, it seemed, took precedence over all.

They left habitation behind them with the mountain of the god to their right, following the road that led towards, and then switched back and forth across, a gradient slightly less steep than the others surrounding the city. They passed the point where the green-brown grass abruptly ended and bare rock began and shortly after reached a plateau that rose vertically at its far side into a cliff face that was as much a hive of activity with its multitude of openings and ledges festooned with pulleys and cranes as the level space was before it, more people performing more tasks than the eye could take in at first glance.

Every group, whatever their task, whether at the cliff, the area before it or the workshops and animal pens to one side, was supervised by priests, conspicuous in their rainbow plumage and with expressions of a sternness more in keeping with those who had performed the sacrifice than with the kindness shown by those they had met in the street temples. Brann shuddered slightly, but not without his attention being drawn to a frame beside many of the priests, coloured and knotted cord hanging on each and the clerics consulting them periodically. He remembered the knotted cords in the room of torture, and his shudder turned to the need to fight against retching as he walked.

Matala-Kitu directed them towards the left side of the area, indicating a spot near that end of the cliff, while the cart headed straight to their destination.

'Would it not be quicker to follow the cart on the direct route?' Gerens said.

'Indeed it would,' Matala-Kitu agreed, 'but much riskier. Only those of the blood of the land can even approach the entrances to the mines, or death ensues without hesitation or challenge. It is the way.'

They headed parallel to the cliff as far from it as they could manage before turning directly in line with the point Matala-Kitu had pointed out. As they drew closer, Brann could make out a low broad opening where the rock face angled away from the cliff towards the more haphazard rock and varying slopes to the side of the plateau.

'We travel through there?' he asked Matala-Kitu.

'We travel through there,' the man confirmed.

'It is the way,' Konall quipped sardonically.

They reached the spot shortly after the slower cart, and gathered before a set of broad low-sided carts, five in number, linked fore and aft with each other. Most curiously, however, was that they sat on a stone road leading into the opening in the rock... or rather within the road. A pair of deep grooves had been cut into the stone with stunning precision, the thick wooden wheels – the rims clad in a band of iron to protect against the wearing of the stone – sitting secure within the grooves.

A similar pair of grooves ran in line alongside and, as they watched, four broad-chested oxen of a sort bigger than any Brann had seen in his travels pulled another set of five carts into the open, laden with nothing more than a dozen men.

A man approached them fast, and Brann reached automatically for the weapons that would have hung from his belt, but were concealed within their own small cart. He corrected the motion, sliding each hand instead towards the opposite elbow, his fingers gratefully finding the knives under his loose sleeves. As he felt the second of the pair of blades, his mind turned to Xamira.

As if on cue, her voice murmured in his ear. 'Relax, not everyone wants to fight you.' She chuckled. 'Note that his hurry is anxious rather than aggressive.'

The man made directly for Matala-Kitu. 'You must hurry.' He indicated the lightening sky above the mountain tops. 'We must leave soon.'

Matala-Kitu nodded and turned to his son. 'Fetch the men to unload the supplies from the cart and to take the tools from the baskets.'

The boy pointed behind them. 'They approach already, Father.'

'Good.' He turned to the rest of them. 'While they are unloading, use the activity to cover you taking our things

382

from the cart to the first carriage. Then, when it is moving, climb in.'

Konall frowned. 'Will that not attract attention? Climbing into the carriage?'

'It will be expected. The first, third and last carriages carry the same cargo as the rest, but with room left for a group of men to help push past slow sections or clear the tracks of debris. We are the party for the first carriage.'

'And your wife, your boy and our invalid?' Gerens said.

'We must mask them as best as we can when they embark.'

There was no time for further discussion. The workers had arrived and in the bustle Brann's group did manage to retrieve their equipment and personal supplies. They threw them into the first carriage and tried to look as if they were loading it further as Marlo and Matala-Kitu's wife and son were helped aboard. Lying flat, the three were quickly covered using loose sacks with no alarm raised, to Brann's surprised relief.

He breathed more easily and made to climb after them, but Matala-Kitu put a swift hand on his shoulder. 'We must help to start the motion.'

Brann frowned, looking at the front of the leading cart. 'But the oxen are not here yet, and they will do that, surely?'

Matala-Kitu was puzzled. 'Why would we require oxen when we have the hills to do the work? This is ready to leave.'

Brann cocked his head in confusion but, before he could ask anything, a shout prompted them to action. Chocks were pulled way and men pulled stout poles from the wagons and inserted them through the thick spokes to lever the wheels forward, while the rest put the shoulders to work and heaved at the collection of carts.

To his surprise, Brann found the carts started to move almost immediately and more easily than he could ever have imagined. The men with the poles threw them back onto the wagons and added their strength to the effort as speed smoothly increased. Brann allowed himself a smile – the greatest difficulty might be in getting himself on board before it picked up too much speed. If that was the most serious danger, however, he would be happy.

As if to prove him a fool for his complacency, Marlo sat upright, wild alarm in his one visible eye and his face almost as pale as the bandage wound at an angle around his head. 'Mother!' he shouted, his voice shrill with fear. 'Mother, the sheep are dancing on the oranges! Stop them! We must stop them!'

Grakk vaulted onto the carriage beside him, placing a calming arm around his shoulders and producing a small vial from inside his tunic. Popping the stopper with a flick of his thumbnail, he lifted it to Marlo's mouth and let him drain the contents and, before he had finished easing the boy back down with soothing words, peaceful sleep had claimed him.

Grakk glanced back at the work area apprehensively, and Brann did likewise, taking care not to trip. The ground sloped very slightly down at this point and they were at the speed of a long lope now and would soon enter the dark opening in the rock, and he was acutely aware that he did not want to fall in front of one of those heavy iron-shod wheels. A priest was striding towards them, and as Brann watched, he pointed and shouted. Warriors, around a dozen, surged past him at a run.

An urgent shout came from the front of the wagon: 'Get on, now! We pick up speed soon.'

Brann was glad of the news but hoped at the same time that 'soon' would be 'very soon'. He grabbed the side of the wagon, the lip slightly below the level of his shoulder, and vaulted, tumbling in an ungainly heap onto heavy hessian sacks of hard lumps that bruised what felt like the length of his body. He rolled to his stomach and saw Konall sitting with perfect ease at the front and facing back, amusement lighting his eyes.

'Good to see you haven't lost your fondness for a comic fall,' the noble boy said drily. 'Marlo will be disappointed to have missed it.'

Brann grunted but too much breath had been knocked from him for him to utter the insult on his lips. He turned and looked back. The warriors were closing, some readying long flexible spears.

'Don't fret,' Konall said. 'No bows. Not even a giant could reach us with a spear from there.'

One man was ahead of the others, and he pulled a short rod, almost the length of his arm, from his belt and seemed to hook one end to the rear of his spear.

Grakk's eyes widened. 'Atlatl!' he shouted. 'Get down!'

Konall frowned. 'Whatl? Whatl?'

Before he could ask more, the wagon jolted and he fell to one side. With a thud that made them all jump, a spear hammered into the wood where Konall's chest had been just a heartbeat before. It flexed with the motion of the cart, fletchings bobbing in front of Brann's face as the wagon entered the opening. Almost immediately they felt the ground drop away more steeply and they picked up speed, plunging into the gloom of a tunnel lit by widely spaced lamps. Two further spears dropped just behind the final wagon.

'Thatl thatl, I assume,' Gerens said flatly.

Brann looked at Konall. 'If you hadn't fallen at that moment...'

Konall looked at the spear. He shrugged. 'It wasn't my time.'

Brann shook his head. 'Halvekans.' It took a hard tug to pull the spear from the wood, and he looked at the weapon, and then at Grakk. 'So, atlatl?'

Grakk looked at the spear, then back at Brann. 'My apologies to all of you. It slipped my mind that they used such weapons.'

'And I,' said Matala-Kitu, equally apologetically. 'I did not know that you were unaware. You do not have such where you come from?'

'Not atlatls, whatever they are, not wagons in grooves, not temperature farms in holes in the ground, not a lot of things, I realise.'

Matala-Kitu looked surprised. 'Really? How do you survive?'

Konall snorted. 'I am beginning to wonder.'

Brann touched the spear, and raised his eyebrows at Grakk.

'Ah, indeed, the atlatl,' the tribesman said. He turned the spear, pointing to a small hollow in the rear end. 'The atlatl is the short stick you saw the thrower hold. It is hooked at the end, which is fixed into here, and its use gives greater speed to the spear and, as you saw, greater range. The spear itself also helps in this respect, being more similar to an oversized arrow than to the javelins we are used to seeing.'

'There is much we could learn here,' Brann mused.

'Indeed,' Grakk agreed. 'But this is not something we could learn, but something we could remember. The records we have tell us that this was a method used in all lands in the distant past. As our larger sized game became more scarce, bows would suffice for the smaller animals remaining. Here, however, the practice has been retained.'

'And these carts in grooved roads?' Brann asked.

Grakk peered at the wagons with fascination as a light patch ahead indicated the end of the tunnel. 'These, I have not seen before.'

Matala-Kitu looked at him. 'Your knowledge reveals a previous time in our lands. But you have not visited our city before? Or at least, not our mine?'

Grakk shook his head. 'Neither.'

The man nodded. 'That makes sense. This track leads from Tucumala to Chula Pexl, the port you seek. The two cities have an agreement – they relish the trade our gold brings, and we need the deep waters of their port to send the gold to Sagia. For centuries, the track has linked the cities.'

They emerged into the morning light, and Brann glanced back along the wagons. He saw the other groups of men and tensed, reaching for his sword. They could not have missed the alarm at the mine, and it would be simple for them now that they could see what they were doing to step along the carriages to reach them.

But the men lay relaxing, their spirits visibly lifting as they reached the light. Matala-Kitu laid his fingers on Brann's hand and pushed it away from the hilt with a gentle smile. 'You think we are the only ones leaving the city today?'

Brann nodded at the man at the front of the wagon. 'And your friend?'

'My cousin.'

'He leaves too?'

'He will have to after the incident at the mine, or he will

find himself the subject of another sacrifice, though maybe a more private and instant one.' He smiled. 'But fortunately he was leaving also. He has no one in Tucumala – my father moved there from Chula Pexl before I was born and Kunakan-Atik joined us five summers ago to work at the mine.'

'And your parents?'

'There was a collapse in the mine not long after I became a father myself. My mother was taking supper to surprise my father when it happened.'

It was said simply but the emotion touched Brann. 'I'm sorry.'

Matala-Kitu looked over the landscape, the rays of the early sun slipping over the mountain ridges to lay a golden haze over the vegetation below them. 'Of course I miss them, but I have the responsibility to protect my family now, and there is no protection in sitting with them in the path of a god's anger when a couple of days' walk will let you witness the aftermath of what happens when gods become angry. Dead cities contain dead citizens, and if the gods will it, it will happen. I worship my gods but that doesn't mean I agree with the words of the current priests. If others believe them, that is their choice to make, but I make mine.' He looked at his cousin. 'Kunakan-Atik is a skilled steersman, but will have more future practising another craft in Chula Pexl, I fear. And openings for a diligent worker are always available when many of the most zealous have answered the call to arms.'

Brann frowned. 'There is war among the cities?'

Matala-Kitu shrugged. 'Not that we have heard, but these are uncertain and fearful times, thanks to the voice of the god within the mountain. Maybe the High Master gathers

holy warriors because he feels it prudent to be prepared.'
He shrugged. 'But I am only a simple workman looking out
for his family – who am I to guess at the motives of a lofty
priest?'

Brann nodded and looked at Kunakan-Atik, kneeling on
a cushion and grasping two vertical poles that extended
down outside the front of the wagon to what appeared to
be hinges near the base of the cart. Periodically he would
gently pull one or both towards him, and as he did so, a
corresponding pole attached to each handle and extending
vertically with a bright rag at the top – the left one red and
the right green – would move in tandem.

'Steersman?' Brann said.

'Indeed. This track moves ever downwards, and on some
occasions speed can become too great for the wagons to
remain on the track, particularly on corners. Those handles
slow the wheels at one side of this wagon or the other. An
assistant steersman in the final wagon,' Brann looked back
and wondered how he hadn't noticed the man before, but
realised that with only the handles and not the poles with
the flags, the man merged with the group around him,
'watches the flags at the front and mimics the movement of
Kunakan-Atik's handles. It is the man at the front who must
feel the motion and predict the track ahead to ensure the
speed is appropriate at all times. It is a skilled job.'

Brann looked at Kunakan-Atik with new appreciation.
'Lives are in his hands.'

'They are, but what is valued more is the gold in the
sacks. To lose any would be to incur the wrath of the gods
and the Empire, and neither is desired. Every trip carries
the same number of sacks, and every sack carries the same
weight of gold, and every shipment is checked under armed

guard as soon as it arrives at Chula Pexl. Should there be a deficit, those armed guards become executioners. Every person on the wagons is held responsible, so all do their utmost to ensure the cargo arrives intact.'

'Harsh.'

Matala-Kitu shrugged. 'It is the way. Riding the wagons carries prestige and bestows rewards, so many are encouraged to take the work and bring integrity and diligence with them.'

Brann looked at the heavy gold at the throats and on the arms of Matala-Kitu and his wife and cousin. 'Gold seems to be plentiful, it seems. Why would anyone be tempted to steal it anyway?'

'It is an adornment to us, worth less than grain or iron, for gold cannot keep you alive or plough a furrow. But it is worth much to those who visit the port, and so can be traded for much in return. There is the temptation.'

Brann nodded. 'And when we reach Chula Pexl, the cargo will be handed over and all aboard with us here will enter the city and disappear into its welcome arms.'

Matala-Kitu smiled. 'Precisely. We are safe now. No one is more skilled than Kunakan-Atik and although others can match him, now that we are clear we cannot be caught. There is a road to Chula Pexl for those who travel normally, on foot or mounted, but this is the quickest route and we will be there before the sun is halfway to its high point.'

Brann glanced at Marlo, still asleep thanks to Grakk's potion. As well as needing the ship for transport, the medical supplies on board would be invaluable. 'That is good,' he said.

Matala-Kitu smiled his gentle smile. 'You should take the chance to rest. By all accounts, you have had an eventful night.'

Brann realised he was right. The horror of the basement seemed distant and vivid at the same time, but the rigours had sapped as much energy as had the lack of sleep. As soon as he lay back, he drifted into sleep, though the memories of Marlo's ordeal saw to it that it was fitful rest at best.

A jolt in their motion jerked him fully awake. He sat up, knife in hand, but saw that Kunakan-Atik was drawing them to a halt in a section that ran between a small group of trees in a more lush area of ground. When they stopped, he pointed ahead, drawing the attention of those around him to what his sharp eye had spotted: a thick branch wedged into one of the track grooves. Should the wheels have been jumped from their secure hold, the consequences would almost certainly have been dire.

Gerens and Konall were already on the ground and quickly levered the branch free, tossing it well to the side. Kunakan-Atik was holding the wagons at a standstill with his handles – presumably aided by his assistant at the rear – and as soon as he let them go, the slope started them rolling once more. The men had dismounted and lent their muscles to the motion, although the steepness of the gradient saw them scramble aboard within a score of paces. Brann's effort was no more graceful than his last attempt, and Konall's amusement was just as great.

Brann sat up and looked back to check that everyone in the other wagons had also jumped in successfully, though why he thought anyone would be more clumsy than he in dragging themselves aboard, he wasn't sure. His eyes drifted further back, following the track winding in shallow curves to adapt to the terrain and marvelling at the level of ingenuity that could maintain a constant downwards slope for the distance they had travelled. His eye caught movement and he straightened.

'Do you see it also?' said Grakk.

Gerens sat up. 'What?'

'Something behind us,' Brann said, squinting.

Konall uncoiled himself and stood, one hand shading his eyes and balancing as if the wagon was solid rock rather than a haphazardly bouncing and rocking wooden platform. 'Shit,' he said. 'Pursuers.'

Matala-Kitu frowned. 'Are you sure? I know of no one who could travel this route quicker than my cousin.'

'Perhaps not with five wagons laden with gold, but this is one wagon on its own, laden with men. And a lot of shiny weapons.'

Matala-Kitu paled. 'How could I not have thought of this?'

'It doesn't matter now,' Brann said, his mind already working. 'Dwelling on what cannot be changed steals time from dealing with what can be.' He looked forwards. They were closing on an area of dense jungle, as Grakk had called it, with their track and the parallel route for ox-drawn wagons to return to the mine cutting a single tunnel of green shadow as sunlight struggled to pierce the thick foliage. 'How far to the city?' he asked.

'Ten minutes,' Kunakan-Atik called over his shoulder. 'The jungle extends for many miles to either side, but it is a narrow stretch ahead to Chula Pexl.'

Matala-Kitu was standing now, in a half crouch as he steadied himself with one hand on Brann's head. 'They are lighter and can take the bends faster.' There was near-panic in his voice, a long way from the calmly courageous outlook they had seen from him until now, and Brann realised the difference was the mortal danger to his wife and son. 'They will catch us in half that time.'

'Then,' Brann said slowly, 'let them.' The others looked at him aghast. 'If we cannot stop them catching us, ensure they do so on our terms, not theirs.'

'Agreed,' said Grakk.

Brann lifted Matala-Kitu's hand from his head, and the man immediately dropped to sit close to his family, a determined look settling over his face and a broad knife, similar to those that had been carried by the thugs who had captured Brann and Marlo, appearing in his hand.

Gerens looked across. 'So what do we do, chief?'

Brann thought for a moment. 'I need to check something with Kunakan-Atik.'

He moved beside the man and conferred quietly, wishing to keep his questions quiet until he was sure of what could be achieved. Satisfied, he turned back.

'Actually, Gerens, you could do something. You are the most nimble of us. Do you think you could make it back to those other wagons and tell the men to join us in this one? Including the steersman.'

Gerens gave a look that indicated his mystification that Brann could hold any doubt over his ability to achieve exactly that, and proceeded without hesitation to prove the fact. The other men took little time to join them, their movement hastened further when Gerens pointed out what followed them.

Brann pointed to the sacks. 'Try to pile those as much as you can, to give us some form of shelter from their spears. Once under the jungle trees, they won't be able to get much elevation in their throws and will just have to rely on flat power. A barrier will help shield us from that.'

They rounded a bend at speed, Kunakan-Atik using skill beyond their understanding just to keep the wagons on the track.

'Why,' said Konall as his knuckles turned white with gripping the side of the wagon for the length of the bend, 'do we go so fast if we want them to catch us?'

Brann grinned, the danger of the ride thrilling through him like the feeling of combat. 'Because we want them to catch us at speed.'

He glanced back, holding tight to the side of the wagon as it bumped and jostled and rattled and shook them as if they were toys in the jaws of the dogs of the gods. The hunters were closing even sooner than he thought. They could have just followed closely, to arrive at the destination where their prey would be caught between them and those waiting, but Brann had wagered that the scent of blood in their nostrils would fuel their zeal. They could have engineered the situation if it hadn't been the case, but the chasers' impatience helped.

He shouted to Kunakan-Atik and the man worked his handles gently, slowing them at an almost imperceptible rate. Brann turned to the occupants crammed into the wagon, their faces alight with excitement or fear... or both. 'When it slows enough, I will give you a shout, and if you want a chance of living, jump. At once.' He shot a quick look to one side, with the broad stone of the parallel tracks, and the other, with the thick jungle foliage. 'If I were you, I would leave at the side of the jungle – there may be a tree amongst the softer branches, but there is nothing but a hard landing on the other side. When you see the opportunity, fall on those behind us.' He glanced at Marlo and the woman and boy beside him. 'Those of us who can, that is.' Gerens and Konall already had Marlo sitting up and gripped between them, so he stilled his next instruction – they had anticipated that he would ask them to assist their friend.

The tracks curved to the left, slowing them further. As they exited it, Brann shouted, 'Jump, now!'

Immediately bodies started throwing themselves over the side, and in moments Brann and the steersman were alone aboard. He let it run a few breaths more, judging that the chasing wagon was entering the bend itself. He clapped Kunakan-Atik on the shoulder and shouted, 'Now!'

The man hauled on both handles, fighting against the momentum that urged them forward. Brann reached past him and grabbed a handle and they took one each, dragging back with both hands clenched and their entire bodies straining. He could feel the handle jumping in his grasp, but he also felt the change beneath his feet. The wagon jerked and jumped, held back in front and pushed from behind. He twisted, watching the wagons behind and the track beyond. The pursuers came into sight, several men with spears poised to throw and the steersman letting the wagon have its head as it careered onto the straight like a slingshot but surprise turning his head involuntarily as he saw the people lying to the side, some on the short sward cut to keep the trail clear, others having tumbled into bushes, some dazed and others already climbing to their feet. The distraction worked in Brann's favour, for it delayed the steersman from realising what was happening.

The third and fourth wagon lifted slightly where they met, and it was enough to jump the wheels from the grooves. The two started to angle to the right as if on a hinge, and Brann worried that they might pull the entire string of wagons free of the tracks, leaving the way clear for the one behind.

He heaved at the handle for a last few seconds, sweat stinging his eyes, leaning back into the pull with his feet planted against the front of the wagon. Muscles trained to this action by leagues of rowing gave all they had, and the wagon responded further. He jerked a look back again and, as the third and fourth wagons continued right, the final carriage was pulled from the tracks. It twisted, tumbling on its side and crashing the opposite way from the two before it.

There was no time for words. Grabbing Kunakan-Atik's tunic, Brann threw himself to the edge of the wagon. As the pair thrust against the lip, the side started to lift beneath them, the wagon being pulled over in the opposite direction. They hurtled away from it, and Brann felt the breath burst from him as he hit the hard ground, rolling and tumbling. He rose to one knee and saw a carriage, or a bit of one, hurtling towards them. He grabbed Kunakan-Atik under the arms as he dived, the other man reacting and pushing away as well. They crashed into the foliage and scrambled further into branches and dirt as they landed, fleeing in panic. The debris tore past without reaching the bushes, however, and they turned to watch.

It was chaos, a turmoil of destruction. Dust and wood twisted and flew and smashed and exploded in a maelstrom of madness, the noise thundering over them and hammering their ears. Wagons rolled and flew, smashing each other into flying shards and piling wreckage while iron-shod wheels and sacks heavy with gold carried even more destructive power, their force crashing into all before them like boulders hurled at a castle wall. It was hell visiting the living.

And into its midst hurtled the wagon pursuing them.

Unable to jump in time, the men aboard pulled and tore at each other in their dread, the steersman pulling on his handles in futile desperation, though his scream spoke of his despair. They disappeared into the cloud of dust, into the destruction, helplessly hurtling to their doom.

Silence fell but for the last movement of alarmed wildlife, before they, too, became still. The dust started to settle. Gerens and Xamira flitted into the dissipating cloud with knives drawn, but the rest of them just sat or stood, stunned by the force of the devastation. Gerens emerged, the face around his dark eyes coated with dark dust smeared by sweat. He looked at Brann and shook his head. 'Not a one.'

They gathered around the wreckage, staring. Then one man spotted a sack, still intact. He stepped onto the broken wood, over a twisted corpse, and lifted it. At the sight, others followed, many finding similarly undamaged sacks and others scooping handfuls of gold into whatever they could find to hold it.

Brann looked at Matala-Kitu. 'I thought gold was not prized by your people.'

Eyes, still stunned, turned to him. 'A future is. And, used wisely, this can buy them that, when they come to Chula Pexl with nothing of their lives before.'

'I take it that your family are unhurt, from your presence beside me.'

Matala-Kitu smiled. 'Bruised, but alive. They would not have been had those men caught us in the manner they intended.'

'And the others?'

'Two broken arms from hitting a tree, one broken neck from hitting the flat ground in the wrong way, and three broken or injured legs, it is hard to tell.'

'Three broken arms,' said Kunakan-Atik, joining them, his offending limb cradled against his chest.

'I'm sorry,' Brann said.

'Sorry?' The man's laugh was strained with pain, but genuine nonetheless. 'Better a broken arm than a spear through the guts.'

Two men approached and laid a sack each at Brann's feet. 'Thank you,' they said, walking without further ado into the jungle with another sack on a shoulder.

'I would take it,' said Matala-Kitu. 'Your friends are entitled to it as much as any of us, and it is because of you that we all have a chance now.'

'Not just me,' Brann said. 'Your kindness in helping us, Kunakan-Atik's skill in steering us and bravery at the end...'

'Still...' Matala-Kitu said, looking down at the gold.

Brann grinned. 'Fair enough. We can only take these two, though – two of us will be needed to help Marlo.'

'Marlo? He is your wounded friend?'

Brann nodded.

'He is fine after the jump?'

Brann turned in alarm and guilt. He was standing chatting and had forgotten his friend. As he rushed back to where the others had landed, however, he breathed again when he saw the boy sitting propped against a tree, Lita ensuring he stayed balanced. Grakk had tended to the broken limbs and was reaching around Kunakan-Atik, putting the finishing touches to a sling improvised from a strip torn from the clothing of a corpse.

'Dead men's tunics are becoming an essential part of every medic's equipment,' Brann quipped as he drew near.

'It has long been so around battlefields,' Grakk said. 'Now we can add torture chambers and wagon wrecks to that.' He clapped Kunakan-Atik on the sound shoulder in satisfied dismissal and moved to Marlo, tipping some herbs from a small pouch and crumbling them into his palm. He held them under Marlo's nose and, as the boy caught the scent, he stirred and moved his head, his eyelid fluttering. 'We have no time to fashion a stretcher from what we can cut,' he said, indicating the jungle plants. 'The noise from that cannot fail to have been noticed, unless the thickly growing flora of the jungle has masked the sound more than we might think. Either way, we cannot take the chance, and we will move more quickly if Marlo can walk supported.'

Two men walked past bearing a section of a cart, around the size of a door, that held sacks of gold in various states of repair.

'On the other hand...' Konall said laconically.

Grakk smiled. 'Excellent, young lord. If you would be so kind...'

Konall and Gerens quickly found a suitable section of wood, and Brann helped Grakk to gently lift the boy onto it. Grakk lifted his head and helped him to drink a few sips from a small vial. 'For the pain,' he said, 'not to bring sleep. He should only sleep now when his body tells him to, not because we want him quiet.'

'Let's hope his mother's oranges are safe, then,' said Konall.

With Marlo laid on his front on the wood and tied securely, they moved quickly from the scene, Gerens and Konall carrying their friend, and Brann and Grakk each with a sack on their shoulders, while Xamira brought up the rear, eyes roving constantly for any signs of approach from any angle. The other erstwhile passengers had already scattered from the scene, and Kunakan-Atik led the way through the jungle, following animal trails that Brann found hard to even spot. The plants were of colours and shapes like nothing Brann had ever seen before, and the air was so thick with water he felt as if he was drinking as he breathed. His eyes widened as an insect of frightening proportions and appearance landed on a plant with thick flat leaves only for the leaf to fold in half, snapping shut to trap the insect within.

'Whichever god designed this place had taken the dream smoke in Sagia, I think,' he gasped. 'Not one thing is familiar, and most are beyond imagination.'

'It is more than merely the plant life, young Brann, although you should be wary not to let yourself be scratched lest it be one that carries more lethal poison than an assassin's toolbelt,' Grakk said seriously. 'There are also the animals: deadly snakes that appear as twigs in your path, waiting to strike, or black cats larger than a hunting hound that lie in wait in branches above; crawling insects that bring death with a bite and their flying cousins who swarm.'

Brann's skittish steps betrayed the fear that swept through him. Grakk smiled and patted him on the shoulder. 'Do not worry, young Brann. 'I will try to spot most of them before you wander into them.'

They emerged onto the dockside, the unchanging expanse of the sea beyond a sudden change to eyes that had become suffused with discovered wonders of the land. Most importantly, four sets of eyes alighted on the masts of two ships with familiar flags, and four sighs of relief were heaved. They turned to their local companions, each expressing thanks.

Matala-Kitu smiled. 'It worked out well. It was more eventful than I had envisaged, but,' he kicked the sack at his feet, 'it has given us more options as we start our new life. I wish you well.'

'And you,' Brann said, embracing him. Farewells were swapped and the family disappeared into the crowd, just two more men with sacks on their shoulders and a woman leading her son.

They hurried to the ships, spotting familiar faces on the one to the right and hurrying up the gangplank. Rodrigo's weathered face split into a wide grin.

'You return, my friends! Did you enjoy your trip to witness the delights of this land? And you bring a new friend, and one so pleasant in appearance will always be welcome on this vessel.' He ignored her venomous glare, but his smile vanished as Brann set down his sack with a metallic clank and eased his aching shoulder. 'Oh, you didn't. Tell me you didn't.'

Grakk stepped forward, his sack effortlessly balanced on his shoulder. 'Perhaps we should discuss this further in your cabin.' He nodded at the slab of wood bearing Marlo. 'There is also the matter of our injured friend.'

The captain's eyes were anxiously sweeping across the teeming dockside, but he saw no sign of aggressive pursuers for the moment. 'Quickly, then. You must get out of sight.' He looked at Marlo. 'Back injury?' he asked, not waiting for an answer, and lifting the collar of his tunic to peer inside. His eyes narrowed and he called over two sailors, telling them to take Marlo to the ship's surgeon. 'Before he came to us, he had been *conscripted*, shall we say, to a company of pirates and as such became skilled, amongst other things, in treating backs laid open to the bone by the lash. If anyone can help your boy, he can. Now come, and bring your accursed luggage with you.'

As soon as the door closed on the captain's cabin, he wheeled. 'Do you not recall the last thing I said before you left? The locals may seem genial, and although I hear the more extremely devout of them have been called away to some gathering or pilgrimage or whatever, but – even in the case of the mildest baker or the most amiable leather-worker – if you insult their gods or show contempt for their hospitality...' He stomped to a window overlooking the quay, anxiously scanning for suspicious movement, then over to the opposite side. 'Your room, as before, is below this and has the same configuration of windows.' He opened a window to the bright waters of the harbour and jerked a thumb in its direction. 'At the first sign of any white-tunics and those big broad jungle-chopping blades they carry coming aboard, those sacks go out there,' he growled. 'And at the second, *you* follow. You understand? Any time between now and this time tomorrow, this is the only option.' He glared around the group.

'Of course,' Grakk smiled reassuringly. 'We will do so without hesitation.'

'Actually,' said Brann, 'we will not.'

The captain looked at him with incredulity turning fast to anger, and Grakk's head swung to do likewise. He glanced at Konall, who merely looked curious, while Gerens regarded him with the same impassive expression of calm trust as ever.

Brann perched on the edge of the desk, sitting before the rear windows in a manner that he hoped was both relaxed and disarming, one leg swinging idly. 'If we leave before this time tomorrow, there is not the opportunity for anyone in white tunics, rainbow capes or any other form of clothing to come aboard.'

Rodrigo stammered in confusion. 'Before tomorrow?'

'Actually, as soon after now as possible.'

Grakk placed a hand on his arm. 'Brann, I know you want...'

Brann shot him a warning look and a shake of the head, and faced the captain once more. 'Would there be a problem with that?'

The burly shoulders shrugged. 'Only if you are threatening me. If you are, my crew and I will have some issue with your presence on our ship at all.'

'There is no threat. Quite the opposite, in fact.'

'In that case,' Rodrigo beamed beatifically, 'there is no dispute. And no question of leaving before tomorrow. This ship's owners have decreed the business that we must conclude here, business that cannot be completed until tomorrow.'

Brann's eyebrows raised and he cocked his head. 'And if the ship were to gain a new owner?' He gently kicked the sack at his feet with his swinging leg.

The captain's eyes widened. 'You are intending to buy this ship?'

Brann's black-bladed dagger appeared in his hand, and the captain flinched. Brann ignored the reaction and leant to slice the top of the sack, plucking forth a rough nugget gleaming yellow. He tossed it to Rodrigo, who just managed to adjust himself in time to catch it. 'This should cover our passage to Sagia.' He lifted the sack and strode across the room to place it in the astonished captain's arms. 'And this should help the new owner with the costs of setting up his fledgling business, if he showed enough acumen to accept his first charter with the alacrity desired by the client.'

The man stared at the sack he cradled, lamplight reflecting on the contents through the narrow slit. 'It may cover an expense or two,' he said, his voice hoarse. He cleared his throat, a small smile on his face. 'The Empire's gold stocks do not swim from here to Sagia, so there would be good work, I would think, for a captain who knows the people and the area and who is in possession of a ship that has been expensively refitted to be more secure and more defendable. And renamed, naturally.'

Brann hit him with his most winning smile. 'And so...?'

Rodrigo opened a stout chest and threw out an assortment of belongings before placing the sack inside and locking it with a key on a thong around his neck. He straightened, looked around them all, and nodded several times. 'Hmm,' he said. 'Yes. Indeed. Yes.' He stared out of the window towards the city, then looked at those around him once more. 'If you gentlemen would excuse me, I have some arrangements to make for our imminent departure.'

He left the door wide open when he exited, his shouts carrying clearly to them. 'Mr Grayson, all are aboard, yes? I know the cargo is not complete, I mean the crew. Yes? Then cast off. Yes, I mean now.'

Moments later, amid the flurry of activity that had ensued, a call came from further away. Rodrigo's bellow came louder to them as he turned towards the stern to answer. 'Of course they want to know why we are leaving. Tell them we have new orders to head to Sagia. They are to proceed as originally planned. They will be happier to follow their route than ours on their own, hugging the coast being safer than the open sea. And do it quickly, before we are too far.'

As if to back up his last comment, the ship lurched as it was pushed from the quayside.

Konall looked at Brann. 'That was a large price you just paid to save twenty-four hours.'

'He saved more than that,' said Grakk. 'We are going

directly to Sagia without the route we would otherwise have followed.' He looked at Brann. 'I can understand the eagerness to be clear of the owners of that gold, but why the extreme haste, and why to Sagia?'

Brann met his eyes. 'Because I know where Loku is going. What this is all about.'

'So,' said Konall as soon as Gerens had shut the door behind them in their own cabin. 'Do you want to tell us what that was all about?'

They could feel the wind fill the sails, and Brann stared from the rear window as the port already began to recede. 'It was several things, but only as we stood in the captain's cabin did they all come together to make sense. It was when Rodrigo was speaking about the devout extremists, and I thought of Loku's fanatical obsession that is driving him in his scheming. It reminded me of something he said: he talked about their *Annals of the Gods*.'

Grakk nodded. 'Their holy texts. The only literature they have that uses writing as we would recognise it. In general, they use—'

'Knotted cords, I know,' Brann said. 'But it is how he referred to them: he called them the *Second Annals of the Gods*.'

Grakk hissed in a rare show of anger. 'You were correct in considering fanatical extremists. There are those amongst these people who believe that there is secret knowledge hidden in previous wisdom handed down from their gods.'

'And is there?' Xamira asked, her curiosity piqued. Brann guessed that the intention behind her presence was to gather intelligence as much as to offer extra protection.

'There has never been any evidence to even indicate it,'

Grakk said, his eyes dark. 'But a lack of evidence has never stopped zealots from believing what it suits them to believe; on some occasions it fuels their belief.'

'In any case,' Brann continued, 'it started me thinking about where Loku might believe the first annals could be if his people did not possess them. And another thing: you do know, don't you, of that sacrifice?'

'Matala-Kitu mentioned it,' Gerens said. His voice was grim, though most things he said did tend to carry a dark tone.

Brann noticed Xamira's lack of comprehension. 'I can tell you of it in detail another time should you wish, but suffice to say that a young man and woman were given to the god.' He drew a slow breath. 'But what you don't know is that it was a ruse, a tactic by Loku.'

Konall's face drained to white fury. 'You mean that was meaningless?'

Brann hesitated, the images still fresh in his mind, as he guessed they long would be. 'To Loku, it wasn't. It achieved what he wanted. In failing to appease the god, he received the mandate from the people to leave, to seek, as he put it, "greater knowledge elsewhere".'

He looked at Grakk. 'So I thought of what you told me, that they believed that the five gods had crossed the sea to these people.' Grakk nodded. 'And their gods reside in mountains of fire. So where across the sea might mountains of fire be found?'

All eyes turned to Grakk, who had become very still.

'It is true,' he said, 'that these people believe that their gods originated from what is now known as the Blacklands. But I cannot understand why Loku might think he could find a fabled tome in what is widely regarded as a wasteland.'

'I would have thought so, too, but for the answers Loku sought when we... when Marlo was brutalised,' Brann said. He cleared his throat, trying to clear the shaking from it. 'He asked three questions: who in Sagia guided and sent us; what we did with the Tribe of the Desert, and what we know of his plans.' Grakk looked up sharply at the second question. 'Yes, I know. In all that was happening at the time, I got confused, thinking that the Tribe was referring to the Deruul, who we travelled with across the Deadlands. But it is worse, I realise now.' His look to Grakk was grim. 'He knows we were with your people, your tribe: the guardians of the knowledge.'

'And what,' said Xamira from behind him, 'answers did they receive to these questions?'

Brann wheeled, eyes blazing. 'You belittle what Marlo endured with that question of your own. Had they received the information, you would not have found us alive.'

'Calm yourself,' she said. 'It is clear that your friend suffered far beyond the point when most would have told their life story twice over, and can only be admired beyond words for it, but we are all learning a lot here. It will be helpful in trying to stay alive ourselves to know what our enemy knows.'

Brann took a breath. She was right. His mind had jumped to the conclusion, but it was only now that he was totally understanding how he had got there. He was thinking as he spoke, piecing together fragments that had been assembled in his thoughts, and was so consumed in doing so that he had forgotten the others would be building the picture in their own heads also.

He smiled at her. 'Now that you mention it, there was one answer Marlo gave.' He enjoyed the tension that dropped over the room. 'He told them that the man at the palace behind our endeavours was Prince Kadmos.'

Xamira spluttered in laughter, and Brann saw the amusement sweep away the disquiet. 'That murderous bully? That is genius! He could be credibly jealous of his brother's rule and be plotting for his own ends. And if any ill falls his way from this, it will not fall undeserved.'

'That boy,' said Gerens, 'increases in my estimation with every passing hour.'

Grakk nodded solemnly. 'We all think we know people we are close to, but we seldom – if ever – understand everything that has formed them in their earlier life. That lad was born strong and has a past that has made him stronger. He is a man, and was so before our eyes were opened to it.' He looked at Brann, his eyes dark. 'But, as you were saying…? About Loku and my people…?'

Brann collected his thoughts once more. 'Yes. He knows we were with them, but has no idea why or what we learnt, or he would not be asking. But he does know something *of* them or, again, he would not be asking.'

'So,' Konall said, quietly, 'when you heard him say that he would seek greater knowledge elsewhere, we can have a strong wager where that might be.'

Grakk's voice was taut. 'Your haste was justified, young Brann.' He sat heavily on a chest, his brow furrowed. His words were almost a whisper. 'He simply cannot find Khardorul.'

The others started speaking at once, adding their thoughts. Brann steadied himself, knowing the worry that he was about to place on Grakk's shoulders. After a long moment, he forced out the words. 'That might not be all.' They fell quiet in an instant, strained faces turned to him. 'When he left the cellar, Loku said that he was going to join those prepared. At the time, I understood this to mean that whatever he intends had been planned for some time, but we know that already. So now I'm wondering: who has been prepared? Matala-Kitu mentioned about the devout followers of their gods being called to arms or conscripted in both Tucumala and Chula Pexl. Gathered for what, and where?' He stood, animated as other memories came to him. 'And the Duke, in Belleville, mentioned that some from the camp had already been sent on to the next stage of their duty...'

Gerens's voice was a low growl. 'And that wee prick, Ove, told Philippe when he was pretending to be Daric that they had sent men away for some purpose, with more due to follow. It sounded like a process of movement was ongoing.'

Grakk stood slowly as well. '*And* when Loku spoke with Daric at the hunting lodge, he told him that they had dispatched men to serve the cause.' His voice was almost a whisper of worry. 'He has been assembling a force.'

'An army,' Brann agreed. 'Whatever level of fighting ability they may or may not have, they will have numbers and the herb-fuelled frenzy we have seen. Add into that the organisation and dedication of those he may have from Tucumala, Chula Pexl and whichever other cities, and there will be a big problem if they move on Khardorul.'

'More than a problem,' Grakk said. What Loku thought he sought was less important than what he may find in the repository of centuries of amassed knowledge. The threat, whether it would be destroyed or fall into the wrong hands, was unthinkable. What could be lost to the world or, worse, how it could be used by a lunatic like Loku...

'We need to warn the Emperor,' Brann said. 'His millens

should cut that force to carrion, but only if they know to go to them.'

'I will speak to Rodrigo,' Grakk said. 'Every scrap of canvas that can be raised on the mast will be helpful.'

As the tribesman turned to leave, however, the door was flung open and a young sailor burst in – just a heartbeat before he found himself on his back with Xamira's knife resting sharp against his throat.

'Might be an idea to knock,' she suggested to his terrified face.

He nodded and spoke in a squeak. 'Healer sent me. The patient has been treated and has awakened.'

They all made for the door, but the sailor piped again: 'He said just one of you at this point. The lad is still very weak.'

Grakk nodded at Brann, and the rest stood aside without a word.

The surgeon was adjusting the bright lamps that had lit his work to bathe his cabin in a softer glow when Brann was let in. A man around Grakk's age, he straightened when he saw Brann, running his hand through thinning grey hair, his movement drawing Brann's eyes from the figure lying curled on the bed.

'Good news and bad news,' he said. 'The bad is that I have seldom seen evidence of suffering such as this young man has endured. But the good is that whoever tended him did a masterful job. His wounds are clean and free from impurity – they in themselves should not sicken. All I had to do was tidy it up, really. Ensuring it is clean still, a bit of stitching and then binding each wound in clean bandages meant for that purpose and not originally intended as clothing... although, as with the treatment, that was also expertly done. Whoever helped the boy, he was a handy person to have around.'

Brann smiled. 'He still is. Frequently, and in many ways.'

'Then you are lucky also, although how fortunate the lad is can only truly be judged when we see the effect his ordeal has had on his mind.' The man's eyes narrowed in curiosity as he washed his hands in a bowl to the side of the room. 'I must say, if I could be left with the recipe for whatever lotion was applied, it would serve as payment in full for my services, for the effect it has had has been incredible.'

Brann felt his face betray his surprise. 'He offers that to every healer we encounter, but usually it is treated with scorn as it is found in his people's lore and not in modern teachings. I am sure he would be delighted if you would take it.'

The surgeon beamed. 'I am of a mind that my place in life is to heal and cure people. If something works, it works, and who am I to deny that to a patient in need?' A nod of his head sent Brann's attention back in the direction of Marlo. 'He is tired, very tired, but he is all yours, for a short time, as long as you think of his interest and leave him when he starts to drift off again. I have left the wounds on his back to breathe for just now, and will return later to bandage those and check him.' He made for the door, drying his hand with a small cloth tucked through his belt. 'I must confess, there was no charge for my services, so I have cheated you out of the secret of the salve.'

With a wink, he slipped from the room, and Brann stepped to Marlo, whose eyes opened at his approach. He crouched at the side of the bunk, gently gripping the boy's arm, his two eyes and Marlo's one at a level as his friend lay curled on his side.

'I'm sorry,' Marlo whispered.

'*You* are sorry?' Brann was thrown.

'I tried not to talk.' A hint of a smile. 'But at least when I did, I let them believe a falsehood.'

Brann laughed. 'That you did. At worst it will cause misdirection amongst Loku's people and protect the identity of our friend, and at best it will cause some considerable discomfort for Kadmos. Your thinking certainly impressed Xamira.'

'Xamira?'

Brann's head readjusted to the point where Marlo's memories would have ended. 'A new friend, though I have the impression she will go her own way before long.' He felt a sudden pang of loss at the thought, but pushed it away. 'As long as *you* are going nowhere, that's all that matters.'

'Don't worry, I am a tiny bit too tired to go for a walk at the moment.'

'You wouldn't get far – we are on a ship out on the Sea of Life.'

'I thought I could feel the movement. And that man: the ship's healer?'

Brann nodded.

'He has done a good job?'

'I believe so.'

Marlo's eye socket had been covered with a pad held in place by a bandage and another was bound around his thigh where he had been stabbed, but Brann stood, his legs stiff from crouching and peered over Marlo at the boy's back. The two great wounds had been stitched with precision and, as the surgeon had indicated, the skin looked as healthy as it could have done. 'I know so. You will have an impressive couple of scars, but apart from that, all looks well.'

412

Marlo gave a soft laugh, surprisingly humorous. 'I only look half as well as I did.' A finger flicked up to indicate his one eye.

Brann found himself laughing with him. 'Only you would think to say that.'

Marlo's face fell as memories struck him. 'I wish I could have acquitted myself better. I squealed like a piglet even before the pain.' Anguish started to fill his face along with something else – shame?

Brann shook his head. 'You have no idea, do you?'

'No idea? Of what?' The words were starting to come slower, and his eyelid was blinking lower.

Brann knelt again and rested his hand on Marlo's shoulder. 'I had thought Philippe's performance as Daric was the bravest thing I had ever seen, but this surpassed it and anything I believe I will ever witness.' He paused, emotion filling his throat. 'You are an inspiration to me.'

'I? To you?' Marlo smiled, and his eye closed.

Brann stood, wiping moisture from his own eyes. Deep in his sleep, Marlo shuddered.

When he returned to the cabin, the redness of his eyes must have been instantly apparent. Grakk and Konall sprang to their feet in alarm and Gerens hovered, the concern in his eyes the most emotion Brann could remember seeing in him. He waved his hand in dismissal of any dire assumptions. 'He's fine, he's fine. Don't worry, it's just me being stupid.'

Konall frowned. 'When you came in like that, I thought…'

Brann smiled weakly. 'I know what you thought. I'm sorry, he is just so… so humbling.'

Gerens shrugged and picked an apple from a bowl in the corner of the room, the matter clearly closed in his mind.

413

'I know he is a cheery wee arse, but I wouldn't go that far.'

Brann sat on a bunk, staring at the wall. 'You don't understand. It's not that. It's just…' He felt emotion welling up again. 'He said…' He coughed roughly. 'After all he'd been through…' His voice broke and he shook his head, embarrassment filling him.

Grakk sat in a chair across from him. 'I suspect I know your quandary. If you would indulge me in just a few questions, I believe I can determine its precise nature.'

An apple flew across the room and only Grakk's honed reactions managed to deflect it up and away from his head.

'He will indulge you not a word,' Xamira growled. 'A pox on your questions. Out!' She wheeled on Konall and Gerens, a glare in her eyes and hands on her hips. 'You also. Out. Out!' She turned to regard Brann, not even watching as they raced each other to the door. 'Men,' she spat. 'Sensitivity of a camel.'

Brann stared at the floor, feeling the heat burn on his face. 'They must think me a fool.'

She bumped down on the bunk beside him. 'I need to ask no questions,' she said, ignoring his comment. Her tone was straightforward. 'Here is what it is. You watched your friend suffer horribly while you were helpless to stop it, or help in any way. Now you remember every minute of it, every cut into his body, every scream from his lips. You wish that it had been you, and when you look at his body now, you feel nothing but guilt that he is lying there and you are walking around.'

Brann nodded. 'How do you know?'

'I have been about. I have seen many people in many situations.'

He frowned. 'You are much the same age as me. How could you have seen so much?'

She shrugged, her fringe dancing above her eyes. 'It is what I do for my employer. What I have done, for some time. You have been in this world for a few years now, but a few short years – I have a start on you. Now enough of that. We are talking about you – don't get diverted.'

He frowned. 'But you just told me what I feel, and you were right. What more is there?'

She rolled her eyes. 'Men,' she lamented again. 'Why are you so shit at this?' She sighed, standing and running her fingers through her hair to gather her thoughts. 'Do you feel any better?'

'No.'

'So that is what more there is.'

He stood also, exasperated, feeling he was in a riddle contest and knew none of the answers. 'So what do I need?'

She turned to face him in a blur and, even faster, her hand grabbed the front of his tunic and jerked him forward. Instinct pulled him backwards, away from the pull and, as he felt her foot strike his legs, he realised his mistake. With the sweep of her leg and a twist of his arm, she neatly flipped him back onto the bunk. Before he could react, she was kneeling astride him, pinning his hips to the bed. He could feel both her against him and his body's reaction, and tried to squirm away. She squeezed with her legs, trapping him, and leant forward, her hair brushing his face. 'If I didn't want that,' she breathed, 'I would not be sitting like this.' He felt his stomach churn more than it had ever done before a fight. 'What do you need?' Her voice was husky, her eyes inches from his. Her hand slipped up under his tunic and he felt her nails scratch up his stomach, then down. She drew closer, and he could feel her breath hot on his lips as she spoke. 'You need to forget.'

'I should not have done that,' he said as they lay together.

She raised herself on an elbow and looked down on him, lean muscles in her arm flexing and wisps of hair the colour of sun-bleached corn dropping across her eyes. 'And yet you wait until now to say that,' she said, a smile twitching the corner of her mouth.

He looked away, shame burning within him. She was right. 'But my heart is with another.'

'I am sure it is. In fact, I know it is.' She saw his look. 'I was sent to watch over you, remember?' She stared at him for a long moment. 'Tell me, do you feel better than you did when I sent the others from the cabin?'

He hated to admit it, but looked into her eyes and could not lie. He nodded. 'In a way.'

Her voice was firm. 'In an important way.' She sighed. 'Look, true love and true fear are the most powerful forces within us, as my teacher drummed into me, and I have seen nothing to refute that in my travels and much to support it. We need them to drive us, to help us to stay alive, to live. But a life of the love the bards sing about is for most people, in their villages and towns, in their festivals and their markets, when they leave for their work and when they return, on their walks on summer nights and their winter evenings together by the fire. If they can find it, they are lucky, and they should cherish it. But we are not them. People like you, and me, and your friends outside the door, and your friends in Sagia, we are in a world – whether we have chosen it or not – where some of us try to let those other people live the life they live, and some try to destroy it – or at least don't care if they do. We see things, we endure things, we hear things, we must do things, and all of them change us, make us different, scar us.'

'So we just make up our own rules?'

'We fight the ones who seek to make their own rules. But in doing so, Nature makes rules for us according to what we live under. All of the scars we are given in here,' she tapped his head, 'we must conquer if we are to carry on. And sometimes we cannot conquer them on our own. Things build, and they need release or they take you under the surface that we all swim to stay above. What you felt today had been seeded long ago, had grown in many places and been fed by many experiences and, when you spoke with your friend, what you saw behind his words became the one last barrel that threatened to sink the ship. You see in your head what he endured, but what is in your head that you don't see is what *you* have endured. And believe me, what your mind must bear after your ordeals since you left your home will last as long and as strongly as the scars that will be visible on your friend.' He tensed and she put a finger on his lips to stay his words. 'No matter what you might say just now.'

'So this was...?'

'When the body and mind bear too much, they need release. And this is the most powerful release there is.'

'You were just doing me a service?'

She shrugged. 'In one way, actually, yes. It was one that was needed. One that we all need now and again, when it all gets too much. We can all dream of the life with our love, by the hearth or hand-in-hand in the sun, and those few of us who are lucky enough will reach that, but until we do we must accept the life we have and do what we must to try to reach the love and the hearth. For you, this was part of that. Sometimes we have to let out some of the dark to make room for the light to come in.'

417

'You speak like a philosopher, not the warrior you appear.'

She grunted. 'That's what happens when you are raised by monks. They taught me to fight but, before, during and after those lessons, they forced me to think. A lot. And then to talk about my thoughts. And then to think again. It becomes a habit.'

He looked at her with narrowed eyes. 'You would get on well with Grakk.'

'Perhaps.' She kissed his cheek softly and rose with a wink. 'But he is not my sort.'

He couldn't drag his eyes from her as she pulled on her breeches and drew her tunic over her head. Men's clothes could not take from her femininity, but her femininity could likewise not take from her bearing as a warrior. The result was intoxicating, and he gasped at a thought to divert his mind. 'When you threw me onto the bunk – was that a move learnt from the monks?' It sounded lame, but he was desperate, and he was actually curious about her training.

She grinned. 'It was a move learnt from having only brothers who decided from an early age that I would learn to fight like a boy. And that served me well when I was taken to the monastery after I survived when they didn't.'

He grew still. 'I'm sorry.'

She shrugged. 'It was a long time ago and I was very young. It was a first step to this life which, harsh as it may be, is not the town of rough shelters and rougher people where I started.'

She threw his clothes at him and he dressed quickly.

'Thank you,' he said quietly.

She frowned. 'Oh, do not think that you were the only one to benefit from this.'

He didn't know how to answer, and fussed with his

weapons, settling them about him and only feeling fully clothed when they were all in place. But his mind still was working. 'It feels like there is a connection between us now.' It was a fact he couldn't deny to himself.

She looked at him askance. 'There is a connection between you and Marlo, and Konall, and Grakk, and especially Gerens for some strange reason. We have a connection of some sort with everyone we have met and some we haven't.'

'That's not what I—'

She cut him off with a laugh, amused rather than mocking. 'I know, I am just playing with you. Of course there is, and all connections are different. This one was there before, but it took today to reveal it to us. We have all sorts of connections with all sorts of people.' Her smile was wicked. 'Though admittedly, this is one of the stronger ones. The forever-strong ones.'

The door was banged roughly and Konall's voice was loud through the heavy wood. 'It's getting blowy on deck. You have had enough time for your girly words, and their hot air will give us some welcome warmth.'

She drew a slow breath and laid her fingers on his arm, speaking quietly. 'This connection does mean, however, that you must have my back as I have had yours.' She reached for the door, casting an even more mischievous grin back over her shoulder. 'Especially after paying so much attention to my front.'

If the others noticed his blush or the dishevelled bunk as they stomped in, they didn't show it.

'Feeling better, chief?' Gerens said. At Brann's nod, Gerens turned the burning darkness of his gaze on Xamira. 'Thank you. There are some things that women handle better than men.'

419

Brann spluttered into a fit of coughing but Xamira maintained her poise, the hardness back in her own eyes. 'Of course there are. That is how men have survived the centuries.'

Konall looked about to debate the point, but Grakk laid a hand on his arm. 'More importantly, we will be in Sagia in a few short days. We should start discussing what we will do there.'

There was a table in the middle of the room and, as Brann pulled out a chair, he kicked a pillow under the nearest bunk.

Grakk grinned.

Xamira slapped his bald head.

Chapter 9

The silver goblet crashed against the wall and bounced across the floor.

'A third millen? And this one? Has he lost his wits?' He grabbed the second goblet on the table and filled it with wine.

'Have you?'

He turned to find anger turning her eyes as hot as her voice was made cold. She stood stock still, glaring at him.

'You would throw the boy to him?'

'He is a man.'

'He is a young man.'

'He is still a man. And his time has come.'

'His time will come and go without him should he be rotting in a cell. Or worse.'

She stormed closer, and he found himself taking a step back. He caught the movement, drawing himself to his full height.

'He will not. His companions are here, so here is where he will come should he survive where he went. Then we

*will learn what he has learnt, know what he has come to
know. If it is of sufficient import, it must sway the fool.'*

'You do not know that it will.'

'It must. It is a risk we have to take.'

*She snorted in disgust. 'It is a risk he will be taking. For
your ends.'*

'For all our good.'

*She spat into the fire, the venom in the action repeated
in her tone. 'For your good.'*

'What does it matter if many gain?'

'It matters to you.'

*'It has to matter to someone, or we will be destroyed by
a madman fighting a fool.'*

She laughed with scorn. 'And watched by an older fool.'

'A fool who trusts your prophecy.'

*'Do not lay the blame for your callousness on the words
of the gods,' she growled.*

*'I do not. Should the gods speak true, he will be the hero
who must stand for us all if we are to defeat what would
otherwise be our doom. He is the key to the downfall of
those of weakness who must fall, and to the door that must
open to those of us who see the title of Emperor as a means
to rule and not an opportunity for a daily banquet of frivolity
and praise and with concern for naught beyond the walls
of this palace.'*

Her voice became a hiss. 'Those of us? Or one of us?'

*'What must be, must be. And what also must be is for
the boy to fulfil his destiny.'*

*'It is not for you to decide the path he takes in doing so.
That is between him and the gods. And whether he achieves
it is down to him alone.'*

His fist thumped on the table, sending the glass decanter

to smash on the stone floor. His voice was a bellow, raw in his aged throat. 'Well, to be allowed that, he must face danger. No one follows a hero who merely proclaims himself as such; he must speak through his actions, and in his deeds he must be seen to achieve what they cannot. What I do, what I have always done, what I will do now in sending him to that fool and what I plan beyond, is present him with the opportunity to do as such.'

'And what good is that should it fail?' she said. 'A dead hero is of use only to the bards.'

'That may be so,' he growled, 'but a living one must give the bards something to sing about, else he is just another soldier.'

****

The ship bumped against the quay amid the early morning chill, and Brann scampered down the gangplank as soon as it was set in place, leaving behind a beaming Rodrigo with a chest full of gold and a head full of plans.

'Keep your hoods up,' he cautioned the others. 'Loku is most probably not here, but his Sagian spies and their thugs will still welcome us with a club or a sword before we can get halfway to what we want to do.'

Xamira gave him a nod and slipped away. They had spoken on the deck as the ship approached the harbour and he knew her duties would take her elsewhere, but still the sight of her drifting into the busy activity of the dockside crowd before she disappeared moments later left a pang of loss in his chest. Neither of them had spoken again about what had transpired in the cabin, but there had been something different in her eyes since; something indicating that

423

it sat at the back of her thoughts in the same way that is sat in the back of his. He shook his head, trying to clear his mind to concentrate on what had to be done.

Their passage to the Pastures, the areas of slums and poverty where Marlo had spent his early years and where the house lay that harboured Einarr, proved uneventful and quick through streets not yet filled, and their welcome there was warm and genuine – all the more so for the unexpectedness of their arrival.

They sat quietly as all from their trip was related, but Einarr's dark expression mirrored that of the others when Brann told of their intentions.

'Have you lost your wits?' he thundered, leaping from his chair with what, Brann noticed, was already remarkably controlled balance for one with only one foot. The lord glared at him with the power inherent in decades of wielding authority. 'You honestly think you will stay alive if you go and present yourself to the very man who accused you of being part of a plot to murder him and sentenced you to what he believed was certain death? Who we then, to all appearances, did try to kill, using an assassin who looked like you? Whose home we struck at the very heart of? Whose niece died in that attack?' He saw the pain in Brann's eyes. 'Look, I am sorry about the hurt that last memory brings you but, believe me, it is nothing to the short but decisive pain of a heavy blade chopping through your neck.'

He shook his head, grabbing his crutch and stomping to the table.

Grakk said softly, 'We believe it is the only way, Einarr. There is no other option. We need his armies. Loku cannot be allowed to find the way to Khardorul. Even if he finds the one item he desires and resists the temptation to grasp the power offered by the rest, which simply would not happen, merely the knowledge released to the world of the existence of that unimaginable archive and all it contains would bring chaos and destruction, such is the callous self-interest that is the manifestation in some of the natural urge to survive by evolving stronger than our peers. What we describe as inhuman is, unfortunately, all too naturally human. The lives of many more than just us few, more than even this entire land, will be in jeopardy.'

Einarr glared at the table in silence.

Brann walked to the other side of the table. 'I agree with all of that,' he said. 'Which is why I will go alone.'

Uproar broke across the room like a wave on rocks. Brann stared around them all, waiting for the noise to subside.

'I know what you are saying,' he said when it did. 'But I am the only one who knows the private way to Alam's room, and think about this: if you find it surprising that I would willingly put myself before the Emperor, think how astonished the Emperor will be. Surely he will see how important the news I bring must be if I place myself in that position.' He paused, before continuing: 'And if the worst does happen, then another two or more people would find themselves in that situation when the message could have been just as well delivered without them.'

Several nods around the room accepted that fact, and all eyes turned to Einarr. His fists were clenched and he hit them gently against the table, several slow times. He looked up at the top of the stairs where Aldis, despite her years unknown, stood straight and steady on the landing, regarding him. His eyes met those of the soothsayer he venerated and something seemed to pass between the pair. When his head turned back to Brann, a resigned sadness was lined across his face. 'There is nothing certain about the views of that man,' he said in a low voice, 'but if you must, you must.'

Brann started to reassure him further, but the look in his eyes stopped him. With a nod, he dropped his weapons on the table, retaining only one knife on his belt. He pulled his cloak about him, cast one last look at Marlo's pale form watching him quietly from a chair by the fire, turned and left the house.

On the walk to the entrance he remembered leading to the sewers, Brann had tried to visualise each turn on the route below the palace, but still he was forced to double back several times after taking a wrong turn in the darkness. What seemed like a day later, he found himself easing through the movable stone panel at the back of the privy and, with a furtive and nerve-filled look, into the corridor close to Alam's chambers.

All was quiet, magnifying to his ears every slight sound he caused as he crept to Alam's door, and he pressed his ear softly against the wood. He could hear nothing, and snatched an anxious look from side to side behind him, expecting a servant or a guard to appear. He eased the latch with painstaking slowness and pushed the door open the slightest crack, listening again, still hearing only silence. He edged the door forward the width of a finger, leaning forward to press an eye to the space.

'Oh, for pity's sake just come in!' the old voice yelled in exasperation.

Brann jumped so violently that the door swung wide, and he almost stumbled into the room.

The former Emperor was sitting in his customary high-backed chair. 'Come in and shut the door, you fool. Or would you rather just call the guards instead?'

Brann stepped in, obediently closing the door and glancing around. They were alone, and he breathed more easily. 'How did you know it was me?'

Alam snorted. 'You need to work on your sneaking. Pulling up a hood may fool Taraloku-Bana's dolts, but I rely on fewer people of higher quality.'

'I need to see Kalos,' Brann blurted. He saw no point in wasting time.

But Alam was less hasty. 'Oh, I see. A hunted fugitive wanders in here and thinks he can demand an audience with the most powerful man in the world.'

'It is vital. His help is vital.'

'And you think he will offer assistance to you, of all people, just like that.'

'Of course not. But it is for the sake of all, including his Empire and, therefore, him.'

Alam sighed and indicated the chair beside him. 'Convince me that I should put you in a position to try to convince him.'

Brann told him the salient points of his journey, from Markethaven to Chula Pexl. Alam had steepled his fingers and, head still and eyes closed, listened in silence, but when Brann added his theory of Loku's aim, the old head snapped up.

'He knows of the City of All Wisdom?'

Brann nodded. 'I believe so. Does the Emperor?'

Alam nodded. 'That secret is passed to each Emperor on his accession by the High Mother of the Oracle. The idea is that he must keep it safe, though the current incumbent is not faring well on that score.'

Brann frowned. 'Is it not a huge risk that one such as Kalos knows what Khardorul harbours? Would he not be tempted to seize the power it could bring, power that dwarves even what he holds now?'

'Each High Mother tends to have decent intuition as to character, which is why one rises to such a position. She who crowned Kalos was no exception. He knows it is a secret place of great holy significance and seclusion in the Blacklands – an area unpleasant enough to hold no attraction for a lover of luxury, and a sanctum of piety is utter anathema to a lover of decadence. It makes him feel important to know there is a secret he alone must protect, and it is easy to keep a secret to yourself if you have no interest in its truth.'

Brann thought of the frivolity that had marked every encounter he had experienced with the Emperor, even in the face of dire circumstances. Alam's words made sense.

The old man looked at him. 'Nevertheless, he has been charged with protecting it, and protect it he will, as he loves the concept of being the Emperor. And so I see that you are not here to ask his help, in actual fact, but to present a situation where it is in his best interest to act. Or, to put it another way, he would see a possible calamity that the dispatch of a couple of his millens would avert.' Brann nodded. 'Very well, but be aware that he is not in the best of moods given that his brother, Kadmos, got himself drunk enough two nights ago to lose his balance on the balcony of his chambers. And, as you know, these Royal residences are fairly high above the courtyard at that side of the building.' He saw the look on Brann's face. 'Oh, don't tell me you had something to do with that also.'

Brann shrugged. 'Maybe.' He couldn't stop a smile

twitching at one corner of his mouth. 'Loku – Taraloku-Bana – may have been led to believe that the person guiding us from within the palace was that very prince.'

The old man pondered that for a short moment, stroking the long wisps of his beard. 'There are advantages: he does not look any more for such a person and he thinks that you and your sorry little band are without highly placed assistance and influence, meaning that he may underestimate you.'

'And Kadmos was a nasty bastard.'

'And Kadmos was indeed a nasty bastard,' Alam agreed. 'And although that is by no means always a bad thing, in his case it was.' He noticed Brann's disapproval. 'You have yourself your own nasty bastard: the boy with the hair like black fire.'

Brann frowned. 'But Gerens is not a vicious bully. He's just matter-of-fact about things.'

A cold smile. 'And so it is, always. A friend is efficiently ruthless, an enemy is a vicious bully; one you love to have on your side, one you hate in opposition; one is a nasty bastard... and so is the other. As I say, it is not always a bad thing. Kadmos enjoyed it and did it for himself, whereas your boy feels nothing and does it all for you. That is the difference: why and how they did it, not what they did. Learn to see what is in front of you, not what you want to be in front of you, and you will appraise people better. And if you can appraise them, you have more of a chance of reading them and predicting them.'

'And controlling them?'

'Of course. What is the point of building years of knowledge of what works and what does not, if you cannot utilise that? And how can you utilise it when your body is weak if not through others?'

'And is that what you do with me?'

'Of course.' He gave a thin smile, but the eyes were hard and Brann saw in that moment the Emperor who had once ruled with a hand as skilled and uncompromising as a captain who guided his ship equally through storm and calm. 'What do you think is in this relationship for me otherwise?'

'I thought you did this out of the goodness of your nature.'

Alam snorted. 'The temples can attend to charity, but can they run an empire? Each has his part to play.'

Brann looked into the empty fireplace as the breeze that stirred the gauze of the curtains brushed over him from, it felt, a land across the sea. 'You sound like someone I met in Tucumala.'

'Then you should listen to what he told you, for you heard wisdom.' He grunted. 'Enough. You want to meet the Emperor, then.'

'I do.'

'Good.' He shuffled to a plaited cord hanging beside the mantelpiece, and pulled on it twice. Moments later a servant girl – around half Brann's age and with a tread as soft as her eyes were sharp – slipped through the doorway.

'Lord?' she said with a slight bow.

'Take this young man to the Lord Chamberpot with information that he was sent by a member of Lord Taraloku-Bana's network with a message of such import that it must be delivered directly to the Emperor himself.'

The girl's voice was cool, confident, but respectful. 'For clarity, lord, you mean me to take this boy and the message to the Lord Chamberlain?'

He gave his customary snort. 'You know what I said, and you know what I meant. Both are full of the same stuff, but the chamberpot is periodically emptied of it.' He looked at Brann. 'Go with the girl. She is one of mine. If I can trust her, so can you, and she has a mind quicker than either of us men.'

Brann blinked at him, still taking in that he was to be meeting the Emperor so quickly. 'What, now?'

Alam sighed deeply, looking at the girl. 'You see? Certainly quicker than his.' His fierce gaze turned back to Brann. 'Go, fool.'

Brann went.

****

She stepped from the balcony into view as soon as the servant had led the boy from the room.

'You did not even have to persuade him.'

'I almost had to restrain his eagerness.'

'Then he is as reckless with his life as you are.'

'And yet he survives each trial.'

'He is knocked down, he gets back up. Every time. He knows no other way.'

'You like him, don't you?'

He gave no answer. Which was the answer.

****

The Lord Chamberlain was as pompous as Alam had suggested, if not more so, but he was nothing if not effective at his job. Within minutes of receiving the message from the girl – and she herself had a knack of presenting the message with just the right tone on the right words to convey that if Brann was not presented to the Emperor at the earliest opportunity, the Lord Chamberlain's head was liable to be requested in his stead – Brann handed his knife to the man and, in moments, found himself being led by the man and accompanied by two fully armoured guards along a passage for which sumptuous would seem an inadequate description of the décor.

It would seem that an overabundance actually achieves less, Brann thought, as he found himself unable to take in any more than a fraction of what he passed: feet sinking into soft floor coverings; eyes caught by statues large and small; gilt in precious metals and lacquered in colours vivid beyond the reality of what they represented, bathed in the light of lamps in shapes and designs beyond the skill of any metalworker he had ever known, casting shapes of light and shadow in patterns both intricate and inventive. *And this is just the corridor.*

He was ushered into an antechamber that made the passageway seem austere, and then a room of assorted but equally ostentatious furniture for reclining and sitting, with a large circular bathing pool set before a window from floor to ceiling allowing a vista of the city. Brann felt relief that, at least, the Emperor was not in the pool.

Instead, Kalos reclined on a divan, clad simply in a blue tunic of fine silk, regalia elsewhere but with the regal bearing naturally displayed only by those born to the role. His relaxation was in stark contrast to the large guards and their bared blades who stood everywhere he looked.

'Ah,' the Emperor said, his tone genial and his smile matching, 'if it isn't our own little indestructible assassin. I take it that you are not, in actual fact, an emissary from my Source of Information's network of gatherers. Rather, you would appear to be somewhat weary of fruitless running and accepting of their decreed fate.'

Brann looked at the floor, unable to resist being intimidated by the man's position. He forced his eyes to rise. 'It is about your Source of Information that I come, Imperial Majesty. There is a great danger within your realm. One that is more important than any risk to my life.'

The man smiled. 'Of course, you are right. Any matter relating to the Empire is more important than your life.' He waved a hand flippantly as if to dismiss such an obvious and insignificant matter. 'However, it does surprise me that you would seek death to tell me that my esteemed advisor has missed some important news, despite his expertise and the resources at his disposal.'

Brann shook his head. 'It is not an omission of the man that I come to you to relate, Imperial Majesty, but a warning I must deliver that there is a dire threat to a resource beyond value – a threat posed by that very same man.'

The Emperor's smile remained, but puzzlement crossed his face. 'Now, you must admit, this seems strange to me.'

'It is true, Imperial Majesty, I assure you.'

Again the dismissive wave. 'No, no, no. I speak of our last official meeting, when your Northern lord, Einarr, similarly levelled a charge of treason and treacherous plotting against the very same man. And here you are, willingly walking your neck towards the headsman's block, and you cannot manage to be imaginative enough to bring me anything new. You could have at least attempted to offer me a little entertainment in the process, doomed as it would have been.'

'Imperial Majesty, perhaps you could agree, then, that if I had any motive other than the truth, I would indeed have brought something new, or made a more extravagant attempt at a tale. But my lack of doing so, helpless in the face of such danger to me, surely indicates the truth in my message. An army has been raised, and only your millens can face it and destroy it.'

Kalos laughed delightedly. 'Now that is better! You see, if you could have tried that from the start rather than lazily directing old insults towards a respected official of the Empire, we would have begun this conversation on a far more positive footing, although you must realise that the outcome would have been the same.' He sighed. 'The two closest millens are already in the North, attempting to restore order and the adequate flow of trade where your own rulers are failing so pitifully to do so, and the millen on garrison rotation here in Sagia just weeks ago left to assist them in accelerating their progress.' He smiled benevolently. 'You should be delighted. You sought before to weaken my forces by luring my millens north, and yet here it has taken place. The only beetle in your wine is that my commanders, and Taraloku-Bana himself, have been able to assure me that there is no culture currently capable of mounting a threat to Sagia, and that the Palace Guard is more than capable of ensuring the safety of those within the keep; so I am, after all, able to attend to the matter of free-flowing trade. But it is now done *for the Empire's sake*, not to your ends.'

Brann felt horror creep through him. The very reason Einarr's party had travelled here in the first place had indeed been to warn of the unrest in the North and, if they were to achieve their most desired aim, to gain military assistance from the Empire in quelling it before it grew further. But now it seemed that this had been Loku's intention from the start. The man had only delayed the Emperor's implementation of it until he himself was ready to act. He had been several steps ahead of them throughout. More than that, he had orchestrated everything, leading them along a path as if he were dropping a trail of bread always a half-dozen paces ahead of a gaggle of geese hungry for every morsel and never lifting their heads to see who had given it.

Kalos spoke again. 'Now, I know not your intention here, but to be honest this interruption to a long and tedious day is now becoming tiresome in itself. Perhaps you may have intended to get close enough to me to attempt a killing blow, or maybe this is just an inept effort to discredit a man of trust and influence, but it is time for this nonsense to be brought to a halt.' He looked at the Lord Chamberlain, who fell to his knees at the glance. 'Dungeons overnight and take his head in the morning.'

'So it shall be, Your Imperial Majesty,' the man's obsequious voiced whined. 'Shall I arrange a spectacle for the execution?'

The Emperor reclined with a languid smile. 'Oh, no need for all that fuss. There is a block in the dungeons. That will suffice.' His hand waved airily.

The Lord Chamberlain bowed in acknowledgement, and Brann felt the unyielding grip of two guards on his arms as he was wrenched towards the door.

'You don't understand,' he shouted in panic, though less for his own safety than for the consequences of doing nothing in the face of Loku's action. He had avoided mentioning in front of the others in the room the name of the city kept in secret from all but a scant and carefully selected few. But he knew that the secret was passed to each Emperor on accession to ensure their assistance in protection, on pain of inevitable assassination by agents of the gods should they seek to abuse that knowledge, and he had no option now but to make a desperate last attempt. 'He is seeking to plunder the knowledge of Khard—'

The Emperor leapt to his feet. Two swords flashing to rest against Brann's chest and one pricking his throat cut off his words.

Kalos's face was grim and, though his voice was as even as ever, it carried a menace that could only stem from deep-burning anger. 'If he utters another noise – coherent word or grunt I care not – cut out his tongue. And put him in a cell only long enough for the headsman to be summoned.'

The haste of the guards to take him redoubled and the trip to the dungeons was rough and rapid, attracting many a startled stare from passing servants, but Brann took care to stay silent. There was nothing possible to gain now from words other than mutilation.

He was flung into a cell with one other occupant, a dishevelled and broken old man of little physical substance and fewer words. Brann looked at the cowering figure in the corner picking at his deep-red hair to remove rotting straw gained, presumably, from sleeping on the floor where more of the lank straw lay on the damp stone, and dismissed him from his attention.

He pressed against the thick wooden door, peering through the small barred window and seeing only a short way along the dimly lit passage of similar doors that he had seen on the way in. His fingers grasped the bars and he shook the door, more in despair and frustration than in any expectation it would move. It rattled slightly.

The man Brann had dismissed spoke with a voice sounding considerably younger than he would have anticipated, had he expected any speech at all. 'You are wasting your time, of course.'

Brann recovered from his surprise and rested his back against the door, his body and his voice weak with despondent helplessness. 'I have made a terrible mistake,' he said.

* * * *

'I have made a terrible mistake,' he said.

He sat on the edge of his bed, body sagging and heavy, as if the weight of the task he had created for himself were only now bearing down upon him. He felt like an old man, and he knew from her face he appeared so. He looked at his hands twitching and fiddling in his lap, unable to meet her eyes.

'I have killed him as surely as if I had put a dagger in his chest when he stood here before me.'

'This is not you. All plans have setbacks, most of them unforeseen. You must have known this was possible; you must have planned alternative measures, other routes to the goal.'

'I have nothing. I could feel he was the one, the chance we had. All I have planned has been built on him, and now I have let that foundation be pulverised. Dust cannot support walls above. The Three were alerted I may need their assistance, but it is now too late to call in their assistance – they would need to have been in position already. I listened not to you and you were right. And now all of it was for nothing. Is for nothing.'

Her voice was soft again. 'You can plan again. It is your way. You do not fail until you stop.'

'It is more than that.'

She waited long moments before speaking, nervous of the emotion behind it.

'You like him, don't you?'
This time he answered.
'Yes.'
A tear ran a wet trail down his dry old cheek.

****

'We all make mistakes.' The voice was not only young, but vibrant with strength.

Brann looked in the man's direction properly for the first time. He was a small figure, insubstantial, with a shock of hair that hadn't seen a comb or even been run through with fingers for as long as it had been growing. His clothes had turned to rags, more missing than remaining, and the skin under the discolouration of dirt was marked by marks that were equally liable to be bruises or the evidence of disease. Brann almost expected him to die in front of him.

But when the eyes lifted to his, he saw bright life and intelligence.

'I shouldn't have ended up in here,' Brann said. 'There are things I must do.'

The narrow shoulders shrugged. 'I think you will find those words on the lips of every resident in these parts.'

'But I never intended this!'

'Again, that's what everyone says.' A grin, exposing teeth remarkably healthy and at odds with the rest of his appearance. 'Well, everyone except me.'

A door of metal clanged open along the corridor. The man stood and stretched his back. 'That will be the headsman. It is our time.'

Brann's stomach lurched. 'Our time?' He pressed his face against the barred aperture once more, straining to see who approached. 'And why in the gods' names are you so cheerful about it?' His legs wanted to run but barely had the strength to stand and he had to fight not to wet himself. He thought with scorn of the way he had walked so willingly into the Emperor's presence. Dire consequences were so much easier to dismiss when they had yet to move from the realms of possibility to those of reality.

A huge angular face with a gap-toothed grin appeared in front of him with a roaring laugh. Brann fell backwards with a yell and felt pain as he tensed instead of relaxing into the impact on the hard floor. Relaxing would have relaxed his bladder as well, and if he was to die he would do so with dignity; bruises wouldn't matter in a few minutes.

As keys sounded in the door, he mocked his thoughts made stupid by fear: he had yet to see a dignified death; he doubted there was such a thing.

The door opened wide to reveal a gangling man the height of Hakon but without his broadness, instead with limbs thick with strength and seeming too long for his body. Hanging loosely in his right hand, he held an axe with a huge blade. Of course he would, Brann thought. He scrambled back, feeling the dread evaporate as the fighting coldness started to fill him. He moved back further, not now from fear but to give him space to evaluate his opponent. The axe was the first danger – if he moved to his left, the man's right, the first swing could only be away from him and that entire side of the man would be exposed before the axe could swing back. The man's weight would be on his right leg as he pushed into the swing, so a stamp to the side of the knee could cripple it. The axe, too, was designed for slicing through a neck in a single cut, and was too heavy to be moved quickly in a fight. All this he read in his first glance but, as his legs tensed to spring, he noticed more.

There were no guards. Nor was the jailer present. Only one man to take two out for execution, and he also to swing the axe, with no assistance in either task. Strange.

And his cellmate strolling past Brann with a nod to the giant, slapping the man approvingly on the shoulder as he moved to the door and coolly inspected the scene outside.

The headsman ignored Brann and turned. 'Was that what you wanted, sir?'

The scruffy man gave a pale smile as Brann – the tension easing from his muscles and the cold from his brain – slid around the headsman in as wide an arc as possible and slipped from the cell. The jailer lay in a large pool of blood a short distance beyond the metal door that was the only exit from the area, a great cleft from the left side of his neck down almost to the right side of his ribs. Brann thought of the power involved in such a wound and looked with even greater appreciation at the man behind him, moving to where he could see both men at once.

The other prisoner nodded absently, his mind clearly partially engaged elsewhere. 'A little messy, but undoubtedly effective.'

The big man beamed, and the prisoner turned to Brann, his smile faint again. 'You see, it always helps when a principal character – in this situation, our headsman here – can be bought, and even more so when he is already in one's employ.' His voice was cool, measured, in keeping with the bearing he now adopted. 'My friend, Happy, has not only been the palace headsman, and a particularly proficient one, as I'm sure you can imagine; beheadings are not an everyday occurrence, and a selection of unfortunate incidents in drinking houses, combined with a certain potential I saw in him, led me to believe that a second job would prove beneficial to him. That second job will now become his primary employment as he will henceforth be resigning from his position of headsman.'

Happy looked across. 'Should I inform them, sir?'

The man looked at their empty cell and the dead jailer. 'I think they will be aware, Happy.'

Brann looked at the big man, then back at his erstwhile cellmate. 'His name is Happy?'

The young man frowned through the grime on his face. 'Does he look unhappy to you?'

The giant beamed at him.

'No,' Brann said, 'I'll grant you that, but—'

'Well,' the man cut in, 'in a situation where he had no memory of ever having a name prior to being appointed headsman, and only referred to by his title thereafter, it seemed natural to find him a name, although it seemed only polite to determine if he wanted one. When I asked: "Would a name make you happy?" he seemed to misunderstand and replied: "Yes, it would. So I am now Happy?" It seemed simpler to let it stick, and he has been Happy ever since, so to speak.'

The big man nodded. 'I am happy to be Happy,' he confirmed.

Brann looked at the door anxiously. 'It is a nice story,' he acknowledged to Happy, 'but should we really be wasting time if we have a chance to escape?'

The young man cocked his head to one side. 'The guard should change shortly. That will allow us to negotiate the planned route unmolested.' He saw Brann's questioning look. 'I have a highly acute sense of the precise passage of time. I have no idea why but even were I to understand it, doing so would not improve the asset in any way, so it would be time wasted in coming to that understanding. Talking of which, we may as well use this pause in our activity to our advantage.'

He looked at the faces, seven in all, peering through the small windows in their cell doors. 'Who do we have here?'

He moved from cell to cell, looking in to inspect the occupants. He stopped beside one, beckoning Happy to join him. 'This one can come with us – he will prove useful in our daily business. Fortunately, he is currently sleeping, so knock him out or put a bag over his head or something.' He glanced around the other cells. 'Kill the rest.'

He nodded Brann's attention towards the doorway and sauntered out. Brann followed as the screaming began, stepping over the corpse of the jailer as the young man perched on a desk, selecting an apple from a small basket of food – presumably the jailer's meal – and offering it to Brann. When Brann shook his head, he took a satisfied bite from the fruit.

Brann looked back at the area where carnage was taking place. 'Is that absolutely necessary?'

The man frowned. 'Of course. They saw me.' He looked at Brann, and smiled his faint smile once more. 'Oh, of course, you are thinking that you have seen me as well. Fear not, my companion. My siblings have assured me that you may know me and, in any case, it would be entirely counterproductive to devise and enact a plan to break you out of the palace dungeons if I were to kill you afterwards for knowing my appearance.'

'Wait, wait, wait...' Brann said. 'Moving on for now from the identity and killing bit, are you saying that this is all to let me escape?'

The man was puzzled. 'Why would I have myself incarcerated here only to break out again?'

Brann's head was starting to spin. 'So if it was for me, how did you know I would be here?'

'When I heard that you were to approach the Emperor, regardless of the subject or content of your conversation, I knew that there would be only one outcome – Kalos is a highly predictable man, though obviously not in your eyes. Since I also knew that Happy was not immediately on hand to carry out the execution for them, they would have to imprison you, even for a short time. A surprisingly small bribe here and there was all that was needed to allow me access to play my part in the cell and ensure the correct man walked out of here when the rest did not. I told Happy that when he was summoned for your execution, he should instead bring me clothes,' he patted a bundle on the desk beside him, 'kill the jailer and open our door (it's best to keep instructions fairly short and simple for him). And here we are.'

'But why? I have never met you before. Who engaged you to rescue me?'

The man set down the half-eaten apple and started to swap his rags for the bundle of clothes on the desk. 'No one. Well, no one directly, to be precise. But a common friend in the palace sent a message recently that our assistance might be needed by you at some point, and to ask us to be prepared to act if our particular brand of services were indeed required. On discovering this situation of yours, it could not have been clearer that help was necessary. If I had not acted now, then there would not have been another opportunity to assist.' He looked at Brann with eyebrows raised pointedly. 'There would not have been a you.'

Happy rejoining them with his axe dripping and an unconscious man slung over one shoulder like a sack merely served to emphasise the last point.

Brann shuddered. The image of his own execution was dispelled, however, by a thought that entered the head he was glad he still possessed. He stared at the young man casually finishing the apple as thoughts fell into place. Meticulous planning. Trusted siblings. High intellect. Criminal activity. Fiercely guarded anonymity. Gods, even the same red hair.

'Abraxus,' he said. 'The Third Triplet.'

The eyes, a curious stillness about them, regarded him as if they could see into every corner of his mind. 'Indeed. You are now one of a group of only five to know my identity, my appearance and even that I genuinely exist. Well, four, I suppose, since I know the first and the last but only my backwards reflection and not my true appearance. I would request that you keep all three of those elements known only to the current number of people, or the number will decrease by one.'

Brann nodded. On recent showing, he believed it would decrease extremely quickly.

Abraxas tossed the apple core onto the desk and walked to an outer door, opening it and turning his head to listen.

A bell rang distantly. Abraxas smiled. 'Our cue, my friends. Let us take our leave.'

He led them with quiet assurance through corridors and up stairs, passing no one but the occasional servants who instantly dropped their eyes at the sight of the headsman.

A guard stopped them only once – at the great gate in the first of the concentric walls that they would pass through. Abraxus had his head down and walked with a stoop and

444

a limp, and Brann tried in his own way to appear common-place.

'Apprentices,' Happy said cheerily to the man.

The guard waved them through with a grunt. 'Rather my job than yours, boys. Still, the job needs done and someone needs to do it. On your way.'

Brann was amazed the man didn't notice the outrageous wink Happy threw their way.

'Excellent, Happy,' Abraxas said. 'Very well done.'

The big man visibly swelled with pride.

A short distance after leaving the palace grounds completely, they turned down an alley. Abraxas found an old sack amongst a pile of broken crates and handed it to Brann.

'Apologies, my good fellow, but it is enough that you know my appearance. I cannot stretch it to knowledge of the route to my current abode. I would be grateful if you would cover your head.'

Brann pulled the sack over his head, trying to ignore the pungent smell of onions, and found himself lifted to Happy's free shoulder as if he were no more than a toddler. The axe must still have been in the man's hand, for the blade came to rest disconcertingly across the top of Brann's back and the back of his head, but he ignored that also as he tried to gauge direction and time, failing completely at both.

An all-too-long period of jostling and bouncing, in which he left behind comfort and dignity and gained a feeling of nausea, ended when he was gently placed on his feet and the sack was pulled from his head, the busy chatter of what sounded like an inn drifting from below.

'Brother. Sister.' Abraxas's voice came from behind him and he turned to see him standing with two others, of similar build and with the same hair, red like the hidden embers that hold the heat of the fire. Now that he saw them alongside each other, he chided himself at not spotting the resemblance – the identical resemblance – between his former cellmate and the two he had met previously, although the time had been long since the last meeting and he had not been in the best of humour then. They were dressed as before: the woman in black with grey detail and the man in the same hues, reversed, while Abraxas had changed into all black, like the shadows he embraced.

The woman nodded with a smile at Abraxas while the man embraced his brother, though Brann noticed that he held himself clear of any areas still caked in dirt. Abraxas noticed also.

'If you will all excuse me, now that I am no longer a prisoner I must scrub away the veneer of one. Happy, I would be grateful if you would be so kind as to find a hovel for your luggage and leave a note with him that he can resume his previous activities to sharpen his skills but that he works for me now, and will be contacted in due course.' As Happy walked across the room, the eyes turned on Brann. 'And please remember the secret that the five conscious people in this room hold, and the consequences of a future lack of discretion.' His ghost of a smile returned Brann's nod and he turned to a separate room. 'Please make yourself at home and enjoy the hospitality of my humble abode,' he called over his shoulder.

Brann felt the woman's eyes studying him. 'Brann of the Arena,' she said, her voice even more cool than that of Abraxas. 'Welcome once more.'

Her brother gave a deep and sweeping bow. 'Though not confined to the Arena, but more worldly-wise now, we hear.'

Brann nodded to each. 'Dareia, Phrixos. Yes, I have travelled a bit.' He looked around the sparsely filled room. 'Your brother lives simply.'

'All that is of value to him, he carries in his head,' Dareia said. 'He needs little else, for his thoughts occupy his time.'

'I can imagine,' Brann said, 'but I was more referring to the lack of armed protection surrounding you.'

Phrixos shrugged, flinging himself into one of the few chairs in the room. 'Our motives may be different but the paths to them run parallel, as we have seen with some success in the past, so what would you have to gain by harming us? And we you?'

Brann nodded at the sounds of splashing water from the next room. 'And it is not deemed a risk that I see the inside of the home of the most secretive man in Sagia?'

Dareia frowned slightly. 'Of course not. If you did mean ill towards him, it would matter not that you have seen this. It would take you more time than you want to spend looking for this place and for no benefit to you. And by the time you did find it, you would meet different inhabitants. This will not be his home by tomorrow. Abraxas prefers to move home with frequency. His nature is indeed a highly private one.'

Brann indicated the floor, from where the hubbub had not abated. 'And yet he chooses rooms above a busy inn?'

'Dear boy,' said Phrixos, leaning back and stretching extravagantly, 'it is far easier to be invisible in a crowd than an empty room or deserted street.'

'So,' Brann said, 'you freed me from the dungeons as part of a working relationship with the man we both know, I understand that. But why the meeting? I could have easily been taken back to my companions.'

447

'Trade, of course,' Phrixos said. 'We have already given you something, and could give more. In exchange, we would know of the land from which you are recently returned. Most specifically about the passage of their mineral commodities to this city.'

The image of the ambition-driven Rodrigo flashed into Brann's mind. 'I might be able to put you into touch with just the man who will soon know the inner workings of that very operation. Though you would have to promise not to touch the cargo on his ship.'

'Do we lecture you on how to best a man with a sword?' Dareia said. 'We may have to touch his goods now and again to maintain the semblance that he is not favoured by us for any reason, but the touch will be lighter than on others.'

It made sense. Brann was satisfied. 'So, I can make the introduction and tell you what I know of the organisation of the transport before it reaches the foreign port. But you mentioned you could help me further?'

The man uncoiled from his chair and moved to a window, placing one foot on the sill to move the drawn curtain just enough to let him see the street below. 'We believe you seek the Source of Information.' He smiled. 'Your abrupt increase in interest confirms my words and his importance to you. Should you meet him and only you walk away, it would not be harmful to our enterprises.'

'And?' Brann said.

Dareia walked across and steered her brother away from the window. 'And there is news of substantial activity approaching the city of Irtanbat.'

It meant nothing to Brann. 'Irtanbat? And what sort of activity?'

'Activity,' said the man, 'much like an army. Apparently, a smaller force landed from the sea and met with the main army that had gathered in the low hills between the desert and the coast.'

'And Irtanbat, for your information,' his sister added, 'is a city four days' ride east of here, capital of the kingdom of Kurkina. It is a sprawling city that grew around a collection of oases, hence its name, which means Twenty Springs, although I suspect there were fewer than that but Twenty was felt to be a nicer number for a name. Its size makes it a valuable trading partner for Sagia; its underground water makes it feasible for a population of its size, and its less than planned or organised growth over the centuries means that it is easy for an army to take but hard to hold.

'And, significantly, it lies directly between the coast and ul-Detina, the City of Ghosts that the agents of a certain Taraloku-Bana's have been asking about across this city.'

'Now you certainly have my interest,' Brann said. 'But how would you know all this?'

'Because I felt some time ago that it would be a sound business move to expand from our own export and import interests with that city to establish a foothold of our own there, and have been building this with care ever since.' Abraxas had emerged from the other room, freshly dressed and meticulously cleaned, and stood towelling his hair. The resemblance to Phrixos was almost perfect but for Abraxas's slightly smaller stature and slighter build. 'Information needs to be full and frequent for that to be successful.'

Brann looked at him, his own mind moving, planning, considering. 'Can you get us there?'

'Of course.'

A thought jumped into his head. 'I suspect we will need

449

more knowledge of armies than any in our group possess, even if we are just to infiltrate one. Can you find someone for me?'

Abraxas frowned. 'Why would you need my help to find the compound of Cassian?'

'I love Cassian dearly,' Brann said. 'But I also know the strengths and... limitations of his mind. I need the same knowledge but from one more direct and, shall I say, straightforward, in stating what needs to be said. It is his brother I have in mind, if he is in the city and willing to accompany us.'

Abraxas's faint smile drifted across his lips. 'I am sure I can find him. And I know that my siblings can persuade him.'

'You are not going to threaten him, are you? Or hurt him?' Brann's shock was compounded by the fact that he was constantly unnerved by a man who dealt death so casually, as a simple means of anonymity. Death happened to all, as he was acutely aware, at the hands of man, chance, or Nature, but for it to be seen as such a minor matter was unsettling.

Abraxas folded the towel precisely and placed it on a shelf. 'Now, now, my friend, not everything must be achieved with brutality. Sometimes it is a far better course just to offer a compelling argument as to the good reasons for making a choice. And, I suspect, given what is asked and for what reason, he will not require a great deal of persuading in any case.' His pale eyebrows drew slightly closer. 'You really should try to curb your violent tendencies.'

Brann didn't know what to say. 'This from a man who... But I didn't mean... I thought...' He sighed. 'Good. Thank you.'

The party reined in their horses at Grakk's signal ahead, waiting as the tribesman led his mount down the rock-studded slope ahead before he could ride back to them. Einarr stopped his horse on one side of Brann, the Northern lord happier on a horse than Brann had seen him for a long time – although he had noticed the man's determination had seen the crutch become almost a part of his body, giving him an adeptness of movement that was scarcely believable – and Ossavian on the other, his eyes blazing strength and purpose as they had done since the first moment he had joined them. Both men sat with patience and without a word, and Brann followed suit.

Grakk galloped up to them. 'Baggage train, supplies for Loku's force. More guards than us, far more.'

Brann nodded. 'We wait and pass behind once they are out of sight. No option.'

'Agreed,' Einarr said.

Ossavian stared at the hilltop. 'Actually, there is another option.'

Brann looked at him and felt Einarr doing likewise. 'As a young officer I fought in the East. Some of the tribes there had their own way of doing battle.'

'What way?' Brann's interest was aroused. Necessity had intervened to stop his lessons with Grakk in recent times and he missed them.

'They had not the numbers to confront the millens in battle, so they did what they could. And what they could was to attack when least expected, where least expected, with the intention of disrupting, demoralising and depleting rather than defeating. They would attack fast and melt away fast, over and again. It was the hardest campaign I ever fought in. Our soldiers were not trained to combat it, and

451

it was only their discipline and adapted tactics that eventually allowed our numbers to tell.'

'And these,' mused Einarr, 'are not trained at all and unlikely to be disciplined.'

'And so...' Ossavian prompted, staring at Brann with eyebrows raised.

Brann frowned, looking from one man to the other. 'Why are you looking at me? One of you is a lord and heir, schooled in military matters since he could walk and having fought around the world, and the other... well, for pity's sake, the other is a general who led armies of the Empire and served in campaigns before I was born. What in the god's names are you looking at me for?'

The two men exchanged a glance, and Einarr sighed. 'Brann, would you take a look at us all, and at yourself? Your actions since you first came onto my ship and your desire to come to this city we are now trying to reach are what have brought every person in this group to this point. We are all here because you are. You appear wholly incapable of seeing it for yourself, but we are following you, which makes you our leader.'

Brann looked at him, talking such nonsense. He frowned. 'We are all good at what we do – that is why we tend to stay alive. Gerens and Marlo, and maybe Hakon, and Philippe, and perhaps one or two of the others, all for different reasons. But you taught me, instructed me... And Grakk knows so much, and is capable of more than we will possibly ever know. Breta and Mongoose are too much their own people. And Cannick – how could I possibly...?' He snorted. 'And Konall. Seriously... Konall?'

With the exception of Marlo who recuperated in their safe house – protected by the same men from Einarr's former crew who already watched over their revered soothsayer Aldis – he looked around the faces as he mentioned their names. And with each one, he received a nod, some with a small smile, some solemn, Hakon with a grin and Breta with a wink. Emotion and fear surged within him in equal measure, torpefying his thoughts.

Cannick's low voice broke through to him. 'We are all at your back, lad.' He nodded ahead. 'But that means you are in front, leading.'

Brann sucked in a deep, sharp breath. If that was the case, they deserved more than a deer paralysed by the sight of a lynx about to pounce. He quickly drew his thoughts together, and turned to Grakk. 'How many wagons? And where are the guards?'

'Thirty wagons, some with canvas canopies, single file, unevenly spaced. Most of the guards are at the front and the rear, around a score in each group and from the fact that those at the front – who were all that were close enough to see in detail at that point – were more interested in chatter and jokes than vigilance and that some of the wagon drivers were close to snoozing, I would hazard a guess that no trouble is expected.'

Ossavian nodded. 'That is a common failing of those who follow behind a host that is thus far unopposed and confident.'

Brann nodded, turning his mind back to the point that morning when they had split from the smugglers they had travelled with, the criminals having brought them close to the city and wanting to preserve the secrecy of their method of entry. It had not presented a problem – the real work had been done in exiting Sagia where squads of soldiers hunted the prisoner who had somehow massacred everyone

in his dungeon before escaping the palace, and in avoiding
unwanted attention on the route from the immediate envi-
rons of the city. 'How far did they say we were from the
city when we left them?'

'Less than two hours' ride in a straight line,' said Einarr.
'And we have done around half that already.'

Brann pictured the scene described by Grakk and cast a
look at the dry brush and short, stunted trees around them.
He gestured to the others to move close, and they manoeu-
vred their horses to do so.

'Quickly grab enough branches to make rough torches.
They won't have to burn long, so don't waste any time on
them. We will hit them fast and leave faster. The target is
only the middle section of wagons, furthest from the guards.
Get the torches into every second wagon – the wood and
canvas of the carts will be so dry in this heat they should
go up quickly – and if we are lucky and the fire spreads to
those between them, it will spread the damage more. Strike
at anyone who comes close, and remember wounding leaves
them someone to tend, so don't worry about having to make
it a killing blow. The most important thing is to pass through
the line unscathed and give your horse its head as you leave
the other side. My hope is that the guards will be torn
between giving chase and fear of leaving the wagons unguarded against any other attack now that the unexpected
will have happened, but I would get out of bowshot as
quickly as you can, and remember that the wagon drivers
will most probably be armed so watch for arrows from
them.'

He saw faces determined and trusting and his breathing
eased slightly. He cast a quick glance at Ossavian who
returned the slightest of nods but otherwise was impassive.

'Good. Let's go.'

Philippe passed him and Brann caught his eye. 'Are you fine with this?' Brann said. 'You came to help Grakk with healing, and I fear I am placing you in a situation you would not have chosen for yourself.'

Philippe's cool eyes met his. 'These may not be the same people who caused my sister's death,' he said, 'but they are the same people, if you understand me.' Brann did, and nodded. 'I may not be able to swing a sword to any great effect, but I am sure that I can throw a bunch of burning twigs. I would not pass up this chance to do so, though I may not be as brave as the rest of you.'

'If you are willing to ride into this knowing that you can't swing a sword, you are braver than the rest of us,' Brann said. 'Thank you, Philippe.'

It took only a few moments to gather the wood but the old general took the chance to do so close to Brann. 'I agree with your plan,' he said in a quiet voice, 'and I want you to know that you can always come to me for advice on anything military, but if I could offer you counsel right now, never seek that advice when you are issuing orders or giving instructions. Those who will risk their lives to follow your instructions need to know that you have assurance and certainty of purpose in your decisions even if you, within yourself, feel differently. A warrior fights very differently with or without confidence, and it is within your power to bestow it or erode it.'

'Such responsibility at every turn,' Brann whispered. 'There are just too many ways to get your people killed.'

'Or to keep them from being killed,' Ossavian smiled, clapping him on the shoulder. 'Imagine if someone else was giving the orders and you could see their folly, that they were taking good people into the clutches of death. You would wish you could change the orders, give the right ones that you know should be given, would you not?' Brann nodded. 'Well be thankful, therefore, that you are in the position where you can.' He grinned. 'And if you are about to walk us into death, don't worry: I'll accidentally knock you out and change it all.'

Brann laughed. 'Thank you.'

A wink came from the broad face and Ossavian walked to his horse. 'Nice touch with the fire, though. Wouldn't have thought of that myself.'

When they galloped down the slope, his bundle of branches flaring beside him and held away from his horse's side, Brann still felt the pride in his chest at Ossavian's last words and reflected briefly on the truth of the effect of confidence. As they closed on the wagons, though, with looks of alarm, and then horror, turning their way, shouts of fear and warning visible in moving mouths and straining throats but unheard above the hoof beats thundering in his ears, Brann felt the familiar fighting coldness settle over him like a well-worn and much-loved suit of mail.

His fiery brand was already burning close to his fingers, but it would last just long enough to reach its target, which was all that mattered. He closed on the centre wagon in an arc, curving left to let his right hand hurl the remnants of the branches into the back of the wagon. He could see it disintegrating as it flew but the flames still flickered, falling among piles of sacks and against the wood of the wagon bed. His sword was in his hand already and he held it wide, barely swinging it but using the momentum of his horse to let it cut into the neck of the cart driver as he turned to bring a crossbow to bear. He let his wrist turn with the impact to lessen the depth of the cut, wary of his sword being pulled from his hand, and then he was wheeling in front of the oxen pulling the wagon, the beasts completely unruffled by the sudden activity around them. He dug his heels into his horse and bent low across its neck, urging it up the rise on the other side of the supply convoy.

Reaching the top of the low hill, he pulled the horse to a turning halt, closely followed by Gerens who, as usual, had followed his every step into combat. All five wagons they had targeted were ablaze, though he was disappointed to see that only one of those carts between burning neighbours had also caught fire. As he watched, though, the canopy on the next one along from the soaring flames and swirling sparks of the foremost burning wagon started to smoke. In seconds, orange started to flicker along it.

'That's another one,' Cannick said with satisfaction, noting his line of sight. 'Either the flames will run down the poles holding the canopy or the thing itself will burn its ties and drop into the cart.'

Ossavian and Philippe joined them, bright excitement in the young man's eyes and brighter blood running down his cheek.

'Don't worry,' Ossavian reassured Brann, 'he just got too close to one of the drivers before I could get just as close. He will survive his first scar.'

Brann nodded at the scene below them. 'Even more successful than I had imagined. Give my thanks to those Eastern tribes.'

The general smiled. 'There is always more to be learnt from defeat than from victory; the trick is to stay alive enough to gain the lesson.'

Brann was fascinated, though. 'Much can evidently be gained extremely quickly.'

'If done the right way, at the right time, with the right knowledge beforehand,' Ossavian cautioned him. 'We had the benefit that they assumed they were in a place of safety and suspected nothing. Had they known we were coming, we may have found that they welcomed us, and that the wagons were carrying archers rather than food and equipment.'

All along the line, their briefest of actions had turned what had been a peaceful caravan into a chaos of commotion and noise, screams mixing with shouts, futile attempts at beating back flames mixing with galloping guards with weapons held ready, and panic infusing every part of it. Men wheeled carts out of line to escape those burning nearby, whipping and yelling at oxen spooked by the roaring flames so close, while others cut the traces of the draught animals attached to blazing wagons. Not all of the oxen were lucky – their carts too fiercely aflame for men to bear the heat, the bellowing animals were condemned to a dreadful death.

Hakon sniffed the air appreciatively as he drew up beside Brann. 'At least they'll eat well tonight.'

Mongoose scowled and kicked him as she rode past, but Breta nodded as if it were the most obvious of opinions. 'Waste is an insult to the gods,' she said seriously.

Sophaya and Grakk cantered up to them from the furthest attacked wagon to complete the group, and Gerens cast a questioning look at the girl, who replied with a sweet smile.

Brann checked around them as a group of guards turned their horses towards them. Everyone was there. 'Time to see how much appetite they have for the chase,' he said.

They needed no encouragement and wheeled their horses

458

as one and launched them towards the rolling hills between them and Irtanbat. They rode fast, initially, to put distance between them and the convoy, but eased to a canter to preserve their mounts' energy, taking as straight a line eastwards as they could over the trackless terrain, either over the shallow hills or around the side of them as the route dictated. They could always gallop again if a short burst was needed – or turn to face their pursuers, although Brann was keen to avoid pointless casualties – but there was no great onus to lose those behind through cunning or deception so he settled for simply outrunning them and kept to the most direct course towards the city. It would be no surprise to those they had attacked that they made for that destination, he presumed.

He noticed Konall looking back several times before speaking to Grakk and taking the oculens from him. He kicked his horse to a gallop and turned at the top of the next rise to point the instrument back past his companions. When they reached him, he grunted. 'I thought they were dropping back,' he said, handing the tube back to Grakk with a nod of thanks. 'No stomach for it – they have just turned back.' He looked at Ossavian as his horse skittered beneath him and he turned it forwards once more. 'You will get used to his plans actually working. You will learn not to underestimate the value of absolutely no proper military education in the slightest, coupled with rampant eccentricity.'

He rode off, leaving the general staring at his back. 'Is he being humorous or serious?' Ossavian asked.

Einarr shook his head slowly. 'My nephew knows nothing other than to be serious,' he said, his tone and face equal in their astonishment.

Brann rode past them. 'He's right, you know,' he said, barely succeeding in keeping his face straight.

It was another half hour before they crested a hill to see a plain lying before them, the glittering of a river and the accompanying greenery that hugged it snaking from the horizon on the right to the start of a city on the left.

'I don't think we need the looking tube this time,' Sophaya said. 'I'm guessing that it is Irtanbat and our enemy, all in one handy spectacle.'

No one replied. No one needed to. A camp, seeming vast in the emptiness of the terrain around the city, nudged against the start of the buildings, and tiny figures could be seen making their way freely between both camp and city.

Cannick spat in the dust and sparse grass at his horse's hooves. 'I would suggest that this time we do not attempt to ride through them.'

'We could, I suppose,' said Brann, 'thought not in as aggressive a manner as we did before. We could try to act as if we belonged and just walk right through them. But...' He started to look at Ossavian but caught the movement in its infancy. He drew a breath. 'But we risk too much for too little gain, when we could merely take longer and ride right round them. They are here already and they look in no hurry, so whoever we seek on the far side of that can wait a few extra hours for our arrival, even more so as we are unexpected.'

'What difference can the addition of the talents of just twelve make against an army, anyway?' said Mongoose.

'The talents of eleven and the bandages of one,' Philippe corrected her.

She didn't turn to him, but continued. 'The talents of twelve. Everyone here has played their part, and I will defy the demeaning of any of us.' She paused. 'Look, I am here because you are, Brann, but I also came for myself, thinking to kill as many of those depraved bags of scum as I could and perhaps, with luck, the devil who leads them. I am sure there will still be plenty for our blades to feast upon whether we join with the defenders now or later.'

Einarr pushed his horse forward. 'We have far more of value to offer than our talents with sword or healing, or our determination to use those. We have knowledge of the enemy, of how they fight, of their characteristics, of their background, of their strengths and their weaknesses – and of their leader. If we can reach those commanding the defence, this will be a greater contribution than any a thousand swords could make.'

'So we head round,' said Hakon. 'But please, can we move now? It is a long time since we ate and the smell of roast ox is still in my nose.'

They looped away from the force, heading south-east, and met not a soul on their passage. It seemed the route the army had taken had followed the road on which they had encountered the supply caravan, and with wagons not able to take the route their party had over the hills, anyone following the army or supplying it was taking the road north until the hills petered out and the way could turn east directly towards the city.

The river was broad and, where they met it, shallow enough to ford. They let the horses drink, and refreshed themselves, although they rested under the shade of slender-trunked trees for only a short time, eager as they were to reach their goal now that it was in sight.

With the river and, more importantly, several miles between them and the army's camp, they felt confident enough to strike north-east, approaching the outskirts. Almost immediately, the sounds of fighting came to their ears. All eyes turned to Brann, and his drawn sword was all the instruction they needed.

They cantered forward in a tight unit until they saw a small group of men facing around two score warriors of the familiar broad-shouldered and barrel-chested build of those from Chula Pexl or the cities around it. The invaders fought with tenacity and formidable strength and they outnumbered those they faced and Brann's group combined, but they were no match for a dozen horse-borne warriors thundering upon them, into them, through them, blades hacking with honed skill and hooves trampling with crushing force. It was over in less than a minute, and not one of the foreigners remained alive at the end.

Chests heaving, they faced the defenders who stared at them with the shock of men who had thought just moments before that their only future was to sell their lives as dearly as they could. Eventually one, a tall gaunt man with blood dripping from a limp arm, spoke. 'I don't know who you are, but you are most welcome for your assistance and, more to the point, the timing of it.'

Brann dismounted and walked forward, but the words he was about to say were drowned out by Ossavian's stentorian roar, startling both parties to similar effect. 'You don't know who?' From the height of his horse, he pointed his short Sagian sword, red-smeared and dripping, at Brann. 'You are looking at Brann of the Arena, the undefeated champion of death matches and duels alike in the greatest of Sagia's spectacles of combat. The only man to fight man and beast in the pits of below the city, where the rules of competition are only either to live or to die, for not days, not weeks but month after month and emerge with his life. The man who crossed the desert and back, who has visited fabled cities and sailed the sea to steal the holy gold from the very men who have just sought to take your lives. Brann of the Black Steel, the man who has come to fight with you, the man who will save your city!'

The local men, as bedraggled a group of fighters as Brann had ever seen, roared and ran to him. He felt for his long knife but not before hands grabbed his, squeezing them in gratitude, seeking just to touch him, words in voices hoarse with emotion thanking him for their lives, for their families, for their city. He found nothing to say in return, but patted their shoulders in what he hoped was an appropriate gesture, until Ossavian's bellow took their attention and saw them step back slightly from him.

'Now go! Tell your comrades! Tell your neighbours. Tell all: Brann of the Arena is here! Brann of the Arena is with you!'

The men nodded and stumbled in their haste to leave, each eager to be the first to spread the news of the man they had met, the words they had heard, the salvation of their city.

Brann looked up at Ossavian. 'What in the gods' names did you just do?'

Ossavian smiled. 'I gave them you. I gave them hope. And that might be the best weapon we will have.'

Brann dropped from his horse and picked up one of the weapons the enemy had used: what appeared to be a wooden sword with slices of black stone – what must be the same material as he had seen used for the tools of the priests at the sacrifice in Tucumala – embedded in the wood in rows along each edge.

He looked up as Grakk rode over. 'Weapons of wood and stone? From a civilisation as advanced in devices and ideas as they are?'

Grakk smiled with his eyes. 'Try the edge.'

Brann ran his finger along one of the segments of stone. Instantly his blood ran over the black stone and his eyes widened as he jerked his hand back in as much surprise as pain. 'I have seen nothing as sharp outside the star metal of my own weapons,' he said in astonishment.

Grakk nodded. 'The heavy-bladed metal weapons you have seen are really tools that they have imported from other cultures further south. Called pangas, they are primarily used for cutting the stubborn undergrowth of their jungles as the metal blade is almost unbreakable, but some there have adopted them as weapons. What you see here, the macuahuitl, is their traditional weapon of war. While that stone can shatter more easily than our metals, it holds an edge of a sharpness that is unparalleled,' he looked at Brann, 'or almost unparalleled. Combined with the weight of the weapon, I have seen these take off many a head with ease. Even, once, the head of a horse with a single swing, though that was with a bigger version, wielded with both hands.'

'One like this?' Hakon said from another corpse nearby. He lifted a weapon identical to the one in Brann's hands but at least half again as long and, while it looked far too cumbersome and heavy to be practical, it moved quickly enough in Hakon's huge hands. 'This,' said the Northern boy through a grin, 'I like.' He swung it experimentally with both hands on the hilt and then – to Brann's amazement – one-handed, and seemed equally pleased with each method. 'The head of a horse, you say? Interesting. Very interesting.'

He lifted the body at his feet into a sitting position and pulled a broad scabbard wrapped in brightly patterned fabric over its head and, after inserting the weapon, he slung it across his own back, quite clearly delighted with his acquisition.

Brann looked at the weapon in his hands with new respect as he dropped it back on the ground to let him take a drink from his water skin. 'I have never seen its like. I suppose advanced thinking is in looking at different ways of doing things, not constrained by what everyone else does.' Hakon had been unable to resist pulling out his new weapon once again and was leaping and swinging it like an uncomplicated child with his first wooden sword. In a way, he was. Brann smiled fondly. 'And I have never seen a sword as big as that.'

'Actually,' Grakk said, 'it is ironic that the only place I have heard of a sword-like weapon of that sort of size is in the mountainous north of your island, where the people live closer to the ways of their ancestors than you soft farmers in the South. They have swords of metal, but some are said to be as tall as a man.'

Brann's eyes widened. 'In Alaria? The Northern tribes are as big as Hakon?'

'Only some of them. The big ones carry the big swords, but all of them are fierce warriors. The not-so-big ones find their own ways to fight men with big swords.' He looked with narrowed eyes at Brann. 'Which does somewhat remind me of someone...'

Hakon strode up. 'What did you say this was called?'

'A macuahuitl,' Grakk said.

Hakon made several attempts at repeating the word. "I'll call it my maqua.'

'Time to go,' said Brann.

They rode – through gaps in walls allowed to crumble through the perceived safety of sitting, of all the kingdoms in the Empire, most in the shadow of Sagia – into a city of discomforting eeriness. With no buffer between them and the enemy, the residents of these first areas had abandoned their homes, fleeing from the atrocities every army brings. Brann stared at houses, some with enclosed gardens glimpsed through doors left gaping, everything perfectly in place but for the inhabitants. Shopfronts, built into the bottom level of buildings, still displayed their wares, and although some had been looted by those seeking supplies as they fled, most still appeared ready for custom. Carts sat in the streets, as if the owners had dropped into a nearby building for just a moment. The only sounds were the buzzing of insects around rotting food and the occasional scuffle of paws of a dog – stray from the city or the larger desert animal encouraged into the empty streets by temptation and curiosity – as it was startled by the noise of the horses' hooves. With no opposition, the enemy forces had clearly been directed where fighting was possible – to control the city, they must subdue the population, Brann realised, not merely occupy empty buildings.

He turned to Grakk, who was riding at his side. 'Why stop here? Why did Loku not just pass the city by? He could have carried on without taking the time it will do to take a whole city.'

'Two reasons, curious young Brann,' the tribesman said. 'From a strategic point of view, he would be wary of leaving a competent force behind him, exposing the less warrior-like part of his army such as we faced on the road and creating the possibility that, as a whole, he could be caught between them and some other assisting force. Safer to annihilate this danger, or at least deplete it to the extent that a portion of his own force can be left to watch the back of those who press forward.

'But probably more importantly to him is the second. He knows that we travelled to ulDetina from those of his men who survived their pursuit of us to that city, but he knows nothing of the route from there to Khardorul. He may stumble on another route across the Blacklands and may even discover which mountain of the countless ones in the Blacklands hides my home city, but relying on chance is not his way. He has planned too much, too intricately, to be a man who is comfortable with anything other than controlling his path to his goal. He knows that a direct route must lead from ul-Detina, the City of Ghosts, to my home in the City of Wisdom, else we would not have gone there. However, he cannot interrogate ghosts in ul-Detina, so he will enquire of the people here in his own particular fashion. Whether it is the route we took or another, he seeks a way to Khardorul, and amongst the thousands in this closest city to the Deadlands, he must be sure there is lore that will reveal it to him, even just in tales passed through generations that are thought to be fanciful entertainment. Remember, he has experience of gathering and disseminating information for the Emperor for many years, and he will extract it here in quantity, and distil what he needs. He will extract it in quantity and at speed.' Brann's face must have revealed his thoughts at that last comment. 'You can never forget, young Brann, what we are dealing with.'

Brann felt the anger rise. 'How could I possibly? How can you think I would?'

'I don't just mean what you experienced and, worse, what

you saw Marlo experience,' Grakk said softly. 'Do not let it cloud your thoughts because it is personal. There are others who have experienced worse, and in numbers greater than we can ever know. This man may believe passionately in his cause or it may be a deception to mask personal gain but, no matter which, it allows him in his mind to see no impediment to, or limit to, the suffering he will inflict on countless innocent people if it will advance him one inch towards his goal.'

Brann's eyes widened in realisation. 'It is not just about Khardorul, and the knowledge within,' he said, 'although the danger is not just in what Loku may discover but in what the world will discover: the city's very existence. But is more. It is the threat of what he might do after. What he will do after.'

Grakk nodded, his eyes fixed on Brann, his voice intense. 'When a man in his later years finally achieves all that he has worked for, he is satisfied and weary, and rests with satisfaction and, often, relief that his work has reached a conclusion while life has allowed him to do so; but when a man in his prime finally achieves all that he has worked for, a hunger is awakened, as is a realisation that he can sate it. He looks for more of the same. And when he is a man with a deep sense of his own righteousness...'

Brann let his own stare leave Grakk and sweep around the unsettling scene of a city street with every element present but people. 'He will not settle. He will not stop. So he must be stopped.'

'For every reason we have, indeed he must. And for all those reasons, it must, somehow, be here. He must not take another step towards Khardorul and its secrets. As important as he gains none of that knowledge is that the world remains ignorant of the city's very existence, and the treasure of knowledge it harbours. What has taken a thousand years or more to collect and preserve must be fed carefully back to the world – there is no culture so civilised that man's baser nature could resist the misuse of power in such abundance. This, here, is where we must make our battleground, young Brann. This is where, of Loku and you, one wins and one fails, and the world takes its next step along with whichever one still stands.'

The unmistakable whirr of an arrow in flight saw them flinch in unison before the missile clattered against the front of a house. A yelp from a rooftop was followed by a short scuffle, then movement descending inside the building. They waited, weapons bared, as the sounds drew closer.

Brann started as Xamira stepped from the doorway, gripping a boy of around twelve summers by the neck of a tunic as dirty as his face and holding a bow in her other hand.

She sighed and looked at Brann, shaking her head in despair. 'It would help if I could actually watch you from afar as my orders dictate rather than having to step in to save your neck again.' She proffered the boy before them, eyebrows raised. 'A dozen pairs of eyes and not one of them lifted above street level. How you have all survived a fraction of your journey is beyond me. And, as for you, you fool,' she shook the terrified boy, and held the bow in front of his face, 'you should only be allowed out with this when you can manage to tell friend from foe.' She dropped boy and bow in disgust on the street.

Grakk look at Brann. 'A lesson, and not just in wariness. We can realise all we like the magnitude of our task, but as easily as that can our plans be ended.'

Brann smiled. 'But likewise for Loku. He is a man. He can die.'

Ossavian had dismounted and ambled over to the boy, who cowered with head down, shaking and not daring to touch his bow. The old man crouched on one knee with a groan of effort, picking up the bow. 'This yours, lad, or did you steal it?'

Anger lifted the eyes in reflex. 'It is mine.'

'Good, good,' Ossavian said quietly, placing one calloused finger under the boy's chin to keep his head up. 'Your father make it for you, or buy it?'

Pride flared in the boy's eyes and his bearing. Brann noticed that the shaking had stopped. 'He made it. He made it last year to mark my achieving years of two digits.'

'He means when he turned ten,' Mongoose murmured to Hakon, who nudged her for her cheek.

Ossavian shot the pair a warning look, then turned back to the boy. He ran his fingers along the wood, sighting along the curve and plucking at the string. 'A fine weapon.' He nodded quietly and placed the weapon back in the boy's hands. 'A fine weapon indeed. Treasure it.'

The boy grasped it with a tightness bordering on desperation, and Ossavian's eyes narrowed. 'Your father?' he said to the boy.

Tears filled the young eyes, and the group watched in silence as the general's thumbs gently wiped them away. 'They killed him,' his voice almost indistinct. 'On the first day they came.'

'Your mother still lives?'

A nod. 'And my sisters.'

'Well, young man, you see your father when you look at the bow, but your mother and sisters see him when they look at you. He lives on in you, now, and you have a chance to make him proud. What you did up there was foolish

470

because you must pick your targets with more care, but it was also courageous. Most would have hidden, but you acted. We will need more like you in the times to come.' He glanced up at Xamira with a wink. 'Just make sure people cannot sneak up on you so easily next time.'

He stood up with a similar groan as when he had crouched, and laid a hand on the boy's shoulder. 'Now, before you go back to the family you must protect now, can you tell me something?' The small face looked up at Ossavian and Brann knew in that instant the boy would move the city for the old soldier if it was within his power to do so. 'Can you tell me where the fighting is?'

The boy nodded vigorously. He pointed ahead. Then to the right. Then to the left.

Konall grunted. 'So basically everywhere except where we have come from.'

Ossavian ignored him, his eyes fixed on the youngster. 'Good boy. One last question: is there somewhere close that is high, where we can see far?'

'The temple tower?' the boy suggested brightly.

'The temple tower would be perfect,' Ossavian smiled. 'But I am afraid I don't know where it is.'

'I can show you!' The small figure was exultant, tugging at the large hand that enveloped his, trying to skip ahead and looking all of his few years.

'Whoa, young fellow!' Ossavian laughed. 'These old legs have a horse for a reason. Give me a moment.' He eased himself back onto his horse and nodded to the lad, who led the way with enthusiasm.

'Masterfully done,' said Einarr.

Ossavian shrugged. 'Only half of being a general is skill in placing soldiers in the right place on a battlefield. The

471

other half is in knowing just exactly what your soldiers need. Reading your own people is just as important as reading the enemy's moves.'

'A lesson for us all,' Einarr agreed.

'Learn from your elders, boy, learn from your elders,' Ossavian laughed. 'Is that not right, Cannick?'

'It's what I've been trying to tell him for years,' Cannick said from behind.

Ossavian guffawed even more heartily.

They rounded their third corner and the boy pointed proudly. From the centre of a building built in a perfect circle soared a tall slender tower, and through the open sides of a roofed platform at its peak, a long conical wooden tube could be seen suspended on two ropes, swinging lazily in the breeze that the height exposed it to. 'There!' the boy said, beaming at Ossavian. 'The priest calls us with his horn from there, but it also has a most excellent view. So my friend's uncle told me.'

'Then,' Ossavian said, 'we are indebted to you and your friend's uncle. Now you run to your family, and you remember to tell them that you saw,' he slapped Brann's horse on the rump to send it jumping forward, 'Brann of the Sagian Arena, come to save your city.'

The boy's eyes widened, and he bowed to Brann. 'I am honoured to meet you. I am Akun of, er, Irtanbat.' He hesitated. 'Are you a great hero?'

'Of course he is!' Ossavian said with grandeur. 'How else could he save your city?'

The boy scampered away almost as fast as his arrow had gone, and Brann looked askance at the old general. 'You place a heavy obligation on me.'

Ossavian raised his eyes to the sky. 'How many times

472

must I tell you? If we tell them that you will save their city, they are more likely to save it themselves. Now you, Konall and Sophaya get yourselves up that tower. Konall and Sophaya have good eyes, and you have decisions to make.'

Grakk tossed his oculens to Sophaya and the three quickly found the stairs within the tower, the cool of the inside of the temple and the top of the tower bringing welcome respite from the baking heat of the streets, where the buildings blocked the air that moved across the open land without.

They stood on the platform, circling slowly to take in the scene. Brann did not need the keen vision of the other two any more than they needed the oculens. The scene was all too evident.

In the distance, across a sea of rooftops, fluttered a banner – they could only presume it was where the king currently made his command – and between here and there were countless pockets of the frantic movements that could only be the struggle of desperate combat; in other streets, the haze of smoke hanging where still shapes must be the corpses of men, death stealing the distinction between friend and foe, the only movement that of the carrion beasts who profited from the slaughter; between them were blazes of active fires and ravaged ruins, where beside them their eyes fell on buildings curiously and inexplicably untouched, as if marked for safety by the mysterious whim of the gods of war.

Between here and there was the struggle for a city.

'This journey of ours,' Brann said, 'may take longer than we thought.'

Chapter 10

She entered as the tall girl left the room. The girl's eyes were downcast, demure, submissive to a servant of superior rank. The older woman's mouth twitched into a smile. She was not fooled.

'You see promise in her,' she said, setting the daily tray bearing the decanter of iced water and two goblets on the table closest to him. She filled both and passed one to him.

He took a slow drink. 'I see it because it is there. I can guide it, but it is within her alone to grow it.'

Her eyebrows arched. 'It grows fast. Already you set her tasks previously entrusted only to your sadly departed man.'

He shrugged. 'Someone has to do them.'

'This someone was a novice in these matters just months ago.'

'As I said, it is dependent on her. If she proves worthy, she is entrusted more greatly. She has proved eager to be worthy, and astute in succeeding in that endeavour.'

They sat in the comfortable silence that only close companionship makes possible.

She finished her water, feeling the last of it trickle cold into her chest. 'How far can she climb?'

He looked at her. 'I cannot live forever. Someone must come after.'

* * * *

The journey took three days. Three days where every step, every breath, took them deeper along a path that led into the hell of every god ever worshipped. It became strange to enter an area where a thin haze of smoke did not mist all around, did not linger on their tongues and in their noses, did not catch in their chests. Silence was mostly their norm; the slightest sound jarring enough to send them turning with a jerk and reaching for weapons.

The first people they encountered was a band of Loku's recruits, frenzied by the herbs they had ingested, hacking at the corpses of a fight that, from the state of the bodies, had finished at least two days earlier. Brann's party fell upon them in silence, the foe so intoxicated that they shouted and laughed that the dead had risen to fight them, even as they themselves were slaughtered. Not one of them rose.

Shortly after, they found city folk barricaded in a row of shops, defending themselves against a large group of Goldlanders, as Hakon had taken to calling them to distinguish them from his name for the other half of the foe: the Scum. Desperation was written across the faces of the locals, and written into their every movement. They fought with cleavers and hunting spears, with knives and smiths' hammers, with anything they could find, men and women shoulder to shoulder, the terrified cries of children muted in the rooms behind. What they lacked in weapons was compensated for by innate instincts of protection towards the children and home at their backs and against those who would take them away. And, Brann noticed, several – many, in fact – of the men fought with a discipline and assurance beyond civilians.

But still they were losing; the heavy broad blades of their enemy cutting through tendon and bone more easily than the branch and vine of the jungle that had been behind their design. The invaders pushed onto them, starting to drive them back, starting to create gaps, starting to overrun them. Until Brann launched himself onto the rearmost without warning, axe-blade cutting and hacking and spraying blood over victims and aggressor alike, and followed in the next instant by his companions.

Caught between enraged warriors and impassioned defenders, the Goldlanders were bested almost immediately, but such was the fury of all that not a one was left alive. No words were spoken after, but for Ossavian's mantra: 'Brann of the Arena comes to save the city. Tell all. Tell all.'

Nods of gratitude were exchanged over heaving chests and, with dazed eyes, mothers clutching children in disbelief at their ability to do so, fathers casting about for further peril, already backing their families away to seek a safer refuge.

Brann's party pushed on. Time was of more value than gold or gems here; time governed the numbers of lives lost.

And so it went. So they went. Scrambling over rubble, falling on the enemy. Wandering through pristine neighbourhoods with barely even a sign of dust or smoke, falling on the enemy. Stumbling upon a campsite at dinner, falling on the enemy. Encountering Irtanbatians, spreading the word of Brann's arrival, falling on the enemy. Falling on the enemy, falling on the enemy, falling on the enemy; for every one they killed, they found ten more. Falling on the enemy, arms too weary to carry a weapon finding new strength to swing that blade. Falling on the enemy, fighting through the enemy, ever forward, ever onward, ever closer.

And then, without warning, they were there. Brann had scrambled up the blackened, jumbled blocks of a building that fire had collapsed. He had fallen, despite his eyes scanning the surface he trod, when a shattered statue shifted under his foot as he crested the pile. He had picked himself up, lifted his head. He saw the camp at the end of the street ahead, saw the soldiers that he knew, just knew, were not the enemy. He stopped.

'We are here,' he said.

Breta stepped up beside him. 'We are here.'

They picked their way down the slope and walked to the first sentries; the first people Brann had approached in recent memory with his weapons sheathed, the sensation now feeling unnatural. A welcome party awaited, a squad of two score soldiers with levelled spears and raised shields and what must be an officer, their once proud armour and plumed helmets now battered and dented with no surface spared. Brann preferred to see it that way – it was worn by survivors.

The officer stepped forward. 'You have been watched in your approach, for some time.' His voice was weary but his eyes were firm.

'We know,' said Grakk.

As Grakk had answered, the man directed his words at him. The rest sat on the ground where they were, uncaring of the spears, uncaring of anything but the fatigue in their bones. 'You do not seem as the other strangers, the invaders.'

'Because we are not they.'

The man regarded him silently with narrowed eyes as he thought. 'You knew the camp was here?'

'We knew it was in this direction.'

'You did not suspect it was close when you saw the watchers?'

'We have been watched often, on our journey through the city. There is much fear.'

The officer nodded. 'That is the truth.' He cocked his head. 'Journey from where?'

'From Sagia.'

'No, from where in the city?'

Grakk shrugged. 'We do not know its name. We entered on the south side.'

The man's eyes widened and a murmur spread through the wary soldiers. One or two spears lowered slightly. The officer's words were slow, disbelieving. 'You have come all the way from the south side? You have made it through from there.'

Grakk smiled wearily. 'I did not say it was easy.'

'I did not think it were possible.'

Grakk's smile became a grin. 'Believe me, there were times when we were of that mind also.'

The officer frowned, then his face cleared as a thought grew. 'Sagia... foreigners... warriors... women who fight as... Our scouts bring rumours of a saviour, one they call Brann of the Arena, a mighty warrior come from the Jewel of the Empire to free us from this horror.' His frown returned. 'But they did not speak of him as a tribesman.'

'There would be a simple reason for that,' Grakk said. 'For I am not he.' The officer's shoulders sagged in disappointment. 'He is he.' His finger pointed at Brann.

The officer's silence drew Brann's eyes up to meet the man's. The eyes he found held anger. 'Do not toy with us. We have been through more than you would imagine. We have seen our families and our city suffer more than we would want to imagine. Do not jest about hope.' He spat in the dirt at their feet, and nodded at the city behind them. 'If you came here to fight, you do not need to join our ranks – you will find it aplenty out there.' He gestured to his men. 'See them away from here.'

Brann stood slowly, easing the stiffness that had already set into aching limbs. 'I have fought my way across your precious city, killing more of your enemy than probably all of you here combined, as has every man and woman you see before you. I am sore; I am tired; I can't remember what it is not to smell blood and smoke, and I can't be arsed debating.' His sword was suddenly in his hand, and the officer took a step back, drawing his own as a rattle from his men spoke of shields and spears being readied for his command. 'You have probably slept four times since we did last, but still, if I have to, I will best you sword to sword if it proves any point you need made obvious.' He noticed the man's eyes flicking to the black blade, its metal seeming to absorb light where every other weapon around him was reflecting it. 'But perhaps you have heard more than just a name. Perhaps you have heard more than just stories of feats. Perhaps you have heard of...' He reversed the sword in one fluid movement, presenting it hilt first to the man.

The officer sheathed his own weapon warily, as if this might be a trick and would find Brann's sword in his gut in a move as quick as the one that had turned it a moment before. But Brann stayed still, and he carefully took the hilt. Surprise crossed his face at the lightness, and he lifted the weapon, testing the edge of the blade against his thumb with a hiss of surprise at its sharpness despite the use the stories attested to. 'Not even a notch,' he said in wonder, holding the blade to the light. 'Care to exchange?'

Brann smiled. 'Perhaps not.'

'A weapon beyond compare.' He nodded in acceptance. 'There cannot be two such.'

'So we may see the king?'

He handed back the weapon and looked around the group with a new respect. 'I will ask. You can certainly enter the camp. I will have a man take you to where you can wash and eat while my message is relayed through those more senior than I.'

Brann slid his sword back into its scabbard. 'That would be appreciated.'

King Ruslan was short and slim of stature, but big of personality. When Brann, Einarr, Ossavian and Grakk were shown in, he was standing at the back of the large pavilion tent that served as his residence, audience chamber and war room simultaneously, poring over a map of the city that filled the entire surface of the table before him and cursing volubly and creatively at the map and at himself, berating both for his lack of opportunities and solutions. A group of officers, five in number, towered over him but their silent reserve and respectful expressions were evidence of the esteem they held for their ruler.

Lost in thought, the king did not notice their presence at first and they stood as patiently as his commanders. Brann did not envy the man his task, not only responsible for the defence of his city but also the wellbeing, feeding, sheltering, sanitation and dozens of other considerations, Brann was certain, of a population fractured and scattered by the invaders and by panic.

To see the man's greeting when he became aware of them, however, he might have had nothing more to ponder than the colour of the new paint scheme for his throne room or whether to have meat or fish for his lunch. His face split into a smile of delight and he came across to greet them without waiting for them to approach him, grasping their arms and nodding his head in delight, his light golden crown pushed back and acting as much as a band to keep his hair from his eyes as it did as a mark of office. Above the waist, he wore only a richly embroidered waistcoat, exposing the hard belly of a man accustomed to exercise, and his arms, cuffs of gem-studded gold below the elbows and rings of the same metal above them, were likewise lean and muscled, while Brann noticed scarred knuckles and calloused palms as Ruslan came to him in turn.

'Welcome, welcome all,' he said, his tone rich, the warmth in it genuine.

Here was a man, Brann thought, who did not shirk his responsibilities but who was at pains to avoid dumping the weight of them on others where it wasn't necessary. Here was a man to follow.

'Please,' the king said, 'come in, come away from the chill. Evening is coming and there is a chill at this time of year. Now, I believe we have a man of repute from the great Arena of Sagia?'

Brann stepped forward, suddenly self-conscious. 'Your Majesty,' he said, not knowing whether to bow or not, resulting in an awkward bend at the waist, more akin to a spasm than a sign of respect.

Ruslan waved a hand with a laugh. 'Oh, don't bother

with all that nonsense. Airs and graces just waste time when I could be telling people what to do and they could be doing it.' His grin was infectious, and Brann found himself smiling back as the king scanned the others. 'And you, I am guessing, must be the renowned General Ossavian.'

Ossavian nodded, his eyes widening slightly in surprise. 'You know me?'

Ruslan shook his head. 'You were spotted as you crossed the camp. I never did have the honour of serving with you, but my son did when he was learning to be a soldier, in your final campaign.'

Ossavian smiled grimly. 'I had thought it the final one, Majesty. But now...'

The king nodded sadly and was introduced to Einarr and Grakk. As he greeted them as warmly as he had Brann and Ossavian, a young officer who could only be the son of the king – he was the image of his father as a young man but with his hair cropped to stubble and his face earnest where his father's was constantly creased in bonhomie – stepped forward and inclined his head to Ossavian. 'General,' he said. 'You will not remember me, but...'

'How is your shoulder, young Serhan?' Ossavian asked.

Brann gawped, and sensed that the others did the same as the silence of surprise dropped across the tent.

'Impressive,' murmured Ruslan.

'Fully healed some three years hence,' said Serhan. 'And yours?'

'The same, young man, the same.' The king was regarding him with an expectant expression, and Brann felt just as curious. Ossavian grinned. 'It is not quite so impressive as it seems – it was impossible to see even the faces of most of the soldiers under my command, never mind learn the

482

names, but people tend to stay in your memory when they throw themselves in the way of an arrow shot at their general from close range. The shaft passed right through the young man's shoulder and lodged in mine, pinning us together, but his movement had taken it away from the centre of my chest where it would otherwise have struck.'

He reached forward and pulled up the loose short sleeve of the prince's tunic, exposing a scar on the front of his left shoulder and a corresponding one on the rear, then pulled across the neck of his own tunic to show the puckered scar on the front of his left shoulder.'

'The things one learns of one's son,' the king mused. 'You never told me of this incident, Serhan. Why ever would you not?'

'Many acts of heroism far greater than that take place in war, father,' the young man said seriously. 'It felt wrong to brag.'

'Cleary his mother's son,' Ruslan explained to the group. 'Had it been me, I would have had my minstrels make a song of it. But tell me, boy, what did you learn from that experience.'

Serhan's voice was as solemn as his face. 'To use my shield.'

The laughter rocked the tent.

'So, General,' King Ruslan said to Ossavian as the amusement subsided, 'what gladdens my heart the most is that the Emperor has come to our aid. How many men have you under your command?'

Ossavian stared at him in confusion. 'The Emperor looks north at this time, Your Majesty, not east. The millens immediately at his disposal have been sent in that direction, not this. I am here in my own capacity, travelling with companions fine, but few. There are no more than a dozen of us.'

The king's face paled and lost its easy geniality in that moment. 'But... but why would a general come without an army?'

'I am no general these days, but I have not lost what is in my head nor my desire to do what is right. The man who leads this horde to your door has been chased by this young man,' he indicated Brann, 'across the known world and back again. It is only through him that we even know this is taking place at your city, and he almost lost his life trying to warn the Emperor that you were under threat. We know this man, we know these enemies, and we are here to do whatever we can to stop him.'

'But with so few? You have not even the numbers to fill the gaps where my own men have been lost.'

Einarr coughed politely. 'If you don't mind me asking, Majesty, what numbers do you have? It is always more useful to consider what we can work with rather than what we would like to work with.'

Ruslan took a deep breath and, when he lifted his head once more, his eyes had regained their thoughtful calm. 'You are right, of course. It was just a... a shock. We have hoped daily for support to arrive, and when I heard that not only a general, but one of the two brothers who are the greatest of generals, was within a party seeking audience, I thanked the gods that my prayers had been answered.' He ticked off on his fingers the few assets he could list as he named them. 'As some of you will know, as vassals of the Empire we are not permitted an army – only the Emperors millens can march the lands – but we are allowed a household guard numbering no more than five hundred, who you will find camped around this tent less those who have fallen already. We also have our citizenry, and as citizens of the Empire as well as of Irtanbat, the men must serve their years in the millens themselves so they know how to hold a weapon. However, with the millens the only armies in the Empire and keeping the peace between kings who, in any case, have no troops themselves to cause trouble amongst each other, there is no real need – especially this close to Sagia – for defences, so our walls have crumbled and allow this enemy to access the city where they will. As a result, we fight on a thousand fronts, having had no warning in the first place to mount a concerted defence. The populace will fight – I know my people, and this is their home – but they are in pockets of a meagre few scattered across this eastern half of the city. In the meantime, the attackers capture who they can and there is talk of mass torture in their camp, though no soul has returned to enlighten us as to the answers they seek.' Brann saw his companions' faces darken and he felt a rage flare within himself, thinking of the innocents suffering – more innocents suffering – in the name of Loku's fanatical quest, but the king noticed not, his eyes sweeping slowly across his map. 'All we can do is resist as long as the gods give us strength and take as many of them as we can before they overrun us.'

Brann shook his head forcibly. 'No, that is never all you can do.' A tense silence fell across all gathered there and Brann realised that every eye was on him. 'Your Majesty,' he added, lamely.

But the king merely smiled with interest. 'And what would you do, Brann of the Arena, you and your small band of warriors?'

Brann drew his confidence to him and forced himself to

walk to the map, gathering his thoughts. He eyed the areas marked like a leopard's hide, presumably an indication of the known zones where citizens gathered and resisted. 'We need to know what we have, we need to communicate. We need to spread hope and let people know they are not alone. And we need to do it fast.' He looked at King Ruslan. 'My companions bring together a certain level of ability and a mix of good fortune, training and experience that has seen us survive situations that many others may not have. Let us form an independent unit, reporting directly to you. Let us bring word and hope to your people and death to any of the foe we encounter on the way.'

'And you lead them?' Ruslan said. 'You speak for them all?'

Brann paused, and looked at the others. He saw the message in their eyes and turned back to the king. He nodded. 'I do.'

The king stared at him, and he held his breath until he realised the eyes were thoughtful rather than provoked to anger. 'Had you brought a thousand soldiers I would have been loth to release such a resource,' he said, 'but what difference will a dozen make to my ranks? If you can help my people, who am I to say you should do otherwise? If you can leave in the morning, I will give you all the assistance you require and my blessing also.'

Brann smiled. 'We can leave in the morning.'

The king's eyebrows raised. 'I expected you to barter for leaving a little later in the day. You have only arrived at my camp, battered and exhausted, a matter of merely hours ago.'

Brann's eyes locked with those of the king. 'With respect, Your Majesty, everyone we have seen in this camp is battered and exhausted. Such is war. We crave rest like nothing else, yet we know that we cannot rest until the man who brought this, who drives this, who designed all of this – we cannot rest until that man is dead. And we will not.'

King Ruslan smiled. 'I believe we are all going to get on famously.'

Brann crouched in the doorway, scanning the street, his eyes moving but his head held still. It was quiet, but that was often the most likely sign of danger. No animals, no birds, noting: no sign of life was the surest indicator that you could lose your own.

His eye stopped on a sack, metal in the form of plates, candlesticks, tools, and the gods only knew what else spilling from it on the roadway in front of a building as empty as the rest in this quarter, as likely to have been abandoned by disturbed looters as by a fleeing family. He glanced at Sophaya, standing beside a window that was no more than a space in the wall, open to the world. Her back was flat against the wall to give her the narrowest angle to see, and be seen from, the street and her bow was in her hand, an arrow ready to meet the string. He hissed, catching her attention, and she followed his gaze to the sack. She nodded and the bow came up, the arrow in place and string drawn in the same movement. The instant it came into position, she loosed, and Brann watched the arrow streak to the target, striking the sack and its contents with savage force, scattering some across the ground around it and clattering the rest against each other. The noise rattled around the street, echoing and lingering in the heavy backdrop of silence for the scant few heartbeats before the world was filled with greater sound, a roar from a score of throats or more as a group, Goldlanders and Scum combined, charged around a corner.

They stopped, meeting no foe. Faces slipped from battle rage to confusion as they turned slowly, the momentum gone from their charge and their heads.

It was the moment.

'Now!' Brann shouted, launching himself from the doorway, sword in one hand and axe in the other. He did not need to look for the others; he knew they would come, closing from various sides on the group now startled at the switch from hunters to prey. Arrows flicked past him and he sensed the movement of two of his companions at the edge of his vision, but he had already fixed on his first targets.

He closed in moments, shortening his stride to improve his agility. His axe swung low at an unprotected leg, cutting deep. His movement took him at an angle and he caught the curve of the blade around the side of the half-severed limb, using it to pull both legs sideways and hurling the man into the one beside him. Before the second man could react, Brann's sword tip had punched in and out of his chest. He turned, axe and body swinging together: the weapon, unwatched, to where he knew lay the throat of the man with the wounded leg, blood spraying high in the afternoon sun; the body to let his head scan for the next danger, his sword already braced to meet it.

He heard movement as he continued to spin in a slight crouch and saw a Goldlander rushing towards him with his macuahuitl poised to swing and the round wooden shield his people favoured swinging as he ran. Wary of the crushing force of the weapon in the hands of the powerful Goldlanders as much as the sharpness of the edges, Brann sprang forward, meeting the man before he was intending to complete his swing. His axe came up to deflect the fearsome weapon and he spun to his left. The stiffened quilted tunics that the Greenlanders wore in battle would considerably slow the slash of a blade so Brann reversed his sword as he spun, driving it point-first past the edge of the shield and through the heavy fabric, up under the ribs. The man coughed blood, Brann feeling it hot on the back of his neck, and he quickly pulled the sword free and stepped away, guarded against a spasmodic final attack from the dying man. The body hit the ground.

Another man was facing directly at him, spear in the action of being launched, when two swords pierced his torso. Gerens and Xamira nodded to each other as they withdrew their weapons.

Brann glanced about him quickly, but their opponents were by now few. Hakon was laying about him to devastating effect with his huge macuahuitl, while Mongoose faced two men with her speed and precision. As she darted, thrust, and parried in a blur, an arrow buried itself in the side of one of the men and she finished the other.

Silence fell, but for their heavy breathing and the moans of two of the Goldlanders; Brann had yet to hear any of them scream, whatever the circumstances. Gerens drew his knife, and the moaning stopped.

Brann cast about, seeing all of his companions standing. Good. He listened, hearing no sounds of anyone else drawn by the noise of the fighting. Nothing: also good. 'Any wounds take them to Grakk and Philippe, the rest of us – well, you know the drill.'

They piled high in the middle of the street as much wood from the empty buildings as they could quickly find and threw the bodies of the Goldlanders on top: disease was the last thing the defenders of the city needed. Once the wounds had been tended, they lit the pyre and left immediately. If the smoke attracted reinforcements for those who burnt, they were better being out of the vicinity; if it brought local people, the message was there in any case. Before they left, though, Brann noticed Ossavian dipping a bunched tunic in blood and daubing a large letter B on the wall closest to the pyre, as determined as ever to make a legend of Brann. He knew it was important to the old general and, while he was discomforted by what he was attempting to achieve, Brann trusted him.

They crouched in the darkness, ten days and twelve ambushes after luring the Goldlanders with Sophaya's arrow into the sack of metal, staring from the top of the building over the square where the enemy, four groups of them in all, had gathered for the night. They had heard tell that these partic-ular squads, Goldlanders and Scum alike, had taken to returning to a certain spot at the end of each day, establishing an ad hoc forward camp deep in the city and secure in their safety among a population that they were terrorising and playing their part in gradually eradicating. They were indeed confident, Brann noted with satisfaction: they had gathered in what had once been a hall for the surrounding commu-nity, a large single storey building with a single entrance of tall, grand doors that opened outwards letting the sounds of their merriment spill even further than the light from the opening. It was clear it had been a building of importance: unlike the majority of structures in the city that were formed of either stone or mud bricks according to their relative status, this was constructed of finely carved wood, a precious commodity in the area. It was also the fact that had generated their strategy, one suggested by Einarr who remembered practices spoken of in the sagas of his people.

Brann's eyes lit upon a tall slender pole that had been erected by the invaders in front of the hall. Close to the top, a man had been impaled, his body having slid partially down the shaft, leaving the sharpened end of the wood protruding above one shoulder. It stood as a macabre standard for the force camping here. Brann's eyes, and his mood, darkened even further as the sight took him back to the camps in the mountains of Halveka, where he had first sighted those they now referred to as the Scum. He growled softly. A man who condones this, who encourages this, could have at his mercy the vast treasury of knowledge housed in Khardorul? Even the image of the Scum rampaging through the sanctity of that idyllic settlement was a sacrilegious horror. It must not be.

He nodded to the others in the moonlight. 'Let's do it.'

It took moments to dispose of the casual sentries, what few there were. Einarr limped with a speed that no longer caused surprise among them alongside Sophaya, Hakon and Xamira to gather in front of the doors, bows strung and ready. Shapes moved above as wooden debris, bundles of hay scooped from stables that Philippe had spotted the previous day and oil from clay jars filched from a defunct shop were spread about the roof in addition to those already in small piles around all four sides of the building. Brann, his back pressed to the wood of the wall to the side of the doorway, waved to the four archers and, without hesitation, they started to send a succession of arrows through the open doorway.

Uproar ensued. Screams mingled with the banging and

scraping of furniture overturning as only those already struck were left in the central area. Three Goldlanders, more brave than the rest, scampered to the doors and pulled them shut. The archers allowed them to do so.

The instant the doors slammed shut, Brann, Philippe, Cannick and Ossavian darted to the doorway, each placing a length of stout wood across its width, holding a long iron nail in position at its end. Breta and Hakon swung large hammers, driving eight nails home with eight thundering swings. The doors were as impenetrable as the walls.

At the eighth hammer blow, light from above glowed across the square and Mongoose, Gerens and Grakk dropped lightly from the roof. The trio ran quickly around the building, setting alight the bundles at the foot of walls splashed in oil, and Brann moved with the others from the door to join the archers who stood with arrows ready in case any should emerge from doors weakened by flames.

But all that emerged were screams of, first, horrified realisation and then horrified agony. Brann looked again at the figure impaled on the pole and then back at the building consumed in fire, and felt nothing for those dying inside.

The fight, an ambush in which they had joined the city folk who had prepared it, hadn't lasted long, their numbers and their passion both outweighing those of the invaders. As they stood over the dead, searching for a lingering threat, a familiar figure approached them and ran directly to Ossavian.

The general smiled and led the boy to Brann, his hand resting on the slight shoulder. 'Akun of Irtanbat would like me to tell the great warrior Brann that three of his arrows felled those who seek to take their city from them.'

Brann pushed aside the regret that one so young should already be so callous about death and able to kill with such ease. It was preferable, he reminded himself, than one finishing his life so young. He smiled. 'In that case, I am not the only great warrior here today. Akun of Irtanbat has indeed made his father proud.'

The boy beamed and bowed to Brann, before scampering away, shouting for his uncle.

'Oh gods,' came Konall's voice from behind. 'Now he'll be wanting us all to bow to him.'

Brann's reply was cut short by a shout from further along the street and he whirled, his sword still in his hand from the fight. A man ran towards them, and he relaxed as he saw that he wore armour of those belonging to Ruslan's guard: a long mail coat with a square plate inset to cover the lower ribs and belly. Brann was amazed the man could run at all in it – he found his own lighter mail a burden enough in the stifling heat.

The man, his face caked in sweat-smeared dust, slowed before them and spoke without preamble. 'King Bahadur has arrived from Tharpia with his five hundred, and Firat, Irtanbat's first warrior, has been found alive after being feared dead in the initial attack. King Ruslan calls a Council, and you are requested to join him.'

They found the camp alive with excitement as much as with the extra bodies brought by the Tharpians. An officer, one of his eyes kept closed by a fresh scar running at an angle across this forehead and half of one ear missing, met them and directed them to a building on the edge of the camp, facing into the open area. It had originally comprised two storeys, but fire had taken away the roof leaving only the lower level as offering any shelter. They entered into one large room stretching from front to back, three tables and an assortment of chairs the furniture at the front, and an even more varied selection of beds arranged near the far wall.

The officer turned to them as he showed them in. 'King Ruslan apologises for the cramped conditions for a party of your size in the tent previously provided. This was hitherto the home of a merchant – the family lived above, and this area was where he welcomed customers and displayed his wares. It is not much, but you have more space than in the tent.'

Brann looked around, feeling the air in the shade inside a touch cooler than in the glare of the sun and seeing shelter where others would have seen dilapidation. 'It is more than we have enjoyed for the past few weeks. Please pass our thanks to the king.'

The officer nodded. 'There is also a walled area at the back of the building where pits have been done to let you…' He glanced at Xamira, Mongoose, Breta and Sophaya and blushed, a curious look on his battle-hardened face. 'Where you can, er…'

Breta walked past, already unstrapping her weapons and flexing her shoulders. 'Where we can shit and piss. It's all right, we do it too, soldier.'

The man blushed even deeper. 'Ah, of course. Yes, you have latrine pits. I am afraid the washing facilities are communal, however, although the women and men of the camp do have separate areas.'

Cannick grunted. 'Communal is an improvement on none, lad, so don't apologise. This is excellent. You do us proud.'

The officer visibly relaxed. 'I am glad. The quartermaster

had it brushed out and he suggests, if you are happy to do so, that you stow your equipment at the rear of the room to allow space at the front to allow you to receive your guests when they arrive.' He inclined his head. 'Now, if that is all, I must attend to my men.'

Ossavian clapped him on the back. 'Then go, young man. They are your primary responsibility, not us. You have more than fulfilled any duties you had to us.'

The man smiled and left. Brann looked at the others with his eyebrows raised. 'Our guests? Who would visit us? Should any come, I hope they arrive and leave in a hurry before we are called to report to the king.'

They had barely stowed their meagre possessions, however, when they heard the noise of a group outside above the hubbub of the camp. Brann groaned, setting down the bow he had been unstringing beside the water skins and food pouch he had already laid down and the carefully folded black cloak of his father that he had placed beside him on his cot. 'What do these people want? Can we not at least wash and feed ourselves?'

'Apparently not,' Konall said, moving to the door with a frown. He stopped abruptly and backed back in without a word.

King Ruslan entered, and Brann sprang to his feet.

'My friends,' the king said. 'It is good to see you have returned safely.' He bathed them all in his welcoming smile. 'Tales of your exploits reach us and inspire the population, and for that you have my gratitude.'

Brann was still dumbfounded by the king's presence. Before he could reply, a voice growled from the doorway. 'Tales are for bards. I would hear this from the source of the stories before my opinion is formed.'

495

A tall man entered, powerful and broad of shoulder. A shirt of armour formed of scales like the skin of a fish could disguise neither a warrior's build nor the slight paunch commensurate with the years that streaked grey through his cropped hair. A long scar beside hard eyes moved as he spoke, as if a venomous snake was poised to remind those he addressed of the danger the man himself exuded.

Ruslan waved an arm at the newcomer. 'May I present King Bahadur of Tharpia on the eastern shore of the Sea of Life.'

Brann bowed in what he hoped was an appropriate way, his eye catching the movement of the others doing likewise. As he straightened, more men filed in, and Ruslan introduced each as he appeared. 'Prince Serhan, you have met.' The young man nodded at his name. 'Firat, our first warrior, feared dead but recently returned to us,' a lean man as hard-faced as Bahadur and a mass of cuts, scrapes and bruises, with the edge of a bandage showing under the edge of his helmet plumed with a horse's tail dyed red. 'Haluk, our former first warrior and himself a champion of the Sagian Arena, who travelled from the farm of his retirement on hearing of the peril facing his mother city,' a man older than Einarr but younger than Ossavian, his impassive expression unchanging as he nodded their way. 'My personal guard, Maktanu, the most feared warrior of Irtanbat who has watched over me since I campaigned as a young officer in the South when I saved his life and he lost his tongue, both in the same incident,' a huge man in every dimension and with skin almost as dark as Brann's sword, a livid scar pulling one corner of his mouth into a constant half smile, though a whole warmth seemed to glow in his eyes. 'And, final in his entrance but not in his standing, my friend Bahadur's first warrior, Shahkam Davar,' a man of medium height but excessive menace, his neatly shaped black beard framing a hooked nose and glaring eyes; he did not acknowledge them. 'Unfortunately, my other friend, King Thanases of Corens, which sits as the nearest city to us in an eastern ride, is unable to join us.'

'On account of the journey having rendered him weary, Your Majesty?' Brann imagined an elderly monarch, braving the hot arid land to come to his fellow king's aid.

'On account,' growled Bahadur, 'of the worship of the coin of commerce rendering him a craven child who pisses his throne at the shadow of a risk to his prosperity.'

'Now, Bahadur,' Ruslan chided. 'We prefer the term cautious.'

The tall man spat on the floor. 'You prefer it. A man who guards his balls leaves his throat exposed. Cut the throat and the balls are treasured no more.' Brann was unable to avoid a smile, catching Bahadur's attention. 'You find that funny?'

Brann smiled wider. 'I find it to be perfect sense. And I find that pleases me.'

Ruslan cut in. 'Thanases did aid us in one respect, it is true. His invitation to good Bahadur here to visit him to discuss a treaty of trade meant that the Tharpian five hundred were close enough to be here now.'

Brann spoke before he could stop himself. 'The entire household guard travelled on a trade mission?'

The tall king's head swivelled to regard him. 'My Invincibles do, as every king's force should, but few see the sense in doing. A soldier does nothing but grow fat and complacent sitting in a barracks. A man needs new sights to remind him there are others in the world who may seek to be better than he.'

Bahadur looked down on Brann with narrowed eyes. 'You are the one taking toll on the invaders?'

'I and my companions, Your Majesty.'

He ignored Brann's point and looked at Shahkam Davar. 'He is not very big.'

'There are plenty of men bigger than me who I have cut to the ground, Majesty,' his first warrior said. His dark eyes fixed on Brann. 'Though I cannot judge at this stage if he would fight or fall.' A sneer crossed his hawk face. 'I have the start of an opinion, however.'

'As have I.' Bahadur looked back at Brann. 'I have been here three days and you and your small group have had more effect in that time than my Invincibles and Ruslan's five hundred combined, and that is not to say there was any lack of valour, effort or proficiency on the part of our soldiers. Ruslan also values your impact, and his is one of three opinions in this Empire that I respect.' He frowned. 'Why else do you think we come for your counsel?'

'You, ah, you come for...?' Brann's thoughts jammed in his head. 'Your Majesties, I am honoured by your presence as we all are, but I don't see...'

Ruslan stepped forward and took Brann by the arm, leading him to the largest of the three tables. 'You have not long arrived, and I know you and your companions need sustenance and rest, young man, which the gods know you have earned many times over. However, we are men who have fought battles on plains and in hills; if city walls are breached, the city is lost. This battle within a city is new to us, but you have been fighting it with great success in these past weeks, so if we can impose on your time and your thoughts for just a short while in a brief discussion, then we monarchs and these great warriors accompanying us would be grateful for your indulgence of our intrusion and we could make whatever preparations prove necessary while you eat and sleep.'

Brann felt the man sit with him at the table, his mind only gradually letting meaning filter through the barricade of concepts that contradicted the world he knew. 'Your gratitude? My indulgence? Your imposition?' His voice seemed distant in his head.

He reached for the reality of the room around him much as he had once reached for the surface of the sea after being freed from entrapment deep underwater. Einarr's voice came from behind him, wonder in its tone. 'When heroes and kings come to call.'

Ruslan turned. 'What was that, Lord Einarr?'

Einarr smiled slightly. 'My apologies, Your Majesty. The past words of an elderly lady dear to us returned to me in this moment.'

'Really?' The king paused briefly. 'Then she is not only dear but extremely helpful. We must talk of her further, at a more convenient time. Now, however,' he turned back to the table and gestured to his son. 'Serhan, if you please.'

The young man stepped forward and spread Ruslan's plan of the city on the table top. The map had been redrawn with the most recent knowledge of the sea of the enemy and the islands of resistance marked in contrasting colours.

The two kings sat across the table from Brann, and their party clustered to the rear of them, as Brann's did behind him.

Brann quickly scanned the map, noting that already some of the positions needed to be changed according to what they had witnessed in the field.

Ruslan spoke. 'The city itself is spread too wide for the

enemy to occupy completely. These pockets of resistance are scattered all over, hundreds, maybe a thousand of them, more than we even have found. Areas where the enemy will not enter without loss, streets they will not walk without meeting death. They are small in the context of the size of the city, but in existing at all they are large in importance. Your attacks on the enemy where they least expect have grown hope in the breasts of my people and sown some doubt in the minds of the invaders; these have opposite effects on the tenacity with which a man,' he glanced at those standing with Brann, 'or woman fights.'

'So now is the time to strike them,' Bahadur said with vigour. 'We need an army. We need to unite them.'

'Indeed,' said Ruslan. 'We take the chance the gods have presented to us.'

Brann was staring at the map, finding areas where he had moved, fought, planned, slept, stalked until they became familiar. His eyes saw drawn markings but in his head he saw buildings, streets, and people. The two kings' words and his own images galvanised him and a memory returned to him of their attack on the supply caravan and Ossavian's lesson at the time. He looked up with fire in his gaze as thoughts tumbled from him in words fast and urgent.

'No.'

Both kings looked at him in surprise and a murmur ran through their entourage, more than one hand reaching for a weapon. Brann ignored it. 'We need to organise our people, use their inspiration, but in the most effective way, not in a battle where we will be swamped and achieve nothing with our deaths.

'Instead, hit the enemy on a thousand fronts one day, and a thousand more the next. The foe may be an army five times our number or more, but it is an army half of drugged lunatics and half of religious fanatics. Let us take the doubts you speak of and feed their superstitions, create their illusions, fill their nightmares. Let us make them fear an army of ghosts, an army of demons, who strike from the shadows and alleys and fade away unseen. Let us cut them away, a piece at a time and with each cut take from them a little more of their confidence and what is left of their sanity. We must bring to them the fear they have brought to others, and we must bring it again and again and again.

'We must, and we will.'

There was silence. Brann felt worry grow in his stomach. He knew this was the only way, but he had overstepped the mark in contradicting them. Bahadur looked at his champion, and Ruslan at each of his group; both received nods in return, even, after a pause, from Shahkam Davar.

Bahadur fixed a level stare on Brann. 'Agreed.'

'And with your few words, Brann of the Arena,' Ruslan said, standing, 'we have our way forward.' He clapped his hands, a smile breaking across his face. 'So it shall be.'

The two kings led their legendary warriors from the dilapidated building, and Brann turned to look at his companions.

'Did that just happen?' he said.

Brann watched as the enemy soldiers crept along the street from both directions, drawing closer to the warehouse building with minute care to avoid alerting those within, eyeing the smoke from the cooking fires drifting from the second and third of the six storeys. He watched as they gathered at its front, massing before the wide goods entrance and the smaller doorway further along the wall. He watched as they were given the signal and slipped silently inside, showing remarkable restraint as more than fifty feet moved quietly, stepping past broken crates, discarded wagon wheels, old ropes lying like giant snakes in the dust, unused work surfaces empty but for more dust and the occasional abandoned tool. He watched as light at the back of the building was disturbed by more entering through the great rear doors designed to allow passage to carts entering and leaving simultaneously. He watched as the first started to climb the two broad stairways, the remainder packing behind in their eagerness. He watched as they rushed, the tension and silence alike broken by a roar of furious power. He watched as they spilled into the empty space, milled in the empty space, officers trying to regain their momentum and force them to the next floor before the advantage of surprise was completely lost.

He watched from the building across the street.

He sprinted from the cover, the others following. Arrows quickly took out those few of the foe who had lingered on the ground floor or who, driven by suspicion at the emptiness one level above, drifted back down the stairs. Swift hands grasped the ends of the ropes so recently stepped over, some able to be reached at the doorways, others having to be retrieved from inside, while Sophaya and Mongoose stood ready with arrows nocked to bowstrings. Hakon and Breta took one rope each, while the rest paired up.

Time was short, and vital. Brann checked that all were outside the building. 'Now!'

They heaved at the ropes. The rough fibres burned against their skin, but they heaved more. Brann felt the support pillar at the other end of the rope pulled by him and Cannick start to shift, the bricks already weakened by them the night before. At the first movement, it gave way with a suddenness that sent them sprawling in the road and they picked themselves up with apprehension, pushing hard with their legs into a run from the building.

The others were running, too, putting as much distance between them and the warehouse as they could, but at the first creak, a groan as if a god were opening a great door with rusted hinges, an irresistible curiosity turned their heads as one. As if time slowed, the building collapsed in upon itself, and in upon those within. There was a terrible power about the way blocks two men could barely lift between them moved as if they floated, and a rumble like the roar of the mightiest of waterfalls shook them to the core of their bones and a cloud of dust swept over them, forcing them to duck and turn as they coughed and spat, covering their streaming eyes too late.

By the time the dust had settled enough for them to see the devastation, the screams had already stopped.

The air hung heavy, and not just from the heat of the sun. They stood in silence, stunned by devastation beyond any of their expectations, and by what they knew lay buried within.

'That is no death for a warrior,' Konall said quietly.

'No warriors lie within,' Brann said. 'Those who seek to murder innocent families are not warriors. Those who glorify suffering are not warriors.' He spat in disgust. 'Those, there, are not warriors. And those, there, will not kill another person in this city.' He shook his head to clear it. 'Come. This will attract more than we can kill. And this is not just about us, and revenge, and our feelings. This is about bringing order to desperate resistance. Let us do so.'

Brann watched as the city folk fell on the invaders. For once, he stood back. It was time to leave this group to it.

It was time for them to know they could succeed by themselves.

It was only a supply store, but it was a supply store behind the enemy front. He had listened while the leaders had planned the attack, and had needed to add no advice, only approval. He had followed as they wound through streets and alleys familiar to them and a maze to invaders. He had watched as the few guards, complacent in the arrogance of the dominant host, fell quickly and in shock. He had watched as casks of water and wine were poisoned, as weapons were bent and broken, as tools were stolen or destroyed, as food was gathered or ruined. He had watched as all that would burn was piled high. He had watched as all was done with determined efficiency and not a second wasted on fruitless celebration or self-congratulation.

Now he watched as the heap was set alight and the group withdrew at speed. The smoke would be a signal that would attract, but it would also – and in this lay its purpose – be a signal that would present a message: that nowhere were the invaders safe.

An hour and a safe distance from the scene, they stopped in safety. Brann turned to the two who led them. The woman looked at him with eager eyes. 'Did we do you proud?'

They did themselves proud, but he was aware of what was vital for them to hear, to be able to carry with them the next time, and the next. 'You did, and more.' He saw the light in their eyes, and knew what he said next to be true. 'You are ready. Do what you must for your city. Over and again.'

The band of defenders, their resolve made firm by previous successes, waited perfectly for the moment. The passing squad, mixed two-to-one in favour of the Goldlanders, reached the marked spot and the city folk burst upon them.

But the Goldlanders were experienced. They were organised. They turned, shields raised, and closed the gaps between them, forming a circle that wheeled steadily to each man's left to turn new defenders all the time to face whatever came at them. The attackers ran onto a barrier of wooden shields and levelled spears. As the momentum of those behind pushed the first attackers hard up against the shields, the wall opened slightly to let Goldlanders in their inner rank wield their macuahuitls to terrible effect. As the attack faltered, the Scum emerged from an unthreatened part of the circle to join the fray in their disordered and frenzied fashion.

Brann leapt from the pile of rubble they had chosen as a vantage point, his sword and axe in hand as he landed. He didn't need to say anything, the others had seen the danger also and there was no time, or need, for a subtle plan, only direct action. They hurled themselves at the nearest flank of the enemy, Hakon striking them first with the roar of a lion and the force of a bull. One man struck by the huge boy's shield was knocked back to lean against those behind and Brann used him as a ramp, running right up him and vaulting into the centre of the circle of invaders. Grakk somehow managed to reach the interior close behind him, as did Gerens, and the three fell with ferocious speed on the Goldlanders, killing many and turning more. The circle disintegrated and the attackers' superior numbers prevailed.

Brann wandered among the corpses of those he had tried to train. Women who had been as eager as their husbands and brothers to play their part lay among the men, and even three young boys, forbidden to join the attack but emboldened by the achievements they had witnessed before and having run amongst the crowd when their elders had been fixated on the target. He felt the resolve within him shake slightly.

'They were not ready,' he said, his voice breaking.

Grakk, placed a hand on his shoulder as it rose and fell, his chest still sucking in air with great gasps. 'These on the ground were not, but those still standing were. War is a harsh instructor, and brutally dismissive of those who learn anything less than instantly. Those here who live, have learned. They are ready.'

Brann looked at the bodies at his feet. 'But these – I should have known.'

Grakk shook his head. 'Sometimes, young warrior, we are not afforded such luxuries. We can only know in the trying.'

Brann sank to his haunches and looked up at his friend. 'This is no way to live, where ordinary people succeed or fail, and the judge of which is Death.'

'Young Brann,' said Grakk gravely, 'right now, that is the only way to live. The alternative is to surely die. Each of us has to find our own reason to persevere.'

Brann stood, and swept his hand over the dead. 'This. This is my reason.'

Brann crouched on the rooftop, three floors up, watching the squad of Goldlanders move slowly up the street. This was a scouting squad, a score in number, rather than the main force that would come after. And they were learning. Rather than bunching, they spread, meaning that arrows and spears had to be accurate and could not just be launched into a crowd to be assured of a hit. And they moved slowly, the advanced members peering around the edges of doorways and windows to ensure that empty buildings were, in fact, empty.

Brann glanced at the girl beside them, no more than thirteen years of age, her bow held ready in a relaxed hand: this was not her first time. Behind them crouched Philippe – the girl had taken a shine to him and he was here as what now proved to be an unnecessary calming influence.

Brann pointed wordlessly at the soldier in the centre of the group, the beaten copper that encased his helmet marking him as the officer. The girl nodded, already raising her bow, the narrow head on the arrow perfect for lancing through the quilted tunics of the enemy. She stood, sighted and loosed. Without waiting to see it strike, she turned and ran on quiet feet back across the rooftop, Brann and Philippe alongside her. The cries of alarm rising behind were all they needed to know. Dead was a bonus – the attack was yet another sign that the invaders were safe nowhere, never. 'Good girl,' Brann murmured as they dropped to a lower roof and then another, several hundred yards from the scouts before they could even start to react. 'Best that they think they can die from a foe unseen. Then they see danger in every cat's shadow, in every flutter of fabric in the breeze, in every reflected sunbeam. Then they fear death brought by ghosts in a haunted city.'

The girl smiled.

Philippe caught his arm and held Brann back a few paces as they loped along an alley. 'You do not worry at introducing one so young to death?'

Brann jerked a thumb back over his shoulder. 'The

invaders introduced the children here to death. We just help them to return the gift. Better to deal it than have it dealt.'

Brann looked at the girl. 'She is ready.'

The tumbling jumble of furniture landed with a mighty crash, pushed from piles on the rooftops facing each other across the narrow street, blocking the way to the height of three men where the fighting column of mainly Scum, supported by a tenth of their number in Goldlanders, had passed just seconds before as they entered the circular plaza with five roads radiating from it in the shape of a star. Five streets that now, with the smashed furniture, were all of them blocked with tangled barricades.

Oil was poured on the newest blockade to render it as the other four. It was then that the force in the plaza, more than two hundred strong, became aware that the dampness beneath their feet was not water, nor even waste. The sliding footing was a clue, and minds clear of narcotic herbs should have been quicker to awareness, but the Goldlanders present had been too busy trying to keep order among the Scum to notice aught else.

They noticed now. Brands were lit and tossed upon the barricades, creating barriers of towering flames. As the fire reached the ground, it kissed the lake of oil filling the square, spreading inwards in five expanding arcs towards the force who shrank towards the centre in horror, eyes transfixed by the advancing death.

Some, emboldened by or mad with the herbs, and many of the Goldlanders broke for the sides of the plaza, seeking sanctuary in the surrounding buildings but finding all openings boarded tight. Above, city folk stepped to the lips of rooftops, and the screaming invaders looked up to meet a rain of arrows, spears and masonry that brought a quicker end to their lives than the flames licking at their legs and catching their clothes. When all on the outskirts lay still, the archers turned their attention to those still breathing in the centre.

When all was motionless in the square, Brann turned to the commander of this group, the largest they had trained. 'This time, leave the bodies. Charred corpses have a certain effect on erstwhile colleagues and, spread as they are, their numbers are clear at first sight. Let the barricades burn away and their comrades will come across this with ease.'

He looked at those lining the rooftops, no reaction on their faces or in their demeanour, merely eyes assessing what had been accomplished and seeking any details that needed to be finished.

He looked at the square. It was a job well done. It was a plan, simple in its devising and precise in its execution, and it was a plan of the people who had lived here, who knew their city and who now knew how to use it against those who would take it from them.

He looked again at the commander, a young man barely older than he was.

'You are ready.'

'Now we are ready for more.' Brann looked at the two kings as they stood around the map table in Ruslan's pavilion. 'Attrition has taken its toll on the numbers and the hearts of our enemy and created soldiers of our people.'

'What more?' Ruslan asked.

Brann felt nerves in his stomach at the thought. 'Battle.'

Bahadur leant both fists on the table. 'First you tell us we should fight one way, and now you tell us we should do what we suggested in the first place. My men tell me of no signs that you were wrong, so why do you?'

Brann shook his head. 'I am not saying it was wrong. That was right then, and it has worked, as your men say. But this is now. And things are different.'

'What is different? They are still here. We still prick at them.'

Ossavian cleared his throat. 'If I may, Your Majesties, that is correct, but it is the where that is changing. We are hurting them, we are unsettling them, but they still have the numbers over us, by far. We have slowed their movement through the city, but we have not stopped it. We hit them and we drift away, but each time we do so we must drift a little further. You have had to move this very camp twice already.' He stepped up to the table and traced a finger across the map. 'These are not quite the most recent positions but you can see what I mean. The small areas of our people are closing in on each other,' he spread his arms wide to the extents of the markings, and drew cupped hands in towards himself as if gathering the pockets of resistance to him, 'and are being pushed back towards the edge of the city. Eventually they will be joined as one mass, and pinned in one corner. Then the invaders can attack en masse and the city environment will not serve us as it does now. Their commanders have shown clearly that results matter more to them than the preservation of their own men's lives, and they know that, while it will be scrappy and messy fighting, their numbers will overwhelm us at that point. They know they just have to be patient and success will come.'

Ruslan folded his arms, the movement drawing his waist-coat closed across his bare chest. 'Forgive my lack of understanding, but if their numbers would defeat us then, why would they not overwhelm us in battle now? Why not wait and see if the situation will change? War invariably brings the unexpected.'

'You are entirely correct in that, Your Majesty,' Ossavian said, 'but there is one thing we definitely know will change: as our forces start to lose room to move as freely within the city, the nature of the fighting will become less of our choosing and we will start to incur greater and greater casualties where, in the circumstances we have chosen up till now, our losses have been minimal. The enemy can afford losses more than we can, and the enemy knows that.'

'Rest assured,' Bahadur growled, 'we two are infinitely more comfortable with the tactics of open battle, but I do not see the sense in seeking death sooner against far superior numbers. Why choose certain defeat now?'

Ossavian's look was sombre. 'The timing is forced upon us. Our people have learned all they can under these circumstances, and will only lose soldiers as this proceeds. We have weakened them slightly in numbers and more in morale, and so we have given them anger to drive their thoughts when they should be using reason. We should make use of that time. Our people may never have the military organisation of a standing army, but neither does half of the invading army.'

Ruslan shook his head in worry. 'But the organised half of their army still outnumbers all of ours. These are my people and I will not send them to be slaughtered by this host.'

'I agree,' said Brann, 'and I have grown close to them too in these past weeks. But we do not choose open battle where those numbers suit them. We choose it where they suit us.'

Ruslan's face lit up. 'You talk of the northern plain, where three rivers converge and limit the space.'

Ossavian and Brann nodded together, and Bahadur's eyes narrowed as his mind considered a more familiar military scenario. 'They cannot manoeuvre as they would wish, and their front would be narrowed?'

Again they nodded. He looked at Ruslan. 'Can we move all of our people, including the civilian fighters, to this place in safety?'

Ruslan grinned. 'If it means having a chance to defeat this threat to my people's existence? In that case, anything can be done.'

Chapter 11

He looked down to where a girl stood on a balcony much like his, watching the horizon. A girl who had travelled from the North, who had risked even greater dangers in slipping into the palace and under his care than she had in the leagues between her Halvekan home and the city. A girl who had killed to be here. A girl who waited for the same one that his own eyes sought in the bare lands stretching across their view.

He walked back into his room where the women had gathered.

Three women.

One from his past, now his most frequent companion, knelt to one side, watching quietly.

One for the future, fast becoming his hands outwith the palace, knelt to her side, learning quietly.

One, oldest of all, Mother to the one from his past, one who brought past, present and future to a single point, in this moment the focus of his being, sat before him, the blood he had sliced from his palm on the tip of her tongue and smeared slightly on her lip.

Her head was tilted back, her eyes closed, her breathing shallow and slow. She gave a low moan, silver jewellery at her brow chiming like tiny bells at an offering to the gods. Silence lay heavy around her.

Her head snapped up. Her eyes opened, staring into his. Her voice was low, deep.

> *'The seed has been nurtured*
> *And the shoot has been fed,*
> *The flower has blossomed,*
> *The man has been bred.'*

A shudder ran through her, and her eyes grew sad. Her voice deepened further.

> *'Evil has grown, as a cloud it has spread,*
> *Death its desire, world enveloped in dread.'*

He leant forward, hands lying tensed on the top of the small table between them. 'Your words and those of my agents are as one. The prophecies come to pass.'

'The prophecies ever come to pass,' she said, her voice distant, as if belonging to another. 'The whether is never in doubt. The mystery is only in the how, the when and the who.' She swayed, her head circling with her body. 'One has played his part: the blood of that one is tasted; blood of one who has lived amongst blood and outlived those who spilt it. One must now play his part: the tears of that one were tasted ere now; salt tears amidst salt water, a storm of nature then, a storm of men now.'

Her back straightened with a jerk, and her hands shot forward to grip his with the strength of a dozen men. Her eyes were shut, and she became still, very still, her breathing imperceptible. Her voice was a whisper.

> *'Nations will stand*
> *Or nations will fall,*
> *When heroes and kings*
> *On the One come to call,*
> *On one they once thought*
> *So small.'*

Her eyes snapped open, locking on his.

He felt drawn, felt that he moved closer to her though neither had stirred an inch, felt one with her.

The words came from his mouth, though he knew not whence they came. But when they came, he realised, they came from her.

'The fates align. The gods watch on. One will stand, one will fall. Two paths await the world; the future can step on one alone. The time—'

She spoke: 'is now.'

****

It had taken two days for their army to gather at the northern side of the city, which was much quicker than Brann had anticipated, but local knowledge and a sense of purpose and anticipation at being able to strike to major effect had seen large numbers of people move through areas both devastated and untouched with alacrity and largely undetected. Brann's group had nibbled at the edge of the invading force in multiple places, occasionally slipping behind their lines to ensure that none felt truly safe, but the emphasis had been on short, quick attacks that had created an impression of danger more than they had inflicted any great harm. Other groups, before they had left for the meeting point, had harried at the south and east of the enemy, adding to the illusion that the defenders' activities had continued as usual as opposed to the reality that these areas were emptying of any opposition. Any skirmishes between the foe and those travelling north would not, they hoped, draw undue attention to that area of the city more than any other.

As the sun dropped towards the horizon, Brann looked over the force now gathered immediately outside the broken wall and tumbled stonework that gave him his vantage point. The soldiers of the two kings' guards went about their business with quiet efficiency while an air of expectation, even occasional excitement, hung over the city folk. He wondered how quickly that would change when the enemy force stood before them.

Goldlander scouts had appeared on hills nearby, but the defenders had let them leave unscathed. It mattered not that Loku would know they were there – more, they wanted him to come, and the sooner, before they had to start worrying about such extra issues as sanitation and additional food, the better. The waiting, too, would take its toll on confidence and eagerness.

Brann glanced at Konall beside him. 'They say the waiting is the worst part.'

The tall boy grunted. 'Then they have never been stabbed with a sword in the part after the waiting.'

Gerens was sitting on a fallen block of masonry, within touching distance of Sophaya and defending distance of Brann. He nodded down at the people massing below. 'Think they can do it?'

Brann shrugged. 'No idea. But I don't know they can't either. And there's a lot to be said for fighting with your home at your back.' He looked over the force: gathered around cooking fires and looking no more warlike than a crowd of families at the Midsummer Festival back at home. His eyes narrowed as they gauged the numbers. 'They are more than I thought they'd be, maybe four thousand even without the women and children, plus the two five-hundreds, but we'll still be outnumbered around three to one if Ruslan's scouts have got the enemy numbers right.'

Xamira was standing further along the wall, one foot resting on a broken rampart as she rested her forearm on her knee. 'And why cannot the women fight? They have done up till now, and acquitted themselves well. Not all of the enemy have died at male hands, remember.'

'You are right,' Cannick's voice came from behind them where he sat, carefully and slowly sharpening his sword. 'But this fighting will be very different. It is a dirty business, with little skill and much brute determination. I have no doubt that yourself, Breta, Mongoose, Sophaya…'

'Not Sophaya,' Gerens cut in. 'We would be weakened without her skill enhancing the ranks of the archers.'

Cannick nodded in acceptance. 'I have no doubt that yourself, Breta and Mongoose, with your experience of various forms of combat could hold your own, but even many of the men who have had military service if not, in many cases, much experience of conflict, will fall cheaply, never mind women who only picked up a spear or an axe a few short weeks ago, despite the bravery they have shown since. Many a great warrior has fallen in battle from an unskilled blow that he did not see coming or a deflected thrust from one of his own comrades, while many a weak and terrified recruit has survived without having to defend a single blow. Call it chance or the will of the gods, but either way you just never know how it will go. All you do know is that it is not pleasant.' He nodded out at the area beyond them, bounded by the three rivers. 'And one thing that is more than certain: there will be no honour or glory out there when it all comes together.'

'Thank you for that reassurance, dear Cannick,' Sophaya said brightly. 'It seems we have lost before the enemy even arrives.'

Cannick sighed. 'Sorry, young lady. I fear I have seen too much of this in my time. Each time, it wears away a little more of you.'

Xamira angrily kicked a piece of the wall loose with the sole of her boot. 'I hate battles. I hate the killing in battles.' She turned at the silence behind her, seeing the expressions her words had prompted. 'What? You think all killing is the same? Kill a man for a good reason or a bad one, and it is your reason. Yours to decide, yours to live with. But battle? Battle is killing for someone else's reason, and usually you don't even know what that reason really is. Usually there is one man on each side who, ultimately, has that reason. Those two decide, but all the rest must live with it – if they live. That is no reason to kill.' She picked up a fragment of stone and flicked it furiously over the edge of the wall. 'And this? This is worse: one man alone has the reason for this battle. One man forces thousands on both sides to fight and die: one side because he tells them to, and the other side because they will die anyway if they succumb. One man should not have that power.'

Brann nodded. 'That is exactly why we seek to stop him.'

They dropped into silence, subdued by her words. Subdued by the truth of her words.

'Oh, my poor city, my poor people!' Ruslan's voice, hoarse in its anguish, turned them towards his approach, the imposing Maktanu and Bahadur's first warrior Shahkam Davar at his back. 'I have neglected the walls and exposed my people.'

Brann looked along the broken structure they stood upon, barely a hundred yards of its visible lengths still standing as it had been built. 'In fairness, Your Majesty, you had five hundred men. You could not have defended more than a fraction of the walls. Within a day, your people would have been fighting the same battle they have fought anyway.'

Xamira grunted. 'And, Your Majesty, it is their duty to stand up to an invader, anyway. No one should stand back and watch another fight for his home.'

Shahkam Davar glared at her but the king spoke with a considered slowness. 'I understand your words, and I cannot argue against them. It is the lot of a ruler to make decisions, and it seemed more prudent to direct my finances towards sewers and water supply, and roads and buildings, than it was to maintain miles of walls that seemed irrelevant with the protective wing of Sagia seeming to cast such a deep shadow over us.' He looked over the crowds below. 'Now, however...' He sighed. 'You are right, I could not have defended the walls with my Five Hundred, but perhaps I could have stockpiled weapons. Perhaps they could have been distributed if the citizens had been able to defend their city from strong walls, rather than in its streets and alleys, hunted like rats in a cellar. Perhaps I could have kept records of all those with service in the millens. Perhaps—'

'Perhaps you could have foreseen the future that no one expected, Your Majesty,' Grakk said softly. 'Or, far more likely, perhaps you could not. No one anticipated this, not even the Emperor with all the resources at his disposal.' He looked at the king, sincerity clear in his eyes. 'Any ruler who cared about his people would have seen the sense in your decisions, and would have made the same choices.'

The king sighed again. 'Wise words, wise words. But when I look at these people, I cannot shake myself free from the guilt at all who will die on this soil, who will end their time here and never return to the homes they will fight for. The mystery is how many that will be.'

They looked up as a rumble of interest rippled across those very people, and Gerens stood, pointing into the distance. A dust cloud was lifting, a cloud of a width too definite to be a product of nature.

'I think,' he said darkly, 'that mystery will be revealed sooner rather than later. Majesty.'

The king stared at the cloud, shaking his head. 'What have we done to the Emperor that is so bad that we are not worthy of his aid? Why does he not recall the millens from the North and send them here? I cannot believe he does not know of this, of a force this size within his Empire. It is not as if we are at the furthest point of his domain.'

Grakk's eyes were also fixed on the signs of the approaching army. 'There are none so blind as those who will not see,' he said, his voice low.' He turned to Ruslan and spoke softly, almost gently. 'The truth is, Your Majesty, that he has been fooled into sending the millens he had at his disposal to the North. Fooled. A man who rules with the assurance of a god cannot be seen to be fallible, to have been tricked. He will ignore this as if it had never happened. A new king will be appointed here, to rule those who are left. A new one will rule in Tharpia. Thanases will know, but will live the lie for he will profit from it. Who else will care, will even be aware? If he has to burn this city and,' he hesitated slightly and looked at Brann, 'any other that Loku may have his eyes on, the Emperor will do so to protect his air of infallibility, and therefore his rule.'

'A ruler who would put his own reputation before the lives of those he governs?' the king's voice was a whisper of disbelief.

Grakk shrugged. 'A ruler closeted from the real world can develop such ideas about how the power of his rule is achieved.'

Brann saw the anger and pain that tensed the king's shoulders. 'Whatever takes the Emperor's attention elsewhere,' he said, 'you are assured of the complete commitment that our group, no matter how small in numbers, will offer to aid you, in any way we can. It is not much, I know, but all we can give, we will give to your cause.'

Ruslan looked around the small band. 'It is much that you offer. My apologies, I should not burden you with my worries, for they are not yours to bear. However events transpire tomorrow, please be assured of my gratitude for your service to my people.'

Brann smiled grimly. 'Anything to see that bastard dead.' His eyes moved to the growing cloud of dust. 'Anything.'

Brann found himself back at the same section of wall when the only light was that from a moon almost full. The embers of fires burning low were scattered amongst the force gathered below him, where he knew there would be many others as wide awake as he, while a separate collection of dots glowing dark orange marked the enemy army. He tried to find the four posts that had been erected at the arrival of Loku's force, but the shadows hid them. He needed no light to see them in his head, though.

Four men of the city had been brought to the front of the enemy host, their clothing ripped from them and cackling men of the Scum holding them spread-eagled while the sharpened end of one of the long slender posts was hammered between their legs. Not one of the doomed men let a sound escape their lips at the agony that, to those who watched, was unimaginable in its extent though clear in its horror, but when the posts were tipped upright and inserted into holes in the hard ground, letting the men's weight take effect, it became more than any willpower could resist. The screams of the four mixed pain and horror in equal measure. They lingered in Brann's ears even now.

Xamira's voice came low from behind. 'What thoughts keep sleep at bay: the sights of yesterday or what waits tomorrow?'

He could not drag his eyes from the enemy camp, but he heard the soft movements draw closer. 'Both, but more than that is the thought of what happens should we fail. It appears we cannot win. No general who ever lived would predict a victory for us, and yet the lives of so many depend on our success. So many here and so many more beyond these horizons who will suffer should the riches at the end of Loku's quest be revealed to him, to the world even. He cannot be allowed to leave here. Whatever happens to anyone tomorrow, he must not move even one step forward. It appears we cannot win, and yet we must.'

'Then,' her hand slipped into his and he felt the breath of her words on his cheek, 'you need your sleep and the renewed strength it brings. Let me help you.'

He turned and saw the bedroll under her arm. 'You think that can solve anything, don't you?'

She frowned. 'Circumstances vary. Very often it causes

more problems in life than solves them. And very often a sharp blade is a better solver of problems.' Her fingers tightened. 'But tonight, in these circumstances, you need to feel in a place apart. You need to lose yourself. And you need the sleep that will bring.'

He felt her pull gently at his hand, and he followed. Again, she was right.

Brann gave Konall a sideways glance. 'You were right about the waiting. Even this part is worse. I'm shitting myself worse than walking into any fight in the Arena.' He wasn't exaggerating: he could feel his bowels clench and his head grow light.

Konall grunted, his horse shifting beneath him. 'In the Arena, you relied only upon yourself. Here, too much is unknown.'

Brann nodded, the urge to talk leaving him as quickly as it had come. He let his eyes leave the enemy host, the solid centre of Goldlanders flanked by the undisciplined crowds of the milling Scum, restless and agitated with whatever concoction of herbs they had ingested today, and move to their own ranks. The elite guards of both kings had been split into sections of one hundred men, with two of those sections being held in reserve along with Brann's unit, to be deployed where support was needed. Brann was certain that this support would be needed frequently and in many places. The remaining eight sections of guards were spread along the line of the main force, with the city folk, armed and armoured in whatever way they could best manage – with most of their equipment having been scavenged from those they had killed in the past gruelling weeks – having been split into seven roughly equal sections of their own and placed between the sections of soldiers. Brann could see the logic: with the regular troops covering both flanks and being positioned alternately with the civilians, every inexperienced section would have toughened and skilled warriors to their left and right. He could also see that more than a few of the city's woman had defied the order to leave the battle to the men and had slipped into the ranks now that it was too late to spend time sending them away. It was their city, their families, too.

Breta edged her horse closer to Brann. 'Now both forces are gathered, the difference in numbers is daunting. Have we any chance?'

Einarr's deep voice came from her other side. 'Neither side has cavalry – not enough of us to count as we aren't trained as cavalry anyway, Goldlanders know only infantry combat and the Scum will have been hard enough to train and control without putting them on horses, while the Empire limits each subordinate king to a guard of foot soldiers to curb what little military power they grant them. This simplifies things as the number of varying factors are reduced – if anything can be straightforward in battle tactics.' He scanned the enemy ranks. 'If inroads can be made into either of their softer flanks, we can get at their soldiers from the side.'

'If...' Konall said.

'*If* is all we have until we know,' Brann said, staring at the small figure on a horse, visible above a guard of Goldlanders. 'And a big *if* is that if we can get to Loku, we might be able to end it all.'

Konall snorted. 'Lot of people between us and him. All we can do is go where we need to and kill whoever we see in front of us.'

Brann found himself unable to argue.

Ruslan rode his horse past them at a walk. He winked at Brann. 'Time to start earning my keep,' he said quietly.

Brann frowned. 'What does he mean?'

'He means,' said Einarr, 'that it is time to help his soldiers forget the horror that will soon engulf this place.' He held up a hand to stop Brann's next question, and nodded to where the king had ridden in front of their lines, turning his horse to face his host.

A hush fell over the troops at the sight, and all eyes fixed upon him. His voice rang out, the confident tone reaching further than Brann had expected.

'Today, those facing us will know the limit of their courage when they witness the depth of ours. What deeds make them quail, we will dare. When they cower, we will charge. When they bow their heads and look only at the ground in despair, we will raise ours and feast our eyes on opportunity presented by the gods who bestow their favour upon those who fight for what is right.

'Yes, some of us will die. But we all die someday. And when those who chose not to take this field draw their final breath as old men, they will know in that moment that they pass from this world just the same, for there is no escape from that final fate, but they will know that there will be no story told of them as generations yet unborn will tell of we who stand here today.

'So tell me.' His voice rose to a defiant shout and, with it, his sword rose high in his hand, the blade flashing. 'Tell me this: will you be forgotten or will you be remembered; will you run for your home or towards those who would take it from you; will you wither in the shadows of time or will you shine as heroes for eternity?'

The roar burst from the army he addressed was as empty of discernible words as it was full of the answer he sought. The kind gave the smile of a proud father and rode back through the ranks, clasping hands and patting shoulders as he went.

Breta grunted. 'I'll admit, he is good.'

'It will see them into their first charge,' Einarr said, 'but that is an important first step to take.'

Movement halted their conversation. The enemy host began to move forward and the defenders were ordered to move also so the momentum was not in one direction alone. Brann looked on as if it was unreal, as if he watched a picture that moved but which he wasn't a part of. Shouts came sporadically from both sides as insults and challenges were hurled, more – Brann guessed – to raise the courage of those who yelled them rather than with any intention of affecting the opposition. Arrows flickered and spears flew to draw cries of pain and shock, though few in number: both commanders had opted, for differing reasons, to put as many men into the main struggle as they could.

As the forces closed, a roar rumbled along each army, increasing in volume like a wave approaching a beach, until its crescendo saw both front lines break into a run, unable to contain themselves any longer.

The lines merged and the murder began.

Men hacked and pulled and snarled and screamed, generations of civilisation vanishing in an instant and animal instincts consuming them. All that mattered was to survive, and the way to survive was to tear and stab and rip and smash all in front of you who would seek to do the same to you. The line where the two armies met became blurred, but looking down from the slight rise in the terrain where they waited, Brann's eyes became accustomed to the ebb and flow of the two masses and he spotted the weakness almost in the same moment as did Bahadur.

'There,' the tall king said to Ruslan, pointing from the platform built to afford them an overview of the proceedings. Both kings looked at Ossavian, standing alongside them. A short distance in from their left flank, the defenders of the city were being pushed back. Should the invaders burst right through their line, they could round on the city soldiers from behind, making their superior numbers tell against that section on two sides rather than just one.

Ossavian nodded. 'There. One hundred.'

Bahadur shouted to an officer of his guard. 'One hundred men, to there.' He pointed again and the man nodded. Brann caught Ossavian's eye and received a nod in turn.

'It is our time,' he shouted to the others, kicking his heels into his horse's sides, and soon overtaking the running reinforcements.

Short of the fighting, however, he slowed his horse enough to leap from its back. To reach the enemy, he would have to pass through their own troops and a charging horse would cause as much damage to them as the enemy. He started running as soon as they struck the ground, pulling his sword and axe free as he moved. The edge of his vision caught the shapes of his companions keeping pace at his side and then he was among their own men, passing through and reaching the heart of the fighting. The impending danger was not those who battled but from those behind, driving through the gaps between the fighting men and ever deeper into the defending force. The city folk fought with passion and a desperation that lent them strength and resolve in abundance, but there were more ranks behind the front line of the invaders than that of the defenders, and so more pushed past fighting men all the time. They had to be stopped.

Brann flew into them like a whirling maelstrom of steel and death, his two blades whirling and cutting without pause. The fighting coldness filled him, and his movements were obvious and certain to him, bringing a devastating speed and deadly precision. The black edges cut through padded armour and flesh and bone with equal ease as his mind saw two, sometimes three, moves ahead, his attention already on the next person even as he struck at the one before. He was unaware of his companions, aware only of those he sought to engage, but he sensed the arrival of the reinforcing soldiers in the shift in momentum.

The enemy were pushed back, leaving their dead and dying as the only sign of their having reached the distance they had, and Brann fought the urge to follow them. Their job was done here, and they would likely be needed by others. They pulled back, leaving the invigorated city folk to renew their efforts to greater effect, having recovered from the surprise at the reality of battle that had given the invaders an initial advantage.

He looked across the maelstrom of hacking metal and screams, seeing Loku, impassive on the far side, watching all from his raised vantage point. So near, but as impossible to reach as a mirage in the desert.

Seven more times Brann's unit were sent in alongside the reserve soldiers to strengthen a point in the line before both armies withdrew to regroup, each foray spreading further among their army the reputation of Brann as an irresistible force and an inspiration, and five more times as a whole the forces clashed and withdrew, the inhuman slaughter becoming an accepted hell but no less chaotic and frenzied for that acceptance. The defenders were pushed back, but their line never sundered. The invaders were repelled and slowed, but their attacks never faltered. When part of the enemy line seemed fragile, extra numbers would pour into the gaps. When one wing of the defending force had been on the verge of being outflanked, a horde of women, led by Sophaya, had poured from a gap in the city wall and fallen upon the foe in vicious passion fired at the sight of their men in such peril, retiring only when the danger had been averted. Fanaticism and the instinct to protect met each other head on, and each met its match. Five more times the armies clashed, neither giving nor receiving the hope of success. Five more times the armies clashed, and it was on that fifth occasion that Cannick fell.

Brann saw the blow, the overhand slash as the stocky veteran parried a blow from another man. He felt no grief at the time, the sight registering only as information in the coldness of his head, but the sorrow hit all the more violently for that when they carried the body as the armies withdrew.

They laid him gently to the ground, and Brann sagged beside his friend, feeling as if his soul had been pulled from him. Einarr, who had fought every blow beside Cannick from the start of the day to the end, came to them, somehow limping with more grace of movement than many men managed with two feet, his face stricken. Konall sank to his knees beside them, weeping silently and openly. Brann saw none of the others who gathered around, his eyes fixed on the familiar lined face that he expected to move with words of calm wisdom as it so often had, his two hands gripping one of Cannick's big calloused hands that had been as quick to clap a shoulder as grasp a sword hilt. He saw none of the others, but he heard their grief. Hakon roared.

Brann closed his eyes, a picture in his head of two figures sitting behind an inn in Belleville, looking at the stars, the gruff voice with a gentle warmth as real for a moment as if they were back there once more. 'If we have lived life as well as we can here, then we can face whatever lies beyond as it comes to us.' *Please, gods, if you exist, let him be welcomed.*

The enemy never came again that day. As darkness fell, the enemy left their dead where they lay, only the carrion beasts attending to them, but the healers from the city brought parties of non-combatants to retrieve the wounded and the dead of their own. A silence fell over the army, no one finding any desire to discuss the battle, and all finding it inappropriate to discuss anything unconnected to the battle.

Not one mind wanted sleep that night, but not one mind could resist the exhaustion that came when the muscles stopped moving. Each slept where they had last stopped, unmindful of where they lay, many of them unaware even that slumber had taken them.

Shortly after dawn, the defenders moved towards the enemy advance, weary from the previous day's exertions but grimly determined not to render their efforts meaningless through even the slightest capitulation.

Brann led his unit into the thick of the fighting where and when directed, falling into a routine of killing and withdrawing, killing and withdrawing. The movements became automatic, their thoughts numbed. He found his cold, fighting self was not fading between bursts of violence.

The battle became a stalemate of attrition where only Death made gains. Men struggled with each other, doing damage to other men their only thought. The ground turned to dark slick mud where blood mixed with hard earth, and bodies – and parts of bodies – conspired with the mud to make the footing as much a danger to being bested as the strength and skill of the man that was faced. And so it went on, time becoming meaningless and a world without lethal toil seeming a distant and faded memory.

Brann lost count of the times they had been inserted into the fray, but it mattered not. He had a job to do, and all that mattered was that he did it. The gore was thick upon his mail, on his face, in his hair; during each withdrawal he wiped it only from the blades to keep them sharp and the grips and his hands to keep them secure. He ducked and twisted; stabbed and cut; sliced with edges and smashed with pommel and haft and knee and elbow and fist; he destroyed balance with his shoulder, knocked legs away with foot and weapon and killed with whatever gave the quickest death. All became one.

And through it all, he heard his name shouted with Ossavian's voice. The enemy was pulling back, he could sense it, so why could he hear Ossavian? Had they been pushed close to the commanders' platform? He killed his man, saw another fall close to him and checked for danger. When he was able to, he turned. Ossavian had ridden as close as he could manage before the footing became too treacherous for his horse, and was hurrying closer on foot.

He saw Brann looking at him, and roared, 'There! An opening!'

Brann's eyes followed the general's pointed finger. In withdrawing, a gap had opened in the enemy force – not an empty path, but a thinning of the crowd. A thinning of the crowd in a direct line to Loku.

Brann reacted instantly, the cool in his mind setting no obstacles to plans and calculations, casting about for the others and shouting to those close enough. He turned back to their goal, but felt anxiety bloom as the moving crowd already seemed to be filling the area they sought. A Goldlander blocked his vision and filled his ears with his roar, rushing at him with weapon poised. Brann's feet shifted without conscious thought, his axe deflecting the blow and his sword driving up into the stomach, the razor sharpness of the black metal slicing through padded armour and the body beyond with equal ease. He twisted to pull the sword free and, in the same movement as he stepped away, the axe swept around to knock the legs away and send the dying man hurtling to the ground. Instinct saw him flinch back as a spear flashed through the space the man's torso had occupied an instant before, though it would not have struck Brann in any case. It did strike a target, though, from the grunted shout behind. Brann saw the look of horror on the face of the man who had thrown it, a man of their own force. He spun.

It had struck Ossavian.

It had not struck deep into the general's side, but Brann knew it was deep enough. Thoughts of reaching Loku were abandoned in a heartbeat – the chance had been slim, and receding, in any case. This was a greater blow. Ossavian may have become a close companion, but he was also the greatest military mind this army possessed. Throughout this battle, the only man on their side of the lines with the experience of commanding an army in full battle had directed the city's makeshift force with the deft touch of a master musician playing a fine instrument, constantly adjusting and adapting to apply pressure to the greatest effect and resistance just where it was needed. While the two forces now were dragging the battle to a contest of wills, still his expertise was vital.

And here he was, gravely wounded in the mud.

Brann was already at his side. Ossavian, his face drawn with the pain and one hand holding the spear still where it entered his side, looked up at him. 'Take that worry from your face, boy. I'll be fine. Gods, I've had worse when I've drunk too much to stay on my feet.'

Brann glanced down at the froth in the blood seeping between the general's fingers, and was just as aware as Ossavian himself that he lied.

Ossavian smiled weakly. 'Just get me back up where I can see what is happening, young man. Can you do that for me?'

Brann nodded. He glanced back, seeing both armies retreating from the field for the first short respite that the day would bring. He waved a passing soldier to help, and the pair took an arm each across their shoulders and eased the general back to the medics who swarmed to help. Ruslan's personal healer, his robes already more bloodstains than not, waved away all but Philippe, citing both the personal connection and the young man's fast-growing skill to explain to the young man why he remained. Brann was waved away also, and he complied without a word. In situations such as these, the healer was a king.

The tending stations, already overwhelmed, accepted more of those too badly injured to continue or, in some cases, to live. The remainder of the army regrouped, hands grasping greedily for liquid of any sort, wounds being roughly bandaged to allow a return to the fight, weapons prepared or replaced.

Brann gratefully accepted a water skin and, gulping, swept his eyes about the scene as, already, the lines began to form once more. No encouragement was needed. This was their home. They would defend it while they still could stand. The two kings, while rocked by Ossavian's injury, were pragmatists and were already absorbed in directing and adjusting where they saw fit.

Brann looked over at the canopy where Ossavian was attended with calm urgency; he looked at the dead and dying strewn across the empty ground that would soon be filled with ever more victims; he looked at the ranks of faces that had come to this field with earnest determination and now stood upon it with a hardened acceptance that they must, for now, live in hell. Xamira's bitter words from the night before filled his head once more. *Battle is killing for someone else's reason.*

Brann's voice came out in a growl. 'Enough.'

Hakon looked up. 'Say again?'

Brann shook his head as his hands checked his weapons. 'No more.'

He walked forward, his stride becoming more definite with every pace. All that he had done, all that he had suffered, all that he had endured, all that he had survived, all that he had become: all now seemed to make sense. All of it aligned, and with a certainty that felt unshakeable, he knew. He knew this was his time.

Gerens's voice came from behind. 'Oh shit. Grakk!'

He walked on, through the ranks of their soldiers, none now considered novices, all around starting to murmur as he passed.

Grakk caught him as he neared the front of their lines. The tribesman looked at him with worried eyes. 'Have a care, young Brann. It appears that while there is madness and a disregard for the lives and suffering of swathes of ordinary people in Loku's thinking, there is a purpose to it and an ingenuity behind it that may exceed that of all of us combined.'

Brann's voice was low and dark. 'The cleverest head thinks less when a sword blade takes it off at the neck.'

Grakk laid a hand softly on his arm. 'Have a care, young warrior, for the blade may miss its mark should the target outsmart the aggressor.'

Brann stared at him. 'My blade will not miss him.'

He passed through the front rank and continued walking into the emptiness between the armies. An emptiness that felt much larger without the press of struggling men around him. He walked past corpses from many cultures, all just men in death. He walked into clear ground. When he was the length of two spear throws from the enemy host, he stopped.

A gaggle of the Scum, no more than a dozen from along the length of the line, broke from their ranks and ran at him. At shouted commands, most stopped and capered back. Another command, and arrows flickered from the enemy and took down those who continued. One alone survived, charging at Brann, his eyes alight with wild lust. A single contemptuous swing of Brann's axe took away that light.

He slowly wiped his axe on the tunic the man wore beneath ill-fitting mail, his eyes never leaving Loku. He pointed his weapon straight at Loku. All eyes turned to the enemy leader; he could not ignore the gesture. The stopping of the men who had run at Brann had already proved that he would not ignore the gesture already made.

Loku slowly walked his horse forward. He passed through

his men, staring at none but Brann. He dismounted at the front rank and walked onto the field. He stopped twenty paces from Brann. Behind him stood a small group of what appeared to be senior officers or priests, and one archer, too far away to accurately strike Brann where he stood, but close enough to be sure of a kill should Brann move close to where Loku now stood. Brann heard noise behind him also and glanced back to see Gerens, Xamira, Grakk and Hakon poised to rush forward. He raised a hand slightly to hold them there, although they had already stopped, wary of provoking a situation that was already tensely balanced.

'So, boy,' came Loku's mocking tone. 'It has come to this. How you must wish that you had realised in those woods that poor Daric was not the real prize.'

'I have you now,' Brann said, his voice flat.

'You do indeed,' Loku said amiably, 'or, at least, you have my curiosity and my attention for as long as my curiosity lasts. Pray speak.'

'This,' Brann swept his hand to encompass both armies and the area of slaughter between, 'serves neither of us.'

'Oh, I don't know.' Loku's tone was flippant. 'Half of my men see it as a religious experience, and the rest positively revel in it. And you know that you will lose. Your people could each kill two of mine before they fall and I would still have a force enough to serve my gods' purposes when all on your side of the field are meeting with their gods.'

'I hope your gods are patient,' Brann said. 'I doubt it serves your purposes to wait overlong at this place, and it suits ours to keep you here.'

Loku's eyes grew serious, though the mocking smile remained. 'Every hour I am here, I grow closer to the information I need for the prize I seek, and then nothing can stop me. And every hour I am here, your new friends from this city grow fewer, so I presume you have a suggestion. A truce? We go on our way, and leave this city?' He barked a harsh laugh. 'I have told my soldiers that the gods will see this city fall to the righteous, and I cannot have them doubt their gods, can I? How could their gods be wrong? And in any case, I still have questions to ask of the locals, and one answer to find. If I ask enough people, one will know.'

Brann felt his face harden. His voice rose, ringing harshly in the still air, reaching at least the closest ranks of the enemy host. 'Let your gods show their power, if they have it! Let there be a fight of champions! Let all watch and all witness the fight that will decide the fate of this city. Let us see if your gods have the strength to prevail. Let us see if your gods are true!'

Loku's lip curled in contempt. 'A clumsy effort boy, but a decent attempt, I suppose, from one at your level of guile. Run along now.'

His words faded, however, as a rumble spread across the enemy lines, developing into a chant.

'Our gods are true! Our gods are true!'

Even the Scum, who had no concept of any gods but for the invented and crudely drawn deities of pain and suffering they had been introduced to in their camps, joined the chant. Loku turned to stare at them, then looked back at Brann, his voice just audible above the noise. 'It seems that my people have a less finely tuned appreciation of guile. You shall have your fight of champions.'

'Prepare yourself,' Brann growled in eagerness. 'You have fifteen minutes before I meet you here.'

He turned to go, but Loku's honeyed tone stopped him. 'Oh, my dear foolish boy, you do not think I would dirty my holy hands on you? Your kings have sent a champion, why would I do different?' He whirled to face his army, his hands held high. The noise quietened, and his voice called clear and strong. 'This hero of the foe has come with a challenge, and we will meet this challenge with the strength of our gods in our hearts and our sword arms!' A roar burst forth, and he waited for it to fall. 'We will accept this challenge in our time-honoured tradition. Five gods, five champions.' The chant took up those four words, and he let it continue for a short while before turning back to Brann. 'Five of ours will meet five of yours.'

Brann was already considering it: the two kings would doubtless insist on their two first warriors, both hardened and skilled warriors as Brann had witnessed in recent times, and the five would be completed by Grakk, himself and Gerens – he knew there would be no chance of keeping away the boy who had made it his purpose to watch over Brann since the moment they had met. He was confident in the talents of each.

Loku continued, his words coming through a delicious smile, turning to his host once more. 'This man before me is the first of their challengers! Salute the bravery of the man who seeks to defeat death five times!'

Brann frowned at this and Loku noted his reaction with undisguised glee. 'Oh, Northerner, do not tell me you are unaware of the custom across these southern lands of combat under the sight of the gods? Allow me to enlighten you. Five champions are chosen from each army. The first two fight, the winner facing the next man, and then the next, until one side has no champions left. In being prepared to fight five men, each of the first pair prove their faith that the gods favour them. And in being prepared to take the place of those who fall, those who follow show their devotion to the one who stepped into the light of the gods first. I commend you on being the first of your people – your faith delights me.'

Brann stared at him, feeling the hatred burn in his eyes. He was trapped into Loku's terms. Brann had sought the confrontation and, in his haste, had neglected to think that customs in the South may vary from those in the Northern sagas he had listened to with a child's shining eyes. To seek to change it in his favour would be catastrophic for the morale of the army behind him, but to die here would be worse for the city and its population. He had no option – Grakk's warning about Loku's ingenuity came back to him too late.

But if this was how it would be, then his fate was set, one way or the other. He spat. 'I will kill your five, and then I will put your head on top of one of your poles.'

Loku's smile broadened. 'Oh, I am sure you will not. But I very much look forward to watching you make the attempt. And my thanks for hastening what had become a tedious affair. Victory here will release my full attention to finding the knowledge to save my people. I need that hastened time, and I thank you for it.'

He turned in a whirl of his robes and returned to the acclaim of his followers.

Brann walked back to his comrades, his mind already committing itself to thoughts of the impending combat. Loku may have forced him into a series of fights of horrendous odds, but Brann had approached him with the basic aim of stopping the wholesale slaughter of the battle by addressing the one reason for it taking place and that, at least, he had achieved. For now.

Gerens grabbed him as soon as he reached them, his voice intense. 'You do not need to do this, chief. You are already the hero you needed to be. What you have done, it has achieved more than all the rest of us combined could have accomplished. If this army can but hold them here to sap their strength, then regroup in the city where a demoralised enemy will enter only with fear, we can turn the tide. He will have failed. Khardorul will be safe.'

Brann stared at the enemy host, at the man standing among them, and shook his head. 'I know why you say it, Gerens, but you cannot blame yourself for not being able to protect me this time. You have discharged that duty more times in the past than was ever necessary. What will be, now, must be.'

Gerens made to speak again, but Grakk's voice came low from behind. 'He is right, young Gerens, though it pains me as much as it does you to watch this unfold.' He looked at Brann. 'You have to stay alive – for all these people. I truly do not know how you can achieve this, but I also do not know all that you have gone through in Sagia. I can only hope that there is something in the terrible things you endured that will have helped you to prepare for this now. For Loku does not even ultimately need his men to win, although it would be best for him were they to do so. He needs to kill you. In doing so, in losing our talisman, the inspiration of all those people behind you, our hope will fade like smoke from a pyre.'

Brann looked at him. 'I only fought to help them in whatever way seemed right at the time. I did not choose to be their hero.'

Grakk smiled sadly. 'No hero ever does.'

Xamira spun him to face her, her look as strong as her tone. 'You have to stay alive for these people.' But her eyes said: '*For me.*'

The four supporting warriors were chosen as Brann had predicted; even Shahkam Davar showed grudging respect for him in his greeting. The five walked forward, the eyes of two armies upon them. Brann was reminded of entering the great Arena of Sagia: there, thousands also had watched him fight. This time, however, he was driven by personal desire: he did this for those who stood behind him, and he did this for Loku.

He reached the appointed spot, noting that no designated area had been marked. The fight would go where it went. He guessed there would be no rules also, but that did not trouble him, either. He had fought, and survived, in the illicit matches below the streets of Sagia, where the only rule was *live or die*.

He checked his weapons: the knife sheaths were all filled and his sword and axe were remarkably undamaged by the intensive fighting, the black metal bearing not even a scratch, never mind a nick. His mail shirt had fared not so well in the intensity of the fighting throughout the previous day, rent in places and battered in others, but it would do and he settled it more comfortably on his shoulders. He noticed as he did so that the kings' three warriors checked their weapons, also: they expected him to fall. Gerens's hands moved to his sword and his two knives, but it signified nothing – that happened every time he thought Brann was in any danger. Grakk alone stood still and impassively. The sun flashed from his bald head as he nodded to Brann.

The tribesman moved closer. 'Remember what you learnt

in your fights in the City Below, not in those of the Arena: there is no fighting clean or fighting dirty, only fighting and winning or fighting and losing. Fighting is simply doing what you have to do to stay alive. And in this sort of a fight, you are at least the equal of any warrior I have known. Remember. Your greatest danger today will be fatigue, your greatest enemies the sun and the time you fight. Do not tarry with any man. And do not relax until the life leaves each one, nor even after the last – we do not know what Loku will do then.'

Brann's laugh emerged harsh and brittle. 'On the bright side, the worst that can happen is that I discover the truth of whether there is an afterlife. That is a fairly momentous consolation.'

'No one living can know the truth of that for sure,' Grakk conceded. 'But as creatures, we are conditioned to strive to our last breath to survive, and the urge to live is greater in you than any I have known.'

Brann's mouth moved awkwardly into a smile. 'You speak as if I will live through this.'

'You had better,' Grakk said, his expression never wavering from solemn. 'I am due to fight second, and I am a little tired today.'

Brann's smile came more easily than he would have expected for the brief moment before he looked across the space to those awaiting him. It faded as the question of afterlife or oblivion, expressed as black humour but spawned by the reality of his situation, filled his thoughts. He forced his head clear – he had no further time to prepare. A member of the Scum was walking forward, sword and round shield ready, and Brann wanted no hesitation on his part to give the man confidence. He examined the man: better built than

542

the majority of his comrades, though no doubt he did possess their outlook on life, and with the balance and easy movement of a fighting man – most probably a mercenary before being attracted to Loku's brand of religion. His eyes fixed eagerly on Brann with a confidence that grew as their eyes met. Brann revised his decision on the hesitation, and turned to Grakk, as if urgently conversing.

'Make as if you push me to him,' he said quietly.

Grakk frowned, but did so with automatic trust, his hands spinning Brann and propelling him a couple of steps towards his opponent. Brann fumbled to draw his sword and almost dropped it as he did.

It almost worked.

The man leapt forward with a roar of triumph and a face alight with glee. In the same moment, Brann's sword came alive in his hand, spearing forwards as he took two steps at an angle on the balls of his feet. A loose rock turned the man's footing and his body, and Brann's blade cut through the space where he would have been, and Brann stepped back out of range as the man swung wildly as he tried to regain his balance. His mind was settling into the coldness of combat; his buried self remembering these types of fight with fondness.

The man regained his poise, a sneer spreading across his lips. 'Now you know the gods are with me today.'

Brann shrugged. 'Perhaps. Or perhaps they wish a proper contest for their entertainment.'

He left his axe for the moment, aiming to sap as little strength from his arms as he could, and moved at his opponent, trading blows and gauging his skill. The shouts that had come from both armies as the two had initially closed now became a roaring of voices, the sound taking Brann back more deeply to his gladiator days.

The man was good – he was a champion, after all – and his basic technique seemed greater than Brann's. He used this, attacking little in favour of a solid defence, moving and parrying, clearly hoping to wear down Brann's energy. With his greater reach and his studded leather tunic, as opposed to Brann's mail, he had a chance of doing so, and Brann switched his sword to his left hand as much to rest his right arm as to try to unsettle the man. His opponent merely changed his position, his smile now gone as he lost himself in concentration – the fight continuing longer than Brann would have wished.

Unsettling a foe steeped in rigid technique was the way to penetrate their defence – he had learnt as much in his early days of fighting in the more mundane fighting pits in the trading areas surrounding Sagia. And the unconventional approach was Brann's natural style: the way he had fought before he knew even how to hold a sword, the approach his mentor, Cassian, had worked so hard to build technique upon, rather than replace. What seemed right at the time.

He slipped into a rhythm of blows, letting the man fall comfortably into the pattern. Without warning, he crouched and reached into his boot for the knife Konall had once given him. Instead of flicking it at the man, which would have produced an instinctive defensive reflex, most probably with the shield and a spin, he lobbed it vertically in front of both of them.

The unexpectedness took the man's eyes upwards to follow it. The point of Brann's sword took him in the throat. The unexpectedness filled the man's face with stunned confusion.

Brann took three steps back, twisting his sword as he

pulled the blade free, and watched from a safe distance as the man fell face down in a spreading pool of his own blood.

The roar from behind surged, while those in front fell silent.

One.

He flexed his shoulders. The work against such a stubborn defence had sapped a little energy, but more than in any fight of that length that he could remember. Previous fights, however, had not come after a day of battle and a third more.

The next man stepped forward, a colossus of a Goldlander, his head seeming to merge with the huge muscles topping his shoulders and leaving no room for a neck. Brann's head tilted to one side and his eyes narrowed as he studied the man. He swung a macuahuitl as large as the one Hakon carried and, while he was not quite as tall as the Northern boy, he was broader. Wearing nothing but a heavy black skirt, no imagination was needed to know that muscle was slabbed on top of muscle in such bulk that the body was as if carved from a massive tree trunk and the limbs did not swing easily or far, but the power... Even just a short backswing would produce a strike that would be like being hit by a giant's hammer – bringing the added problem that there would be little warning of such a strike being launched.

Brann again left his axe for now, needing the speed of attack and retreat the sword afforded, but his first action was to dart and grab the shield still gripped by the man he had killed, the body lying where it had fallen. He did not intend to remain in the path of that fearsome weapon that flicked like a switch in the massive paw, but it would be no disadvantage to carry a little extra protection.

545

The man lumbered towards him, the eyes beneath the heavy brow expressionless of emotion but with a glint suggesting an animal cunning. The man plodded at him with relentless determination, and Brann scampered back to howls of derision from Loku's men. He was gauging the large man's movement, though, judging his mobility and, most importantly, his change of balance.

Brann let the big man close the gap and the swing came as he knew it would. He dropped to his right, under the weapon, and immediately rolled to his left, tucking his shield under him and rising in the same movement, his sword flicking out and leaving a crimson trail across the side of the lower ribs. The man seemed not to notice. He turned towards his prey and trudged ever forward.

Brann jinked one way and then the other, seeking an opening past the flashing swings of the macuahuitl. He darted in the way he had once watched Mongoose do, barely evading the weapon but unable to avoid the thump of a shoulder, or an elbow, or a knee, the impact like that of a stone-headed club but preferable to the damage threatened by the sharp edges of the blades on the macuahuitl. His mind worked continuously, dismissing moves that proved futile, seeking ways of creating the chance he needed. But the huge man was not stupid, and he also noticed. As he feinted to one side and came back to the other, Brann noticed too late the halted swing crossways of the macuahuitl and the sudden downwards swipe that knocked his sword completely from his hand. He dropped to reach for it, raising the shield, and was jarred through every bone as the Goldlander punched with a battering ram of a blow directly onto the banded wood. Another punch before Brann could recover shattered the shield and almost wrenched Brann's arm from his shoulder. A large sandalled foot stomped forward, between him and the sword, and his crouch was too low to allow him to draw the axe. He would have to create distance to rise and give himself space to pull forth that weapon – but he didn't have the time. The step forward changed the angle of the man's stance and Brann knew that the next blow would be with the other hand, the one bearing the macuahuitl. He snatched at the knife in the sheath on his forearm bearing the broken shield and stabbed it down through the huge foot so hard that a third of the blade drove into the hard earth beneath.

This time the man did scream, jerking back instinctively, and Brann dived and scrambled, turning back to the danger with his axe in hand. The giant was howling, the paces he had staggered driving the point of the knife against the ground and forcing the blade back up through his foot. He stopped, lifting one leg to hunch forward and grab at the knife, wobbling in his stance. Brann was already running and launched himself into a leap to reach the man before he rose upright once more. As he came down, so did the axe. The black metal of the axe head cut deeper than any blade had a right to do, but still it only cleaved halfway through where the neck ought to have been. Halfway was enough.

Both armies fell silent as the giant dropped, stunned by the ferocity of the battle.

Brann put a foot on the shoulder and, chest heaving and his entire body aching, he wrenched the axe free.

Two.

He retrieved his sword and retired to seek water from his companion warriors. He looked at Grakk as he was handed a water skin, and nodded, his emotions still detached and pushed aside. 'I am not so easy to kill as they maybe thought.'

Grakk shook his head. 'Be wary, young Brann. Those two were never meant to kill you.'

Brann looked at him. 'They made a damn good attempt at achieving what they weren't meant to do.'

Grakk's voice was intent. 'Think, remember: he cares not whether the four who come after you live and defeat his remaining champions, only that you die. When you are gone, he will let loose his army once more, for he knows that without your legend among them, these people will fight but their belief will have gone and with it any chance they had of ultimately resisting.' He indicated the two bodies in the dirt. 'The first was to tire you, and the second to weaken you. They did not know that, but they have done their job. He has chosen the order wisely. All you can do is keep your wits and know that, if anyone can do this, it is you. I believe this.'

'As do I.' It was Shahkam Davar's deep voice, and Brann looked up in surprise. The man placed his hand on Brann's shoulder and, as Grakk followed suit, so did the other two. Brann felt no swell of pride, for his emotions were at bay, but he felt the cold calm flow through him more keenly, as if radiating from their confidence in him. He nodded, and turned.

A tall man of the Scum, lanky and absurdly long-limbed, stood twirling a spear with a speed and skill that defied the eye. A manic laugh issued from his leering face. 'Had enough already, champion? Too weary for more. Come here and I will hasten the sleep you seek, though not the type you crave.'

Brann swivelled his head to ease his neck, and strode forward.

548

The fight was not without injury on his part, the spear point nicking him in a dozen places or more through his torn mail and on his arms and legs, but when his axe in his left hand eventually slammed across and down to hammer the shaft towards the ground, he was able to continue the movement into a spin and slash his sword into the side of the thin head. The leer became permanent, though misshapen.

Three.

He did not wait for the next, or stop for refreshment. He was feeling more fatigue than a short rest would dispel, and needed to hide the fact. He wiped his sword on the dead man's tunic and walked towards the enemy, sword and axe swinging loosely in his hands, and stared.

A comparatively wiry Goldlander stepped forward, still broader of shoulder and chest than most men of Brann's land but with a speed of movement greater than any of the three who had come before.

A macuahuitl hung at his belt and he carried a quiver over one shoulder but no bow. As he approached, the man reached over his shoulder and his arm flashed forwards. Brann dived to the side and a dart the length of his arm whirred past. He rolled without waiting, staggering to his feet as a second dart buried its head in the dirt he had vacated. A third, as he dodged, glanced off his mailed side. He could not wait for a fourth and he let his axe and sword drop, his hand reaching behind his head to the throwing knife strapped at the back of his neck. Had he been given time to think, his throw would undoubtedly have been clumsy and askew, but instinct moved him and the blade flew true. It missed its mark – the man's chest – but struck him in the shoulder of his throwing arm as he reached for his next missile. Brann had already followed the blade and, at a full run, launched himself into his opponent, landing on top of him. He pushed one knee down to raise himself up and, as the man snarled through gritted teeth and reached hard fingers for Brann's throat, Brann jerked the knife free from the shoulder and plunged it into one of the wildly staring eyes. He prised away the fingers that had spasmed against his throat and pulled the knife free, wiping it clean and replacing it. He moved quickly to gather his sword and axe lest the next opponent be sent without pause, but he was allowed to seek a drink. This time he did take the opportunity.

Four.

He stood, slightly swaying as he drank. The gentle eyes of Maktanu regarded him as he cautioned Brann to drink sparingly and slowly.

'You do not wish to be slowed, or to spew,' he said gravely.

Brann knew it was true, and resisted the urge to gulp.

'Oh shit,' said Grakk, and Brann looked to see a man of average height, in a black tunic and breeches and bare feet, walk calmly into the area. Two slim, slightly curved swords, similar to those favoured by Grakk, were cradled in his arms.

'He has found himself a Master of Steel,' Grakk said. 'A religious order, with whom I learnt my skills of the blade, though I could never attain the levels achieved by those who had lived there since infancy. This man is one of their ilk. Loku has prepared you, now he serves you up.' He looked at Brann, his eyes troubled. 'You must find a way, young Brann. You must.'

Brann nodded. 'I know. I will, for these people. And for your people.'

Grakk shook his head. 'No, for me. I could not bear the thought of this day should I see you fall after all you have achieved, nor therefore could I live beyond it. My heart would burst.'

Brann nodded and shrugged. 'No man is invincible. Not I,' he looked across the open ground, 'and not he. Let today be his for that discovery.'

Without another word, he drew his two favoured weapons and turned to the man, glad in this moment for the lightness of the star metal.

The man rose, and bowed. Behind him, in the front line of the enemy host, Loku smiled triumphantly.

The cold in Brann's mind kept his thoughts analytical as he walked. He felt his legs weary, his arms heavy, but it did not dismay him. He felt the heat of the sun eat into his energy, but it did not worry him. Facts were to be considered – to worry wasted time and diverted thoughts, blinded awareness, slowed reactions. You can only ride the horse you sit upon, he had once been told, not the one you covet, so find a way to coax from the mount you have the speed it possesses.

The man would be fast, he knew. He would have moves Brann had never before seen, never mind faced. He would be single-minded. He would be dedicated to his goal. His technique, of sword and body and mind, would be flawless.

But he had been reared learning, and practising, and fighting those with the same attributes. Those like him.

Brann was not like him. Therein lay his chance. Perhaps his only chance. One chance was better than none, but only if the chance can be taken.

The man bowed, his swords still cradled across his chest, his eyes never leaving Brann. Brann nodded curtly. Respect is for training; when reality comes into play, what is necessary to live is all that matters.

The man stepped back, starting a complex set of movements with the swords, a ritual of preparation, almost beautiful in its grace.

Brann struck.

He cut with a swing of his axe, controlled but with flashing speed, forcing the man to parry and step aside. He did so with ease, but Brann's intent had been achieved: not an insult to the ritual, not to try to gain an unexpected opening, for a master of such elevated ability would never be beaten by such, but the interruption of the preparation. It was possible that the man had started every fight in his life with that rite – if Brann had cut short the accustomed preparation, the forming of a mindset, then it eroded slightly the advantage. And even the slightest erosion was of value.

The man came at him in a smooth series of blows, slower than Brann had expected until he realised that he was being himself assessed. He deflected and moved, evading all while giving away as little as he could about his ability.

He registered also, though, the slight sluggishness in his own movements, the extra effort needed to react. He could not win this by defending, and he could not wait until his energy had diminished significantly before he himself attacked.

He turned a sword thrust with his axe and used the movement to swivel his own weapon, stabbing the end of the handle at the man's face. The speed of his opponent saw the blow miss its target, but it struck his shoulder. Brann spun in the same instant, moving out of range. For all the man's prowess, Brann had landed the first blow to be landed. At the sight, the defenders of the city added their roar to that of the invaders, but Brann wasn't fooled. The blow had caused no damage.

He defended more and slipped an angled thrust of his sword at the man's leg, his axe swinging at the gap left by the parry. The man drifted away from the move and came back, his blades moving with incredible speed. Brann deflected, swayed, parried, and spun, his whole world narrowing to the movement in front of him as all the noise and sights beyond it were shut out, but he felt himself slowing and three swift cuts left the marks of their deftness, one on his ribs, one on his leg and one on his cheek.

He knew what he had to do, just to keep himself in the fight. He swung wildly with both weapons at once, surprising his opponent with the bizarre move, then rammed his shoulder against the lean hardness of the man's chest. It was a suicidal move and that in itself saved him – no student of the art would expect it. A student of the art adjusts quickly, however, so as soon as he felt the man stumble back, Brann leapt away, running to his companions. A roar of triumph and derision at his cowardice erupted from the invaders but Brann cared not.

'Cut the straps,' he shouted desperately. 'I need to lose my mail.'

If they were mystified or disagreed, they wasted no time in disobeying. He dropped his weapons and bent forward and, in seconds, the mail shirt had been dragged over his head and he retrieved his weapons as he straightened, the heat of the high sun fresh on his skin rather than stifling, draining. His padded tunic went with it, leaving him bare chested, but he welcomed the relative cool and the release of the weight. He knew he had slowed the loss of energy, but he also knew that *slowed* was not *reversed* nor even *stopped.* Time was his enemy as much as the man before him.

He felt the blood from the three wounds run on his bare skin as he walked back to the fight, his own people now roaring at the sight of his return. They were nicks, really, no threat to his ability, but he and his opponent knew that the relevance of the cuts lay in the shared knowledge that the man could penetrate his defence. He saw the man's eyes rest briefly on the dragon tattoo on his right arm, the eyes widening slightly – the first reaction that Brann had witnessed from him – though the face returned almost instantly to its expression of focused calm. He clearly knew the tattoo's significance and the knowledge may have been of interest, but not sufficiently so to distract him.

More importantly, the man would know that time was against Brann, and would know Brann would have to come out fighting. There was no option, however – sometimes you just have to do the obvious if there is no alternative available.

He went for the man with a flashing whirl of attacks, controlled but at a speed hard to follow. The man was unperturbed, moving smoothly and carefully backwards to absorb Brann's motion, his eyes watching with care, his swords moving even faster than Brann's, a silver net of steel woven in front of him, every stroke made with precision and purpose and following complex patterns far beyond any teaching Brann had known.

Brann felt his muscles start to cramp and redoubled his efforts. The defending army saw the blows increase but knew not the truth behind the surge, cheering their encouragement.

His opponent knew the truth. He started slipping a thrust

among his defensive moves, a cut, a stab, a flick of a wrist, a flash of light. Blood now dripped from a dozen parts of Brann, and the twin blades found further targets with increasing ease. Brann felt the strength seep from him with the blood, but the cold logic in his mind registered it and ignored it as unable to be dealt with at this time. He forced his hands and feet to move, thwarting the killing strikes but unable to avoid the multiple slices and pricks. He knew what the man was doing – he would do it himself.

His head started to swim, and he fell to one knee, flinging the axe around in a wild low swipe, the unexpectedness of the accident taking the man by surprise for the first time. The man threw himself backwards, arching his back as he flipped his feet off the ground barely in time to avoid the sweep of the axe. Brann launched backwards himself, staggering to his feet and lurching away towards his companions, his eyes still fixed on his opponent as the man rose in a smooth movement.

He reached his own people, stretching his arm behind him. 'Water.' His voice was a croak. He felt the water skin pressed into his hand and half turned to take it, movement beyond catching his eye as he did. A stretcher was being carried towards them, with a familiar figure upon it. A dozen paces from him, a gruff command had it set down and the man started to rise. Supported by the two soldiers who had borne the stretcher, Ossavian walked slowly towards him, effort and strain in every movement and a crimson stain on the bandage wrapped around his waist and stomach. Despite all, his bearing was as proud as ever.

Brann drank quickly, then glanced at his opponent. The man stood patiently waiting, so Brann saw no reason not to walk to meet Ossavian. The match had to be finished in any case, whether they restarted now or minutes from now. One of them would die, and the survivor would not be concerned with the time of day at that point.

Ossavian reached out and grasped Brann's arm, his hand shaking but his grip strong. Brann felt himself swaying, and caught himself, but the old general had noticed. His eyes locked on Brann's and his free hand came up, Brann feeling the rough fingers against his cheek.

'Oh my poor boy,' he said. 'What has he done to you?' He coughed, a spray of fine red spots caught on the sleeve he raised to shield his mouth. 'I have watched from afar, but now I come close, for my sight is dimming.'

The coldness formed Brann's thoughts even now, and he regarded the man: the shaking, the seeping wound, the blood on the breath, and then the darkening sight – this man was strong indeed to still be breathing.

'I have watched from afar and even from there I know well the style of such a man. All I can give you is this: for such as he all is in balance, all is perfection. *Even* is aligned, *odd* is imbalance. Always, the moves of his weapon in even numbers and with two weapons, moves in total of four, of eight, of twelve must therefore be followed. It is ingrained over years, nothing else feels natural to him.' His other hand came up, and Brann felt his head held with urgent strength. 'If you remember anything, boy, remember what my brother Cassian believed: remember the power of six. Three with each hand keeps you even, but unsettles him. Remember my brother's six.'

Brann nodded. The man meant well. 'If you say so.'

Ossavian smiled gently, swaying slightly himself, and lowered his hands. He drew a figure six in the blood on the back of each of Brann's hands, and Brann looked at them blankly. He frowned, but left them as they were. There was no need, nor reason, to wipe them away.

'I say so.' His eyes were sad. 'One other thing, boy. Let me travel on my path alone today. Do not accompany me.'

Brann nodded. The words did not make sense to his logic, and he discarded them, but clapped the man on the shoulder in thanks. Ossavian was trying to be kind, and there was no reason to be rude in return. He returned to Grakk and reached again for the water.

As he drank, he assessed himself. His strength was low – even walking left a fatigue in his legs, and the half-empty water skin felt heavy. The sun felt hot, and pain was every-where. He looked at his opponent, impassive patience and calm assurance in his relaxed stance. He looked at Grakk, and he could see that the tribesman suspected what was coming. Brann considered his situation, his capabilities, his choices. And he knew.

'I have one option alone,' he said to Grakk. 'If I live but do not... *return*, will you care for me?'

Grakk's eyes bore the sadness of one who knew he must watch what he dreaded, but would watch out of love. 'Of course I will.'

Brann nodded. 'That is all I need to know.'

He dropped the water skin, it being already forgotten. Shahkam Davar handed him his sword and axe, inclining his head in respect. He took them, his hands feeling complete once more. He walked into the emptiness between the armies – an emptiness but for four bodies and one man awaiting him with swords cradled in his arms.

He stopped. He bowed his head. He closed his eyes. He drew in a deep breath, and slowly let it drift out.

He felt for the other within him. The other part of him.

The part whose essence drifted through him when he fought. He felt for the source of the essence.

He found it.

He set it free.

His head came up with a deep gasp. His eyes opened. He saw the crowds around, and drank in their eagerness. He saw the wounds on his body, combining to threaten his life in time, but not now. And not impairing – that was what mattered. The pain was immaterial. The pain was good. Dead men felt no pain. He saw the man before him, competent, skilled, agile, dangerous: a challenge. He forced strength into his muscles; either way, he would rest later. He smelt the blood on his body. He tasted the blood on his teeth. He ran his tongue along his teeth, savouring the taste. He looked at the man.

He smiled.

He strode at the man and swung his sword. Taken slightly aback at Brann's renewed vigour, the man stepped back several paces before the two fell into a rhythm of blows. Brann's mind worked as he fought. The man was good, but fought only with his swords. Perhaps his skill had been gained at the loss of any awareness of other ways of killing. Perhaps the skill had meant he had never required any other ways of killing.

A sword lanced forward past the axe and caught the back of Brann's wrist. It was trivial, but Brann's eyes caught a number drawn on the back of his hand, a strange thing to see. His mind shrugged. Six was as good a number as any for him.

He hit with groups of six blows. Alternate, three with each, then withdraw. Two with the sword, an axe, a sword, an axe, a sword, withdraw. Straight back in, two sword, axe, two sword, axe, withdraw. He liked this. Axe, parry with sword, axe, sword, sword, axe, withdraw. Two, two, one, one. Always six. It felt good. It felt better when he sensed the stutter in the other's rhythm; he knew not why, but why was immaterial. That it was there was enough.

Be unexpected. Predictable brings death. Assumption brings death. Opportunity brings death for the other. Unexpected brings opportunity.

Six, then six, then six. He waited for the stutter again. It came, and with it a hesitation, a blink in the concentration. In that instant, Brann swept both of his weapons high out to the sides and down in great arcs, back up in gathering speed to rise as one between them. They were aimed not at the man, but at the sky, and the two swords they crashed into, braced as they were with years of training for attacks coming inward, were knocked towards the sky with the passage of Brann's weapons.

The way was open to the head, to the chest. It was the chance. He knew it. The man knew it. And as the man twisted to bring down one sword to protect it, Brann ignored the chance.

He dropped to one knee, letting go of his sword and axe, useless as they were at this range. He grabbed the black-bladed knife from his belt and stabbed hard and fast into the groin before him. Even before the man's scream started, he had sliced across the back of one knee, buckling the already weak legs and rose as the man started to sag. Without pause, the black blade cut the throat as if it were silk.

There was no roar from either half of the crowd, only the soft patter of blood drops on the hard earth, and Brann's own heavy breathing. In the silence, he looked at the man at his feet. He looked at the four other bodies he knew had been sent to kill him. He looked up and saw a man in a cloak of many-coloured feathers standing before a crowd of men broad of build and powerful. The broad men started to hum, a deep oppressive sound. The man in the feathered cloak stared at Brann, his eyes wide with an emotion Brann did not recognise or understand. He knew, though he did not know how he knew, that this man had sent the five.

He looked at the bodies. They were too heavy to drag quickly, so he lifted his axe. The dark metal cut through each neck with ease.

He walked to the man five times, and each time placed a head before him.

He looked into the man's eyes. 'Now I need yours.'

The man turned, stumbling backwards. He stopped and looked at Brann as if a thought occurred. 'My people,' he said, his voice almost a whisper. 'Who will they survive? Who, but me, can save them?'

Brann cocked his head in curiosity. Why did the man not understand such an obvious answer? 'People who want to live, find a way. Sometimes it works, sometimes it doesn't, but if many people try, someone finds the way. It is what we do. It is within us not to welcome death, but to fight it.' He frowned at the man, lifting his axe slightly. 'You do not know this? Do you welcome death?'

The man said nothing, but his answer was clear in his widened eyes and his flight into the crowd behind.

Brann did not follow. The man's people were too many to defeat. But the man's people hummed louder, stronger.

The man pushed aside people in his way. Brann noticed his movements were becoming more frantic, and the willing-ness to move of those he pushed was becoming less willing. Then the people stopped moving out of his way. Still the humming grew.

The man was part way up a slope when Brann saw the people close tight around the feathered cloak. Tight enough to halt it. The humming grew deeper still.

The man screamed and beat at the unmoving people. They remained unmoving. The humming rose louder than ever.

The man turned and looked at Brann. Even at that distance, the hatred blazed like fire from the man. Then, at the final moment, it turned to terror. A weapon rose, then fell. Another, then another, then another, all rose and fell, rose and fell. The feathered cloak fell with them. The humming stopped.

The feathered cloak was one colour. Blood red.

There were others with the broad men, others with a wild look in their eyes and movement of restless twitches. He had seen their like before in the City Below, his home. He had fought their like before. The fights had not lasted long. Those who needed to chew herbs to find the courage to fight were not natural fighters, nor competent ones.

The broad men fell on these others without warning. All along that crowd, the others fell as the feathered man had done, shouts of surprise quickly turning to screams of horror; those few who escaped fleeing in any direction that took them from the fearsome slaughter.

Brann turned to see if the crowd behind him would turn to such violence also, but found them slumping to the ground as if a great weariness had settled over them. He wondered if they had drunk too much of the fermented juice he had been given after a victory in the pits.

The broad men, thousands of them, had finished their killing. Turning towards Brann, they dropped their weapons and sank to their knees. A strange action, he thought.

A man, his bald head covered in tiny black symbols, moved to Brann's side. He recognised him – he was a friend.

'Grakk,' he said to the man. The man nodded. 'Why do they not cheer? The crowd should cheer. The crowd normally cheers.'

The man's smile seemed sad. 'When people are faced with the unexpected, they do not know what to do. What they don't do, is what they would normally do.'

Brann looked at the headless body of the man with the two swords. 'He found the truth in that.'

The friend Grakk clapped his shoulder. 'That he did, young man, that he did.'

Two men accompanied by warriors aplenty strode to the pair, the shorter one bare-chested other than for a waistcoat, the tall one with a metal tunic resembling a fish's skin, and both wearing a simple crown.

'We are in your debt, Brann of the Arena,' the shorter one said.

The tall one fixed pale eyes on him for a long moment. 'This will not be forgotten, I will ensure as much. I have never seen its like. Not one of us has.'

Brann frowned. He had won fights before, and this reaction seemed a little excessive, especially given the lack of cheering. 'Thank you,' he said. It seemed appropriate.

The tall man looked at the huge crowd of men kneeling amongst the bodies of their erstwhile comrades. 'What about them?'

Grakk looked at them. 'Let them go,' he said softly.

'What?' The word burst from the shorter man, while his taller companion merely stared.

Grakk's voice was even, measured, as he seemed to think as he spoke. 'The path taken by a religious fanatic is usually that which is shown to them by one claiming to be a representative of their gods, and where it is a path of pain and suffering inflicted on non-believers, that representative tends to be one who serves personal aims more than those of the heavenly masters, no matter how much the self has been deluded otherwise. The zealot has not a mind of his own but has been cleverly manipulated to believe that the thoughts of another are actually his but, for that very same reason, he will follow a path of good just as easily as one of evil. We can hope that the next religious leader these people follow will be one of a more caring and peaceful nature. Most immediately, one who believes the people of Tucumala are best moving out of the path of a god's anger.'

The smaller man thought for a moment. 'It makes sense. And, in any case, we have enough mouths to feed and shattered lives to rebuild to keep us busy without the administrative bother of them to add to it all.'

The tall man looked at him, then nodded. 'Very well.'

Another friend, with wild black hair, ran to him, closely followed by a young woman whose hair the colour of the sun flew behind her. Each looked as worried as the other.

Brann knew them. 'Gerens. Xamira.'

'How do you feel?' the boy Gerens said, concern filling eyes that burned like cold dark fire.

Brann looked around at the scene. 'I feel right.' He nodded to himself. 'Just... right, as if this makes sense. As if the gods approve.'

A look passed between Grakk and Gerens, and though Brann did not know what it signified, the black-haired boy seemed to understand. 'At least you live,' he said. He turned to the woman and spoke in a low voice. She nodded, understanding passing over her face also.

Grakk said, 'Come, Brann. I made a promise, and I will keep it. We have a journey ahead of us, but first you must rest.'

Xamira, however, stepped between them. 'I have something that may work.'

Brann was puzzled, but many things were puzzling him and he accepted that, if he needed to know, they would tell him.

The boy Gerens looked at Grakk, raising his eyebrows. Grakk shrugged. 'It cannot do any harm, I suppose.' He passed a small jar to the girl.

She took him by the hand and Brann let her lead him through the crowd. Men and the few women among them moved to clap his back, grasp his hands, and say words of gratitude and admiration. Maybe this was what they did instead of cheering in this place, he mused. She led him from the crowd and to the city wall beyond, finding a gap in the structure. The buildings were empty, and she found one with a well. Raising water and ripping a sheet she had found in the house, she gently bathed his wounds and spread the salve contained in the jar Grakk had given her. It was absorbed quickly and she bound the wounds tightly and with care, one by one, with strips cut from the sheet. She examined her handiwork and nodded, satisfied.

'Come,' she said, leading him to the bed where she had found the sheet.

It was not the twining of their bodies that brought him back, nor the pleasure that came with it, overwhelming though it was. It was the look in her eyes in the instant before she kissed him, long and deep, and in the instant after. He looked there, and saw his soul reflected, and in the reflecting, it was returned.

He saw her from deep within himself, felt himself drawn to the world, to his memories, to his awareness, to her. A slow surge of energy, growing in a wave of vitality, rose through him, filling mind and body alike.

He was alive, in every way. He knew himself once more, and he smiled.

When they lay in each other's arms, peace settling through him, he raised himself on one elbow and looked at her, stroking a stray lock from her eyes.

One corner of her mouth twitched into a smile, a look of melancholy. 'Now you must go to her.'

He frowned, his thoughts in turmoil, love producing longing and guilt and confusion in equal measure. He gathered the thoughts slowly, trying to make sense of them, or at least set them into some order. 'I love her. But there is something with you also. I cannot justify it, or even rationalise it, but I also cannot deny its existence.'

'Your time has been with me, but now is with her.' He looked at her. 'Would you have had her in all this? In the blood and the gore and the biting and stabbing and screaming?'

'She *can* fight, you know. Women like you, Breta and Mongoose are rare around here, but in her land, all women are taught to bear arms just as the men are.'

She looked at him with narrowed gaze. 'Maybe so, but would you have had her be a part of *this*?'

He took a while to answer, but when he did, he looked into her eyes. 'No.'

'Then go to her. I am for the life you were forced to have, but she is for the life you deserve. You need her love, and you deserve the chance to give her yours.'

He stared through the window at the clear sky, as if seeing

that life being lived. 'I would like that,' he said softly. His eyes found her face again, and he touched his fingers to her cheek. 'But I will leave a piece of me with you. I will miss you.'

She laughed, her blue eyes dancing. 'Oh, of course you will. You will not be rid of me that easily, Brann of the Arena. We will meet again. There are some things a woman just knows. Now go, live your life.'

He had never had cause to doubt her words before, and he found himself glad that he felt the strength of their certainty yet again.

He reined his horse on the side of the hill, above the village, figures moving on unknown tasks and voices heard in the cool of the summer morning. However, it was a spot to one side of them, no more than a dozen paces away, that his eyes sought. A spot where a crossbow bolt had taken his brother from him. He silently sent a greeting to Callan, but said nothing to the others. It was not their sorrow to carry. He hoped there was indeed an afterlife, that Callan and Cannick could meet there as they had not while alive. Perhaps Ossavian, too. He thought they would like each other, and the thought made him smile.

He thought of the others, Philippe, in Derden, taking to his training as a healer as if born to it, Breta and Mongoose accompanying the Halvekans to their homeland where a shared outlook on life would, he was sure, await them. The four with him sat quietly as he scanned the village, his eyes lighting on a boy and girl, not as small as he remembered them, as a slender woman ushered them into a mill, rebuilt similar but not identical to the one in his memory. As they chased each other inside, the children dodged around a broad-shouldered man carrying a grain sack on his shoulder as easily as if it were filled with feathers. A fierce yearning, too long buried, surged within him.

Brann smiled at Valdis, the happiness filling him as it did each time he saw her at his side. 'Ready to meet the family?'

'Absolutely! Lead on, I'm starving!' came Marlo's voice from behind. He still sat awkwardly on his horse, but his wounds had healed enough to see him through the sea voyages to and from Halveka and, having managed that, he had been determined not to miss this final journey.

Brann was glad, the chance to watch over his friend's recuperation as important to him as the cheer the boy had somehow never let escape him.

Gerens shook his head in despair at Marlo, but Sophaya struck the back of his head with an admonishing slap. Brann laughed and Valdis laughed with him, lifting his heart higher. The girl slid smoothly from her horse and reached to untwist a strap on the saddle to stop it irritating the animal. She caught Brann looking at her and winked.

Unbidden, the memory of a wink in a creased and weathered face in the yard behind an inn slipped into his head. A wink and a gravelly voice. *When you don't know if there is something or nothing awaiting you in death, it puts a little warmth in an old heart to know you have left something of you in those who come after.*

He wiped a sleeve across his eyes. Gerens moved his horse alongside him, his voice unusually soft. 'Cannick or Ossavian?'

Brann shrugged. 'Either. Both.' He looked at his friend. 'Mostly Cannick.' At saying the name, his throat caught and he had to fight to control the rising surge of emotion. He stared down at his horse's neck, feeling his face flush.

Gerens stare was as level as his tone. 'We all die. We just hope it is with dignity, and remembered.'

Brann grunted. 'And not too soon.'

Gerens looked into the distance. 'You will always find something yet undone or still to be seen that will render it too soon.'

'You know what I mean.' He cleared his throat. 'I will miss them. Him especially.'

The dark eyes turned once more on Brann. 'We all want to be missed. They would be glad to know that they are.'

Brann nodded and grinned suddenly. 'Mind you, it would be good to hear the good things people feel for you occasionally without having to die first.'

'You want me to tell you I love you, chief?' He was frowning, but the ghost of a smile drifted across one corner of his mouth.

A small stone flickered past Brann and bounced off Gerens's shoulder. 'Save that for Sophaya, big boy,' Valdis scolded him, climbing back into her saddle. 'This one's mine.'

Gerens turned the cold fire of his eyes upon her. 'That's a relief.'

Brann laughed. 'Enough chat. Let us take our memories to those who will treasure them anew.' He glanced at Marlo. 'And our hunger to those who will feed it.'

He pulled the black cloak around him, fingering the repaired tear near the hem, nodded quietly to the spot twelve paces away, and nudged his horse towards his home.

****

She sat beside him, sipping from her goblet of water. He held his, not drinking, his eyes fixed on the horizon beyond the balcony.

Her sand-dry voice broke the silence. 'So he was indeed the one.'

He nodded. 'He was. Your seeds of destiny flowered.'

'And you feel vindicated for the horrors you set upon him?'

He frowned. What a stupid question. 'Had I not, he would be dead.'

She sat quietly, declining to answer. He snorted in irritation. The silence was more of a rebuke than any angry words.

'You are angry that your plans did not come to fruition? That the ruler still rules? That you still sit here?'

He shrugged, spilling a little of his water on his robe. It did not matter; the heat would dry it before he had finished speaking. 'A danger arose in the enacting of the last plan, a danger of such gravity that it became the focus of everything. Current plans often need to be altered. Former plans can be made anew.'

'Nevertheless, he is still in power.'

'Weakened power. He left the city without a garrison. No Emperor before has failed the city in that way. No Emperor should. Many know that.' He snorted once more. 'Weakened power in one who sees what suits his purpose, rather than building his purpose upon what he sees to be true. Where there was dire threat to the foundations of civilisation, to the order of the Empire and beyond, he sees a rebellion crushed by a loyal vassal king and the heroic death of a Source of Information who brought warning to that king.' He looked at her, a fierceness in his eyes harking back to a time of power wielded. 'A ruler who is led by what he wants to hear is a ruler ruled. Such opportunity attracts ambition from many quarters, ambition in the form *of many voices, each vying to be the one heard and trusted. Tie many boats to a single mooring post and when a storm comes, the post becomes a shattered shard. We will wait for our time, plan for our time, act at that time.'*

'And will that action choose to involve the same instrument of fate as this past one?'

He looked at her. 'Why should it?'

'Because,' she said, 'there is a fourth prophecy.'

He dropped his goblet.

'It says what?'

'It says nothing, yet. It has yet to be uttered. But we know it will come. And with it, the child of this particular destiny.'

'Woman!' he spat. 'Why must you always speak in riddles and half-truths?'

But he would have her no other way. And his mind was already starting to plan.

She smiled.

Epilogue

The storyteller swept in a circle as he uttered the final words, savouring the silence of the moment before the applause. Then savouring the applause still more, he pulled his hood to shroud his face in shadow and swept without another word up the steps between the villagers risen to their feet in appreciation. It was always good to carry a final sense of mystery and drama as you left, to be remembered for your return.

His horse was waiting, as requested, saddled and with his payment and fresh food in his saddlebags. The dawn sun was rising and bringing with it the delicate first light of day, and as he paused to rest his eyes on the soothing colours of nature, his attention caught the mounted figures sitting silently at the top of the hill. His hand strayed to the sword hanging on his saddle but his shout of alarm stilled in his throat. There was a familiarity about the figures.

He smiled.

He had kicked the horse into motion before his feet were even in the stirrups, and urged it into a canter up the slope.

As he drew up before them, he threw back his hood, revealing the smile that had become a grin and the intricate symbols covering his scalp.

The man on the horse at the front, much the same as he remembered as if the intervening years had never passed, laughed in delight. 'Grakk of Khardorul, you are a hard man to find. It has been too long, my friend.'

Grakk scowled with mock anger. 'Then you seek as poorly as you fight, Brann of the Arena.' He looked fondly at the faces at Brann's back, also as familiar to his eyes as if he had supped with them the night before. One was unexpected. Valdis winked at him, as if to say that Brann would not gallivant this time without her. He looked back at the boy, now grown to man. 'But the reason for your seeking?'

Brann looked at him with the same good humour in his eyes as ever. 'We have been summoned, would you believe.'

'You mean *you* have been summoned.'

Brann shrugged. But Grakk noticed he did not deny it. Brann did, however, grin mischievously. 'Do you think you might be ready for another adventure?'

Grakk smiled. 'Always.'

Acknowledgements

And so I find myself somewhere in my 'real' life that, not so long ago, seemed as imaginary as were the trials, tribulations and adventures that awaited Brann and his companions: I am at the end of the Seeds of Destiny trilogy. It worked out differently from the story I had envisaged when I wrote the first words of the first draft of Hero Born, but then all of my stories evolve and change as they are written, so there is no surprise in that. However, Hero Risen would not have worked out *at all* if it were not for certain significant and crucial people, and it is with gratitude that goes beyond the written word that I acknowledge them – well, with gratitude and the fear that, should their huge, vital and indispensable contributions go unmentioned, I would deserve to be hunted down by someone with the cold tenacity and colder brutality of Gerens. And we all know that Gerens is far better as a friend than an enemy.

And therefore, I extend my warmest and most whole-hearted thanks to...

My wife, Valerie, who I have previously described as my

confidence and my reality check, my rock and my refuge, and this remains as true as ever, though I would add to that my inspiration and my energy; and my family, Martyn, Johnny, Melissa, Nicky, Adam and Nathan, and the still-younger ones – Joshua, Riah, Jayden, Ashton and Clayton – who continue to encourage me, make me laugh, fill me with wonder and, most importantly, keep me rooted in the important parts of life.

My parents, Ian and Diane, and my brother, Gordon, whose enthusiasm for my writing keeps my spirits high when pressure weighs heavy and, not least, for being my chief publicists; and my parents-in-law, Frank and Nan, whose relationship with me is a such a vital part of my life and, as with my own parents, whose relationship with each other is an inspiration.

My first-two-chapter-testers, Claire and Melissa, whose opinions are so critical and whose enthusiasm for the stories and the characters is appreciated and humbling in equal measure.

And, of course, to those professionals, skilled beyond my understanding, who made it all possible: Lily Cooper, Richenda Todd and Janette Currie, who edited with keen eyes and deft 'red pens' that showed not just technical skill in their craft but a feel and a care for the characters and the story; Ben Gardiner, whose evocative cover design was yet again classy and just right for this book while at the same time maintaining the distinctive style of the previous covers in the series; Anne-Janine Nugent, who had the unenviable task of making me look more human than wooden in my publicity photos, and found the talent to somehow achieve it; everyone at HarperVoyager whose work goes unseen by me but is no less appreciated for it; and, of course,

Natasha Bardon, who oversees all with a personal touch and who, when Hero Born was just a submission and a dream, saw something in it and launched me on the path that has brought me to this point.

And, of course, the readers: those who have bought each book and enjoyed it enough to move onto the next. A story can only be told if there is someone to tell it to, and a writing a book without readers is like crafting a ship in the desert. Thank you for allowing me to sail my ship on waters that continue to be a glorious wonder to me.

Printed by RR Donnelley at Glasgow, UK